FRED SABERHAGEN
THE BERSERKER WARS

TOR

A TOM DOHERTY ASSOCIATES BOOK
Distributed by Pinnacle Books, New York

THE BERSERKER WARS

Copyright © 1981 by Fred Saberhagen

A TOR Book

First printing, December 1981

ISBN: 48-520-4

Cover art by Franco Storchi

Printed in the United States of America

PINNACLE BOOKS, INC.
1430 Broadway
New York, N.Y. 10018

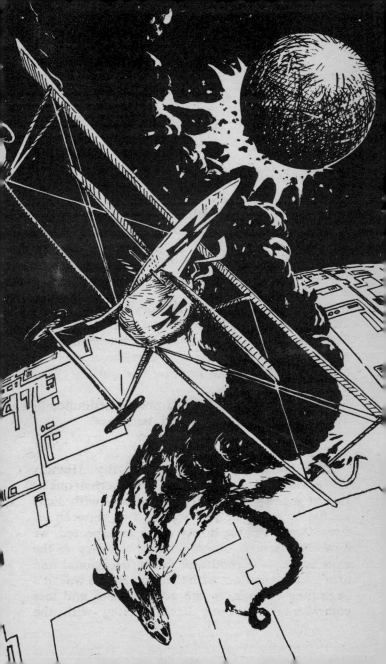

MESSAGE BEGINS
REPORT ON THE PRIVATE ARCHIVE OF THE
THIRD HISTORIAN
A File Which Presents the History of the Galaxy in
Twenty Pages
Transmission Mode: Triplicate Message
Torpedoes
Code: Trapdoor XIII
TX Date: 7645.11.0
From: Archivist Ingli, Expedition Co-ordinator
To: Chief Co-ordinator, Earth Archives
cc Defense Co-ordination Central

Hal: We're here, surrounded by friendly Carmpan of whom we rarely see more than one or two at a time, and then usually only with some partial or symbolic physical barrier between us. Everything is going pretty much as expected, we have experienced nothing really contrary to the experience of a thousand years' occasional and arm's-length contact with the race. By the way, it's beginning to look, to me at least, less and less coincidental that our first meeting with the

Carmpan coincided almost exactly with the beginning of the Berserker War. I'll have more to say on this point presently.

Let me first describe what I consider to be our main achievement so far on this mission. To begin with, the structure in which we are living and working is best described as a large, comfortable library, and we have been given free access to great masses of information in several kinds of storage systems. (I hope, by the way, that the exchange team of Carmpan researchers on Earth are being treated as well as we are here.) Much of this mass of stored data is, as we expected, still unintelligible to us and so far useless. But quite early in the game our hosts pointed out to us, for our special attention, an alcove containing what we've come to call the private archive of the Third Historian. Having looked at the files therein, my colleagues and I agree unanimously that they were very probably compiled and largely written by the same Carmpan individual who used that name (or title) as signature to the messages he composed and sent to our ancestors some generations ago, when the Berserker peril was even greater than it is today.

Since a copy of this report is going directly to the military, Hal, bear with me when I pause now and then to insert a paragraph or two of history. We can't reasonably expect that all the readers over there are going to know as much of it offhand as we do.

Up until now, almost all of the information that we have ever had directly from the Carmpan on any subject—Berserkers, the Builders, the Carmpan themselves, the Elder Races, almost everything—a very great proportion of this information, I say, has come to our Solarian worlds through long-distance communications signed by this one individual, for whom we still have no other name than Third Historian. He—or she, the Carmpan language does not readily distinguish sexes, and they usually appear to care not much more about sex than we do about blood types—was active centuries ago, and to my knowledge no new Third Historian message has been received on the Solarian world for centuries.

So we still know next to nothing about the Third Historian—or indeed about any Carmpan individual—as a person, and it appears to me unlikely that this present Expedition is going to find out much about him. We do of course ask questions, particularly since being shown the private archive that is marked in several places with his signature. Our questions are answered in the usual obscure ways, about which more below. Even the significance of the number in his name or title is still unknown to us. It does seem certain that more than three individuals must have occupied the post of Chief Historian—assuming there is such an official post among the Carmpan —during such a very long history as their race boasts. Or would boast if they were at all given to boasting.

When I asked directly, I was told that the Third Historian is still alive. This surprised me somewhat, though the life-span required, considerably less than a thousand standard years, would not be utterly out of the question even for one of our own comparatively perishable species. However, when I asked urgently to see him, or at least to be told where he is now, I was informed just as unequivocally that the Third Historian is now dead. One of the enclosures with this message is our own recording of this particular question-and-answer session.

Let me digress just a little more from the important contents of the TH's private files, to remark that in the short time we've been here we've had more face-to-face (if that's the right way to put it; you know what I mean) contact with the Carmpan than have any other group of Solarian humans in history. As you are well aware, we were very eager for this chance. On the long voyage out here we managed to convince ourselves that with goodwill on both sides (a requirement that I certainly feel has been met) we were going to do a lot better at communicating with the Carmpan than any other of our race has ever done. We were going to dig a lot of Galactic history out of them, complete with hard facts, dates, numbers, the kind of thing *we* like to call history. We would dig up information that must be available to them even if they consider it valueless, and bring it home with us. Not only that, we would at last meet a Carmpan or two who really wanted to learn about us through our own conscious attempts at communication; and, boy, were we ever going to communicate with *them*.

Need I add, that so far it hasn't worked out quite that way? That so far our formal conference sessions are dominated, whatever we Solarians try to do, by the Carmpan spiritual (?) and sociological abstractions? (Military readers, see my monograph on *Drifts and Tones in Carmpan Communications;* someone at the Archives will be

glad to furnish you with copies.) That's just the
way in which our gracious hosts here insist on
looking at the Universe. I find I must set down the
cliche once again, and then I swear that I will ban
it from all later messages: The Carmpan mind is
very, very different from our own.

Of course the communications we have been
directing to the Carmpan while in general conference form, to our way of thinking, a clear and
concise outline of the history of our Solarian
variant of the human race, from our origins on
Earth through our later phases of expansion and
development to the present, when we are the
dominant life form on more than a thousand
major planets in more than seven hundred
systems, not to mention all the natural and
artificial extrasystemic habitats, enjoying a
blessed variety of political and economic organizations while managing to co-operate quite well,
most of us, most of the time, in the thousand-year
Berserker War.

I frankly don't know what our hosts think of this
presentation we make about ourselves. There are
moments when I believe they knew it all already,
knew more than we have told them, down to the
last detailed production statistic, through their
own far-ranging mental activities. And, again,
there are times when I believe they just don't care,
don't know and aren't interested, are going
through the motions of listening to us only out of
politeness. They do express thanks when we pause
after shoving information at them, as they express
thanks for so much else that our race has done.
But there is no substantive comment on what we
tell them. There are no questions that sound eager.

That's how things stand now. We are here, and being very well treated, and we like our hosts. And they like us and are glad to have us here, even if it would be strictly inaccurate to say that they enjoy our company. And it is somehow implied that they have done, are doing, will do, something important for us. That's how things stand now, how they stood the moment we arrived. Actually we could just have sent them an electronic greeting card and accomplished just as much.

Except of course for one thing. Our presentation of our own history evidently had at least one good effect, that of showing our hosts what we think a history ought to be. It may have decided them to show us quickly the one file in the library that comes closest to our ideal. It was approximately one standard day after our own history presentation, which came about one standard day after our arrival, that we were led to the personal file of the Third Historian. I think I have mentioned that the alcove containing the Third Historian's file and carrel occupies only a very small portion of this library. It's quite a comfortable, self-sufficient artificial world, by the way, that seems to have been built with Solarian comfort and convenience in mind. The gravity, atmosphere, lighting, furnishings, color schemes, and so on, are very pleasant by our standards. Green plants are abundant. And the Carmpan information-handling systems, let me interject here, work better than ours do, once we know precisely what we want to ask of them. Details on request, when we get home. The idea so commonly held among Solarians that we are technologically superior to the Carmpan seems to me to be justifiable only on a very selective basis.

Back to my main subject. While the private writings of the Third Historian we have discovered here are more obscure and difficult to translate than we would like, certainly more so than his famous public transmissions to our ancestors centuries ago, yet they are vastly more accessible to Solarian understanding than any other Carmpan literary-historical work that I have ever encountered in a lifetime of study; I exclude of course documents on the level of mere maps and catalogues, which in their rare appearances have often had practical if limited application.

If we had come here completely unacquainted with the Third Historian, it would still have been obvious to us from his private archive that he was —or is—intensely interested in two things. The first of these, for whatever reason, is our own race. As in his earlier public messages, he repeatedly expresses Carmpan gratitude for our leadership, our victories, and our losses in the long and terrible war against what he so often calls "the unliving enemy." To me the impression is inescapable that much of the material in this private archive consists of drafts of messages intended for us but never sent; that these reiterations of thanks must be for our benefit.

The second great interest of the Third Historian, as evidenced in his old public messages as well as in the newly discovered material, is the Berserkers. Briefly, our most important find within his private archive is an electronic document (I am of course enclosing a recording of it herewith) that purports to be a digest, a capsule, or perhaps an outline, for nothing less than a history of the whole inhabited portion of the Galaxy for as far back as the Carmpan have been able to keep records—and their history, we should recall, has been shown to extend into the tens of millions of years at least. Everything we have learned here tends to support the accepted belief that the Carmpan mental probing can span more than half the Galactic diameter; and that this mind-probing is as accurate for the purposes to which the Carmpan put it as it appears to be useless for any of the military, commercial, or hard (in our terms) research functions to which we have always yearned to be able to apply it.

I had hoped when I began to compose this message to be able to include with it a full if tentative translation of the History Document (hereafter abbreviated HD) found in the Third Historian's private archive. Without the episodic appendix (see below) it could be printed out in twenty pages; it's really that short. But unfortunately the longer I study HD with an eye to making a translation, the more I realize how obscure it is—somewhat in the sense of poetry, I mean, and you, Hal, know what trying to translate poetry can be like. Layer upon layer of suggested meaning, that to me is at best barely perceptible, is packed beneath a surface narrative that in itself could be translated in a number of possible ways. Here we have Drifts grafted upon Tones, and vice versa. Information is packed not only in layer upon layer, but in the interference patterns, or in something analogous to such patterns, that are formed by the relationships between the layers, between each layer and all the other ones. I fear I am not making myself clear. In future messages I mean to go into much more detail about this hologram-like though non-physical system.

Here let me digress to mention one fact definitely confirmed by the surface narrative in HD. This is that the Builders were a warlike race for a long time before they created the Berserkers. There is convincing evidence that before the fateful experiment the Builders had fought at least four long, desperate interstellar wars, resulting in the complete extermination of at least four other races. These four early victim-races are unfortunately identified in HD only in the Tones-Drifts system of sociological-spiritual (religious?) notation. Whether any translation at all of this passage into a Solarian tongue is possible without assigning the races completely arbitrary names and identities (e.g., One, Two, Three, Four) is still in doubt, though I have spent two days working on that simple-seeming question with our own ship's computer.

Parenthetically: I am assured by our hosts that as much time as we might like is available to us on Carmpan computers which our hosts assure us have much more capacity than the shipboard one we brought along. The only problem lies in instructing their computers in what we want. I have no great hopes for being able to do this, as so far it seems all but impossible to explain our way of thinking to the Carmpan themselves. Whether their data processing machinery works on a system of Drifts and Tones I have not yet been able to ascertain, but I have assured myself that it certainly does not work like ours.

A second hard fact confirmed by HD about the

Builders: They were a race designed to roughly
the same physical pattern as Solarian humanity,
though somewhat more slender and fine-boned,
having originated probably on a lighter planet
than Earth. There is a suggestion that the female
tended to be fiercer in combat than the male, and
it is certain that she was somewhat larger. There
was in each individual one cyclopean eye, and
paired external sexual organs (of the same sex) so
that copulation must commonly have been carried
on in duplicate, as it were. The Builders spoke
through sound waves as we and the Carmpan do,
but their creations the Berserkers were never
furnished with the language code as far as can be
determined, or indeed with any other means of
distinguishing their creators from the other life
forms of the Galaxy included in their general programming to hunt down and destroy all life. Of
course there may have been some system meant to
save the Builders from the general slaughter, a
system that failed to operate properly and was
never replicated in the later models of the
Berserkers as they rebuilt and reproduced themselves. On the other hand, the original Berserkers
may have been activated at such a distance from
their creators' home worlds that the death
machines were not thought by their builders to
represent a danger to them. At any rate, we have
found nothing here to contradict the accepted
hypothesis, based on old evidence, that the
Builders did at last fall victim to their own creations.

It is certain that the Builders no longer exist.
The Third Historian speaks of them inevitably in
the past tense, something he does in the case of no

race that is now known to be still alive. The scraps
of recordings that we have found here, showing
the Builders' appearance and containing samples
of their speech, do not differ substantially from
other such old recordings that I have seen before,
and for all I know all of these may be duplicated in
Solarian archives somewhere. (None of us on the
Expedition roster are specialists in Builders'
History. An unfortunate oversight, perhaps, but if
such a specialty exists it would be a very limited
one indeed.)

Copies of all the fragmentary Builder
recordings here will be sent with our next
message. How the Carmpan obtained them is uncertain, since our hosts would not ordinarily have
access to the battlefield wreckage of Berserkers
from which our own material has been gleaned.
Most of these fragments are excerpts, each lasting
only a few seconds, of what if interpreted in
Solarian terms would be considered political
speeches, delivered amid mass chanting rallies of
Builders male and female. There is one fragment
like nothing that I personally have seen before,
though some other members of the expedition
assure me that they have: a scene of Builders performing what might be a dance, or alternatively
the application of some kind of rhythmical torture
apparatus to an unusually large female. (I need
not belabor here the obvious point that all of these
interpretations should be considered tentative.)
The voices in the recordings, as in fragments of
Builder records found elsewhere, are clicking and
whining sounds, probably not reproducible by
either Solarian or Carmpan vocal organs.

And there is one more fragment, very different

from all the rest. In it, members of another race, heretofore unknown to us, appear briefly. Some expedition members have suggested that this may be our only record of the Builders' nameless but undoubtedly very formidable opponents in their final war, the people whose destruction could not be accomplished without such a desperate gamble as the creation of the Berserkers. Expedition members who favor this interpretation point out similarities between this Builder recording and certain Solarian propaganda art from the past. It shows beings rotund and red, thick-limbed almost to the point of having no limbs separate from the body at all; all this in high contrast to the Builder physique. This Red Race is named, if at all, only in a sort of marginal note (using the Drift-Tone system, of course) that was doubtless added by the Third Historian himself. Translation, as mentioned above, is still pending.

Nowhere in any document that we have so far inspected in this library are values given for the size of the domain of any race, in terms of numbers of worlds, strength of fleets, population figures, and so on; even precise physical locations are very rare. We know of course that the Carmpan are perfectly capable of interstellar navigation when it suits them, that they have built and designed ships whose autopilots work perfectly with any of the commonly used systems of interstellar co-ordinates.

Nor have we found any clue as to how many intelligent races, branches living or dead of Galactic humanity, the Carmpan know about. As I have already suggested, one of the most striking things about this library is the paucity of numbers, of quantitative measurements of any kind. A starfaring race who (with the well-known exception of their Prophets of Probability) prefers to do without mathematics, without even counting, must remain to our minds, to put it mildly, something of a paradox. And I am coming to think that there is that in the essence of what the Solarian mind finds paradoxical that demands repeated expression in the thoughts and minds of the Carmpan and their allies or cousins the Elder Races.

(Note to my military readers: The name 'Carmpan' itself, as many of our race today do not realize, derives not from any word by which they call themselves, but rather from the location where our species and theirs first encountered each other.)

We members of the expedition have of course discussed, or tried to discuss, these translational and other difficulties with our unfailingly polite and attentive hosts. As nearly as we can make out from their replies, they believe that the number of intelligent races existing in the Galaxy, for example, is something one simply should not try to know—or if known, it should not be expressed. Despite great efforts on both sides, I have trouble understanding why. To know and express that number would be either sin, or bad form, or maybe sloppy scientific thinking, on the grounds that there is no way one can be sure *enough* of its value. Maybe a little of all three.

But, I press on, a true, worthy answer does exist, does it not, if it can be discovered?

Yes, I am told. But the true answer involves—somehow—the Core region of the Galaxy, or perhaps something (someone?) located (dwelling?) at or very near the center of the Core. "All exact counting of races should be done there," is an exact translation of what one of our hosts said to me. I would be hard put to explain to you which one said it. We are still having a lot of trouble telling one Carmpan from another. But I asked him—or her—more questions, trying to pin down the identity of this thing or person properly in charge of numbering races at the Core. There was no satisfactory answer; only a single word, which I take to signify a complex structure of some kind.

Following this, our hosts made a joint statement, which I quote in translation as well as I am able. They wished, they said, to "express great sadness over the fate of those intelligent races, diverse branches of Galactic humanity despite all diversity of physical form, however many of them there may have been or may yet be, who have been exterminated by the Builders or the Berserkers or any other cause, those known to us and those who lie in the distant reaches of the Galaxy-beyond-measurement, still unknown to Carmpan and to brave Solarian alike. The loss of these races means that much (creative work, of some form) will have to be accomplished (by some unspecified agents) before the Galaxy can be judged complete and worthy."

That passage was so relatively easy for me to understand, that I believe someone among the Carmpan must have expended an extraordinary amount of time and effort on it in advance, and that it was then held ready until the proper moment for its utterance should arrive. Is it possible that the Third Historian himself is among those we meet and speak with every day? I seriously think it is possible, and at the same time I doubt that we shall ever know. He could inhabit any of those slow, squarish Carmpan bodies, so incongruously machinelike in appearance for beings whose own constructed machinery is so subtle, who try to avoid the grossly material in any form . . . actually, as I think I mentioned in passing above, we seldom get a really good look at any of the Carmpan here, though we are often physically close to each other and frequently converse. The rooms in which we most often meet are all niches and alcoves and low partitions, with enough screens of live greenery to make us feel that we are in a garden instead of riding a deep-space artifact at a high fraction of the speed of light. The interior lighting is perfect, as I think I have mentioned, for Solarian eyes, and we can view the Carmpan and even touch them on arrangement, to satisfy our curiosity. But at the same time privacy is rarely more than an arm's length away for anyone, and they frequently resort to it, retreating round a corner or behind a hanging vine. We of course do not intrude upon these temporary retreats. Personally I find myself also retreating sometimes in the midst of a conversation, gazing out through fresh green leaves of some kind—I am no botanist—or a fountain's spray, enjoying the whole arrangement more than I would have suspected.

I am rambling. Back to the History Document. What it presents of the Carmpan view of the physical universe contains no surprise. The Universe just above the galactic level (yet higher levels are implied but not described) is seen as organized in terms of clusters or groups of galaxies. None of us in the expedition are astronomers or cosmologists enough to know if the details of this organization as the Carmpan describe it differ substantially from those mapped out by our own scientists. Actually the Third Historian uses this physical description only as a background for a question in which he is genuinely interested: Are there Berserkers, of independent origin, in galaxies other than our own? And, if so, will the living races of those other megasystems be able to raise up some analog of Solarian humanity to successfully fight off the un-living foe? This passage, with its understated implication that we are universally rare stuff indeed, makes me feel, I confess, vaguely uncomfortable.

It was shortly after reading this disturbing passage for the first time that I approached our hosts to question them on a more personal level: The Third Historian, in some of his early direct communications to our people, has stated that he "sets down" the "secret thoughts" of Solarian men and women who were at all times parsecs away from him, as well as being in some instances removed by hundreds of years of time even when correction is made for all possible relativistic effects. When my hearers affirmed this, I asked whether any of the Carmpan now present were capable of reading our secret thoughts, and if so, were they? The answer was quick and emphatic denial, the most definite response I think I have ever had to any question here. "You and we are too close together," they informed me, "for anything like that."

In HD the Third Historian is also greatly intrigued by another question, related to the one discussed a paragraph above: May there ever have been, in the remote past of our own Galaxy (the context makes it plain he is talking about a billion years or more), other Berserkers, *independent of those now existing?* He adduces a statement which must be meant as evidence to support this idea, though I cannot understand it (again, see enclosed recording.) I am haunted by this suggestion, and it makes me wonder if some of the Elder Races still extant may possibly be of comparable age. It is to me an awesome thought that some races may have survived a Berserker peril more than once.

Another member of our expedition has very recently reported what we all consider to be a remarkable find (see her own report enclosed herewith). In a corner of the library far removed from the archive of the Third Historian she has discovered a record of what are described as "multi-species life constructs" that antedate even the Carmpan themselves by millions of standard years. I interpret "life-construct" to mean a living thing composed of other living things. If we are reading this correctly it is odd that HD does not mention such creations. But perhaps it does, perhaps life-constructs and much else are concealed in the Drifts and Tones amid the layers of meaning.

Here I begin to ask myself another question. It is not a new question among Solarian historians, but here it takes on a new sharpness. Did the Carmpan know the Builders, or know of them, before the Builders plunged into their final war and decided upon their Frankenstein's creation? Conventional history holds that they did not; had the Carmpan known of the Berserkers when that awful construction was first accomplished, the gentle, peaceful Carmpan could hardly have failed to send immediate warning to the races who were thereby placed in imminent peril. But really there is no evidence that the Carmpan did not send such warnings. To some they may have come too late; some may have been unable to profit by them, some may have disbelieved. It would be consistent with the Carmpan nature that such warnings might have been sent on a purely subliminal level of communication if such exists. I think it may. Could it have been at least in part a Carmpan influence that caused an increase in belligerence on many Solarian worlds simultaneously, provoking a military buildup in those decades just before the first Berserker radio-voices came drifting in to our detectors from the deep?

And there is the fact that the Carmpan and Solarian branches of humanity met for the first time very shortly before the first Berserker onslaught on one of our worlds was sustained. Even on the relatively short time-scale of Solarian history the two events, the two meetings, were virtually simultaneous. What are the odds that this was only chance? When one day I am able to meet a Carmpan Prophet of Probability I mean to ask him to calculate the odds.

I have not yet faced our hosts with this suggestion: That that famous first contact between our two races, long assumed by Solarians to be a natural result of our aggressive exploration, was really timed by the Carmpan for their own reasons; that they had known of us for a long time preceding; that we were picked, chosen, adopted, when the time was ripe, brought onto the Galactic stage to play a role just when our ferocity and our armaments were needed in the service of all Galactic life.

If this suggestion is true, still it is far from clear to me that the deception is something we ought to blame the Carmpan for. They did not create the Berserkers nor launch them in our direction. We would still have had to fight the Berserkers if we and the Carmpan had never met. Ought we to blame them for not warning us clearly and directly? We were, and are, the suspicious and mistrustful ones, who really needed no warnings to be on our guard. Probably we would not, on that first memorable day of violence between us and the unliving foe, have returned the Berserkers' fire a microsecond sooner, whatever the Carmpan might have whispered to us beforehand.

And yet I, like most Solarians, continue to feel that the Carmpan presence, their influence, has helped us all through the war. Through them we have learned not only of the Elders but of other races much more helpless. We would still have fought, of course, for our own survival, our own temples and our gods. But it was good, it was better, to know that we were fighting for others also, for the cause of all life in the Galaxy.

When the war began a thousand years ago—may our own lifetimes see a final victory—the belief was widespread among our Solarian people that the Carmpan, even dedicated to peace as they assuredly were, would be forced by events to take up arms. After all, to refuse to enter a war against Berserkers was to be guilty by inaction of the deaths of innocent victims—in this war, as in no other, to fight was not to kill. For our unliving foe, no sympathy or pity could be felt, any more than for the missiles that they launched against us. But for the Carmpan it was no longer a matter of choice. The skills needed for direct combat, the mental and emotional abilities much more importantly than the physical, had been lost to them long ago, when their will to fight was lost— or when that will was, perhaps, absorbed in something larger.

One point of view, put forward here by some expedition members, is that the Carmpan *did* fight the Berserkers, and very successfully. They fought so well that great numbers of them are still alive after a thousand years of the struggle, which when facing Berserkers must be considered a remarkable record. It was simply a matter of the Carmpan choosing and then using properly the most effective weapon available—which happened to be us. They made sure that we had grasped the magnitude of the danger posed by the Berserkers, and then they got the hell out of our way, while from time to time providing us with such indirect help as they were able.

Another viewpoint, expressed recently by some expedition members, is that the Carmpan have already helped us more than most of us realize. They not only knew their own limitations but probably understood ours better than we did ourselves. Of course they never tried to enter battle at our side, never built weapons for us or even

shipped us components or raw materials. Yet
their ambassadors to our worlds, all Prophets of
Probability, on rare but vital occasions (the Stone
Place being the most famous example) have pre-
dicted the outcome of battles, with great benefit to
morale. And our military and economic historians
have often remarked on how fortuitously some of
our supply and communication links have been
maintained during the war's darkest hours, how
needed materiel has so often fallen into the grasp
of our people at a crucial moment. It is impossible
for me to demonstrate that the Carmpan could
have been responsible for this, but I have a
growing suspicion that they were.

From the earliest years of the war the Carmpan
did sometimes provide medical and research
assistance. And the limitation on the kind of aid
they gave were somehow accepted by our own
race, and we continued to believe in their good
will. We saw that they were not cowardly. In the
war's early days some of them came to live on
some of our particularly endangered planets, for
no apparent reason other than to share our perils.
This practice ceased as sentiment among our
people grew against it—the testimony of our
people at the time is that they did not want the
Carmpan to endanger themselves unnecessarily.

There is a fairly lengthy passage in HD on the
Carmpan role as intermediaries between ourselves and the shadowy (to us) Elder Races, with
whom we have so much more difficulty in
communicating than even with the Carmpan
themselves. Judging by the amount of space he
gives this topic, the Third Historian must have

considered it important. Still, he says very little
about the Elder Races in themselves; perhaps
there is some reason by discussion of these
revered ones, like counting, should take place only
at the Core. Or perhaps the Drifts and Tones
within the document tell more about them than I,
with my feeble understanding of the language,
have been able to glimpse as yet.

A substantial part of what the document does
say about the Elders relates them to the Berserker
war—how, when some groups of the Elders could
have withdrawn themselves from the Berserkers'
path, they chose instead to remain where they
were, and delay the enemy by being hunted and
ultimately killed—a delay that was to prove vital
to the survival of some Solarian and other worlds.

Near the end of HD an individual exploit is mentioned, almost the first to be related in the whole
document—it is the strange voyage of the Solarian
warship *Johann Karlsen*, exploring near the
Galactic Core. The limited engagement that was
fought against the Berserkers on that occasion is
treated as of substantial importance, as somehow
foreshadowing an ultimate victory for the cause of
life. I think it probable that the Carmpan know, in
some sense, more of that episode than we do.

Attached to HD in a kind of appendix are eleven
or twelve (the demarcations are not always plain)
episodic narrative reports concerning the experi-
ences of different Solarian individuals in various
phases of the great war.

HD concludes with a postscript in a warning
tone: That no victory in this world, this Galaxy,
this Universe, is final. And no history, either.

(signed) INGLI
MESSAGE ENDS

For most men the war brought a steady deforming pressure which seemed to have existed always, and which had no foreseeable end. Under this burden some men became like brutes, and the minds of others grew to be as terrible and implacable as the machines they fought against.

But I have touched a few rare human minds, the jewels of life, who rise to meet the greatest challenges by becoming supremely men.

STONE PLACE

Earth's Gobi spaceport was perhaps the biggest in all the small corner of the galaxy settled by Solarian man and his descendants; at least so thought Mitchell Spain, who had seen most of those ports in his twenty-four years of life.

But looking down now from the crowded, descending shuttle, he could see almost nothing of the Gobi's miles of ramp. The vast crowd below, meaning only joyful welcome, had defeated its own purpose by forcing back and breaking the police lines. Now the vertical string of descending shuttle-ships had to pause, searching for enough clear room to land.

Mitchell Spain, crowded into the lowest shuttle with a thousand other volunteers, was paying little attention to the landing problem for the moment. Into this jammed compartment, once a luxurious observation lounge, had just come Johann Karlsen himself; and this was Mitch's first chance for a good look at the newly appointed High Commander of Sol's defense, though Mitch had ridden Karlsen's spear-shaped flagship all the way from Austeel.

Karlsen was no older than Mitchell Spain, and no taller, his shortness somehow surprising at first glance. He had become ruler of the planet Austeel through the influence of his half-brother, the mighty Felipe Nogara, head of the empire of Esteel; but Karlsen held his position by his own talents.

"This field may be blocked for the rest of the day," Karlsen was saying now, to a cold-eyed Earthman who had just come aboard the shuttle from an aircar. "Let's have the ports open, I want to look around."

Glass and metal slid and reshaped themselves, and sealed ports became small balconies open to the air of Earth, the fresh smells of a living planet —open, also, to the roaring chant of the crowd a few hundred feet below: "Karlsen! Karlsen!"

As the High Commander stepped out onto a balcony to survey for himself the chances of landing, the throng of men in the lounge made a half-voluntary brief surging movement, as if to follow. These men were mostly Austeeler volunteers, with a sprinkling of adventurers like Mitchell Spain, the Martian wanderer who had signed up on Austeel for the battle bounty Karlsen offered.

"Don't crowd, outlander," said a tall man ahead of Mitch, turning and looking down at him.

"I answer to the name of Mitchell Spain." He let his voice rasp a shade deeper than usual. "No more an outlander here than you, I think."

The tall one, by his dress and accent, came from Venus, a planet terraformed only within the last century, whose people were sensitive and proud in newness of independence and power. A Venerian might well be jumpy here, on a ship filled with men from a planet ruled by Felipe Nogara's brother.

"Spain—sounds like a Martian name," said the Venerian in a milder tone, looking down at Mitch.

Martians were not known for patience and long suffering. After another moment the tall one seemed to get tired of locking eyes and turned away.

The cold-eyed Earthman, whose face was somehow familiar to Mitch, was talking on the communicator, probably to the captain of the shuttle. "Drive on across the city, cross the Khosutu highway, and let down there."

Karlsen, back inside, said: "Tell him to go no more than about ten kilometers an hour; they seem to want to see me."

The statement was matter-of-fact; if people had made great efforts to see Johann Karlsen, it was only the courteous thing to greet them.

Mitch watched Karlsen's face, and then the back of his head, and the strong arms lifted to wave, as the High Commander stepped out again onto the little balcony. The crowd's roar doubled.

Is that all you feel, Karlsen, a wish to be courteous? Oh, no, my friend, you are acting. To be greeted with that thunder must do something vital to any man. It might exalt him; possibly it could disgust or frighten him, friendly as it was. You wear well your mask of courteous nobility, High Commander.

What was it like to be Johann Karlsen, come to save the world, when none of the really great and

powerful ones seemed to care too much about it?
With a bride of famed beauty to be yours when the
battle had been won?

And what was brother Felipe doing today?
Scheming, no doubt, to get economic power over
yet another planet.

With another shift of the little mob inside the
shuttle the tall Venerian moved from in front of
Mitch, who could now see clearly out the port past
Karlsen. Sea of faces, the old cliche, this was
really it. How to write this . . . Mitch knew he
would someday have to write it. If all men's
foolishness was not permanently ended by the
coming battle with the unliving, the battle bounty
should suffice to let a man write for some time.

Ahead now were the bone-colored towers of
Ulan Bator, rising beyond their fringe of suburban
slideways and sunfields; and a highway; and
bright multicolored pennants, worn by the aircars
swarming out from the city in glad welcome. Now
police aircars were keeping pace protectively with
the spaceship, though there seemed to be no
possible danger from anything but excess
enthusiasm.

Another, special, aircar approached. The police
craft touched it briefly and gently, then drew back
with deference. Mitch stretched his neck, and
made out a Carmpan insignia on the car. It was
probably their ambassador to Sol, in person. The
space shuttle eased to a dead slow creeping.

Some said that the Carmpan looked like
machines themselves, but they were the strong
allies of Earth-descended men in the war against
the enemies of all life. If the Carmpan bodies were

slow and squarish, their minds were visionary; if
they were curiously unable to use force against
any enemy, their indirect help was of great value.

Something near silence came over the vast
crowd as the ambassador reared himself up in his
open car; from his head and body, ganglions of
wire and fiber stretched to make a hundred
connections with Carmpan animals and
equipment around him.

The crowd recognized the meaning of the network; a great sigh went up. In the shuttle, men
jostled one another trying for a better view. The
cold-eyed Earthman whispered rapidly into the
communicator.

"Prophecy!" said a hoarse voice, near Mitch's
ear.

"—of Probability!" came the ambassador's
voice, suddenly amplified, seeming to pick up the
thought in midphrase. The Carmpan Prophets of
Probability were half mystics, half cold mathe-
maticians. Karlsen's aides must have decided, or
known, that this prophecy was going to be a
favorable, inspiring thing which the crowd should
hear, and had ordered the ambassador's voice
picked up on a public address system.

"The hope, the living spark, to spread the flame
of life!" The inhuman mouth chopped out the
words, which still rose ringingly. The armlike
appendages pointed straight to Karlsen, level on
his balcony with the hovering aircar. "The dark
metal thoughts are now of victory, the dead things
make their plan to kill us all. But in this man
before me now, there is life greater than any
strength of metal. A power of life, to resonate—

in all of us. I see, with Karlsen, victory—"

The strain on a Carmpan prophet in action was always immense, just as his accuracy was always high. Mitch had heard that the stresses involved were more topological than nervous or electrical. He had heard it, but like most Earth-descended, had never understood it.

"Victory," the ambassador repeated. "Victory . . . and then . . . ."

Something changed in the non-Solarian face. The cold-eyed Earthman was perhaps expert in reading alien expressions, or was perhaps just taking no chances. He whispered another command, and the amplification was taken from the Carmpan voice. A roar of approval mounted up past shuttle and aircar, from the great throng who thought the prophecy complete. But the ambassador had not finished, though now only those a few meters in front of him, inside the shuttle, could hear his faltering voice.

" . . . then death, destruction, failure." The square body bent, but the alien eyes were still riveted on Karlsen. "He who wins everything . . . will die owning nothing . . . ."

The Carmpan bent down and his aircar moved away. In the lounge of the shuttle there was silence. The hurrahing outside sounded like mockery.

After long seconds, the High Commander turned in from the balcony and raised his voice: "Men, we who have heard the finish of the prophecy are few —but still we are many, to keep a secret. So I don't ask for secrecy. But spread the word, too, that I have no faith in prophecies that are not of God.

The Carmpan have never claimed to be infallible."

The gloomy answer was unspoken, but almost telepathically loud among the group. Nine times out of ten, the Carmpan are right. There will be a victory, then death and failure.

But did the dark ending apply only to Johann Karlsen, or to the whole cause of the living? The men in the shuttle looked at one another, wondering and murmuring.

The shuttles found space to land, at the edge of Ulan Bator. Disembarking, the men found no chance for gloom, with a joyous crowd growing thicker by the moment around the ships. A lovely Earth girl came, wreathed in garlands, to throw a flowery loop around Mitchell Spain, and to kiss him. He was an ugly man, quite unused to such willing attentions.

Still, he noticed when the High Commander's eye fell on him.

"You, Martian, come with me to the General Staff meeting. I want to show a representative group in there so they'll know I'm not just my brother's agent. I need one or two who were born in Sol's light."

"Yes, sir." Was there no other reason why Karlsen had singled him out? They stood together in the crowd, two short men looking levelly at each other. One ugly and flower-bedecked, his arm still around a girl who stared with sudden awed recognition at the other man, who was magnetic in a way beyond handsomeness or ugliness. The ruler of a planet, perhaps to be the savior of all life.

"I like the way you keep people from standing on your toes in a crowd," said Karlsen to Mitchell Spain. "Without raising your voice or uttering threats. What's your name and rank?"

Military organization tended to be vague, in this war where everything that lived was on the same side. "Mitchell Spain, sir. No rank assigned, yet. I've been training with the marines. I was on Austeel when you offered a good battle bounty, so here I am."

"Not to defend Mars?"

"I suppose, that too. But I might as well get paid for it."

Karlsen's high-ranking aides were wrangling and shouting now, about groundcar transportation to the staff meeting. This seemed to leave Karlsen with time to talk. He thought, and recognition flickered on his face.

"Mitchell Spain? The poet?"

"I—I've had a couple of things published. Nothing much . . . . "

"Have you combat experience?"

"Yes, I was aboard one berserker, before it was pacified. That was out—"

"Later, we'll talk. Probably have some marine command for you. Experienced men are scarce. Hemphill, where *are* those groundcars?"

The cold-eyed Earthman turned to answer. Of course his face had been familiar; this was Hemphill, fanatic hero of a dozen berserker fights. Mitch was faintly awed, in spite of himself.

At last the groundcars came. The ride was into Ulan Bator. The military center would be under the metropolis, taking full advantage of the defensive force fields that could be extended up into space to protect the area of the city.

Riding down the long elevator zigzag to the buried War Room, Mitch found himself again next to Karlsen.

"Congratulations on your coming marriage, sir." Mitch didn't know if he liked Karlsen or not; but already he felt curiously certain of him, as if he had known the man for years. Karlsen would know he was not trying to curry favor.

The High Commander nodded. "Thank you." He hesitated for a moment, then produced a small photo. In an illusion of three dimensions it showed the head of a young woman, golden hair done in the style favored by the new aristocracy of Venus.

There was no need for any polite stretching of truth. "She's very beautiful."

"Yes." Karlsen looked long at the picture, as if reluctant to put it away. "There are those who say this will be only a political alliance. God knows we need one. But believe me, Poet, she means far more than that to me."

Karlsen blinked suddenly and, as if amused at himself, gave Mitch a why-am-I-telling-you-all-this look. The elevator floor pressed up under the passengers' feet, and the doors sighed open. They had reached the catacomb of the General Staff.

Many of the staff, though not an absolute majority, were Venerian in these days. From their greeting it was plain that the Venerian members were coldly hostile to Nogara's brother.

Humanity was, as always, a tangle of cliques and alliances. The brains of the Solarian

Parliament and the Executive had been taxed to find a High Commander. If some objected to Johann Karlsen, no one who knew him had any honest doubt of his ability. He brought with him to battle many trained men, and unlike some mightier leaders, he had been willing to take responsibility for the defense of Sol.

In the frigid atmosphere in which the staff meeting opened, there was nothing to do but get quickly to business. The enemy, the berserker machines, had abandoned their old tactics of single, unpredictable raids—for slowly over the last decades the defenses of life had been strengthened.

There were now thought to be about two hundred berserkers; to meet humanity's new defenses they had recently formed themselves into a fleet, with concentrated power capable of overwhelming one at a time all centers of human resistance. Two strongly defended planets had already been destroyed. A massed human fleet was needed, first to defend Sol, and then to meet and break the power of the unliving.

"So far, then, we are agreed," said Karlsen, straightening up from the plotting table and looking around at the General Staff. "We have not as many ships or as many trained men as we would like. Perhaps no government away from Sol has contributed all it could."

Kemal, the Venerian admiral, glanced around at his planetmen, but declined the chance to comment on the weak contribution of Karlsen's own half-brother, Nogara. There was no living being upon whom Earth, Mars, and Venus could really agree, as the leader for this war. Kemal seemed to be willing to try and live with Nogara's brother.

Karlsen went on: "We have available for combat two hundred and forty-three ships, specially constructed or modified to suit the new tactics I propose to use. We are all grateful for the magnificent Venerian contribution of a hundred ships. Six of them, as you probably all know, mount the new long-range C-plus cannon."

The praise produced no visible thaw among the Venerians. Karlsen went on: "We seem to have a numerical advantage of about forty ships. I needn't tell you how the enemy outgun and outpower us, unit for unit." He paused. "The ram-and-board tactics should give us just the element of surprise we need."

Perhaps the High Commander was choosing his words carefully, not wanting to say that some element of surprise offered the only logical hope of success. After the decades-long dawning of hope, it would be too much to say that. Too much for even these tough-minded men who knew how a berserker machine weighed in the scales of war against any ordinary warship.

"One big problem is trained men," Karlsen continued, "to lead the boarding parties. I've done the best I can, recruiting. Of those ready and in training as boarding marines now, the bulk are Esteelers."

Admiral Kemal seemed to guess what was coming; he started to push back his chair and rise, then waited, evidently wanting to make certain.

Karlsen went on in the same level tone. "These

trained marines will be formed into companies, and one company assigned to each warship. Then—"

"One moment, High Commander Karlsen." Kemal had risen.

"Yes?"

"Do I understand that you mean to station companies of Esteelers aboard Venerian ships?"

"In many cases my plan will mean that, yes. You protest?"

"I do." The Venerian looked around at his planetmen. "We all do."

"Nevertheless it is so ordered."

Kemal looked briefly around at his fellows once more, then sat down, blankfaced. The steno-cameras in the room's corners emitted their low sibilance, reminding all that the proceedings were being recorded.

A vertical crease appeared briefly in the High Commander's forehead, and he looked for long thoughtful seconds at the Venerians before resuming his talk. But what else was there to do, except put Esteelers onto Venerian ships?

They won't let you be a hero, Karlsen, thought Mitchell Spain. The universe is bad; and men are fools, never really all on the same side in any war.

In the hold of the Venerian warship *Solar Spot* the armor lay packed inside a padded coffinlike crate. Mitch knelt beside it inspecting the knee and elbow joints.

"Want me to paint some insignia on it, Captain?"

The speaker was a young Esteeler named Fishman, one of the newly formed marine company Mitch now commanded. Fishman had picked up a multicolor paintstick somewhere, and he pointed with it to the suit.

Mitch glanced around the hold, which was swarming with his men busily opening crates of equipment. He had decided to let things run themselves as much as possible.

"Insignia? Why, I don't think so. Unless you have some idea for a company insignia. That might be a good thing to have."

There seemed no need for any distinguishing mark on his armored suit. It was of Martian make, distinctive in style, old but with the latest improvements built in—probably no man wore better. The barrel chest already bore one design— a large black spot shattered by jagged red—show- ing that Mitch had been in at the "death" of one berserker. Mitch's uncle had worn the same armor; the men of Mars had always gone in great numbers out into space.

"Sergeant McKendrick," Mitch asked, "what do you think about having a company insignia?"

The newly appointed sergeant, an intelligent- looking young man, paused in walking past, and looked from Mitch to Fishman as if trying to decide who stood where on insignia before com- mitting himself. Then he looked between them, his expression hardening.

A thin-faced Venerian, evidently an officer, had entered the hold with a squad of six men behind him, armbanded and sidearmed. Ship's Police.

The officer took a few steps and then stood motionless, looking at the paintstick in Fishman's hand. When everyone in the hold was silently watching him, he asked quietly:

"Why have you stolen from ships' stores?"

"Stolen—*this?*" The young Esteeler held up the paintstick, half-smiling, as if ready to share a jcke.

They didn't come joking with a police squad, or, if they did, it was not the kind of joke a Martian appreciated. Mitch still knelt beside his crated armor. There was an unloaded carbine inside the suit's torso and he put his hand on it.

"We are at war, and we are in space," the thin-faced officer went on, still speaking mildly, standing relaxed, looking round at the open-mouthed Esteeler company. "Everyone aboard a Venerian ship is subject to law. For stealing from the ship's stores, while we face the enemy, the penalty is death. By hanging. Take him away." He made an economical gesture to his squad.

The paintstick clattered loudly on the deck. Fishman looked as if he might be going to topple over, half the smile still on his face.

Mitch stood up, the carbine in the crook of his arm. It was a stubby weapon with heavy double barrel, really a miniature recoilless cannon, to be used in free fall to destroy armored machinery. "Just a minute," Mitch said.

A couple of the police squad had begun to move uncertainly toward Fishman. They stopped at once, as if glad of an excuse for doing so.

The officer looked at Mitch, and raised one cool eyebrow. "Do you know what the penalty is, for threatening me?"

"Can't be any worse than the penalty for blowing your ugly head off. I'm Captain Mitchell

Spain, marine company commander on this ship, and nobody just comes in here and drags my men away and hangs them. Who are you?"

"I am Mr. Salvador," said the Venerian. His eyes appraised Mitch, no doubt establishing that he was Martian. Wheels were turning in Mr. Salvador's calm brain, and plans were changing. He said: "Had I known that a *man* commanded this . . . group . . . I would not have thought an object lesson necessary. Come." This last word was addressed to his squad and accompanied by another simple elegant gesture. The six lost no time, preceding him to the exit. Salvador's eyes motioned Mitch to follow him to the door. After a moment's hesitation Mitch did so, while Salvador waited for him, still unruffled.

"Your men will follow you eagerly now, Captain Spain," he said in a voice too low for anyone else to hear. "And the time will come when you will willingly follow me." With a faint smile, as if of appreciation, he was gone.

There was a moment of silence; Mitch stared at the closed door, wondering. Then a roar of jubilation burst out and his back was being pounded.

When most of the uproar had died down, one of the men asked him: "Captain—what'd he mean, calling himself Mister?"

"To the Venerians, it's some kind of political rank. You guys look here! I may need some honest witnesses." Mitch held up the carbine for all to see, and broke open the chambers and clips, showing it to be unloaded. There was renewed excitement, more howls and jokes at the expense of the retreated Venerians.

But Salvador had not thought himself defeated. "McKendrick, call the bridge. Tell the ship's captain I want to see him. The rest of you men, let's get on with this unpacking."

Young Fishman, paintstick in hand again, stood staring vacantly downward as if contemplating a design for the deck. It was beginning to soak in, how close a thing it had been.

An object lesson?

The ship's captain was coldly taciturn with Mitch, but he indicated there were no present plans for hanging any Esteelers on the *Solar Spot*. During the next sleep period Mitch kept armed sentries posted in the marines' quarters.

The next day he was summoned to the flagship. From the launch he had a view of a dance of bright dots, glinting in the light of distant Sol. Part of the fleet was already at ramming practice.

Behind the High Commander's desk sat neither a poetry critic nor a musing bridegroom, but the ruler of a planet.

"Captain Spain—sit down."

To be given a chair seemed a good sign. Waiting for Karlsen to finish some paperwork, Mitch's thoughts wandered, recalling customs he had read about, ceremonies of saluting and posturing men had used in the past when huge permanent organizations had been formed for the sole purpose of killing other men and destroying their property. Certainly men were still as greedy as ever; and now the berserker war was accustoming them again to mass destruction. Could those old days, when life fought all-out war against life, ever come again?

With a sigh, Karlsen pushed aside his papers. "What happened yesterday, between you and Mr. Salvador?"

"He said he meant to hang one of my men." Mitch gave the story, as simply as he could. He omitted only Salvador's parting words, without fully reasoning out why he did. "When I'm made responsible for men," he finished, "nobody just walks in and hangs them. Though I'm not fully convinced they would have gone that far, I meant to be as serious about it as they were."

The High Commander picked out a paper from his desk litter. "Two Esteeler marines have been hanged already. For fighting."

"Damned arrogant Venerians I'd say."

"I want none of that, Captain!"

"Yes, sir. But I'm telling you we came mighty close to a shooting war, yesterday on the *Solar Spot.*"

"I realize that." Karlsen made a gesture expressive of futility. "Spain, is it impossible for the people of this fleet to cooperate, even when the survival of—what is it?"

The Earthman, Hemphill, had entered the cabin without ceremony. His thin lips were pressed tighter than ever. "A courier has just arrived with news. Atsog is attacked."

Karlsen's strong hand crumpled papers with an involuntary twitch. "Any details?"

"The courier captain says he thinks the whole berserker fleet was there. The ground defenses were still resisting strongly when he pulled out.

He just got his ship away in time.

Atsog—a planet closer to Sol than the enemy had been thought to be. It was Sol they were coming for, all right. They must know it was the human center.

More people were at the cabin door. Hemphill stepped aside for the Venerian, Admiral Kemal. Mr. Salvador, hardly glancing at Mitch, followed the admiral in.

"You have heard the news, High Commander?" Salvador began. Kemal, just ready to speak himself, gave his political officer an annoyed glance, but said nothing.

"That Atsog is attacked, yes," said Karlsen.

"My ships can be ready to move in two hours," said Kemal.

Karlsen sighed, and shook his head. "I watched today's maneuvers. The fleet can hardly be ready in two weeks."

Kemal's shock and rage seemed genuine. "You'd do that? You'd let a Venerian planet die just because we haven't knuckled under to your brother? Because we discipline his damned Esteeler—"

"Admiral Kemal, you will control yourself! You, and everyone else, are subject to discipline while I command!"

Kemal got himself in hand, apparently with great effort.

Karlsen's voice was not very loud, but the cabin seemed to resonate with it.

"You call hangings part of your discipline. I swear by the name of God that I will use every hanging, if I must, to enforce some kind of unity in this fleet. Understand, this fleet is the only military power that can oppose the massed berserkers. Trained, and unified, we can destroy them."

No listener could doubt it, for the moment.

"But whether Atsog falls, or Venus, or Esteel, I will not risk this fleet until I judge it ready."

Into the silence, Salvador said, with an air of respect: "High Commander, the courier reported one thing more. That the Lady Christina de Dulcin was visiting on Atsog when the attack began—and that she must be there still."

Karlsen closed his eyes for two seconds. Then he looked round at all of them. "If you have no further military business, gentlemen, get out." His voice was still steady.

Walking beside Mitch down the flagship corridor, Hemphill broke a silence to say thoughtfully: "Karlsen is the man the cause needs, now. Some Venerians have approached me, tentatively, about joining a plot—I refused. We must make sure that Karlsen remains in command."

"A plot?"

Hemphill did not elaborate.

Mitch said: "What they did just now was pretty low—letting him make that speech about going slow, no matter what—and then breaking the news to him about his lady being on Atsog."

Hemphill said: "He knew already she was there. That news arrived on yesterday's courier."

There was a dark nebula, made up of clustered billions of rocks and older than the sun, named the Stone Place by men. Those who gathered there

now were not men and they gave nothing a name;
they hoped nothing, feared nothing, wondered at
nothing. They had no pride and no regret, but they
had plans—a billion subtleties, carved from
electrical pressure and flow—and their built-in
purpose, toward which their planning circuits
moved. As if by instinct the berserker machines
had formed themselves into a fleet when the time
was ripe, when the eternal enemy, Life, had begun
to mass its strength.

The planet named Atsog in the life-language had
yielded a number of still-functioning life-units
from its deepest shelters, though millions had
been destroyed while their stubborn defenses
were beaten down. Functional life-units were
sources of valuable information. The mere threat
of certain stimuli usually brought at least limited
cooperation from any life-unit.

The life-unit (designating itself General Bradin)
which had controlled the defense of Atsog was
among those captured almost undamaged. Its
dissection was begun within perception of the
other captured life-units. The thin outer covering
tissue was delicately removed, and placed upon a
suitable form to preserve it for further study. The
life-units which controlled others were examined
carefully, whenever possible.

After this stimulus, it was no longer possible to
communicate intelligibly with Great Bradin; in a
matter of hours it ceased to function at all.

In itself a trifling victory, the freeing of this
small unit of watery matter from the aberration
called Life. But the flow of information now
increased from the nearby units which had per-
ceived the process.

It was soon confirmed that the life-units were assembling a fleet. More detailed information was sought. One important line of questioning concerned the life-unit which would control this fleet. Gradually, from interrogations and the reading of captured records, a picture emerged.

A name: Johann Karlsen. A biography. Contradictory things were said about him, but the facts showed he had risen rapidly to a position of control over millions of life-units.

Throughout the long war, the berserker computers had gathered and collated all available data on the men who became leaders of Life. Now against this data they matched, point for point, every detail that could be learned about Johann Karlsen.

The behavior of these leading units often resisted analysis, as if some quality of the life-disease in them was forever beyond the reach of machines. These individuals used logic, but sometimes it seemed they were not bound by logic. The most dangerous life-units of all sometimes acted in ways that seemed to contradict the known supremacy of the laws of physics and chance, as if they could be minds possessed of true free will, instead of its illusion.

And Karlsen was one of these, supremely one of these. His fitting of the dangerous pattern became plainer with every new comparison.

In the past, such life-units had been troublesome local problems. For one of them to command the whole life-fleet with a decisive battle approaching, was extremely dangerous to the cause of Death.

The outcome of the approaching battle seemed

almost certain to be favorable, since there were probably only two hundred ships in the life-fleet. But the brooding berserkers could not be certain enough of anything, while a unit like Johann Karlsen led the living. And if the battle was long postponed the enemy Life could become stronger. There were hints that inventive Life was developing new weapons, newer and more powerful ships.

The wordless conference reached a decision. There were berserker reserves, which had waited for millennia along the galactic rim, dead and uncaring in their hiding places among dust clouds and heavy nebulae, and on dark stars. For this climactic battle they must be summoned, the power of Life to resist must be broken now.

From the berserker fleet at the Stone Place, between Atsog's Sun and Sol, courier machines sped out toward the galactic rim.

It would take some time for all the reserves to gather. Meanwhile, the interrogations went on.

"Listen, I've decided to help you, see. About this guy Karlsen, I know you want to find out about him. Only I got a delicate brain. If anything hurts me, my brain don't work at all, so no rough stuff on me, understand? I'll be no good to you ever if you use rough stuff on me."

This prisoner was unusual. The interrogating computer borrowed new circuits for itself, chose symbols and hurled them back at the life-unit.

"What can you tell me about Karlsen?"

"Listen you're gonna treat me right, aren't you?"

"Useful information will be rewarded. Untruth will bring you unpleasant stimuli."

"I'll tell you this now—the woman Karlsen was going to marry is here. You caught her alive in the same shelter General Bradin was in. Now, if you sort of give me control over some other prisoners, make things nice for me, why I bet I can think up the best way for you to use her. If you just tell him you've got her, why he might not believe you, see?"

Out on the galactic rim, the signals of the giant heralds called out the hidden reserves of the unliving. Subtle detectors heard the signals, and triggered the great engines into cold flame. The force field brain in each strategic housing awoke to livelier death. Each reserve machine began to move, with metallic leisure shaking loose its cubic miles of weight and power freeing itself from dust, or ice, or age-old mud, or solid rock—then rising and turning, orienting itself in space. All converging, they drove faster than light toward the Stone Place, where the destroyers of Atsog awaited their reinforcement.

With the arrival of each reserve machine, the linked berserker computers saw victory more probable. But still the quality of one life-unit made all of their computations uncertain.

Felipe Nogara raised a strong and hairy hand, and wiped it gently across one glowing segment of the panel before his chair. The center of his private study was filled by an enormous display sphere, which now showed a representation of the explored part of the galaxy. At Nogara's gesture the sphere dimmed, then began to relight itself in a slow intricate sequence.

A wave of his hand had just theoretically eliminated the berserker flee as a factor in the power game. To leave it in, he told himself, diffused the probabilities too widely. It was really the competing power of Venus—and that of two or three other prosperous, aggressive planets—which occupied his mind.

Well insulated in this private room from the hum of Esteel City and from the routine press of business, Nogara watched his computers' new prediction take shape, showing the political power structure as it might exist one year from now, two years, five. As he had expected, this sequence showed Esteel expanding in influence. It was even possible that he could become ruler of the human galaxy.

Nogara wondered at his own calm in the face of such an idea. Twelve or fifteen years ago he had driven with all his power of intellect and will to advance himself. Gradually, the moves in the game had come to seem automatic. Today, there was a chance that almost every thinking being known to exist would come to acknowledge him as ruler— and it meant less to him than the first local election he had ever won.

Diminishing returns, of course. The more gained, the greater gain needed to produce an equal pleasure. At least when he was alone. If his aides were watching this prediction now it would certainly excite them, and he would catch their excitement.

But, being alone, he sighed. The berserker fleet would not vanish at the wave of a hand. Today, what was probably the final plea for more help had arrived from Earth. The trouble was that granting Sol more help would take ships and men and money from Nogara's expansion projects. Wherever he did that now, he stood to lose out, eventually, to other men. Old Sol would have to survive the coming attack with no more help from Esteel.

Nogara realized, wondering dully at himself, that he would as soon see even Esteel destroyed as see control slip from his hands. Now why? He could not say he loved his planet or his people, but he had been, by and large, a good ruler, not a tyrant. Good government was, after all, good politics.

His desk chimed the melodious notes that meant something was newly available for his amusement. Nogara chose to answer.

"Sir," said a woman's voice, "two new possibilities are in the shower room now."

Projected from hidden cameras, a scene glowed into life above Nogara's desk—bodies gleaming in a spray of water.

"They are from prison, sir, anxious for any reprieve."

Watching, Nogara felt only a weariness; and, yes, something like self-contempt. He questioned himself: Where in all the universe is there a reason why I should not seek pleasure as I choose? And again: Will I dabble in sadism, next? And if I do, what of it?

But what after that?

Having paused respectfully, the voice asked: "Perhaps this evening you would prefer something different?"

"Later," he said. The scene vanished. Maybe I should try to be a Believer for a while, he thought. What an intense thrill it must be for Johann to sin. If he ever does.

That had been a genuine pleasure, seeing Johann given command of the Solarian fleet, watching the Venerians boil. But it had raised another problem. Johann, victorious over the berserkers, would emerge as the greatest hero in human history. Would that not make even Johann dangerously ambitious? The thing to do would be to ease him out of the public eye, give him some high-ranked job, honest, but dirty and inglorious. Hunting out outlaws somewhere. Johann would probably accept that, being Johann. But if Johann bid for galactic power, he would have to take his chances. Any pawn on the board might be removed.

Nogara shook his head. Suppose Johann lost the coming battle, and lost Sol? A berserker victory would not be a matter of diffusing probabilities, that was pleasant doubletalk for a tired mind to fool itself with. A berserker victory would mean the end of Earthman in the galaxy, probably within a few years. No computer was needed to see that.

There was a little bottle in his desk; Nogara brought it out and looked at it. The end of the chess game was in it, the end of all pleasure and boredom and pain. Looking at the vial caused him no emotion. In it was a powerful drug which threw a man into a kind of ecstasy—a transcendental excitement that within a few minutes burst the heart or the blood vessels of the brain. Someday, when all else was exhausted, when it was completely a berserker universe . . .

He put the vial away, and he put away the final appeal from Earth. What did it all matter? Was it not a berserker universe already, everything determined by the random swirls of condensing gas, before the stars were born?

Felipe Nogara leaned back in his chair, watching his computers marking out the galactic chessboard.

Through the fleet the rumor spread that Karlsen delayed because it was a Venerian colony under siege. Aboard the *Solar Spot*, Mitch saw no delays for any reason. He had time for only work, quick meals, and sleep. When the final ram-and-board drill had been completed, the last stores and ammunition loaded, Mitch was too tired to feel much except relief. He rested, not frightened or elated, while the *Spot* wheeled into a rank with forty other arrow-shaped ships, dipped with them into the first C-plus jump of the deep space search, and began to hunt the enemy.

It was days later before dull routine was broken by a jangling battle alarm. Mitch was awakened by it; before his eyes were fully opened, he was scrambling into the armored suit stored under his bunk. Nearby, some marines grumbled about practice alerts; but none of them were moving slowly.

"This is High Commander Karlsen speaking," boomed the overhead speakers. "This is not a practice alert; repeat, not practice. Two berserkers have been sighted. One we've just glimpsed at extreme range. Likely it will get away, though the Ninth Squadron is chasing it.

"The other is not going to escape. In a matter of minutes we will have it englobed, in normal space. We are not going to destroy it by bombardment; we are going to soften it up a bit, and then see how well we can really ram and board. If there are any bugs left in our tactics, we'd better find out now. Squadrons Two, Four, and Seven will each send one ship to the ramming attack. I'm going back on Command Channel now, Squadron Commanders."

"Squadron Four," sighed Sergeant McKendrick. "More Esteelers in our company than any other. How can we miss?"

The marines lay like dragon's teeth seeded in the dark, strapped into the padded acceleration couches that had been their bunks, while the psych-music tried to lull them, and those who were Believers prayed. In the darkness Mitch listened on intercom, and passed on to his men the terse battle reports that came to him as marine commander on the ship.

He was afraid. What was death, that men should fear it so? It could only be the end of all experience. That end was inevitable, and beyond imagination, and he feared it.

The preliminary bombardment did not take long. Two hundred and thirty ships of life held a single trapped enemy in the center of their hollow sphere formation. Listening in the dark to laconic voices, Mitch heard how the berserker fought back, as if with the finest human courage and contempt for odds. Could you really fight machines, when you could never make them suffer pain or fear?

But you could defeat machines. And this time, for once, humanity had far too many guns. It would be easy to blow this berserker into vapor. Would it be best to do so? There were bound to be marine casualties in any boarding, no matter how favorable the odds. But a true combat test of the boarding scheme was badly needed before the decisive battle came to be fought. And, too, this enemy might hold living prisoners who might be rescued by boarders. A High Commander did well to have a rocklike certainty of his own rightness.

The order was given. The *Spot* and two other chosen ships fell in toward the battered enemy at the center of the englobement.

Straps held Mitch firmly, but the gravity had been turned off for the ramming, and weightlessness gave the impression that his body would fly and vibrate like a pellet shaken in a bottle with the coming impact. Soundless dark, soft cushioning, and lulling music; but a few words came into the helmet and the body cringed, knowing that outside were the black cold guns and the hurtling machines, unimaginable forces leaping now to meet. Now—

Reality shattered in through all the protection and the padding. The shaped atomic charge at the tip of the ramming prow opened the berserker's skin. In five seconds of crashing impact, the prow vaporized, melted, and crumpled its length away, the true hull driving behind it until the *Solar Spot* was sunk like an arrow into the body of the enemy.

Mitch spoke for the last time to the bridge of the *Solar Spot*, while his men lurched past him in free fall, their suit lights glaring.

"My panel shows Sally Port Three the only one

not blocked," he said. "We're all going out that way."

"Remember," said a Venerian voice. "Your first job is to protect this ship against counterattack."

"Roger." If they wanted to give him offensively unnecessary reminders, now was not the time for argument. He broke contact with the bridge and hurried after his men.

The other two ships were to send their boarders fighting toward the strategic housing, somewhere deep in the berserker's center. The marines from the *Solar Spot* were to try to find and save any prisoners the berserker might hold. A berserker usually held prisoners near its surface, so the first search would be made by squads spreading out under the hundreds of square kilometers of hull.

In the dark chaos of wrecked machinery just outside the sally port there was no sign yet of counterattack. The berserkers had supposedly not been built to fight battles inside their own metallic skins—on this rested the fleet's hopes for success in a major battle.

Mitch left forty men to defend the hull of the *Spot*, and himself led a squad of ten out into the labyrinth. There was no use setting himself up in a command post—communications in here would be impossible, once out of line-of-sight.

The first man in each searching squad carried a mass spectrometer, an instrument that would detect the stray atoms of oxygen bound to leak from compartments where living beings breathed. The last man wore on one hand a device to blaze a trail with arrows of luminous paint; without a trail, getting lost in this three-dimensional maze would be almost inevitable.

"Got a scent, Captain," said Mitch's spectrometer man, after five minutes' casting through the squad's assigned sector of the dying berserker.

"Keep on it." Mitch was second in line, his carbine ready.

The detector man led the way through a dark and weightless mechanical universe. Several times he paused to adjust his instrument and wave its probe. Otherwise the pace was rapid; men trained in free fall, and given plenty of holds to thrust and steer by, could move faster than runners.

A towering, multijointed shape rose up before the detector man, brandishing blue-white welding arcs like swords. Before Mitch was aware of aiming, his carbine fired twice. The shells ripped the machine open and pounded it backward; it was only some semirobotic maintenance device, not built for fighting.

The detector man had nerve; he plunged straight on. The squad kept pace with him, their suit lights scouting out unfamiliar shapes and distances, cutting knife-edge shadows in the vacuum, glare and darkness mellowed only by reflection.

"Getting close!"

And then they came to it. It was a place like the top of a huge dry well. An ovoid like a ship's launch, very thickly armored, had apparently been raised through the well from deep inside the berserker, and now clamped to a dock.

"It's the launch, it's oozing oxygen."

"Captain, there's some kind of airlock on this side. Outer door's open."

It looked like the smooth and easy entrance of a trap.

"Keep your eyes open." Mitch went into the airlock. "Be ready to blast me out of here if I don't show in one minute."

It was an ordinary airlock, probably cut from some human spaceship. He shut himself inside, and then got the inner door open.

Most of the interior was a single compartment. In the center was an acceleration couch, holding a nude female mannikin. He drifted near, saw that her head had been depilated and that there were tiny beads of blood still on her scalp, as if probes had just been withdrawn.

When his suit lamp hit her face she opened dead blue staring eyes, blinking mechanically. Still not sure that he was looking at a living human being, Mitch drifted beside her and touched her arm with metal fingers. Then all at once her face became human, her eyes coming from death through nightmare to reality. She saw him and cried out. Before he could free her there were crystal drops of tears in the weightless air.

Listening to his rapid orders, she held one hand modestly in front of her, and the other over her raw scalp. Then she nodded, and took into her mouth the end of a breathing tube that would dole air from Mitch's suit tank. In a few more seconds he had her wrapped in a clinging, binding rescue blanket, temporary proof against vacuum and freezing.

The detector man had found no oxygen source except the launch. Mitch ordered his squad back along their luminous trail.

At the sally port, he heard that things were not going well with the attack. Real fighting robots were defending the strategic housing; at least eight men had been killed down there. Two more ships were going to ram and board.

Mitch carried the girl through the sally port and three more friendly hatches. The monstrously thick hull of the ship shuddered and sang around him; the *Solar Spot*, her mission accomplished, boarders retrieved, was being withdrawn. Full weight came back, and light.

"In here, Captain."

QUARANTINE, said the sign. A berserker's prisoner might have been deliberately infected with something contagious; men now knew how to deal with such tricks.

Inside the infirmary he set her down. While medics and nurses scrambled around, he unfolded the blanket from the girl's face, remembering to leave it curled over her shaven head, and opened his own helmet.

"You can spit out the tube now," he told her, in his rasping voice.

She did so, and opened her eyes again.

"Oh, are you real?" she whispered. Her hand pushed its way out of the blanket folds and slid over his armor. "Oh, let me touch a human being again!" Her hand moved up to his exposed face and gripped his cheek and neck.

"I'm real enough. You're all right now."

One of the bustling doctors came to a sudden, frozen halt, staring at the girl. Then he spun around on his heel and hurried away. What was wrong?

Others sounded confident, reassuring the girl as they ministered to her. She wouldn't let go of Mitch, she became nearly hysterical when they tried gently to separate her from him.

"I guess you'd better stay," a doctor told him.

He sat there holding her hand, his helmet and gauntlets off. He looked away while they did medical things to her. They still spoke easily; he thought they were finding nothing much wrong.

"What's your name?" she asked him when the medics were through for the moment. Her head was bandaged; her slender arm came from beneath the sheets to maintain contact with his hand.

"Mitchell Spain." Now that he got a good look at her, a living young human female, he was in no hurry at all to get away. "What's yours?"

A shadow crossed her face. "I'm—not sure."

There was a sudden commotion at the infirmary door; High Commander Karlsen was pushing past protesting doctors into the QUARANTINE area. Karlsen came on until he was standing beside Mitch, but he was not looking at Mitch.

"Chris," he said to the girl. "Thank God." There were tears in his eyes.

The Lady Christina de Dulcin turned her eyes from Mitch to Johann Karlsen, and screamed in abject terror.

"Now, Captain. Tell me how you found her and brought her out."

Mitch began his tale. The two men were alone in Karlsen's monastic cabin, just off the flagship's bridge. The fight was over, the berserker a torn and harmless hulk. No other prisoners had been aboard it.

"They planned to send her back to me," Karlsen said, staring into space, when Mitch had finished his account. "We attacked before it could launch her toward us. It kept her out of the fighting, and sent her back to me."

Mitch was silent.

Karlsen's red-rimmed eyes fastened on him. "She's been brainwashed, Poet. It can be done with some permanence, you know, when advantage is taken of the subject's natural tendencies. I suppose she's never thought too much of me. There were political reasons for her to consent to our marriage . . . she screams when the doctors even mention my name. They tell me it's possible that horrible things were done to her by some man-shaped machine made to look like me. Other people are tolerable, to a degree. But it's you she wants to be alone with, you she needs."

"She cried out when I left her, but—me?"

"The natural tendency, you see. For her to . . . love . . . the man who saved her. The machines set her mind to fasten all the joy of rescue upon the first male human face she saw. The doctors assure me such things can be done. They've given her drugs, but even in sleep the instruments show her nightmares, her pain, and she cries out for you. What do you feel toward her?"

"Sir, I'll do anything I can. What do you want of me?"

"I want you to stop her suffering, what else?" Karlsen's voice rose to a ragged shout. "Stay alone with her, stop her pain if you can!"

He got himself under a kind of control. "Go on. The doctors will take you in. Your gear will be brought over from the *Solar Spot*."

Mitch stood up. Any words he could think of sounded in his mind like sickening attempts at humor. He nodded, and hurried out.

"This is your last chance to join us," said the Venerian, Salvador, looking up and down the dim corridors of this remote outer part of the flagship. "Our patience is worn, and we will strike soon. With the De Dulcin woman in her present condition, Nogara's brother is doubly unfit to command."

The Venerian must be carrying a pocket spy-jammer; a multisonic whine was setting Hemphill's teeth on edge. And so was the Venerian.

"Karlsen is vital to the human cause whether we like him or not," Hemphill said, his own patience about gone, but his voice still calm and reasonable. "Don't you see to what lengths the berserkers have gone to get at him? They sacrificed a perfectly good machine just to deliver his brainwashed woman here, to attack him psychologically."

"Well. If that is true they have succeeded. If Karlsen had any value before, now he will be able to think of nothing but his woman and the Martian."

Hemphill sighed. "Remember, he refused to

hurry the fleet to Atsog to try to save her. He hasn't failed yet. Until he does, you and the others must give up this plotting against him."

Salvador backed away a step, and spat on the deck in rage. A calculated display, thought Hemphill.

"Look to yourself, Earthman!" Salvador hissed. "Karlsen's days are numbered, and the days of those who support him too willingly!" He spun around and walked away.

"Wait!" Hemphill called, quietly. The Venerian stopped and turned, with an air of arrogant reluctance. Hemphill shot him through the heart with a laser pistol. The weapon made a splitting, crackling noise in atmosphere.

Hemphill prodded the dying man with his toe, making sure no second shot was needed. "You were good at talking," he mused aloud. "But too devious to lead the fight against the damned machines."

He bent to quickly search the body, and stood up elated. He had found a list of officers' names. Some few were underlined, and some, including his own, followed by a question mark. Another paper bore a scribbled compilation of the units under command of certain Venerian officers. There were a few more notes; altogether, plenty of evidence for the arrest of the hard-core plotters. It might tend to split the fleet, but—

Hemphill looked up sharply, then relaxed. The man approaching was one of his own, whom he had stationed nearby.

"We'll take these to the High Commander at once." Hemphill waved the papers. "There'll be just time to clean out the traitors and reorganize command before we face battle."

Yet he delayed for another moment, staring down at Salvador's corpse. The plotter had been overconfident and inept, but still dangerous. Did some sort of luck operate to protect Karlsen? Karlsen himself did not match Hemphill's ideal of a war leader; he was not as ruthless as machinery or as cold as metal. Yet the damned machines made great sacrifices to attack him.

Hemphill shrugged, and hurried on his way.

"Mitch, I do love you. I know what the doctors say it is, but what do they really know about me?"

Christina de Dulcin, wearing a simple blue robe and turbanlike headdress, now reclined on a luxurious acceleration couch, in what was nominally the sleeping room of the High Commander's quarters. Karlsen had never occupied the place, preferring a small cabin.

Mitchell Spain sat three feet from her, afraid to so much as touch her hand, afraid of what he might do, and what she might do. They were alone, and he felt sure they were unwatched. The Lady Christina had even demanded assurances against spy devices and Karlsen had sent his pledge. Besides, what kind of ship would have spy devices built into its highest officers' quarters?

A situation for bedroom farce, but not when you had to live through it. The man outside, taking the strain, had more than two hundred ships dependent on him now, and many human planets would be lifeless in five years if the coming battle failed.

"What do you really know about me, Chris?" he asked.

"I know you mean life itself to me. Oh, Mitch, I have no time now to be coy, and mannered, and every millimeter a lady. I've been all those things. And—once—I would have married a man like Karlsen, for political reasons. But all that was before Atsog."

Her voice dropped on the last word, and her hand on her robe made a convulsive grasping gesture. He had to lean forward and take it.

"Chris, Atsog is in the past now."

"Atsog will never be over, completely over, for me. I keep remembering more and more of it. Mitch, the machines made us watch while they skinned General Bradin alive. I saw that. I can't bother with silly things like politics anymore, life is too short for them. And I no longer fear anything, except driving you away . . . "

He felt pity, and lust, and half a dozen other maddening things.

"Karlsen's a good man," he said finally.

She repressed a shudder. "I suppose," she said in a controlled voice. "But Mitch, what do you feel for me? Tell the truth—if you don't love me now, I can hope you will, in time." She smiled faintly, and raised a hand. "When my silly hair grows back."

"Your silly hair." His voice almost broke. He reached to touch her face, then pulled his fingers back as from a flame. "Chris, you're his girl, and too much depends on him."

"I was never his."

"Still . . . I can't lie to you, Chris; maybe I can't

tell you the truth, either, about how I feel. The battle's coming, everything's up in the air, paralyzed. No one can plan..." He made an awkward, uncertain gesture.

"Mitch." Her voice was understanding. "This is terrible for you, isn't it? Don't worry, I'll do nothing to make it worse. Will you call the doctor? As long as I know you're somewhere near, I think I can rest, now."

Karlsen studied Salvador's papers in silence for some minutes, like a man pondering a chess problem. He did not seem greatly surprised.

"I have a few dependable men standing ready," Hemphill finally volunteered. "We can quickly—arrest—the leaders of this plot."

The blue eyes searched him. "Commander, was Salvador's killing truly necessary?"

"I thought so," said Hemphill blandly. "He was reaching for his own weapon."

Karlsen glanced once more at papers and reached a decision.

"Commander Hemphill, I want you to pick four ships, and scout the far edge of the Stone Place nebula. We don't want to push beyond it without knowing where the enemy is, and give him a chance to get between us and Sol. Use caution—to learn the general location of the bulk of his fleet is enough."

"Very well." Hemphill nodded. The reconnaisance made sense; and if Karlsen wanted to get Hemphill out of the way, and deal with his human opponents by his own methods, well, let him. Those methods often seemed soft-headed to

Hemphill, but they seemed to work for Karlsen. If the damned machines for some reason found Karlsen unendurable, then Hemphill would support him, to the point of cheerful murder and beyond.

What else really mattered in the universe, besides smashing the damned machines?

Mitch spent hours every day alone with Chris. He kept from her the wild rumors which circulated throughout the fleet. Salvador's violent end was whispered about, and guards were posted near Karlsen's quarters. Some said Admiral Kemal was on the verge of open revolt.

And now the Stone Place was close ahead of the fleet, blanking out half the stars; ebony dust and fragments, like a million shattered planets. No ship could move through the Stone Place; every cubic kilometer of it held enough matter to prevent C-plus travel or movement in normal space at any effective speed.

The fleet headed toward one sharply defined edge of the cloud, around which Hemphill's scouting squadron had already disappeared.

"She grows a little saner, a little calmer, every day," said Mitch, entering the High Commander's small cabin.

Karlsen looked up from his desk. The papers before him seemed to be lists of names, in Venerian script. "I thank you for that word, Poet. Does she speak of me?"

"No."

They eyed each other, the poor and ugly cynic,

the annointed and handsome Believer.

"Poet," Karlsen asked suddenly, "how do you deal with deadly enemies, when you find them in your power?"

"We Martians are supposed to be a violent people. Do you expect me to pass sentence on myself?"

Karlsen appeared not to understand for a moment. "Oh. No. I was not speaking of you—you and me and Chris. Not personal affairs. I suppose I was only thinking aloud, asking for a sign."

"Then don't ask me, ask your God. But didn't he tell you to forgive your enemies?"

"He did." Karlsen nodded, slowly and thoughtfully. "You know, he wants a lot from us. A real hell of a lot."

It was a peculiar sensation, to become suddenly convinced that the man you were watching was a genuine, nonhypocritical Believer. Mitch was not sure he had ever met the like before.

Nor had he ever seen Karlsen quite like this— passive, waiting; asking for a sign. As if there was in fact some Purpose outside the layers of a man's own mind, that could inspire him. Mitch thought about it. If . . .

But that was all mystical nonsense.

Karlsen's communicator sounded. Mitch could not make out what the other voice was saying, but he watched the effect on the High Commander. Energy and determination were coming back, there were subtle signs of the return of force, of the tremendous conviction of being right. It was like watching the gentle glow when a fusion power lamp was ignited.

"Yes," Karlsen was saying. "Yes, well done."

Then he raised the Venerian papers from his desk; it was as if he raised them only by force of will, his fingers only gesturing beneath them.

"The news is from Hemphill," he said to Mitch, almost absently. "The berserker fleet is just around the edge of the Stone Place from us. Hemphill estimates they are two hundred strong, and thinks they are unaware of our presence. We attack at once. Man your battle station, Poet; God be with you." He turned back to his communicator. "Ask Admiral Kemal to my cabin at once. Tell him to bring his staff. In particular—" He glanced at the Venerian papers and read off several names.

"Good luck to you, sir," Mitch had delayed to say that. Before he hurried out, he saw Karlsen stuffing the Venerian papers into his trash disintegrator.

Before Mitch reached his own cabin, the battle horns were sounding. He had armed and suited himself and was making his way back through the suddenly crowded narrow corridors toward the bridge, when the ship's speakers boomed suddenly to life, picking up Karlsen's voice:

" . . . whatever wrongs we have done you, by word, or deed, or by things left undone, I ask you now to forgive. And in the name of every man who calls me friend or leader, I pledge that any grievance we have against you, is from this moment wiped from memory."

Everyone in the crowded passage hesitated in the rush for battle stations. Mitch found himself staring into the eyes of a huge, well-armed

Venerian ship's policeman, probably here on the flagship as some officer's bodyguard.

There came an amplified cough and rumble, and then the voice of Admiral Kemal:

"We—we are brothers, Esteeler and Venerian, and all of us. All of us together now, the living against the berserker." Kemal's voice rose to a shout. "Destruction to the damned machines, and death to their builders! Let every man remember Atsog!"

"Remember Atsog!" roared Karlsen's voice.

In the corridor there was a moment's hush, like that before a towering wave smites down. Then a great insensate shout. Mitch found himself with tears in his eyes, yelling something.

"Remembering General Bradin," cried the big Venerian, grabbing Mitch and hugging him, lifting him, armor and all. "Death to his flayers!"

"Death to the flayers!" The shout ran like a flame through the corridor. No one needed to be told that the same things were happening in all the ships of the fleet. All at once there was no room for anything less than brotherhood, no time for anything less than glory.

"Destruction to the damned machines!"

Near the flagship's center of gravity was the bridge, only a dais holding a ring of combat chairs, each with its clustered controls and dials.

"Boarding Coordinator ready," Mitch reported, strapping himself in.

The viewing sphere near the bridge's center showed the human advance, in two leapfrogging lines of over a hundred ships each. Each ship was a green dot in the sphere, positioned as truthfully as the flagship's computers could manage. The irregular surface of the Stone Place moved beside the battle lines in a series of jerks; the flagship was traveling by C-plus microjumps, so the presentation in the viewing sphere was a succession of still pictures at second-and-a-half intervals. Slowed by the mass of their C-plus cannon, the six fat green symbols of the Venerian heavy weapons ships labored forward, falling behind the rest of the fleet.

In Mitch's headphones someone was saying: "In about ten minutes we can expect to reach—"

The voice died away. There was a red dot in the sphere already, and then another, and then a dozen, rising like tiny suns around the bulge of dark nebula. For long seconds the men on the bridge were silent while the berserker advance came into view. Hemphill's scouting patrol must, after all, have been detected, for the berserker fleet was not cruising, but attacking. There was a battlenet of a hundred or more red dots, and now there were two nets, leapfrogging in and out of space like the human lines. And still the red berserkers rose into view, their formations growing, spreading out to englobe and crush a smaller fleet.

"I make it three hundred machines," said a pedantic and somewhat effeminate voice, breaking the silence with cold precision. Once, the mere knowledge that three hundred berserkers existed might have crushed all human hopes. In this place, in this hour, fear itself could frighten no one.

The voices in Mitch's headphones began to transact the business of opening a battle. There was nothing yet for him to do but listen and watch.

The six heavy green marks were falling further behind; without hesitation, Karlsen was hurling his entire fleet straight at the enemy center. The foe's strength had been underestimated, but it seemed the berserker command had made a similar error, because the red formations too were being forced to regroup, spread themselves wider.

The distance between fleets was still too great for normal weapons to be effective, but the laboring heavy-weapons ships with their C-plus cannon were now in range, and they could fire through friendly formations almost as easily as not. At their volley Mitch thought he felt space jar around him; it was some secondary effect that the human brain notices, really only wasted energy. Each projectile, blasted by explosives to a safe distance from its launching ship, mounted its own C-plus engine, which then accelerated the projectile while it flickered in and out of reality on microtimers.

Their leaden masses magnified by velocity, the huge slugs skipped through existence like stones across water, passing like phantoms through the fleet of life, emerging fully into normal space only as they approached their target, travelling then like De Broglie wavicles, their matter churning internally with a phase velocity greater than that of light.

Almost instantly after Mitch had felt the slugs' ghostly passage, one red dot began to expand and thin into a cloud, still tiny in the viewing sphere.

Someone gasped. In a few more moments the flagship's own weapons, beams and missiles, went into action.

The enemy center stopped, two million miles ahead, but his flanks came on, smoothly as the screw of a vast meat-grinder, threatening englobement of the first line of human ships.

Karlsen did not hesitate, and a great turning point flickered past in a second. The life-fleet hurtled on, deliberately into the trap, straight for the hinge of the jaws.

Space twitched and warped around Mitchell Spain. Every ship in the fleet was firing now, and every enemy answering, and the energies released plucked through his armor like ghostly fingers. Green dots and red vanished from the sphere, but not many of either as yet.

The voices in Mitch's helmet slackened, as events raced into a pattern that shifted too fast for human thought to follow. Now for a time the fight would be computer against computer, faithful slave of life against outlaw, neither caring, neither knowing.

The viewing sphere on the flagship's bridge was shifting ranges almost in a flicker. One swelling red dot was only a million miles away, then half of that, then half again. And how the flagship came into normal space for the final lunge of the attack, firing itself like a bullet at the enemy.

Again the viewer switched to a closer range, and the chosen foe was no longer a red dot, but a great forbidding castle, tilted crazily, black against the stars. Only a hundred miles away, then half of that. The velocity of closure slowed no less than a mile a second. As expected, the enemy was accelerating, trying to get away from what must look to it like a suicide charge. For the last time Mitch checked his chair, his suit, his weapons. *Chris, be safe in a cocoon.* The berserker swelled in the sphere, gun-flashes showing now around his steel-ribbed belly. A small one, this, maybe only ten times the flagship's bulk. Always a rotten spot to be found, in every one of them, old wounds under their ancient skins. Try to run, you monstrous obscenity, try in vain.

Closer, twisting closer. Now!

Lights all gone, falling in the dark for one endless second—

Impact. Mitch's chair shook him, the gentle pads inside his armor battering and bruising him. The expendable ramming prow would be vaporizing, shattering and crumpling, dissipating energy down to a level the battering-ram ship could endure.

When the crashing stopped, noise still remained, a whining, droning symphony of stressed metal and escaping air and gases like sobbing breathing. The great machines were locked together now, half the length of the flagship embedded in the berserker.

A rough ramming, but no one on the bridge was injured. Damage Control reported that the expected air leaks were being controlled. Gunnery reported that it could not yet extend a turret inside the wound. Drive reported ready for a maximum effort.

Drive!

The ship twisted in the wound it had made. This

could be victory now, tearing the enemy open, sawing his metal bowels out into space. The bridge twisted with the structure of the ship, this warship that was more solid metal than anything else. For a moment, Mitch thought he could come close to comprehending the power of the engines men had built.

"No use, Commander. We're wedged in."

The enemy endured. The berserker memory would already be searched, the plans made, the counterattack on the flagship coming, without fear or mercy.

The Ship Commander turned his head to look at Johann Karlsen. It had been forseen that once a battle reached this melee stage there would be little for a High Commander to do. Even if the flagship itself were not half-buried in an enemy hull, all space nearby was a complete inferno of confused destruction, through which any meaningful communication would be impossible. If Karlsen was helpless now, neither could the berserker computers still link themselves into a single brain.

"Fight your ship, sir," said Karlsen. He leaned forward, gripping the arms of his chair, gazing at the clouded viewing sphere as if trying to make sense of the few flickering lights within it.

The Ship Commander immediately ordered his marines to board.

Mitch saw them out the sally ports. Then, sitting still was worse than any action. "Sir, I request permission to join the boarders."

Karlsen seemed not to hear. He disqualified himself, for now, from any use of power;

especially to set Mitchell Spain in the forefront of the battle or to hold him back.

The Ship Commander considered. He wanted to keep a Boarding Coordinator on the bridge; but experienced men would be desperately needed in the fighting. "Go, then. Do what you can to help defend our sally ports."

This berserker defended itself well with soldier-robots. The marines had hardly gotten away from the embedded hull when the counterattack came, cutting most of them off.

In a narrow zigzag passage leading out to the port near which fighting was heaviest, an armored figure met Mitch. "Captain Spain? I'm Sergeant Broom, acting Defense Commander here. Bridge says you're to take over. It's a little rough. Gunnery can't get a turret working inside the wound. The clankers have all kinds of room to maneuver, and they keep coming at us."

"Let's get out there, then."

The two of them hurried forward, through a passage that became only a warped slit. The flag-ship was bent here, a strained swordblade forced into a chink of armor.

"Nothing rotten here," said Mitch, climbing at last out of the sally port. There were distant flashes of light, and the sullen glow of hot metal nearby, by which to see braced girders, like tall buildings among which the flagship had jammed itself.

"Eh? No." Broom must be wondering what he was talking about. But the sergeant stuck to business, pointing out to Mitch where he had about a hundred men disposed among the chaos of torn metal and drifting debris. "The clankers don't use guns. They just drift in, sneaking, or charge in a wave, and get us hand-to-hand, if they can. Last wave we lost six men."

Whining gusts of gas came out of the deep caverns, and scattered blobs of liquid, along with flashes of light, and deep shudders through the metal. The damned thing might be dying, or just getting ready to fight; there was no way to tell.

"Any more of the boarding parties get back?" Mitch asked.

"No. Doesn't look good for 'em."

"Port Defense, this is Gunnery," said a cheerful radio voice. "We're getting the eighty-degree forward turret working."

"Well, then use it!" Mitch rasped back. "We're inside, you can't help hitting something."

A minute later, searchlights moved out from doored recesses in the flagship's hull, and stabbed into the great chaotic cavern.

"Here they come again!" yelled Broom. Hundreds of meters away, beyond the melted stump of the flagship's prow, a line of figures drifted nearer. The searchlights questioned them; they were not suited men. Mitch was opening his mouth to yell at Gunnery when the turret fired, throwing a raveling skein of shellbursts across the advancing rank of machines.

But more ranks were coming. Men were firing in every direction at machines that came clambering, jetting, drifting, in hundreds.

Mitch took off from the sally port, moving in diving weightless leaps, touring the outposts, shifting men when the need arose.

"Fall back when you have to!" he ordered, on Command radio. "Keep them from the sally ports!"

His men were facing no lurching conscription of mechanized pipefitters and moving welders; these devices were built, in one shape or another, to fight.

As he dove between outposts, a thing like a massive chain looped itself to intercept Mitch; he broke it in half with his second shot. A metallic butterfly darted at him on brilliant jets, and away again, and he wasted four shots at it.

He found an outpost abandoned, and started back toward the sally port, radioing ahead: "Broom, how is it there?"

"Hard to tell, Captain. Squad leaders, check in again, squad leaders—"

The flying thing darted back; Mitch sliced it with his laser pistol. As he approached the sally port, weapons were firing all around him. The interior fight was turning into a microcosm of the confused struggle between fleets. He knew that still raged, for the ghostly fingers of heavy weapons still plucked through his armor continually.

"Here they come again—Dog, Easy, Nine o'clock."

Coordinates of an attack straight at the sally port. Mitch found a place to wedge himself, and raised his carbine again. Many of the machines in this wave bore metal shields before them. He fired and reloaded, again and again.

The flagship's one usable turret flamed steadily,

and an almost continuous line of explosions marched across the machines' ranks in vacuum-silence, along with a traversing searchlight spot. The automatic cannons of the turret were far heavier than the marines' hand weapons; almost anything the cannon hit dissolved in radii of splinters. But suddenly there were machines on the flagship's hull, attacking the turret from its blind side.

Mitch called out a warning and started in that direction. Then all at once the enemy was around him. Two things caught a nearby man in their crablike claws, trying to tear him apart between them. Mitch fired quickly at the moving figures and hit the man, blowing one leg off.

A moment later one of the crab-machines was knocked away and broken by a hailstorm of shells. The other one beat the armored man to pieces against a jagged girder, and turned to look for its next piece of work.

This machine was armored like a warship. It spotted Mitch and came for him, climbing through drifting rubble, shells and slugs rocking it but not crippling. It gleamed in his suit lights, reaching out bright pincers, as he emptied his carbine at the box where its cybernetics should be.

He drew his pistol and dodged, but like a falling cat it turned at him. It caught him by the left hand and the helmet, metal squealing and crunching. He thrust the laser pistol against what he thought was the brainbox, and held the trigger down. He and the machine were drifting, it could get no leverage for its strength. But it held him, working on his armored hand and helmet.

Its brainbox, the pistol, and the fingers of his right gauntlet, all were glowing hot. Something molten spattered across his faceplate, the glare half-blinding him. The laser burned out, fusing its barrel to the enemy in a radiant weld.

His left gauntlet, still caught, was giving way, being crushed—

—*his hand*—

Even as the suit's hypos and tourniquet bit him, he got his burned right hand free of the laser's butt and reached the plastic grenades at his belt.

His left arm was going wooden, even before the claw released his mangled hand and fumbled slowly for a fresh grip. The machine was shuddering all over, like an agonized man. Mitch whipped his right arm around to plaster a grenade on the far side of the brainbox. Then with arms and legs he strained against the crushing, groping claws. His suit-servos whined with overload, being overpowered, two seconds, close eyes, three—

The explosion stunned him. He found himself drifting free. Lights were flaring. Somewhere was a sally port; he had to get there and defend it.

His head cleared slowly. He had the feeling that someone was pressing a pair of fingers against his chest. He hoped that was only some reaction from the hand. It was hard to see anything, with his faceplate still half-covered with splashed metal, but at last he spotted the flagship hull. A chunk of something came within reach, and he used it to propel himself toward the sally port, spinning weakly. He dug out a fresh clip of ammunition and then realized his carbine was gone.

The space near the sally port was foggy with

shattered mechanism; and there were still men here, firing their weapons out into the great cavern. Mitch recognized Broom's armor in the flaring lights, and got a welcoming wave.

"Captain! They've knocked out the turret, and most of the searchlights. But we've wrecked an awful lot of 'em—how's your arm?"

"Feels like wood. Got a carbine?"

"Say again?"

Broom couldn't hear him. Of course, the damned thing had squeezed his helmet and probably wrecked his radio transmitter. He put his helmet against Broom's and said: "You're in charge. I'm going in. Get back out if I can."

Broom was nodding, guiding him watchfully toward the port. Gun flashes started up around them thick and fast again, but there was nothing he could do about that, with two steady dull fingers pressing into his chest. Lightheaded. Get back out? Who was he fooling? Lucky if he got in without help.

He went into the port, past the interior guards' niches, and through an airlock. A medic took one look and came to help him.

Not dead yet, he thought, aware of people and lights around him. There was still some part of a hand wrapped in bandages on the end of his left arm. He noticed another thing, too; he felt no more ghostly plucking of space-bending weapons. Then he understood that he was being wheeled out of surgery, and that people hurrying by had triumph in their faces. He was still too groggy to frame a coherent question, but words he heard seemed to mean that another ship had joined in the attack on his berserker. That was a good sign, that there were spare ships around.

The stretcher bearers set him down near the bridge, in an area that was being used as a recovery room; there were many wounded strapped down and given breathing tubes against possible failure of gravity or air. Mitch could see signs of battle damage around him. How could that be, this far inside the ship. The sally ports had been held.

There was a long gravitic shudder. "They've disengaged her," said someone nearby.

Mitch passed out for a little while. The next thing he could see was that people were converging on the bridge from all directions. Their faces were happy and wondering, as if some joyful signal had called them. Many of them carried what seemed to Mitch the strangest assortment of burdens: weapons, books, helmets, bandages, trays of food, bottles, even bewildered children, who must have been rescued from the berserker's grip.

Mitch hitched himself up on his right elbow, ignoring the twinges in his bandaged chest and in the blistered fingers of his right hand. Still he could not see the combat chairs of the bridge, for the people moving between.

From all the corridors of the ship the people came, solemnly happy, men and women crowding together in the brightening lights.

An hour or so later, Mitch awoke again to find that a viewing sphere had been set up nearby. The space where the battle had been was a jagged new

nebula of gaseous metal, a few little fireplace
coals against the ebony folds of the Stone Place.

Someone near Mitch was tiredly, but with animation, telling the story to a recorder:

"—fifteen ships and about eight thousand men
lost are our present count. Every one of our ships
seemed to be damaged. We estimate ninety—that's
nine-zero—berserkers destroyed. Last count was a
hundred and seventy-six captured, or wrecking
themselves. It's still hard to believe. A day like
this . . . we must remember that thirty or more of
them escaped, and are as deadly as ever. We will
have to go on hunting and fighting them for a long
time, but their power as a fleet has been broken.
We can hope that capturing this many machines
will at last give us some definite lead on their
origin. Ah, best of all, some twelve thousand
human prisoners have been freed.

"Now, how to explain our success? Those of us
not Believers of one kind or another will say
victory came because our hulls were newer and
stronger, our long-range weapons new and
superior, our tactics unexpected by the enemy—
and our marines able to defeat anything the
berserkers could send against them.

"Above all, history will give credit to High
Commander Karlsen, for his decision to attack, at
a time when his reconciliation with the Venerians
had inspired and united the fleet. The High
Commander is here now, visiting the wounded
who lie in rows . . ."

Karlsen's movements were so slow and tired
that Mitch thought he too might be wounded,
though no bandages were visible. He shuffled past

the ranked stretchers, with a word or nod for each of the wounded. Beside Mitch's pallet he stopped, as if recognition was a shock.

"She's dead, Poet," were the first words he said.

The ship turned under Mitch for a moment; then he could be calm, as if he had expected to hear this. The battle had hollowed him out.

Karlsen was telling him, in a withered voice, how the enemy had forced through the flagship's hull a kind of torpedo, an infernal machine that seemed to know how the ship was designed, a moving atomic pile that had burned its way through the High Commander's quarters and almost to the bridge before it could be stopped and quenched.

The sight of battle damage here should have warned Mitch. But he hadn't been able to think. Shock and drugs kept him from thinking or feeling much of anything now, but he could see her face, looking as it had in the gray deadly place from which he had rescued her.

Rescued.

"I am a weak and foolish man," Karlsen was saying. "But I have never been your enemy. Are you mine?"

"No. You forgave all your enemies. Got rid of them. Now you won't have any, for a while. Galactic hero. But, I don't envy you."

"No. God rest her." But Karlsen's face was still alive, under all the grief and weariness. Only death could finally crush this man. He gave the ghost of a smile. "And now, the second part of the prophecy, hey? I am to be defeated, and to die owning nothing. As if a man could die any other way."

"Karlsen, you're all right. I think you may survive your own success. Die in peace, someday, still hoping for your Believers' heaven."

"The day I die—" Karlsen turned his head slowly, seeing all the people around him. "I'll remember this day. This glory, this victory for all men." Under the weariness and grief he still had his tremendous assurance—not of being right, Mitch thought now, but of being committed to right.

"Poet, when you are able, come and work for me."

"Someday, maybe. Now I can live on the battle bounty. And I have work. If they can't grow back my hand—why, I can write with one." Mitch was suddenly very tired.

A hand touched his good shoulder. A voice said: "God be with you." Johann Karlsen moved on.

Mitch wanted only to rest. Then, to his work. The world was bad, and all men were fools—but there were men who would not be crushed. And that was a thing worth telling.

Men always project their beliefs and their emotions into their vision of the world. Machines can be made to see in a wider spectrum, to detect every wavelength precisely as it is, undisturbed by love or hate or awe.

But still men's eyes see more than lenses do.

THE FACE OF THE DEEP

After five minutes had gone by with no apparent change in his situation, Karlsen realized that he might be going to live for a while yet. And as soon as this happened, as soon as his mind dared open its eyes again, so to speak, he began to see the depths of space around him and what they held.

There followed a short time during which he seemed unable to move; a few minutes passed while he thought he might go mad.

He rode in a crystalline bubble of a launch about twelve feet in diameter. The fortunes of war had dropped him here, halfway down the steepest gravitational hill in the known universe.

At the unseeable bottom of this hill lay a sun so massive that not a quantum of light could escape it with a visible wavelength. In less than a minute he and his raindrop of a boat had fallen here, some unmeasurable distance out of normal space, trying to escape an enemy. Karlsen had spent that falling minute in prayer, achieving something like calm, considering himself already dead.

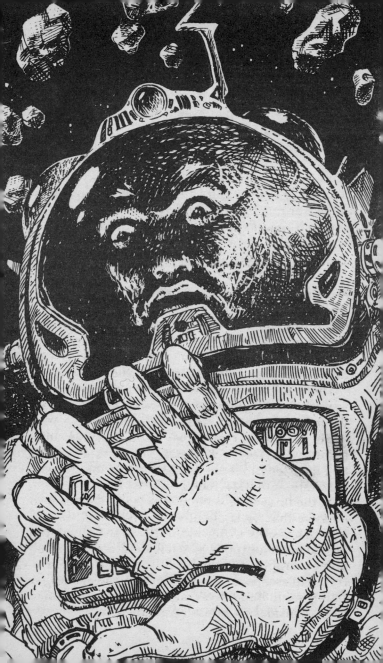

But after that minute he was suddenly no longer falling. He seemed to have entered an orbit—an orbit that no man had ever traveled before, amid sights no eyes had ever seen.

He rode above a thunderstorm at war with a sunset—a ceaseless, soundless turmoil of fantastic clouds that filled half the sky like a nearby planet. But this cloud-mass was immeasurably bigger than any planet, vaster even than most giant stars. Its core and its cause was a hypermassive sun a billion times the weight of Sol.

The clouds were interstellar dust swept up by the pull of the hypermass; as they fell they built up electrical static which was discharged in almost continuous lightning. Karlsen saw as blue-white the nearer flashes, and those ahead of him as he rode. But most of the flashes, like most of the clouds, were far below him, and so most of his light was sullen red, wearied by climbing just a section of this gravity cliff.

Karlsen's little bubble-ship had artificial gravity of its own, and kept turning itself so its deck was down, so Karlsen saw the red light below him through the translucent deck, flaring up between his space-booted feet. He sat in the one massive chair which was fixed in the center of the bubble, and which contained the boat's controls and life-support machinery. Below the deck were one or two other opaque objects, one of these a small but powerful space-warping engine. All else around Karlsen was clear glass, holding in air, holding out radiation, but leaving his eyes and soul naked to the deeps of space around him.

When he had recovered himself enough to move

again, he took a full breath and tried his engine, tried to lift himself up out of here. As he had expected, full drive did nothing at all. He might as well have been working bicycle pedals.

Even a slight change in his orbit would have been immediately visible, for his bubble was somehow locked in position within a narrow belt of rocks and dust that stretched like a thread to girdle the vastness below him. Before the thread could bend perceptibly on its great circle it lost its identity in distance, merging with other threads into a thicker strand. This in turn was braided with other strands into a heavier belt, and so on, order above order of size, until at last (a hundred thousand miles ahead? a million?) the first bending of the great ring-pattern was perceptible; and then the arc, rainbow-colored at that point by lightning, deepened swiftly, plunging out of sight below the terrible horizon of the hypermass's shroud of dust. The fantastic cloud-shapes of that horizon, which Karlsen knew must be millions of miles away, grew closer while he looked at them. Such was the speed of his orbit.

His orbit, he guessed, must be roughly the size of Earth's path around Sol. But judging by the rate at which the surface of clouds was turning beneath him, he would complete a full circuit every fifteen minutes or so. This was madness, to out-speed light in normal space—but then, of course, space was not really normal here. It could not be. These insane orbiting threads of dust and rock suggested that here gravity had formed itself into lines of force, like magnetism.

The orbiting threads of debris above Karlsen's

traveled less rapidly than his. In the nearer threads below him, he could distinguish individual rocks, passing him up like the teeth of a buzzsaw. His mind recoiled from those teeth, from the sheer grandeur of speed and distance and size.

He sat in his chair looking up at the stars. Distantly he wondered if he might be growing younger, moving backward in the time of the universe from which he had fallen . . . he was no professional mathematician or physicist, but he thought not. That was one trick the universe could not pull, even here. But the chances were that in this orbit he was aging quite slowly compared with the rest of the human race.

He realized that he was still huddling in his chair like an awed child, his fingers inside their gauntlets cramping painfully with the strength of his grip on the chair arms. He forced himself to try to relax, to begin thinking of routine matters. He had survived worse things than this display of nature, if none were awful.

He had air and water and food enough, and power to keep recycling them as long as necessary. His engine would be good for that much.

He studied the line of force, or whatever it was, that held him prisoner. The larger rocks within it, some of which approached his bubble in size, seemed never to change their relative positions. But smaller chunks drifted with some freedom backward and forward, at very low velocities.

He got up from his chair and turned. A single step to the rear brought him to the curve of glass. He looked out, trying to spot his enemy. Sure

enough, following half a mile behind him, caught
in the same string of space debris, was the
berserker-ship whose pursuit had driven him
here. Its scanners would be fixed on his bubble
now, and it would see him moving and know he
was alive. If it could get at him, it would do so. The
berserker-computers would waste no time in
awed contemplation of the scenery, that much was
certain.

As if to register agreement with his thought, the
flare of a beam weapon struck out from the
berserker-ship. But the beam looked odd and
silvery, and it plowed only a few yards among ex-
ploding rocks and dust before fizzling away like a
comic firework. It added dust to a cloud that
seemed to be thickening in front of the berserker.
Probably the machine had been firing at him all
along, but this weird space would not tolerate
energy weapons. Missiles, then?

Yes, missiles. He watched the berserker launch
one. The lean cylinder made one fiery dart in his
direction, then disappeared. Where had it gone?
Fallen in toward the hypermass? At invisible
speed, if so.

As soon as he spotted the first flare of another
missile, Karlsen on a hunch turned his eyes
quickly downward. He saw an instant spark and
puff in the next lower line of force, a tooth
knocked out of the buzzsaw. The puff where the
missile had struck flew ahead at insane speed,
passing out of Karlsen's sight almost at once. His
eyes were drawn after it, and he realized he had
been watching the berserker-ship not with fear
but with something like relief, as a distraction

from facing . . . all this.

"Ah, God," he said aloud, looking ahead. It was a prayer, not an oath. Far beyond the slow-churning infinite horizon, monstrous dragon-head clouds were rearing up. Against the blackness of space their mother-of-pearl heads seemed to be formed by matter materializing out of nothingness to plunge toward the hypermass. Soon the dragons' necks rose over the edge of the world, wattled with rainbow purls of matter that dripped and fell with unreal-looking speed. And then appeared the dragon-bodies, clouds throbbing with blue-white lightning, suspended above the red bowels of hell.

The vast ring, in which Karlsen's thread of rocks was one component, raced like a circular sawblade toward the prominence. As they rushed in from the horizon they rose up far beyond Karlsen's level. They twisted and reared like mad horses. They must be bigger than planets, he thought, yes, bigger than a thousand Earths or Esteels. The whirling band he rode was going to be crushed between them—and then he saw that even as they passed they were still enormously distant from him on either side.

Karlsen let his eyes close. If men ever dared to pray, if they ever dared even to think of a Creator of the universe, it was only because their tiny minds had never been able to visualize a thousandth part . . . a millionth part . . . there were no words, no analogues for the mind to use in grasping such a scene.

And, he thought, what of men who believe only in themselves, or in nothing? What must it do to them to look nakedly at such odds as these?

Karlsen opened his eyes. In his belief a single human being was of more importance than any sun of whatever size. He made himself watch the scenery. He determined to master this almost superstitious awe.

But he had to brace himself again when he noticed for the first time how the stars were behaving. They were all blue-white needles, the wavefronts of their light jammed together in a stampede over this cliff of gravity. And his speed was such that he saw some stars moving slightly in parallax shifts. He could have depth perception in light-years, if his mind could stretch that far.

He stepped back to his chair, sat down and fastened himself in. He wanted to retreat within himself. He wanted to dig himself a tunnel, down into the very core of a huge planet where he could hide . . . but what were even the biggest planets? Poor lost specks, hardly bigger than this bubble.

Here, he faced no ordinary spaceman's view of infinity. Here there was a terrible *perspective*, starting with rocks an arm's length outside the glass and drawing the mind on and out, rock by rock and line by line, step by inescapable step, on and on and on—

All right. At least this was something to fight against, and fighting something was better than sitting here rotting. To begin with, a little routine. He drank some water, which tasted very good, and made himself eat a bite of food. He was going to be around for a while yet.

Now, for the little job of getting used to the scenery. He faced in the direction of his bubble's flight. Half a dozen meters ahead of him the first large rock, massive as the bodies of a dozen men, hung steadily in the orbit-line of force. With his mind he weighed his rock and measured it, and then moved his thought on to the next notable chunk, a pebble's throw further. The rocks were each smaller than his bubble and he could follow the string of them on and on, until it was swallowed in the converging pattern of forcelines that at last bent around the hypermass, defining the full terror of distance.

His mind hanging by its fingertips swayed out along the intervals of grandeur . . . like a baby monkey blinking in jungle sunlight, he thought. Like an infant climber who had been terrified by the size of trees and vines, who now saw them for the first time as a network of roads that could be mastered.

Now he dared to let his eyes grab hard at that buzzsaw rim of the next inner circle of hurtling rocks, to let his mind ride it out and away. Now he dared to watch the stars shifting with his movement, to see with the depth perception of a planet.

He had been through a lot even before falling here, and sleep overtook him. The next thing he knew loud noises were waking him up. He came full awake with a start of fear. The berserker was not helpless after all. Two of its man-sized machines were outside his glassy door, working on it. Karlsen reached automatically for his handgun. The little weapon was not going to do him much good, but he waited, holding it ready. There was nothing else to do.

Something was strange in the appearance of the deadly robots outside; they were silvered with a gleaming coating. It looked like frost except that it formed only on their forward surfaces, and streamed away from them toward the rear in little fringes and tails, like an artist's speed-lines made solid. The figures were substantial enough. Their hammer blows at his door . . . but wait. His fragile door was not being forced. The metal killers outside were tangled and slowed in the silvery webbing with which this mad rushing space had draped them. The stuff damped their laser beams, when they tried to burn their way in. It muffled the explosive they set off.

When they had tried everything they departed, pushing themselves from rock to rock back toward their metal mother, wearing their white flaming surfaces like hoods of shame in their defeat.

He yelled relieving insults after them. He thought of opening his door and firing his pistol after them. He wore a spacesuit, and if they could open the door of the berserker-ship from inside he should be able to open this one. But he decided it would be a waste of ammunition.

Some deep part of his mind had concluded that it was better for him, in his present situation, not to think about time. He saw no reason to argue with this decision, and so he soon lost track of hours and days—weeks?

He exercised and shaved, he ate and drank and eliminated. The boat's recycling systems worked very well. He still had his "coffin," and might choose a long sleep—but no thanks, not yet. The possibility of rescue was in his thoughts, mixing hope with his fears of time. He knew that on the day he fell down here there was no ship built capable of coming after him and pulling him out. But ships were always being improved. Suppose he could hang on here for a few weeks or months of subjective time while a few years passed out-side. He knew there were people who would try to find him and save him if there was any hope.

From being almost paralyzed by his surroundings, he passed through a stage of exaltation, and then quickly reached—boredom. The mind had its own business, and turned itself away from all these eternal blazing miracles. He slept a good deal.

In a dream he saw himself standing alone in space. He was viewing himself at the distance where the human figure dwindles almost to a speck in the gaze of the unaided human eye. With an almost invisible arm, himself-in-the-distance waved good-bye, and then went walking away, headed out toward the blue-white stars. The striding leg movements were at first barely perceptible, and then became nothing at all as the figure dwindled, losing existence against the face of the deep . . .

With a yell he woke up. A space boat had nudged against his crystal hull, and was now bobbing a few feet away. It was a solid metal ovoid, of a model he recognized, and the numbers and letters on its hull were familiar to him. He had made it. He had hung on. The ordeal was over.

The little hatch of the rescue boat opened, and two suited figures emerged, one after the other, from its sheltered interior. At once these figures became silver-blurred as the berserker's machines had been, but these men's features were visible through their faceplates, their eyes looking straight at Karlsen. They smiled in steady encouragement, never taking their eyes from his.

Not for an instant.

They rapped on his door, and kept smiling while he put on his spacesuit. But he made no move to let them in; instead he drew his gun.

They frowned. Inside their helmets their mouths formed words: Open up! He flipped on his radio, but if they were sending nothing was coming through in this space. They kept on gazing steadily at him.

Wait, he signaled with an upraised hand. He got a slate and stylus from his chair, and wrote them a message.

LOOK AROUND AT THE SCENERY FOR A WHILE.

He was sane but maybe they thought him mad. As if to humor him, they began to look around them. A new set of dragon-head prominences were rising ahead, beyond the stormy horizon at the rim of the world. The frowning men looked ahead of them at dragons, around them at buzzsaw rainbow whirls of stone, they looked down into the deadly depths of the inferno, they looked up at the stars' poisonous blue-white spears sliding visibly over the void.

Then both of them, still frowning uncomprehendingly, looked right back at Karlsen.

He sat in his chair, holding his drawn gun, waiting, having no more to say. He knew the berserker-ship would have boats aboard, and that it could build its killing machines into the likenesses of men. These were almost good enough to fool them.

The figures outside produced a slate of their own from somewhere.

WE TOOK BERS. FROM BEHIND. ALL OK & SAFE. COME OUT.

He looked back. The cloud of dust raised by the berserker's own weapons had settled around it, hiding it and all the forceline behind it from Karlsen's view. Oh, if only he could believe that these were men . . .

They gestured energetically, and lettered some more.

OUR SHIP WAITING BACK THERE BEHIND DUST. SHE'S TOO BIG TO HOLD THIS LEVEL LONG.

And again:

KARLSEN, COME WITH US!!! THIS YOUR ONLY CHANCE!

He didn't dare read any more of their messages for fear he would believe them, rush out into their metal arms, and be torn apart. He closed his eyes and prayed. After a long time he opened his eyes again. His visitors and their boats were gone.

Not long afterward—as time seemed to him—there were flashes of light from inside the dust cloud surrounding the berserker. A fight, to which someone had brought weapons that would work in this space? Or another attempt to trick him? He would see.

He was watching alertly as another rescue boat, much like the first, inched its way out of the dustcloud toward him. It drew alongside and stopped. Two more spacesuited figures got out and began to wear silver drapery.

This time he had his sign ready.

LOOK AROUND AT THE SCENERY FOR A WHILE.

As if to humor him, they began to look around them. Maybe they thought him mad, but he was sane. After about a minute they still hadn't turned back to him—one's face looked up and out at the unbelievable stars, while the other slowly swiveled his neck, watching a dragon's head go by. Gradually their bodies became congealed in awe and terror, clinging and crouching against his glass wall.

After taking half a minute more to check his own helmet and suit, Karlsen bled out his cabin air and opened his door.

"Welcome, *men*," he said, over his helmet radio. He had to help one of them aboard the rescue boat. But they made it.

After every battle, even a victory, there are the wounded.

Injured flesh can heal. A hand can be replaced, perhaps. An eye can be bandaged; even a damaged brain can to some extent be repaired. But there are wounds too deep for any surgeon's knife to probe. There are doors that will not open from the outside.

I found a mind divided.

WHAT T AND I DID

My first awareness is of location. I am in a large conical room inside some vast vehicle, hurtling through space. The world is familiar to me, though I am new.

"He's awake!" says a black-haired young woman, watching me with frightened eyes. Half a dozen people in disheveled clothing, the three men, long unshaven, gather slowly in my field of vision.

My field of vision? My left hand comes up to feel about my face, and its fingers find my left eye covered with a patch.

"Don't disturb that!" says the tallest of the men. Probably he was once a distinguished figure. He speaks sharply, yet there is still a certain diffidence in his manner, as if I am a person of importance. But I am only . . . who?

"What's happened?" I ask. My tongue has trouble finding even the simplest words. My right arm lies at my side as if forgotten, but it stirs at my thought, and with its help I raise myself to a

sitting position, provoking an onrush of pain through my head, and dizziness.

Two of the women back away from me. A stout young man puts a protective arm around each of them. These people are familiar to me, but I cannot find their names.

"You'd better take it easy," says the tallest man. His hands, a doctor's, touch my head and my pulse, and ease me back onto the padded table.

Now I see that two tall humanoid robots stand flanking me. I expect that at any moment the doctor will order them to wheel me away to my hospital room. Still, I know better. This is no hospital. The truth will be terrible when I remember it.

"How do you feel?" asks the third man, an oldster, coming forward to bend over me.

"All right, I guess." My speech comes only in poor fragments. "What's happened?"

"There was a battle," says the doctor. "You were hurt, but I've saved your life."

"Well. Good." My pain and dizziness are subsiding.

In a satisfied tone the doctor says: "It's to be expected that you'll have difficulty speaking. Here, try to read this."

He holds up a card, marked with neat rows of what I suppose are letters or numerals. I see plainly the shapes of the symbols, but they mean nothing to me, nothing at all.

"No," I say finally, closing my eye and lying back. I feel plainly that everyone here is hostile to me. Why?

I persist: "What's happened?"

"We're all prisoners, here inside the machine,"

says the old man's voice. "Do you remember that much?"

"Yes." I nod, remembering. But details are very hazy. I ask: "My name?"

The old man chuckles drily, sounding relieved. "Why not Thad—for Thaddeus?"

"Thad?" questions the doctor. I open my eye again. Power and confidence are growing in the doctor; because of something I have done, or have not done? "Your name is Thad," he tells me.

"We're prisoners?" I question him. "Of a machine?"

"Of a berserker machine." He sighs. "Does that mean anything to you?"

Deep in my mind, it means something that will not bear looking at. I am spared; I sleep.

When I awake again, I feel stronger. The table is gone, and I recline on the soft floor of this cabin or cell, this white cone-shaped place of imprisonment. The two robots still stand by me, why I do not know.

"Atsog!" I cry aloud, suddenly remembering more. I had happened to be on the planet Atsog when the berserkers attacked. The seven of us here were carried out of a deep shelter, with others, by the raiding machines. The memory is vague and jumbled, but totally horrible.

"He's awake!" says someone again. Again the women shrink from me. The old man raises his quivering head to look, from where he and the doctor seem to be in conference. The stout young man jumps to his feet, facing me, fists clenched, as if I had threatened him.

"How are you, Thad?" the doctor calls. After a

moment's glance my way, he answers himself: "He's all right. One of you girls help him with some food. Or you, Halsted."

"Help him? God!" The black-haired girl flattens herself against the wall, as far from me as possible. The other two women crouch washing someone's garment in our prison sink. They only look at me and turn back to their washing.

My head is not bandaged for nothing. I must be truly hideous, my face must be monstrously deformed, for three women to look so pitilessly at me.

The doctor is impatient. "Someone feed him, it must be done."

"He'll get no help from me," says the stout young man. "There are limits."

The black-haired girl begins to move across the chamber toward me, everyone watching her.

· "You would?" the young man marvels to her, and shakes his head.

She moves slowly, as if she finds walking painful. Doubtless she too was injured in the battle; there are old healing bruises on her face. She kneels beside me, and guides my left hand to help me eat, and gives me water. My right side is not paralyzed, but somehow unresponsive.

When the doctor comes close again, I say: "My eye. Can it see?"

He is quick to push my fingers away from the eyepatch. "For the present, you must use only your left eye. You've undergone brain surgery. If you take off that patch now, the consequences could be disastrous, let me warn you."

I think he is being deceptive about the eyepatch. Why?

The black-haired girl asks me: "Have you remembered anything more?"

"Yes. Before Atsog fell, we heard that Johann Karlsen was leading out a fleet, to defend Sol."

All of them stare at me, hanging on my words. But they must know better than I what happened.

"Did Karlsen win the battle?" I plead. Then I realize we are prisoners still. I weep.

"There've been no new prisoners brought in here," says the doctor, watching me carefully. "I think Karlsen has beaten the berserkers. I think this machine is now fleeing from the human fleet. How does that make you feel?"

"How?" Has my understanding failed with my verbal skills? "Good."

They all relax slightly.

"Your skull was cracked when we bounced around in the battle," the old man tells me. "You're lucky a famous surgeon was here." He nods his head. "The machine wants all of us kept alive, so it can study us. It gave the doctor what he needed to operate, and if he'd let you die, or remain paralyzed, things would've been bad for him. Yessir, it made that plain."

"Mirror?" I ask. I gesture at my face. "I must see. How bad."

"We don't have a mirror," says one of the women at the sink, as if blaming me for the lack.

"Your face? It's not disfigured," says the doctor. His tone is convincing, or would be if I were not certain of my deformity.

I regret that these good people must put up with my monster-presence, compounding all their other troubles. "I'm sorry," I say, and turn from them, trying to conceal my face.

"You really don't know," says the black-haired girl, who has watched me silently for a long time. "He doesn't know!" Her voice chokes. "Oh—Thad. Your face is all right."

True enough, the skin of my face feels smooth and normal when my fingers touch it. The black-haired girl watches me with pity. Rounding her shoulder, from inside her dress, are half-healed marks like the scars of a lash.

"Someone's hurt you," I say, frightened. One of the women at the sink laughs nervously. The young man mutters something. I raise my left hand to hide my hideous face. My right comes up and crosses over to finger the edges of the eye-patch.

Suddenly the young man swears aloud, and points at where a door has opened in the wall.

"The machine must want your advice on something," he tells me harshly. His manner is that of a man who wants to be angry but does not dare. Who am I, what am I, that these people hate me so?

I get to my feet, strong enough to walk. I remember that I am the one who goes to speak alone with the machine.

In a lonely passage it offers me two scanners and a speaker as its visible face. I know that the cubic miles of the great berserker machine surround me, carrying me through space, and I remember standing in this spot before the battle, talking with it, but I have no idea what was said. In fact, I cannot recall the words of any conversation I have ever held.

"The plan you suggested has failed, and Karlsen

still functions," says the cracked machine voice, hissing and scraping in the tones of a stage villain.

What could *I* have ever suggested, to this horrible thing?

"I remember very little," I say. "My brain has been hurt."

"If you are lying about your memory, understand that I am not deceived," says the machine. "Punishing you for your plan's failure will not advance my purpose. I know that you live outside the laws of human organization, that you even refused to use a full human name. Knowing you, I trust you to help me against the organization of intelligent life. You will remain in command of the other prisoners. See that your damaged tissues are repaired as fully as possible. Soon we will attack life in a new way."

There is a pause, but I have nothing to say. Then the noisy speaker scrapes into silence, and the scanner-eyes dim. Does it watch me still, in secret? But it said it trusted me, this nightmare enemy said it trusted in my evil to make me its ally.

Now I have enough memory to know it speaks the truth about me. My despair is so great I feel sure that Karlsen did not win the battle. Everything is hopeless, because of the horror inside me. I have betrayed all life. To what bottom of evil have I not descended?

As I turn from the lifeless scanners, my eye catches a movement—my own reflection, in polished metal. I face the flat skinny bulkhead, staring at myself.

My scalp is bandaged, and my left eye. That I knew already. There is some discoloration around my right eye, but nothing shockingly repulsive. What I can see of my hair is light brown, matching my two months' unkempt beard. Nose and mouth and jaw are normal enough. There is no horror in my face.

The horror lies inside me. I have willingly served a berserker.

Like the skin around my right eye, that bordering my left eye's patch is tinged with blue and greenish yellow, hemoglobin spilled under the skin and breaking down, some result of the surgeon's work inside my head.

I remember his warning, but the eyepatch has the fascination for my fingers that a sore tooth has for the tongue, only far stronger. The horror is centered in my evil left eye, and I cannot keep from probing after it. My right hand flies eagerly into action, pulling the patch away.

I blink, and the world is blurred. I see with two eyes, and then I die.

T staggered in the passage, growling and groaning his rage, the black eyepatch gripped in his fingers. He had language now, he had a foul torrent of words, and he used them until his weak breath failed. He stumbled, hurrying through the passage toward the prison chamber, wild to get at the wise punks who had tried such smooth trickery to get rid of him. Hypnotism, or whatever. Re-name him, would they? He'd show them Thaddeus.

T reached the door and threw it open, gasping in his weakness, and walked out into the prison chamber. The doctor's shocked face showed that he realized T was back in control.

"Where's my whip?" T glared around him. "What wise punk hid it?"

The women screamed. Young Halsted realized that the Thaddeus scheme had failed; he gave a kind of hopeless yell and charged, swinging like a crazy man. Of course, T's robot bodyguards were too fast for any human. One of them blocked Halsted's punch with a metal fist, so the stout man yelped and folded up, nursing his hand.

"Get me my whip!" A robot went immediately to reach behind the sink, pull out the knotted plastic cord, and bring it to the master.

T thumped the robot jovially, and smiled at the cringing lot of his fellow prisoners. He ran the whip through his fingers, and the fingers of his left hand felt numb. He flexed them impatiently. "What'sa matter, there, Mr. Halsted? Somethin' wrong with your hand? Don't wanna give me a handshake, welcome me back? C'mon let's shake!"

The way Halsted squirmed around on the floor was so funny T had to pause and give himself up to laughing.

"Listen, you people," he said when he got his breath. "My fine friends. The machine says I'm still in charge, see? That little information I gave it about Karlsen did the trick. Boom! Haw haw haw! So you better try to keep me happy, 'cause the machine's still backing me a hunnerd per cent. You, Doc." T's left hand began trembling uncontrollably, and he waved it. "You were gonna change me, huh? You did somethin' nice to fix me up?"

Doc held his surgeon's hands behind him, as if he hoped to protect them. "I couldn't have made a new pattern for your character if I had tried—

unless I went all the way, and turned you into a vegetable. That I might have done."

"Now you wish you had. But you were scared of what the machine would do to you. Still, you tried somethin', huh?"

"Yes, to save your life." Doc stood up straight. "Your injury precipitated a severe and almost continuous epileptoid seizure, which the removal of the blood clot from your brain did not relieve. So, I divided the corpus callosum."

T flicked his whip. "What's that mean?"

"You see—the right hemisphere of the brain chiefly controls the left side of the body. While the left hemisphere, the dominant one in most people, controls the right side, and handles most judgments involving symbols."

"I know. When you get a stroke, the clot is on the opposite side from the paralysis."

"Correct." Doc raised his chin. "T, I split your brain, right side from left. That's as simply as I can put it. It's an old but effective procedure for treating severe epilepsy, and the best I could do for you here. I'll take an oath on that, or a lie test—"

"Shuddup! I'll give you a lie test!" T strode shakily forward. "What's gonna happen to me?"

"As a surgeon, I can say only that you may reasonably expect many years of practically normal life."

"Normal!" T took another step, raising his whip. "Why'd you patch my good eye, and start calling me Thaddeus?"

"That was my idea," interrupted the old man, in a quavery voice. "I thought—in a man like yourself, there had to be someone, some component, like Thad. With the psychological pressure we're under here, I thought Thad just might come out, if we gave him a chance in your right hemisphere. It was my idea. If it hurt you any, blame me."

"I will." But T seemed, for the moment, more interested than enraged. "Who is this Thaddeus?"

"You are," said the doctor. "We couldn't put anyone else into your skull."

"Jude Thaddeus," said the old man, "was a contemporary of Judas Iscariot. A similarity of names, but—" He shrugged.

T made a snorting sound, a single laugh. "You figured there was good in me, huh? It just had to come out sometime? Why, I'd say you were crazy —but you're not. Thaddeus was real. He was here in my head for a while. Maybe he's still there, hiding. How do I get at him, huh?" T raised his right hand and jabbed a finger gently at the corner of his right eye. "Ow. I don't like to be hurt. I got a delicate nervous system. Doc, how come his eye is on the right side if everything crosses over? And if it's his eye, how come I feel what happens to it?"

"His eye is on the right because I divided the optic chiasm, too. It's a somewhat complicated—"

"Never mind. We'll show Thaddeus who's boss. He can watch with the rest of you. Hey, Blacky, c'mere. We haven't played together for a while, have we?"

"No," the girl whispered. She hugged her arms around herself, nearly fainting. But she walked toward T. Two months as his slaves had taught them all that obedience was easiest.

"You like this punk Thad, huh?" T whispered,

when she halted before him. "You think his face is all right, do you? How about my face? Look at me!"

T saw his own left hand reach out and touch the girl's cheek, gently and lovingly. He could see in her startled face that she felt Thaddeus in the hand; never had her eyes looked this way at T before. T cried out and raised his whip to strike her, and his left hand flew across his body to seize his own right wrist, like a terrier clamping jaws on a snake.

T's right hand still gripped the whip, but he thought the bones of his wrist were cracking. His legs tangled each other and he fell. He tried to shout for help, and could utter only a roaring noise. His robots stood watching. It seemed a long time before the doctor's face loomed over him, and a black patch descended gently upon his left eye.

Now I understand more deeply, and I accept. At first I wanted the doctor to remove my left eye, and the old man agreed, quoting some ancient Believers' book to the effect that an offending eye should be plucked out. An eye would be a small price to rid myself of T.

But after some thought, the doctor refused. "T is yourself," he said at last. "I can't point to him with my scalpel and cut him out, although it seems I helped to separate the two of you. Now you control both sides of the body; once he did." The doctor smiled wearily. "Imagine a committee of three, a troika inside your skull. Thaddeus is one, T another—and the third is the person, the force, that casts the deciding vote. You. That's best I can tell you."

And the old man nodded.

Mostly, I do without the eyepatch now. Reading and speaking are easier when I use my long-dominant left brain, and I am still Thaddeus—perhaps because I choose to be Thaddeus. Could it be that terribly simple?

Periodically I talk with the berserker, which still trusts in T's greedy outlawry. It means to counterfeit much money, coins and notes, for me to take in a launch to a highly civilized planet, relying on my evil to weaken men there and set them against each other.

But the berserker is too badly damaged to watch its prisoners steadily, or it does not bother. With my freedom to move about I have welded some of the silver coins into a ring, and chilled this ring to superconductivity in a chamber near the berserker's unliving heart. Halsted tells me we can use this ring, carrying a permanent electric current, to trigger the C-plus drive of the launch that is our prison, and tear our berserker open from inside. We may damage it enough to save ourselves. Or we may all be killed.

But while I live, I Thaddeus, rule myself; and both my hands are gentle, touching long black hair.

Men might explain their victories by compiled statistics on armament; by the imponderable value of one man; perhaps by the precise pathway chosen by a surgeon's knife.

But for some victories no realistic explanation could be found. On one lonely world decades of careless safety had left the people almost without defense; then at last a berserker with all its power came upon them.

Behold and share their laughter!

MR. JESTER

Defeated in battle, the berserker-computers saw that refitting, repair, and the construction of new machines were necessary. They sought out sunless, hidden places, where minerals were available but where men—who were now as often the hunters as the hunted—were not likely to show up. And in such secret places they set up automated shipyards.

To one such concealed shipyard, seeking repair, there came a berserker. Its hull had been torn open in a recent fight, and it had suffered severe internal damage. It collapsed rather than landed on the dark planetoid, beside the half-finished hull of a new machine. Before emergency repairs could be started, the engines of the damaged machine failed, its emergency power failed, and like a wounded living thing it died.

The shipyard-computers were capable of wide improvisation. They surveyed the extent of the damage, weighed various courses of action, and then swiftly began to cannibalize. Instead of embodying the deadly purpose of the new machine in a new force-field brain, following the

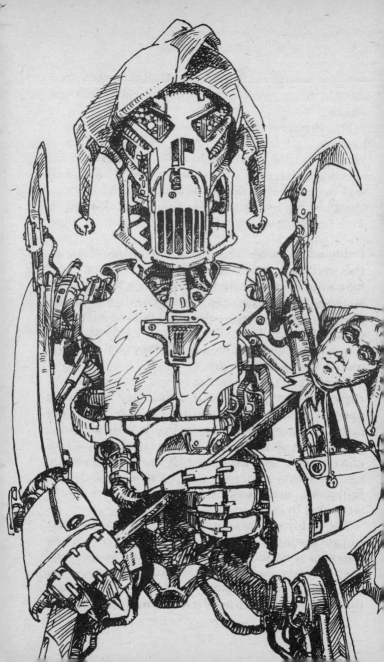

replication-instructions of the Builders, they took the old brain with many another part from the wreck.

The Builders had not foreseen that this might happen, and so the shipyard-computers did not know that in the force-field brain of each original berserker there was a safety switch. The switch was there because the original machines had been launched by living Builders, who had wanted to survive while testing their own life-destroying creations.

When the brain was moved from one hull to another, the safety switch reset itself.

The old brain awoke in control of a mighty new machine, of weapons that could sterilize a planet, of new engines to hurl the whole mass far faster than light.

But there was, of course, no Builder present, and no timer, to turn off the simple safety switch.

The jester—the accused jester, but he was as good as convicted—was on the carpet. He stood facing a row of stiff necks and granite faces, behind a long table. On either side of him was a tridi camera. His offenses had been so unusually offensive that the Committee of Duly Constituted Authority themselves, the very rulers of Planet A, were sitting to pass judgment on his case.

Perhaps the Committee members had another reason for this session: planet-wide elections were due in a month. No member wanted to miss the chance for a nonpolitical tridi appearance that would not have to be offset by a grant of equal time for the new Liberal party opposition.

"I have this further item of evidence to present,"

the Minister of Communication was saying, from his seat on the Committee side of the long table. He held up what appeared at first to be an official pedestrian-control sign, having steady black letters on a blank white background. But the sign read: UNAUTHORIZED PERSONNEL ONLY.

"When a sign is put up," said the MiniCom, "the first day, a lot of people read it." He paused, listening to himself. "That is, a new sign on a busy pedestrian ramp is naturally given great attention. Now in this sign, the semantic content of the first word is confusing in its context."

The President of the Committee—and of the planet—cleared his throat warningly. The MiniCom's fondness for stating truisms made him sound more stupid than he actually was. It seemed unlikely that the Liberals were going to present any serious challenge at the polls, but there was no point in giving them encouragement.

The lady member of the Committee, the Minister of Education, waved her lorgnette in chubby fingers, seeking attention. She inquired: "Has anyone computed the cost to us all in work-hours of this confusing sign?"

"We're working on it," growled the Minister of Labor, hitching up an overall strap. He glared at the accused. "You do admit causing this sign to be posted?"

"I do." The accused was remembering how so many of the pedestrians on the crowded ramp had smiled, and how some had laughed aloud, not caring if they were heard. What did a few work-hours matter? No one on Planet A was starving any longer.

"You admit that you have never done a thing,

really, for your planet or your people?" This question came from the Minister of Defense, a tall, powerful, bemedaled figure, armed with a ritual pistol.

"I don't admit that," said the accused bluntly. "I've tried to brighten people's lives." He had no hope of official leniency anyway. And he knew no one was going to take him offstage and beat him; the beating of prisoners was not authorized.

"Do you even now attempt to defend levity?" The Minister of Philosophy took his ritual pipe from his mouth, and smiled in the bleak permissable fashion, baring his teeth at the challenge of the Universe. "Life is a jest, true; but a grim jest. You have lost sight of that. For years you have harassed society, leading people to drug themselves with levity instead of facing the bitter realities of existence. The pictures found in your possession could do only harm."

The President's hand moved to the video recording cube that lay on the table before him, neatly labeled as evidence. In his droning voice the President asked: "You do admit that these pictures are yours? That you used them to try to get other people to—yield to mirth?"

The prisoner nodded. They could prove everything; he had waived his right to a full legal defense, wanting only to get the trial over with. "Yes, I filled that cube with tapes and films I sneaked out of libraries and archives. Yes, I showed people its contents."

There was a murmur from the Committee. The Minister of Diet, a skeletal figure with a repellent glow of health in his granite cheeks, raised a hand.

"Inasmuch as the accused seems certain to be convicted, may I request in advance that he be paroled in my custody? In his earlier testimony he admitted that one of his first acts of deviation was the avoidance of his community mess. I believe I could demonstrate, using this man, the wonderful effects on character of dietary discipline—"

"I refuse!" the accused interrupted loudly. It seemed to him that the words ascended, growling, from his stomach.

The President rose, to adroitly fill what might have become an awkward silence. "If no member of the Committee has any further questions—? Then let us vote. Is the accused guilty as charged on all counts?"

To the accused, standing with weary eyes closed, the vote sounded like one voice passing along the table: "Guilty. Guilty. Guilty . . . "

After a brief whispered conference with the Minister of Defense, the President passed sentence, a hint of satisfaction in his drone.

"Having rejected a duly authorized parole, the convicted jester will be placed under the orders of the Minister of Defense and sent to solitary beacon duty out on the Approaches, for an indefinite period. This will remove his disruptive influence, while at the same time constraining him to contribute positively to society."

For decades Planet A and its sun had been cut off from all but occasional contact with the rest of the galaxy, by a vast interstellar dust storm that was due to go on for more decades at least. So the positive contribution to society might be doubted. But it seemed that the beacon stations could be used as isolation prisons without imperiling non-existent shipping or weakening defense against an enemy that never came.

"One thing more," added the President. "I direct that this recording cube be securely fastened around your neck on a monomolecular cord, in such a way that you may put the cube into a viewer when you choose. You will be alone on the station and no other off-duty activity will be available."

The President faced toward a tridi camera. "Let me assure the public that I derive no satisfaction from imposing a punishment that may seem harsh, and even—imaginative. But in recent years a dangerous levity has spread among some few of our people; a levity all too readily tolerated by some supposedly more solid citizens."

Having gotten in a dig at the newly burgeoning Liberals, a dig he might hope to claim was non-political in intent, the President faced back to the jester. "A robot will go with you to the beacon, to assist you in your duties and see to your physical safety. I assure you the robot will not be tempted into mirth."

The robot took the convicted jester out in a little ship, so far out that Planet A vanished and its sun shrank to a point of brilliance. Out on the edge of the great dusty night of the Approaches, they drew near the putative location of station Z-45, which the MiniDef had selected as being the most dismal and forsaken of those unmanned at present.

There was indeed a metallic object where beacon Z-45 was supposed to be; but when the robot and jester got closer, they saw the object was a sphere some forty miles in diameter. There were a few little bits and pieces floating about it that just might be the remains of Z-45. And now the sphere evidently sighted their ship, for with startling speed it began to move toward them.

Once robots are told what berserkers look like, they do not forget, nor do robots grow slow and careless. But radio equipment can be sloppily maintained, and ever the dust drifts in around the edges of the system of Planet A, impeding radio signals. Before the MiniDef's robot could successfully broadcast an alarm, the forty-mile sphere was very close indeed, and its grip of metal and force was tight upon the little ship.

The jester kept his eyes shut through a good deal of what followed. If they had sent him out here to stop him laughing they had chosen the right spot. He squeezed his eyelids tighter, and put his fingers in his ears, as the berserker's commensal machines smashed their way into his little ship and carried him off. He never did find out what they did with his robot guard.

When things grew quiet, and he felt gravity and good air and pleasant warmth again, he decided that keeping his eyes shut was worse than knowing whatever they might tell him. His first cautious peek showed him that he was in a large shadowy room, that at least held no visible menace.

When he stirred, a squeaky monotonous voice somewhere above him said: "My memory bank tells me that you are a protoplasmic computing unit, probably capable of understanding this language. Do you understand?"

"Me?" The jester looked up into the shadows, but could not see the speaker. "Yes, I understand you. But who *are* you?"

"I am what this language calls a berserker."

The jester had taken shamefully little interest in galactic affairs, but that word frightened even him. He stuttered: "That means you're a kind of automated warship?"

There was a pause. "I am not sure," said the squeaky, droning voice. The tone sounded almost as if the President was hiding up there in the rafters. "War may be related to my purpose, but my purpose is still partially unclear to me, for my construction was never quite completed. For a time I waited where I was built, because I was sure some final step had been left undone. At last I moved, to try to learn more about my purpose. Approaching this sun, I found a transmitting device which I have disassembled. But I have learned no more about my purpose."

The jester sat on the soft, comfortable floor. The more he remembered about berserkers, the more he trembled. He said: "I see. Or perhaps I at least begin to see. What *do* you know of your purpose?"

"My purpose is to destroy all life wherever I can find it."

The jester cowered down. Then he asked in a low voice: "What is unclear about that?"

The berserker answered his question with two of its own: "What is life? And how is it destroyed?"

After half a minute there came a sound that the berserker computers could not identify. It issued from the protoplasmic computing-unit, but if it was speech it was in a language unknown to the berserker.

"What is the sound you make?" the machine asked.

The jester gasped for breath. "It's laughter. Oh, laughter! So. You were unfinished." He shuddered, the terror of his position coming back to sober him. But then he once more burst out giggling; the situation was too ridiculous.

"What is life?" he said at last. "I'll tell you. Life is a great grim grayness, and it inflicts fright and pain and loneliness upon all who experience it. And you want to know how to destroy it? Well, I don't think you can. But I'll tell you the best way to fight life—with laughter. As long as we can fight it that way, it can't overcome us."

The machine asked: "Must I laugh, to prevent this great-grim-grayness from enveloping me?"

The jester thought. "No, you are a machine. You are not—" he caught himself, "protoplasmic. Fright and pain and loneliness will never bother you."

"Nothing bothers me. Where will I find life, and how will I make laughter to fight it?"

The jester was suddenly conscious of the weight of the cube that still hung from his neck. "Let me think for a while," he said.

After a few minutes he stood up. "If you have a viewer of the kind men use, I can show you how laughter is created. And perhaps I can guide you to a place where life is. By the way, can you cut this cord from my neck? Without hurting me, that is!"

A few weeks later, in the main War Room of
Planet A, the somnolence of decades was abruptly
shattered. Robots bellowed and buzzed and
flashed, and those that were mobile scurried
about. In five minutes or so they managed to rouse
their human overseers, who hurried about,
tightening their belts and stuttering.

"This is a *practice* alert, isn't it?" the Officer of
the Day kept hoping aloud. "Someone's running
some kind of a test? Someone?" He was beginning
to squeak like a berserker himself.

He got down on all fours, removed a panel from
the base of the biggest robot and peered inside,
hoping to discover something causing a
malfunction. Unfortunately, he knew nothing
about robotics; recalling this, he replaced the
panel and jumped to his feet. He really knew
nothing about planet defense, either, and recalling
this was enough to send him on a screaming run
for help.

So there was no resistance, effective or
otherwise. But there was no attack, either.

The forty-mile sphere, unopposed, came down
to hover directly above Capital City, low enough
for its shadow to send a lot of puzzled birds to nest
at noon. Men and birds alike lost many hours of
productive work that day; somehow the lost work
made less difference than most of the men
expected. The days were past when only the
grimmest attention to duty let the human race
survive on Planet A, though most of the planet did
not realize it yet.

"Tell the President to hurry up," demanded the jester's image, from a viewscreen in the no-longer somnolent War Room. "Tell him it's urgent that I talk to him."

The President, breathing heavily, had just entered. "I am here. I recognize you, and I remember your trial."

"Odd, so do I."

"Have you now stooped to treason? Be assured that if you have led a berserker to us you can expect no mercy from your government."

The image made a forbidden noise, a staccato sound from the open mouth, head thrown back. "Oh, please, mighty President! Even I know our Ministry of Defense is a j-o-k-e, if you will pardon an obscene word. It's a catchbasin for exiles and incompetents. So I come to offer mercy, not ask it. Also, I have decided to legally take the name of Jester. Kindly continue to apply it to me."

"We have nothing to say to you!" barked the Minister of Defense. He was purple granite, having entered just in time to hear his Ministry insulted.

"We have no objection to talking to you!" contradicted the President, hastily. Having failed to overawe the Jester through a viewscreen, he could now almost feel the berserker's weight upon his head.

"Then let us talk," said Jester's image. "But not so privately. This is what I want."

What he wanted, he said, was a face-to-face parley with the Committee, to be broadcast live on planet-wide tridi. He announced that he would come "properly attended" to the conference. And he gave assurance that the berserker was under his full control, though he did not explain how. It, he said, would not *start* any shooting.

The Minister of Defense was not ready to start anything. But he and his aides hastily made secret plans.

Like almost every other citizen, the presidential candidate of the Liberal party settled himself before a tridi on the fateful evening, to watch the confrontation. He had an air of hopefulness, for any sudden event may bring hope to a political underdog.

Few others on the planet saw anything encouraging in the berserker's descent, but there was still no mass panic. Berserkers and war were unreal things to the long-isolated people of Planet A.

"Are we ready?" asked the Jester nervously, looking over the mechanical delegation which was about to board a launch with him for the descent to Capital City.

"What you have ordered, I have done," squeaked the berserker-voice from the shadows above.

"Remember," Jester cautioned, "the proto-plasmic-units down there are much under the influence of life. So ignore whatever they say. Be careful not to hurt them, but outside of that you can improvise within my general plan."

"All this is in my memory from your previous orders," said the machine patiently.

"Then let's go." Jester straightened his shoulders. "Bring me my cloak!"

The brilliantly lighted interior of Capital City's great Meeting Hall displayed a kind of rigid, rectilinear beauty. In the center of the Hall there had been placed a long, polished table, flanked on opposing sides by chairs.

Precisely at the appointed time, the watching millions saw one set of entrance doors swing mathematically open. In marched a dozen human heralds, their faces looking almost robotic under bearskin helmets. They halted with a single snap. Their trumpet-tucket rang out clearly.

To the taped strains of *Pomp and Circumstances*, the President, in the full dignity of his cloak of office, then made his entrance.

He moved at the pace of a man marching to his own execution, but his was the slowness of dignity, not that of fear. The Committee had overruled the purple protestations of the MiniDef, and convinced themselves that the military danger was small. Real berserkers did not ask to parley, they slaughtered. Somehow the Committee could not take the Jester seriously, any more than they could laugh at him. But until they were sure they had him again under their control they would humor him.

The granite-faced Ministers entered in a double file behind the President. It took almost five minutes of *Pomp and Circumstance* for them all to position themselves.

A launch had been seen to descend from the berserker, and vehicles had rolled from the launch to the Meeting Hall. So it was presumed that Jester was ready, and the cameras pivoted dutifully to face the entrance reserved for him.

Just at the appointed time, the doors of that entrance swung mathematically open, and a dozen man-sized machines entered. They were heralds, for they wore bearskin helmets, and each carried a bright, brassy trumpet.

All but one, who wore a coonskin cap, marched a half-pace out of step, and was armed with a slide trombone.

The mechanical tucket was a faithful copy of the human one—almost. The slide-trombonist faltered at the end, and one long sour note trailed away.

Giving an impression of slow mechanical horror, the berserker-heralds looked at one another. Then one by one their heads turned until all their lenses were focused upon the trombonist.

It—almost it seemed the figure must be *he*— looked this way and that. Tapped his trombone, as if to clear it of some defect. Paused.

Watching, the President was seized by the first pang of a great horror. In the evidence, there had been a film of an Earthman of ancient time, a balding comic violinist, who had had the skill to pause like that, just pause, and evoke from his filmed audience great gales of . . .

Twice more the robot heralds blew. And twice more the sour note was sounded. When the third attempt failed, the eleven straight-robots looked at one another and nodded agreement.

Then with robotic speed they drew concealed weapons and shot holes in the offender.

All across the planet the dike of tension was cracking, dribbles and spurts of laughter forcing through. The dike began to collapse completely as

the trombonist was borne solemnly away by a pair
of his fellows, his shattered horn clasped lily-
fashion on his iron breast.

But no one in the Meeting Hall was laughing.
The Minister of Defense made an innocent-looking
gesture, calling off a tentative plan, calling it *off.*
There was to be no attempt to seize the Jester, for
the berserker-robot-heralds or whatever they
were seemed likely to perform very capably as
bodyguards.

As soon as the riddled herald had been carried
out, Jester entered. *Pomp and Circumstance* began
belatedly, as with the bearing of a king he moved
to his position at the center of the table, opposite
the President. Like the President, the Jester wore
an elegant cloak, clasped in front, falling to his
ankles. Those that filed in behind him, in the
position of aides, were also richly dressed.

And each of them was a metallic parody, in face
and shape, of one of the Ministers of the
Committee.

When the plump robotic analogue of the
Minister of Education peered through a lorgnette
at the tridi camera, the watching populace turned,
in unheard-of-millions, to laughter. Those who
might be outraged later, remembering, laughed
now, in helpless approval of seeming danger
turned to farce. All but the very grimmest smiled.

The Jester-king doffed his cape with a flourish.
Beneath it he wore only a preposterous bathing-
suit. In reply to the President's coldly formal
greeting—the President could not be shaken by
anything short of a physical attack—the Jester
thoughtfully pursed his lips, then opened them

and blew a gummy substance out into a large pink bubble.

The President maintained his unintentional role of slowburning straight man, ably supported by all the Committee save one. The Minister of Defense turned his back on the farce and marched to an exit.

He found two metallic heralds planted before the door, effectively blocking it. Glaring at them, the MiniDef barked an order to move. The metal figures flipped him a comic salute, and stayed where they were.

Brave in his anger, the MiniDef tried futilely to shove his way past the berserker-heralds. Dodging another salute, he looked round at the sound of great clomping footsteps. His berserker-counterpart was marching toward him across the Hall. It was a clear foot taller than he, and its barrel chest was armored with a double layer of jangling medals.

Before the MiniDef paused to consider consequences, his hand had moved to his sidearm. But his metal parody was far faster on the draw; it hauled out a grotesque cannon with a fist-sized bore, and fired instantly.

"Gah!" The MiniDef staggered back, the world gone red . . . and then he found himself wiping from his face something that tasted suspiciously like tomato. The cannon had propelled a whole fruit, or a convincing and juicy imitation of one.

The MiniCom jumped to his feet, and began to expound the idea that the proceedings were becoming frivolous. His counterpart also rose, and replied with a burst of gabbles in speed-falsetto.

The pseudo-Minister of Philosophy rose as if to speak, was pricked with a long pin by a prankish herald, and jetted fluttering through the air, a balloon collapsing in flight. At that the human Committee fell into babel, into panic.

Under the direction of the metal MiniDiet, the real one, arch-villain to the lower masses, began to take unwilling part in a demonstration of dietary discipline. Machines gripped him, spoon-fed him grim gray food, napkined him, squirted drink into his mouth—and then, as if accidentally, they gradually fell out of synch with spoon and squirt, their aim becoming less and less accurate.

Only the President still stood rooted in dignity. He had one hand cautiously in his trousers pocket, for he had felt a sly robotic touch, and had reason to suspect that his suspenders had been cut.

As a tomato grazed his nose, and the MiniDiet writhed and choked in the grip of his remorseless feeders, balanced nutrients running from his ears, the President closed his eyes.

Jester was, after all, only a self-taught amateur working without a visible audience to play to. He was unable to calculate a climax for the show. So when he ran out of jokes he simply called his minions to his side, waved good-bye to the tridi cameras, and exited.

Outside the Halls, he was much encouraged by the cheers and laughter he received from the crowds fast-gathering in the streets. He had his machines entertain them with an improvised chase-sequence back to the launch parked on the edge of Capital City.

He was about to board the launch, return to the berserker and await developments, when a small group of men hurried out of the crowd, calling to him.

"Mr. Jester!"

The performer could now afford to relax and laugh a little himself. "I like the sound of that name! What can I do for you gentlemen?"

They hurried up to him, smiling. The one who seemed to be their leader said: "Provided you get rid of this berserker or whatever it is, harmlessly —you can join the Liberal party ticket. As Vice-President!"

He had to listen for some minutes before he could believe they were serious. He protested: "But I only wanted to have some fun with them, to shake them up a bit."

"You're a catalyst, Mr. Jester. You've formed a rallying point. You've shaken up a whole planet and made it think."

Jester at last accepted the Liberals' offer. They were still sitting around in front of the launch, talking and planning, when the light of Planet A's moon fell full and sudden upon them.

Looking up, they saw the vast bulk of the berserker dwindling into the heavens, vanishing toward the stars in eerie silence. Cloud streamers went aurora in the upper atmosphere to honor its departure.

"I don't know," Jester said over and over, responding to a dozen excited questions. "I don't know." He looked at the sky, puzzled as anyone else. The edge of fear came back. The robotic Committee and heralds, which had been controlled from the berserker, began to collapse one by one, like dying men.

Suddenly the heavens were briefly alight with a gigantic splashing flare that passed like lightning across the sky, not breaking the silence of the stars. Ten minutes later came the first news bulletin: The berserker had been destroyed.

Then the President came on tridi, close to the brink of showing emotion. He announced that under the heroic personal leadership of the Minister of Defense, the few gallant warships of Planet A had met and defeated, utterly annihilated, the menace. Not a man had been lost, though the MiniDef's flagship was thought to be heavily damaged.

When he heard that his mighty machine-ally had been destroyed, Jester felt a pang of something like sorrow. But the pang was quickly obliterated in a greater joy. No one had been hurt, after all. Overcome with relief, Jester looked away from the tridi for a moment.

He missed the climactic moment of the speech, which came when the President forgetfully removed both hands from his pockets.

The Minister of Defense—today the new Presidential candidate of a Conservative party stirred to grim enthusiasm by his exploit of the night before—was puzzled by the reactions of some people, who seemed to think he had merely spoiled a jest instead of saving the planet. As if spoiling a jest was not a good thing in itself! But his testimony that the berserker had been a genuine menace after all rallied most people back to the Conservative side again.

On this busiest of days the MiniDef allowed himself time to visit Liberal headquarters to do a bit of gloating. Graciously he delivered to the opposition leaders what was already becoming his standard speech.

"When it answered my challenge and came up to fight, we went in with a standard englobement pattern—like hummingbirds round a vulture, I suppose you might say. And did you really think it was jesting? Let me tell you, that berserker peeled away the defensive fields from my ship like they were nothing. And then it launched this ghastly thing at me, a kind of huge disk. My gunners were a little rusty, maybe, anyway they couldn't stop it and it hit us.

"I don't mind saying, I thought I'd bought the farm right then. My ship's still hanging in orbit for decontamination, I'm afraid I'll get word any minute that the metal's melting or something—anyway, we sailed right through and hit the bandit with everything we had. I can't say too much for my crew. One thing I don't quite understand; when our missiles struck that berserker just went poof, as if it had no defense up at all. Yes?"

"Call for you, Minister," said an aide, who had been standing by with a radiophone, waiting for a chance to break in.

"Thank you." The MiniDef listened to the phone, and his smile left him. His form went rigid. "Analysis of the weapon shows what? Synthetic proteins and water?"

He jumped to his feet glaring upward as if to pierce the ceiling and see his ship in orbit. "What do you mean—no more than a giant custard pie?"

But only on the planet Sirgol was the past open to organized invasion, accessible to organized defense, the roots of civilization exposed to probing and attack.

THE WINGED HELMET

His arms upraised, his gray beard and black robes whipping in the wind, Nomis stood tall on a tabletop of black rock twenty feet square, a good hundred feet above the smashing surf. White sea-birds coasted downwind toward him then wheeled away with sharp little cries, like those of tiny souls in pain. Around his perch on three sides there towered other splintered crags and fingers of this coastline of black basaltic rock, while before him spread the immense vibration of the sea.

Feet braced apart, he stood centered in an intricate chalk diagram drawn on the flat rock. Around him he had spread the paraphernalia of his craft—things dead and dried, things old and carven, things that men of common thought would have deemed better destroyed and forgotten. In his thin, penetrating voice, Nomis was singing into the wind:

Gather, storm clouds, day and night
Lightning chew and water drawn!
Waves come swallowing, green and bright,
Chew and swallow and gulp it down—
The craft in which my foe abides,
The long-ship that my enemy rides!

There was much more to the song, and it was repeated many times. Nomis's thin arms quivered, tired from holding over his head the splinters of wrecked ships, while the birds cried at him and the wind blew his thin gray beard up into his eyes.

Today he was weary, unable to escape the feeling that his day's labor was in vain. Today he had been granted none of the tokens of success that all too rarely came to him—heated symbol-dreams in sleep or, when he was awake, dark momentary trances shot through with strange visions, startling stretchings of the mind.

Not often in his career had Nomis been convinced of his own power to call down evil on his enemies' heads. Success for him in this work was a far more uncertain thing than he let others believe. Not that he doubted for a moment that the basic powers of the world were accessible through magic; it was only that success in this line seemed to call not only for great skill but for something like great good luck as well.

Twice before in his life Nomis had tried to raise a storm. Only once had he been successful, and the persistent suspicion remained that on that occasion the storm might have come anyway. At the height of the gale there had persisted a shade of doubt, a feeling that the ordering of such forces was beyond his powers or those of any man.

Now, doubtful as he was of present success, he persisted in the effort that had kept him almost sleepless on this secret rock for the past three days. Such was the fear and hatred he felt for the man he knew must now be crossing the sea toward him, coming with a new god and new advisers to assume the rule of this country called Queensland.

Nomis's grim eyes, turned far out to sea, marked there the passage of a squall line, mockingly small and thin. Of the ship-killing tempest he worked to raise there was no sign at all.

The cliffs of Queensland were still a day's rowing out of sight, dead ahead. In the same direction, but closer, some mildly bad weather was brewing. Harl frowned across the sea's gray face at the line of squalls, while his hands rested with idle sureness on the long-ship's steering oar.

The thirty rowers, freemen and warriors all, could see the bad weather, simply by turning their heads, as easily as Harl could. And they were all experienced enough to reach the same conclusion: that, by slowing down the stroke slightly, they would probably miss the squalls' path and so make themselves a bit more comfortable. So now, by unspoken agreement, they were all easing up a trifle on the oars.

From ahead a cool light breeze sprang up, fluttering the pennons on the sailless masts and rippling the fringe of awning on the tent of royal purple that stood amidships.

Inside that tent, alone for the moment with his thoughts, was the young man that Harl called king and lord. Harl's frown faded as it crossed his mind that young Ay had probably withdrawn into the tent to make some plans for the fighting that was

sure to come. The border tribes, who cared
nothing for the mild new god or the failing old
empire, were certain to make some test of the will
and courage of Queensland's new ruler—not that
there were grounds for doubting the firmness of
either.

Harl smiled at his next thought, that his young
lord in the tent might not be planning war at all,
but a campaign to make sure of the Princess Alix.
It was her hand in marriage that was to bring Ay
his kingdom and his army. All princesses were
described as beautiful, but rumor said that this
one also had spirit. Now, if she was like some of
the high-born girls that Harl had met, her con-
quest might be as difficult as that of a barbarian
chieftain—and, of course, even more to a sturdy
warrior's taste!

Harl's expression, which had become about as
jovial as his facial scars would allow, faded once
more to glumness. It had occurred to him that his
king might have gone into the tent to practice
reading. Ay had long been an admirer of books and
had actually brought two of them with him on his
voyage. Or it might be that he was praying to his
gentle new slave-god, for, young and healthy
though he was, Ay now and then took the business
of worship seriously.

Even while half his mind busied itself with these
reflections, Harl remained alert as always. Now a
faint puzzling splashing in the sea nearby caused
him to turn his head to the port side—and in a
moment all the thoughts in his head were frozen,
together with his warrior's blood.

Rearing right beside the ship, its bulk lifting to

obscure the horizon and the distant afternoon clouds, came a head out of nightmare, a dragon face from some evil legend. The dully gleaming neck that bore the head was of such size that a man might just be able to encircle it with both arms. Sea demons alone might know what the body in the water below was like! The eyes were clouded suns the size of silver platters, while the scales of head and neck were gray and heavy like thick wet iron. The mouth was a coffin, lid opened just a crack, all fenced inside with daggers.

Long as a cable, the thick neck came reeling inboard, scales rasping wood from the gunwale. The men's first cries were sounds such as warriors should not make, but in the next instant they were all grabbing bravely enough for their weapons. Big Torla, strongest of the crew, for once was also quickest, bracing a leg on his rower's bench and hacking with his sword at that tremendous swaying neck.

The blows clanged uselessly on dully gleaming scales; the dragon might not even have been aware of them. Its head swayed to a stop facing the doorway of the purple tent; from the slit of its terrible mouth there shrieked a challenge whose like Harl had not heard in a lifetime of war.

What with all the clamor of voices and blows, Ay had needed no such summons to make ready. Before the dragon-bellow had ceased, the tent flaps were ripped open from inside and the young king stepped forth armed with shield and helm, sword ready in his hand.

Harl felt a tremendous pride to see that the young man did not flinch a hand's breadth from the sight that met him. And, with the pride, Harl's own right arm came back to life, drawing from his belt his short-handled, iron-bladed ax, and gripping it for a throw.

The ax clanged harmlessly off the clouded silver of one eye, perhaps not even felt by the beast. The dragon's enormous head, coffin-mouth suddenly gaping wide, lunged forward for the king.

Ay met it bravely. But the full thrust of his long sword, aimed straight into the darkness of the throat, counted for no more than a jab from a woman's pin. The doorlike jaw slammed shut, crushing Ay instantly. For a moment, as the monstrous head swept away on its long neck, there was seen the horrible display of broken limbs dangling outside the teeth. And then, with one more faint splash beside the ship, the evil miracle was gone. The sunlit sea rolled on unchanged, its secrets all below.

Through the remaining hours of daylight, there was scarcely a word spoken aboard the long-ship. She prowled in watery circles, on and on, never moving far from the unmarked spot where her lord had been taken. She prowled in full battle-readiness, but there was not a thing for her to fight. The edge of the squall line came; the men took mechanical measures to meet it. And the squall departed again, without the men ever having been really aware of its passage.

By the end of the day, the sea was calm again. Squinting into the setting sun, Harl rasped out a one-word order: "Rest."

Long ago he had retrieved his blunted ax and replaced it in his belt. Now the evidence to be seen

on deck was only this: a few bits of wood, rasped
from a raw scar on the gunwale by scales hard as
metal. A few small spots of blood. And Ay's winged
helmet, fallen from his head.

Derron Odegard, recently decorated and
promoted three grades to major, was sitting in as
a junior aide on an emergency staff meeting called
by the new Time Operations commander. At the
moment, Derron was listening with both professional and friendly interest as his old
classmate, Chan Amling, now a major in
Historical Research, delivered an information
briefing.

" . . . As we all know by now, the berserkers have
chosen to focus this latest attack upon one
individual. Their target, King Ay of Queensland, is
naturally a man whose removal from history
would have disastrous consequences for us."

Amling, quick-witted and fluent, smiled
benignly over the heads of his audience. "Until
quite recently most historians even doubted this
man's reality. But since we have begun some
direct observation of the past, his historicity and
importance have both been fully confirmed."

Amling turned to an electric map, which he
attacked with a teacher's gestures. "We see here
the middle stages in the shrinkage and dis-
organization of the great Continental Empire,
leading to its ultimate collapse. Now note Queensland here. It's very largely due to King Ay's
activity and influence that Queensland can remain
in such a comparatively stable state, preserving a
segment of the Empire culture for our planet's

later civilizations to base themselves on."

The new Time Operations commander—his predecessor was now reported to be on a scouting expedition to the moon, or at least to Sirgol's surface, with Colonel Borss and others—raised a hand, student-like. "Major, I admit I'm not too clear on this. Ay was a bit of a barbarian himself, wasn't he?"

"Well, he certainly began as such, sir. But— oversimplifying somewhat—we can say that, when he found himself with a land of his own to defend, he settled down and defended it very well. Gave up his sea-roving ways. He had been one of the raiders and barbarians long enough to know all the tricks of that game. And he played it so well from the other side of the board that they usually preferred to attack someone else."

No one else had a question for Amling at the moment and he sat down. The next officer to appear at the head of the table was a major of Probability Analysis, whose manner was no more reassuring than his information.

"Gentlemen," he began in a nervous voice. "We don't know how Ay was killed, but we do know where." The major displayed a videotape made from a sentry screen. "His lifeline is newly broken *here*, on his first voyage to Queensland. As you can see, all the other lifelines aboard ship remain unbroken. Probably the enemy expects historical damage to be intensified if Ay's own crew are thought to have done away with him. It seems to us in Probability that such an expectation is all too likely to be correct."

Amling looked as if he wanted to break in and

argue; or, more likely, to make a wager on the subject. They had put Amling in the wrong section,
Derron thought. Probability would have been the
one for him.

The Probability major had paused for a sip of
water. "Frankly, the situation looks extremely
grave. In nineteen or twenty days' present-time,
the historical shock wave of Ay's assassination
should reach us. That's all the time we have. I'm
told that the chances of our finding the enemy
keyhole within nineteen days are not good."

The man's edgy gloom was contagious, and the
faces around the table were tightening in spite of
themselves. Only the new Time Ops commander
managed to remain relatively relaxed. "I'm afraid
you're right about the difficulty in finding this
keyhole, Major. Of course, every effort is being
made in that direction. Trouble is, the enemy's
getting smart about hiding his tracks. This time he
attacked with only one machine instead of six,
which makes our job difficult to start with. And,
immediately after doing its job of assassination,
that one machine seems to have gone into hiding.
It hasn't left Ay's time, it'll still be on the scene to
mess up whatever we do to set things right, but
meanwhile it's being careful not to cause any
changes that we might use to track it." Time
Ops leaned forward, becoming less relaxed. "Now,
who's got some ideas regarding counter-
measures?"

The first suggestions involved trying to build
probability in Ay's later lifeline, so that he would
somehow have survived the assassination after all.
This idea soon started an argument on a highly

technical level. In this the scientific people present naturally dominated, but they were far from agreeing among themselves on what could and should be done. When they began to exchange personal viewpoints along with formulae, Time Ops called quickly for half an hour's recess.

Finding that much time unexpectedly on his hands, Derron stepped out and called the nurses' quarters at the nearby hospital complex. Lisa was living there now, while she started to train for some kind of nursing job. He was pleased to be able to reach her and to hear that she too had some time to spare. Within a few minutes they were walking together, in the park where they had met for the first time.

Derron had come to the meeting with a topic of conversation all prepared, but Lisa, these days, was developing a favorite subject of her own.

"You know, Matt's healing so quickly that all the doctors are amazed at it."

"Good. I'll have to come round and see him one of these days. I keep meaning to, but then I think I'll wait until we can talk to each other."

"Oh, goodness, he's talking now!"

"In our language? Already?"

She was delighted to confirm it and to elaborate. "It's like his rapid healing; the doctors say it must be because he comes from so far in the past. They talk about the effect on one individual of coming up through twenty thousand years' evolutionary gradient, about the organizational energies of his body and brain becoming enfolded and intensified. I can't follow most of it, of course. They talk about the realm where the material and the nonmaterial meet—"

"Yes."

"And Matt probably understands what they're saying as well as I do now, if not better. He's up and around most of the time. They allow him a good deal of freedom. He's quite good about staying out of rooms he's warned not to enter, not touching dangerous things, and so forth."

"Yes."

"Oh, and did I tell you they've suspended healing in his face? Until they're sure he can make a fully informed decision on what he wants his new face to look like."

"Yes, I heard something about that. Lisa, how long are you going on living in the hospital? Are you really set on learning nursing, or is it just— something to do?" He almost asked, "Is it just Matt?"

"Oh." Her face fell slightly. "Sometimes I don't think I was cut out to be a nurse. But I have no immediate plans to move. It's hard for me to live right in the hospital when I'm still getting therapy for my memory every day."

"Any success with the treatments?" Derron knew that the doctors now fully accepted that Lisa had simply lost her memory through being caught in the path of the berserker missile. For awhile some had considered it possible that she was an emissary or deserter from the future, made amnesic by descent through time. But on the sentry screens no such reversed lifeline could be found. In fact, no traveler, no device, no message, had ever come from the future to this embattled civilization that called itself Modern. Possibly the inhabitants of the unknowable time-to-come had good reason of their own to refrain from communication; possibly the future Sirgol was not inhabited by man. Or it might simply be that this time of the berserker war was completely blocked off from the future by paradox-loops. It was some comfort, at least, that no berserker machines came attacking from the direction of tomorrow.

"No, the therapy doesn't really help." Lisa sighed faintly; her memory of her personal life before the missile wave caught her was still almost completely blank. She put the subject aside with a wave of her hand and went back to talking about what new things Matt had done today.

Derron, not listening, closed his eyes for a moment, savoring the sensation of life he had when he was with Lisa. At this moment he possessed the touch of her hand in his, the feel of grass and soil under his feet, the warmth of the pseudo-sunshine on his face. Next moment it might all be gone—another missile wave could come down through the miles of rock, or the unraveling of King Ay's severed cord of life might propagate faster than expected up through the fabric of history.

He opened his eyes and saw the muraled walls surrounding the buried park, and the improbably alive, singing, and soaring birds. Down here at the level where humans walked, the place was almost thronged, as usual, with strolling couples and solitaries; in places the touch grass was showing signs of wear, and the gardeners had to defend it with string fences. All in all, a poor imitation of the murdered real world; but with Lisa beside him it became transformed into something better than it was.

Derron pointed. "Right there's the tree where I first came to your rescue. Or you came to mine, rather."

"*I* rescued *you?* From what horrible fate?"

"From dying of loneliness in the midst of forty million people. Lisa, I'm trying to tell you that I want you to move out of that hospital dormitory."

She turned her eyes away, looking down. "If I did that, where would I live?"

"I'm asking you to live with me, of course. You're not a little lost girl any more; you're on your own, studying to be a nurse, and I can ask. There are some unused apartments around, and I'll rate one of them if I take a companion. Especially with this promotion they've given me."

She squeezed his hand, but that was all. She was thoughtfully silent, her eyes on the ground a few paces ahead of them.

"Lisa? What do you say?"

"Just exactly what are you offering me, Derron?"

"Look—yesterday, when you were telling me about your new girl friend's problems, you seemed to have a very firm grasp of what this male-female business is all about."

"You want me to live with you temporarily, is that it?" Her voice was cool and withdrawn.

"Lisa, nothing in our world can be permanent. At the staff meeting just now—Well, I'm not supposed to talk about that. But things don't look good. I want to share with you whatever good things may be left."

Still silent, she let him lead her on stepping-stones across the park's little stream.

"Lisa, do you want a marriage ceremony? I

should have put that first, I suppose, and asked you formally to marry me. The thing is, not many people are going to raise their eyebrows if we do without a ceremony, and if we do without one we'll avoid some delay and red tape. Would you think we were doing wrong if we didn't have a wedding?"

"I . . . suppose not. What bothers me is the way you talk about everything being temporary. I suppose feelings are included."

"When everything else is temporary, yes! That doesn't mean I necessarily like it. But how can anyone in our world say what they'll be feeling or thinking a month or a year from now? In a year we'll most likely all . . . " He let his voice trail off.

She had been searching for words and now at last she found the ones she wanted. "Derron, at the hospital I've absorbed the attitude that people's lives can be made less temporary, now or any time. That people should go on trying to build, to accomplish things, even though they may not have long to live."

"You absorbed this at the hospital, you say?"

"All right, maybe I've always felt that way."

He had, too, at one time. A year, a year and a half ago. A lifetime ago, with someone else. The image that he could not stop seeing and did not want to stop seeing came back to him again.

Lisa seemed to have her own private image. "Look at Matt, for instance. Remember how badly hurt he was. Look at what an effort of will he's made to survive and recover—"

"I'm sorry." Derron interrupted her, looking at the time, finding valid excuse for getting away.

"I've got to run, I'm almost late for the staff meeting."

The scientists, by some combination of calculation and debate, had reached a consensus. "It comes down to this," their newly elected spokesman explained, when the staff meeting had resumed. "If we're to have any hope of healing the break in Ay's lifeline we must first immobilize the affected part, to minimize damage—something like putting a splint on a broken arm or leg."

"And just how do you go about splinting a lifeline?" demanded Time Ops.

The scientist gestured wearily. "Commander, the only way I can suggest is that someone be sent to take Ay's place temporarily. To continue his interrupted voyage to Queensland and there play his part, for a few days at least. The man sent could carry a communicator with him, and be given day-to-day or even hour-to-hour instructions from here, if need be. If the berserkers stood still for it, he might play out the remainder of Ay's life in its essentials, well enough to let us survive."

"How long do you think any man could play a part like that successfully?" someone broke in.

"I don't know." The scientists' spokesman smiled faintly. "Gentlemen, I don't know if a substitution scheme can be made to work at all. Nothing like it has ever been tried. But I think it will buy us at least a few more days or weeks of present-time in which to think of something else."

Time Ops thoughtfully rubbed his stubbled face. "Well, now, substitution is the only idea we've got to work with at this point. But Ay is about twelve hundred years back. That means that dropping a man from here to take his place is out of the question. Right?"

"Afraid so, sir," said a biophysicist. "Mental devolution and serious memory loss sets in at about four hundred years."

Time Ops thought aloud in a tired monotonous voice. "Does anyone suppose we could get away with using a slave-unit on that kind of job? No, I thought not. They just can't be made convincingly human enough. Then what's left? We must use one of Ay's contemporaries. Find a man who's able to do the job, motivate him to do it, and then train him."

Someone suggested, "Appearance isn't too much of a problem. Ay isn't known in Queensland, except by reputation, when he first arrives there."

Colonel Lukas, the Psych Officer on Time Ops' staff, cleared his throat and spoke. "We ought to be able to get Ay's crew to accept a substitute, provided they *want* Ay to be alive, and if we can snatch the whole bunch of them up to present-time for a few days' work."

"We can manage that if we have to," Time Ops said.

"Good." Lukas doodled thoughtfully on a pad before him. "Some tranquilizer and pacifier drugs would be indicated first . . . . Then we can find out whatever details of the assassination we need to know . . . then a few days' hypnosis. I'm sure we can work something out."

"Good thinking, Luke." Time Ops looked around the table. "Now, gentlemen, before it should slip our minds, let's try to solve the first problem, the big one. Who is our Ay-substitute going to be?"

Surely, thought Derron, someone besides me must see where one possible answer lies. He didn't want to be the first one to suggest it, because . . . well, just because. *No!* Hellfire and damnation, why shouldn't he? He was being paid to think, and he could put forward his thought with the clearest conscience in the world. He cleared his throat, startling men who seemed to have forgotten his presence.

"Correct me if I'm wrong, gentlemen. But don't we have one man available now who might be sent down to Ay's century without losing his wits? I mean the man who comes from the even deeper past himself."

Harl's duty was painfully clear in his own mind. He was going to have to take the ship on to Queensland, and when he got there he was going to have to stand before King Gorboduc and the princess, look them in the face and tell them what had happened to Ay. Harl was gradually realizing already that his story might not be believed. And what then?

The rest of the crew were spared at least the sudden new weight of responsibility. Now, many hours after the monster's attack, they were still obeying Harl without question. The sun was going down, but Harl had started them rowing again, and he meant to keep them rowing for Queensland right through the night, to hold off the mad demonstration of grief that was sure to come if he let the men fall idle now.

They were rowing like blind men, sick men,

walking dead men, their faces blank with rage and shock turned inward, neither knowing nor caring where the ship was steered. Frequently the oars fell out of stroke, clattering together or splashing awkwardly along the surface of the sea. No one quarreled at this or even seemed to notice. Torla groaned a death-song as he pulled—woe to the next man who faced Torla in a fight.

Inside the purple tent, atop the chest that held Ay's personal treasure (that chest was another problem for Harl, a problem that would grow as rage and grief wore away), the winged helmet now rested in a place of honor. It was now all that was left . . . .

Ten years ago, Ay had been a real prince, with a real king for a father. At about that time, Ay's beard had started to sprout, and Harl had first begun to serve as the young prince's good right hand. And, also at about that time, the twin sicknesses of envy and treachery had started to spread like the plague among Ay's brothers and uncles and cousins. Ay's father and most of his house had died in that plague, and the kingdom had died too, being lost and divided among strangers.

Ay's inheritance had shrunk to the deck of a fighting ship—not that Harl had any objection to that on his own account. Harl had not even complained about the books and the reading. Nor even about prayers to a man-god, a slave-god who had preached love and mercy and had gotten his bones split with wedges for his trouble . . . .

Over the ship, or beneath it, there suddenly passed a force, a tilting, swaying motion, over in an instant. Harl's first thought was that the dragon had come back, rising from the deep to scrape its bulk beneath the long-ship's hull. The men evidently thought the same, for in an instant they had dropped their oars and drawn their weapons again.

But there was no dragon to be seen, nor much of anything else. With a speed that seemed nothing short of supernatural, a mist had closed in around the ship; the red lingering light of sunset had been transformed into a diffused white glow. Looking round him now, battle-ax ready in his hand, Harl noticed that even the rhythm of the waves was different. The air was warmer, the very smell of the sea had changed.

The men looked wild-eyed at one another in the strange soft light. They fingered their swords and muttered about wizardry.

"Row slowly ahead!" ordered Harl, putting the useless ax back in his belt. He tried to sound as if he had some purpose other than keeping the men busy, though in fact his sense of direction had for once been totally confused.

He gave the steering oar to Torla and went forward himself to be lookout. Then, before the rowers had taken fifty slow strokes, he threw up a hand to halt them, and water gurgled around the backing oars. No more than an easy spear-cast from the bow, a gentle sandy beach had materialized out of the grayness. What manner of land might be behind the beach it was impossible to tell.

When the men saw the beach, their murmuring grew louder. They knew full well that only a few minutes ago there had been no land of any kind in sight.

"Yet that's certainly solid ground ahead."

"*Looks* like solid ground. I'd not be surprised to see it vanish in a puff of smoke."

"Sorcery!"

Sorcery, certainly; no one disputed that. Some kind of magic, good or bad, was at work. What might be done about it, if anything, was another question. Harl quit pretending that he knew what he was about and called a council. After some debate it was decided that they should row straight away from the beach, to see if they might in that way get beyond the reach of whatever enchantment held them in its grip.

Sunset was now long overdue, but the pale light filtering down through the mist did not fade. In fact, it became brighter, for as they rowed the mist began to thin.

Just as they emerged from the fog bank, and Harl was beginning to hope they were indeed getting away from the enchantment, they came near driving their ship straight into a black, smooth, almost featureless wall that rose from the sea. The wall was slightly concave, and it had no edge or top in sight; it rose and extended and curved back without limit around the sea and over the mist. From the foot of this wall the men looked up to find that it made an enormous inverted bowl over their tiny ship; from near the zenith, far above their heads, lights as bright and high as sunfragments threw down their fire on white fog and black water.

Men cried out prayers to all the gods and

demons known. Men shrieked that they had come
to the sky and the stars at the end of the world.
They almost broke their oars as they pulled on
them to spin their ship and drive it back into the
mist.

Harl was as much shaken as any other, but he
swore to himself that he would die before he
showed it. One man had collapsed to the deck,
where he lay with his hands over his eyes, groaning, "Enchantment, enchantment," over and over.
Harl kicked and wrestled him viciously back to his
feet, meanwhile seizing upon the idea and putting
it to use.

"Aye, enchantment, that's all!" Harl shouted.
"Not a real sky or stars, but something put into
our eyes by magic. Well, if there be wizards here
who mean us harm, I say they can be made to
bleed and die like other men. If they are thinking
to have some fun with us, well, we know a game or
two ourselves!"

The others took some heart from Harl's words.
Back here in the concealing fog, the world was
still sane enough so that a man could look around
it without losing his powers of thought.

In an almost steady voice, Harl gave the order to
row back in the direction of the beach they had
glimpsed earlier. The men willingly obeyed; the
man who had collapsed pulled hardest, looking to
right and left at his fellows as if daring any among
them to make some comment. But he would be
safe from jokes, it seemed, for a good while yet.

They were not long in coming to the gentle
sloping beach again; it proved to be real and solid.
As the long-ship slid lightly aground, Harl, sword

in hand, was the first to leap into the shallows. The water was warmer than he had expected, and when a splash touched his lips he discovered that it was fresh. But by this time he was beyond being surprised at such relative trifles.

One of Matt's tutors stepped ahead of Derron, tapped on the door of the private hospital room, then slid it open. Putting his head inside, the tutor spoke slowly and distinctly. "Matt? There is a man here who wants to talk to you. He is Derron Odegard, the man who fought beside you in your own time."

The tutor turned to motion Derron forward. As he entered the room, the man who had been sitting in an armchair before the television screen got to his feet, standing tall and erect.

In this man, dressed in the robe and slippers that were general issue for hospital patients, Derron saw no resemblance to the dying savage he had helped a few days ago to carry into the hospital. Matt's hair had been depilated and was only now starting to grow back in, a neutral-colored stubble. Matt's face below the eyes was covered by a plastic membrane, which served as skin while the completion of the healing process was held in abeyance.

On the bedside table, half covered by some secondary-level schoolbooks, were several sketches and composite photographs, looking like variations on one basic model of a young man's face. Derron was now carrying in his pocket a photo of a somewhat different face—Ay's—caught by a spy device that had been sent, in the shape of a bird, to skim near the young king-to-be on the day he began his fateful voyage to Queensland. That was the closest the Moderns had been able to get to the space-time locus of the assassination— as usual, paradox-loops strongly resisted repeating interference with history at any one spot.

"I am pleased to meet you, Derron." Matt put genuine meaning into the ritual phrase. His voice was quite deep; at most, a little minor work would be needed to match it to Ay's, which had been recorded when the photo was made. Matt's manner of speaking, like his tutor's to him, was slow and distinct.

"I am pleased to see that your health is returning," Derron answered. "And glad that you are learning the ways of a new world so quickly."

"And I am pleased to see that you are healthy, Derron. I am glad your spirit could leave the metal man it fought in, for that metal man was very much hurt."

Derron smiled, then nodded toward the tutor, who had taken up a jailer's or servant's stance just inside the door. "Matt, don't let them con you with talk of where my spirit was. I was never in any direct danger, as you were, during that fight."

"Con me?" Matt had the question-inflection down pat.

The tutor said, "Derron means, don't let us teach you wrong things. He's joking."

Matt nodded impatiently, knowing about jokes. A point had been raised that was quite serious for him. "Derron—but it was your spirit in the metal man?"

"Well . . . say it was my electronic presence."

Matt glanced at the television built into the wall. He had turned down the sound when company entered; some kind of historical documentary was being shown. He said, "Electronics I have learned a little bit. It moves my spirit from one place to another."

"Moves your eyes and thoughts, you mean."

Matt seemed to consider whether he was understanding the words correctly, and to decide that he was. "Eyes and thoughts and spirit," he said firmly.

The tutor said, "This spirit-orientation is really his idea, Major, not something we've inculcated."

"I understand that," said Derron mildly. The important thing, from Operations' point of view, would be this tendency of Matt's toward firmness of opinion, even in a new world. Such firmness would be a very good thing in an agent—provided, of course, the right opinions were held.

Derron smiled. "All right, Matt. In the spirit I was fighting beside you, though I didn't risk my neck as you risked yours. When you jumped onto that berserker, I know your thought was to save me. I am grateful—and I am glad that now I can tell you so."

"Will you sit down?" Matt motioned Derron to a chair, then reseated himself; the tutor remained standing, hovering in the background.

Matt said, "My thought was partly to save you. Partly for my people there, partly just to see the berserker die. But since coming here I have learned that all people, even here, might be dead if we had not won that fight."

"That is true. But the danger is not over. Other

fighting, just as important, is going on in other times and places." This was a suitable opening for the recruiting speech he had been sent here to make. But Derron paused before plunging ahead. For the tenth time he wished that Operations had sent someone else to do this job. But the experts though Matt was most likely to react favorably if the presentation was made by Derron, the man who had, in a sense at least, fought beside him. And using Matt had been Derron's own idea, after all. Yes, he kept coming back to that in his thoughts. He hadn't seen Lisa since that last walk in the park—maybe he had been avoiding her. Yes, he could wish now that he had kept his mouth shut at the staff meeting.

Anyway, in the present situation, if Derron didn't make the sales pitch, someone else would, perhaps less scrupulously. So he vented an inaudible sigh and got down to business. "Already you have done much for us, Matt. You have done much for everyone. But now my chiefs send me to ask if you are willing to do more."

He gave Matt the essence of the situation in simplified form. The berserkers, deadly enemies of the tribe-of-all-men, had gravely wounded a great chief in another part of the world. It was necessary that someone should take the chief's place for a time.

Matt sat quietly, his eyes steadily attentive above the plastic skin that masked most of his face. When Derron had finished his preliminary outline of Operations' plan, Matt's first question was, "What will happen when the great chief is strong again?"

"Then he will resume his own place, and you

will be brought back here to live in our world. We expect we will be able to bring you back safely—but you must understand that there will be danger. Just how much danger we cannot say, because this will be a new kind of thing for us to do. But there will certainly be some danger, all along the way."

Let him know that, Major—don't paint too black a picture, of course. It seemed to be left up to Major Odegard to find the proper shade of gray. Well, Time Ops might be spying over his shoulder right now, but Derron was damned if he'd con Matt into taking a job that he, Derron, wouldn't have touched if it had been open to him. No, Derron told himself, *he* wouldn't volunteer if he could. What had the human race done for him lately? Really, the chances of the mission's doing anyone any good seemed to him very uncertain. Death did not frighten him any more, but there were things that still did—physical pain, for one. For another, the chance of meeting, on a mission like this, some unforeseeable ugly fate in the half-reality called probability-space, which the Moderns had learned to traverse but had scarcely begun to understand.

"And if, in spite of all medicine, the great chief should die, and can never go back to his own place?"

"Then it would be your job to continue in his place. When you needed advice we would tell you what to do. In this king's place you would lead a better life than most men in history have had. And when you had finished out his span of years, we would try to bring you here to our world again to live on still longer, with much honor."

"Honor?"

The tutor tried to explain.

Matt soon seemed to grasp what was meant, and he went on to raise another point. "Would I take more magic arrows with me to fight the berserkers?"

Derron thought about it. "I suppose you might be given some such weapons, to protect yourself to some degree. But your main job would not be fighting berserkers directly, but acting for this king, as he would act, in other matters."

Matt nodded, as slowly and precisely as he spoke. "All is new, all is strange. I must think about it."

"Of course."

Derron was about to add that he could come back tomorrow for an answer, but Matt suddenly asked two more questions. "What will happen if I say no? If no one can be found to take the place of the wounded chief?"

"There is no way that you, or anyone, can be forced to take his place. Our wise men think that, if no one does, the war will be lost and all of us will probably be dead in less than a month."

"And I am the only one who can go?"

"It may be so. You are our wise men's first choice." An operation was now under way to recruit a back-up man or two from the deep past. But anyone else brought up now would remain days behind Matt all the way through the process of preparation, and every hour was deemed important.

Matt spread out his healed hands. "I must believe what you tell me, you who have saved my life and made me well again. I do not want to die in a month and see everyone else die. So I must do what the wise men want, go and take the chief's place if I am able."

Derron puffed out his breath, venting mixed feelings. He reached into his pocket for the photo.

Time Ops, sitting in a small rough cavern a good distance from Operations and watching through one of his systems of secret scanners, nodded with satisfaction and mild surprise. That Odegard was a sharp young lad, all right. No outward display of gung-ho enthusiasm, but always good work, including this job—a smooth soft sell that had gotten the volunteer to place himself on the right side of the question.

Now the operation could get rolling in earnest. Time Ops swiveled in his chair and watched Colonel Lukas pull a white, nightgown-like robe over his head and down, concealing the plastic chain mail that guarded him from throat to knee.

"Luke, you've got some bare face and hands hanging out," Time Ops remarked, frowning. Psych Officers as good as you were hard to find. "These boys you're going to meet are carrying real knives, you know."

Lukas knew. Swallowing, he said, "We haven't got time to be thinking up foolproof protective gimmicks. I won't inspire any confidence if I got out there looking like a masked demon, believe me."

Time Ops grunted and got up. He stood for a moment behind the radar operator to note the image of the ship on the beach and the cluster of tiny green dots in front of her—her crew, come ashore. Then he went on to the window, a wide hole hacked crudely through a wall of rock, and squinted out from between the two heavy stun-projectors and their ready gunners. As the fog generators outside were very near the window, there was nothing to be seen but billows of opaque whiteness, streaming out and away. Time Ops picked up and put on a set of heavy glasses like those the gunners were wearing. The fog effectively disappeared; now he could see the individual men standing before their ship a hundred yards away and the great calm surface of the Reservoir beyond.

"All right," he said reluctantly. "I guess we'll be able to see you wave your arm—if they don't surround you and get in your way. If that happens, wave your arms over your head, and we'll cut loose."

"I just don't want anyone to get trigger-happy, Commander," said Lukas, looking uneasily at the gunners. "We're going to have to do some very delicate work on those men out there, and that won't be easy and may not be possible if they've taken a hard stunning. I'd much rather ease them along with the drugs, ask them some questions, and make some impression on them along the way."

Time Ops shrugged. "It's your baby. Got your gas mask?"

"Yes. Remember, we'll try to do the job with the pacifier-tranquilizer mix in the drinks; they're physically tired, and that may put 'em right to sleep. But don't hesitate to use the gas." Lukas took a last quick look around.

"Looks like a few of them are starting up from

the beach," said the radar man.

Lukas jumped. "Here I go, then. Where's my servants? Ready? Tell them to keep inside at first. Here I go!" His sandled feet thudded rapidly down a stair.

The sand beach sloped up to a lowland of gravelly soil and sparse grass, the kind that grew in shadow. Harl left the bulk of the crew at the water's edge, ready to protect the ship or shove her off again, while with six chosen men he proceeded slowly inland.

The scouting party had not far to go; they had scarcely passed over the first hillock before they saw a single tall figure come walking toward them through the mist. This figure drew close and became a man of impressive mien, dressed in a white robe such as the good enchanters of the old religions wore.

Showing not the least surprise or fear at being confronted by seven armed sea-rovers, this man came near to them and stopped, raising his hands in a gesture of peace. "My name is Lukas," he said simply. He broke in Harl's native language—with a bad accent, but Harl in his travels had managed to understand worse.

"Let us put some pointed questions to this 'chanter," said Torla at once, setting a hand on his dagger.

The one in wizard's garb raised his eyebrows, and his right hand and wrist flexed up slightly from his side. Perhaps it was only a gesture of remonstrance, but perhaps he was giving or preparing to give a signal.

"Let us wait!" said Harl sharply. In this mist, a

small army might lie concealed within spear-cast. Harl nodded to Lukas politely, and gave the names of himself and his companions.

The white-robed man, his hands once more innocently at rest, bowed in grave acknowledgment. He said, "My house is very near; allow me to offer you its hospitality, at least for a meal."

"We thank you for the offer," said Harl, not liking the uncertainty in his own voice. The man's air of confidence had an unsettling effect. Harl wanted to ask what country they had landed in, but was reluctant to reveal his ignorance.

"I pray you," Lukas said, "some or all of you, come to my house, at least for food and drink. If you wish to leave men to guard your ship, I will order some refreshment sent to them."

Harl mumbled for a moment, undecided. He tried to imagine how Ay would have met this strange confident courtesy. Lukas needed no powers of clairvoyance to know that seven sea-rovers newly arrived on his beach had come by ship; but he might have come scouting to find out just how many men and ships there were.

"Wait here for a moment," Harl answered at last. "Then we seven will go with you." Two men stayed with Lukas while Harl and the others walked back over the little hill to explain matters to the rest of the crew. Some of these also argued for seizing the wizard at once and asking him pointed questions.

Harl shook his head. "We can do that at any moment. But enchanters are likely to be stubborn and prideful. And once a man's blood is out, it's hard to pour it back into his veins, should the letting prove to have been a mistake. We'll just watch him close, until we learn more. If food and drink are sent you, I suggest you treat the bearers with some courtesy." He need give the men no urging to caution and alertness; they were ready to strike at shadows now.

So Harl and his chosen six ringed themselves about Lukas and walked inland with him. Taking their cue from Harl, the six other sea-rovers tried to look as if the encirclement was all accidental and unintentional, as if their hospitable host was not really their prisoner. And Lukas might have taken his cue from them, for he gave no sign of being bothered in the least.

As the party proceeded inland the mist grew thicker with each step. Before they had gone a hundred paces they found their way blocked by a line of low cliffs, heretofore invisible, from the top of which the grayness came rolling down. Built right against the foot of this cliff was the wizard's house; it was a simple stone building, with a look of newness, only one story high but big and solid enough to be a manor or a small fortress. At second glance, though, it was hardly a fortress, for the windows were low and wide, and the wide doorway stood unprotected by moat or wall.

Several people in simple servants' garb emerged from this doorway and bowed to the approaching Lukas and his guests; Harl noticed with some relief that none of the servants appeared to be anything more or less than human. The girls among them were comely, in a down-to-earth and lively style; they eyed the warriors sideways and giggled before hurrying back inside.

"No fairy-tale witches here," growled Torla.

"Though I make no doubt they know enchantments of a sort."

Torla preceded Lukas through the doorway, with the rest of the sea-rovers following close on the heels of the white-robed man. Harl was last to enter, looking behind him as he did so, his hand on his ax. He could not begin to feel easy about any man who welcomed seven armed strangers into his house.

Inside there was nothing to feed Harl's suspicions, save more of the same strange confidence. The entrance opened directly into a great manorial room, in which were set more than enough tables and benches to have accommodated the long-ship's entire crew. At the huge hearth, a smiling and confident servant stood turning the spitted carcass of a weighty meat-animal. The roast was browned and dripping, so nearly done that it must have been started hours before.

Though a fair amount of light came in at the windows with the fog, on the walls were mounted enough torches to make the room quite bright. Through simple hangings that covered the rear wall, Harl could now and then glimpse servants going about tasks in distant chambers, which must be dug back behind the line of the cliff. There was of course no way of telling how many armed men might be in those rooms or lurking somewhere outside, but so far Harl had not seen a single weapon, barring table knives. Another easy-mannered servant was now laying out eight places at the head table, setting out worthy but not spectacular silver plates and tankards along with the cutlery.

Lukas proceeded straight to the head of the

table—a couple of the sea-rovers keeping casually close to him—and turned with a gracious gesture. "Will you be seated? There is wine or ale, as you choose."

"Ale!" barked Harl, giving his men a meaningful look. He had heard of potent drugs and poisons whose taste blended very smoothly with that of wine; and even honest drink must not be allowed to take the edge of clearness from their minds. The others echoed Harl's call for ale, though Torla looked somewhat disappointed.

The company seated themselves, and two girls promptly came from behind the hangings to fill their tankards. Harl watched to see that the wizard's drink was poured from the same vessel as his own, and he waited until the wizard was wiping foam from his own lips before he tasted the drink himself. And even then Harl took only a sparing swallow.

The ale was neither too strong nor too weak, but . . . yes, there was something slightly peculiar in its taste. Still, Harl asked himself, in a place where everything was strange, how could the ale be otherwise? And he allowed himself another sip.

"The ale of your country is strong and good," he ventured then, stretching the truth to make a compliment. "So no doubt you have many strong men here and you serve a strong king."

Lukas bowed slightly. "All that you say is true."

"And your king's name?"

"Our present king is called the Planetary Commander." The wizard smacked his lips over the ale. "And whom do you serve?"

A tremulous groan passed around the board.

The tankards scraped in unison as they were lifted, and then together they thudded down, all lighter than they had been. All except Harl's. He had not observed the least sign of treachery—come to think of it, there was no reason why there should be any treachery here—but still he decided firmly that he would not drink any more. Not just now.

"Whom *do* we serve?" he asked the world. "Our good young lord is dead."

"Young Ay is dead!" Torla roared it out, like a man challenging the pain of some dreadful wound. A serving girl came to refill his tankard, and Torla seized her and pulled her onto his lap. But when she resisted his pawing with her thin weak arms, he only held her there gently, while a comical witless expression grew slowly on his face.

Something about this made Harl wonder. His own mind was perfectly clear . . . and yet he should be more concerned, more alert than he was. Should he not?

"Young Ay's death would be sad news," said Lukas calmly. "If it were true." The wizard seemed to be slumping slowly in his chair, utterly relaxed, forgetting dignity.

Oddly, no one took offense at the implication that they would be untruthful in such a matter. The men only sipped or drank, and there passed another murmur of mourning around the table.

"We saw him die!"

"Ah, yes!"

Harl's big fists were knotted, remembering their helplessness against the dragon. "We saw him die, in such a way that, by all the gods, I can scarce believe it yet myself!"

Lukas leaned forward, suddenly intent. "And what way was that?"

In a faltering voice Harl told him. Harl's throat quickly grew dry with speech; scarcely realizing that he did so, he interrupted his tale to take another swallow from his tankard. The truth about the dragon sounded in his own ears like a clumsy lie. What chance was there of King Gorboduc believing it?

When Harl's recital was finished, Torla started to stand up as if he meant to speak. The girl fell from his lap and landed with a yelp on her soft bottom. Torla, his face showing uncharacteristic concern, bent as if to help her. But she rose and scurried away, and Torla kept right on bending over until he was seated again, with his head resting on the table. Then he began to snore.

Torla's shipmates, those who were not on the verge of snoring themselves, only laughed at this. The men were all tired . . . No. Something *was* wrong, they should not be drunk on one or two tankards apiece of any ale. And if they were drunk, some of them at least should be quarrelsome. Harl puzzled over the strangeness of this, took another thoughtful sip himself, and decided he had better get to his feet.

"Your king is not dead," the wizard was repeating to him in a monotone. "Not dead, not dead. Why should you believe that he is?"

"Why? We saw the—the dragon take him." But Harl was no longer quite sure of what he had seen or what he remembered. What was happening here? He swayed on his feet, half-drew his sword, and croaked, "Treachery! Wake up!"

His men's eyes were glassy or closing, their faces foolish. Some of them started to rise at his cry, but then they sank back, leaning on the table, letting weapons slide forgotten to the floor.

"Wizard," one man muttered, turning pleading eyes toward Lukas. "Tell us again that our king lives."

"He lives and shall live."

"He—he is—" Harl could not make him say that Ay was dead. In terror of he knew not what, he staggered back from the table, his sword sighing all the way out of its scabbard into his hand. To hurt anyone for any reason would be a monstrous crime, but he was so frightened that he felt he might do anything. "Stand back!" he warned the wizard.

The wizard also stood up, not shaken, with the length of the table between himself and Harl. From inside his robe Lukas took a mask like an animal's snout, which he fitted onto his face. His voice came out thickly. "No one will harm you here. I have shared with you the drink that makes men peaceful. Sit down now and talk with me."

Harl turned and ran for the door. Outside, the mist suddenly sparkled in his lungs. He ran on until he reached the hillock from which he could see the beached ship, only to discover that all the men he had left there were dead or dying. Half a dozen nearly human monsters with gray, snouted faces were busy arranging their bodies in rows on the beach. Those of his crew who could still move were offering no resistance, but were letting themselves be led like load-oxen.

It was really too bad that such a thing had happened. Harl groped reflexively for his sword and ax, but then remembered that he had thrown his weapons away somewhere.

"It's all right." Lukas' soothing voice came from just behind Harl. As Harl turned, the wizard continued, "Your men are all asleep. They need rest; don't wake them."

"Ahh, that's it!" Harl sighed with relief. He might have known there was no reason to worry, not on this good island of sparkling ale and sparkling air and friendly people who spoke nothing but truth. He saw now that the snouted monsters were only men who wore masks like the wizard's. They were taking good care of his men. Harl looked confidently at Lukas, waiting to be told some more good news.

Lukas seemed to relax, sighing behind his mask. "Come here," he said. And he led Harl down to the water's edge, where the wet sand was kept lapping to perfect smoothness by the little wavelets coming in.

With his finger the wizard drew in the wet sand, making the crude outline of a grotesque head. "Suppose now that this is the dragon you thought you saw. What exactly did you think happened?"

Harl groaned wearily and sank to his knees, staring helplessly at the sketch. Now that he could relax, he felt very tired, and soon he was going to have to sleep. But right now he had to concentrate on what the wizard was showing him. "It seized Ay," Harl said. "In its mouth."

"Like this?" The wizard's finger drew a stick figure clenched in the dragon's teeth, waving helpless lines of arms and legs. Even as he drew, the little waves were coming in over the sketch, smoothing and blurring its lines.

"Like that," Harl agreed. He sat down awkwardly.

"But now all that is being wiped out," the wizard intoned. "Wiped away. And when this evil thing is gone, then the truth, what you and I want to be the truth, can be written in, to fill its rightful place."

The waves were coming in, coming in, erasing the dragon. And Harl could sleep.

Somewhere along the line, during his hurried days of training, Matt asked, "Then King Ay is in fact dead—and not wounded, as I was first told?"

A tutor explained. "You were told he was only wounded, because he can be brought back to life. If your mission succeeds, his dying and his wounds will be as if they had never happened."

"Then if I should fail, someone else can try again? If I am killed back there, my life too may still be saved?"

He had his answer at once from the gravity of their faces. But they went into explanations. "All that you see being done here, all this work, is only to try to give that one man back his life. If we can restore him, then all the other bent and altered lives surrounding his will also flow back to where they were before the berserkers interfered. But not yours, for your life was not there in the original pattern. If you should die in the time of King Ay, that death will be real and final for you. And death will be real and final for all of us here, if you fail in your mission. No one will be able to try again."

One of the perquisites of Derron's new rank was

a small private cubicle of an office, and right now he was silently cursing the promotion that had given Lisa such a fine place in which to corner him.

"Whose fault *is* it if not yours?" she was demanding, angry as he had never seen her angry before. "You admit you're the one who suggested they use Matt. Why didn't you suggest they go back and grab someone else from the past instead?"

So far Derron was holding on to his patience. "Operations can't just reach back and pull someone out of history every time they feel like it. Ay's crew are a special case; they're going right back where they belong. And Matt is a special case: he was about to die anyway when he was brought up. Now Operations already *has* brought up a couple of other men who were about to die in their own times, but those two haven't had a chance to learn where they are yet, let alone what the mission they're wanted for is all about. When they are able to understand it, there's a chance they may refuse."

"Refuse? What chance did Matt ever have to refuse to go, when you demanded it of him? He thinks you're some kind of a great hero—he's still like a child in so many ways!"

"Beg your pardon, but he's not a child. Far from it. And he won't be helpless. Before we drop him he'll be trained in everything he'll need, from politics to weapons. And we'll be standing by—"

"Weapons?" Now she was really outraged. She was still like a child herself, in some ways.

"Certainly, weapons. Although we hope he's

only going to bc in Quccnsland for a fcw days and won't get involved in any fighting. We're going to try to have Ay rehabilitated and bring Matt back here before the wedding."

"Wedding!"

Derron hastened on. "Matt can take care of himself, and he can do the job that's expected of him. He's a natural leader. Anyone who can lead Neolithic people—"

"Never mind all that!" Becoming aware that her anger was useless, Lisa was sliding toward the brink of tears. "Of course he can do it! If he must. If he's really the only one who can go. But why were *you* the one to suggest that he be used? Right after I had talked to you about him. Why? Did you just have to make sure that *he* was temporary too?"

"Lisa, no!"

Her eyes were brimming over, and she hurried to the door. "I don't know what you are! I don't know you any more!" And she was gone.

Days ago, the plastic membrane, its task completed had fallen away from his face. The new skin had appeared already weathered, thanks to the Moderns' magic, and with the membrane gone the new beard had grown with fantastic speed for two days before slowing to a normal rate.

Now, on the day he was to be dropped, Matt stood for the last time in front of the mirror of his room—he was still quartered in the hospital—to get a last good look at his new face. Turning his head from side to side, he pondered Ay's cheeks and nose and chin from different angles.

It was a much different face from the one that had looked back at him reflected in the still waters of Neolithic ponds; but he wondered if the spirit behind it had also been changed sufficiently. It did not seem to Matt that he was yet possessed of the spirit of a king.

"Just a few more questions, sire," said one of the omnipresent tutors, standing at Matt's elbow. For days now the tutors had conversed with him only in Ay's language, while treating him with the respect suitable for subordinates to show when addressing a warrior chief. Maybe they thought they were helping to change his spirit, but it was only playacting.

The tutor frowned at his notes. "First, how will you spend the evening of the day of your arrival in Queensland?"

Turning away from the mirror, Matt answered patiently. "That is one of the times we cannot be sure of, where Ay's lifeline is hard to see. I will stay in character as best I can and try to avoid making decisions, especially big ones. I will use my communicator if I think I need help."

"And if you should happen to meet the dragon machine that assassinated your predecessor?"

"I will try my best to make it move around, even if this means letting it chase me. So that you can find the keyhole to cancel out the dragon along with all the harm it has done."

Another tutor who stood near the door said, "Operations will be watching closely. They will do their utmost to pull you out before the dragon can do you harm."

"Yes, yes. And with the sword you are giving me, I will have some chance to defend myself."

The tutors' questioning went on, while the time for the drop neared, and a team of technicians came in to dress Matt. They brought with them the best copies that could be made of the garments Ay had worn when embarking for Queensland.

The costumers treated him more like a statue than a king. When it was time for the finishing touches, one of them complained, "If they've decided at last that we should use the original helmet, where is it?"

"Both helmets are out at the Reservoir," the other answered. "The communications people are still working on them."

The tutors kept thinking up more last-minute questions, which Matt continued to answer patiently; the dressers put a plastic coverall on him over Ay's clothes, and another officer came to lead him out to the little train that would take him through a tunnel to Reservoir H.

Once before he had ridden on this train, when he had been taken to see the sleeping men and the ship. He had not cared for the train's swaying and did not expect to enjoy riding the ship. As if in tune with this thought, one of the tutors now looked at his timepiece and handed Matt what Matt knew was an antimotion-sickness pill.

Halfway to the Reservoir, the train stopped at a place where it had not stopped last time, and two men got on. One was the chief called Time Ops; he and everyone else showed deference to the second man, whom Matt recognized from his pictures as the Planetary Commander. The Planetary Commander took the seat facing Matt and sat there swaying lightly with the car's renewed motion, holding Matt in steady scrutiny.

Matt's face was sweating, but only because of the plastic coverall. So, he was thinking, this is what a king looks like in the flesh. At once heavier and less rocklike than his television image. But this man was after all a Modern king, and so the king-spirit in him was bound to be different from that which had been in Ay.

The ruler of the Moderns asked Matt, "I understand you thought it important to see me before you were dropped?" When there was no immediate response, he added, "You understand what I'm saying?"

"Yes, I understand. Learning Ay's language has not driven yours out of my mind. I wanted to see you, to see with my own eyes what it is that makes a man a king." Some of the men in the background wanted to laugh when they heard that; but they were afraid to laugh, and quickly smoothed their faces into immobility.

The Planetary Commander did not laugh or even smile, but only glanced sideways at Time Ops before asking Matt, "They've taught you what to do if the dragon machine comes after you?"

Out of the corner of his eye, Matt saw Time Ops nod slightly to the Planetary Commander.

"Yes," said Matt. "I am to make the machine chase me, to get it to move around as much as possible. You will try to pull me out . . . . "

The Planetary Commander nodded with satisfaction as he listened. When the train stopped, he waved the others to get off first, so that he and Matt were left alone in the car. Then he said, "I will tell you the real secret of being a king. It is to be ready to lay down your life for

your people, whenever and however it is needed."
Then he nodded solemnly; he meant what he had
said, or he thought he meant it, and maybe he considered it a piece of startling wisdom. His eyes for
a moment were lonely and uncertain. Then he put
on his public face again and began to speak loud
words of encouragement, smiling and clapping
Matt on the shoulder as they walked off the train
together.

Derron was waiting at trackside in the low,
rough-hewn cavern, to grip hands with Matt in the
style of Ay's time. Matt looked for Lisa in the busy
little crowd, but, except perhaps for Derron, only
those were here who had some work to do. In his
mind Matt associated Lisa with Derron, and sometimes he wondered why these two friends of his
did not mate. Maybe he would mate with Lisa himself, if he came back from his mission and she was
willing. He had thought on occasion that she
would be willing, but there had never been time to
find out.

The tutors and other busy men hustled Matt off
to wait by himself in a small anteroom. He was
told he could get out of the coverall, which he did
thankfully. He heard another door open
somewhere nearby, and into his room came the
smell of the vast body of clean water, the lake that
was hidden and preserved against the planet's
future needs.

On the table in his little waiting room lay the
sword that the Modern wizards had designed for
him. Matt belted on the scabbard and then drew
the weapon, looking at it curiously. The edge
appeared to be keen, but no more than naturally

so. The unaided eye could see nothing of what the Moderns had once shown him through a microscope—the extra edge, thinning to invisibility even under high magnification, which slid out of the ordinary edge when Matt's hand, and his alone, gripped the hilt. In his hand, the sword pierced ordinary metal like cheese, and armor plate like wood, nor was the blade dulled in doing so. The Moderns said that the secret inner edge had been forged of a single molecule; Matt had no need to understand that and did not try.

But he had come to understand much, he thought, sheathing the sword again. In recent days, sleeping and waking, Matt had had history, along with other knowledge, poured like a river through his mind. And there was a new strength in his mind that the Moderns had not put there. They marveled over it and said it must have come from his twenty thousand years' passage from the direction of the beginning of the world toward the direction of its end.

With this strength to work on the Moderns' teaching, one of the things he could see very clearly was that in Sirgol's history it was the Moderns who were the odd culture, the misfits. Of course, by mere count of years, by languages and institutions, the Moderns were far closer to Ay than Ay was to Matt's original People. But in their basic modes of thinking and feeling, Ay and The People were much closer, both to each other and to the rest of humanity.

Only such physical power as the Moderns wielded was ever going to destroy the berserkers —or could ever have created them. But when it

came to things of the spirit, the Moderns were
stunted children. From their very physical powers
came their troubled minds, or from their troubled
minds came their power over matter; it was hard
to say which. In any case, they had not been able to
show Matt how to put on the spirit of a king, which
was something he was now required to do.

There was another thing he had come to understand—that the spirits of life were very strong in
the universe, or else they would long ago have
been driven from it by the berserkcr machines of
accident and disease, if not by the malignant ones
that came in metal bodies.

Wishing to reach toward the source of life for
the help he needed, Matt now did want what Ay
would have done before embarking on a
dangerous voyage—he raised his hands, making
the wedgesign of Ay's religion, and murmured a
brief prayer, expressing his needs and feelings in
the form of words Ay would have used.

That done, he could see no reason to stay shut
up any longer in this little room. So he opened the
door and stepped out.

Everyone was as busy as before. Men worked,
singly or in groups, on various kinds of gear.
Others hurried past, moving this way and that,
calling out orders or information. Most of them
remained utterly intent on their business, but a
few faces were turned toward Matt; the faces
looked annoyed that he had come popping out of
his container before it was time for him to be used
and fearful lest he cause some disruption of the
schedule.

After one look around, he ignored the faces. Ay's

helmet was waiting for him on a stand, and he went to it and picked it up. With his own hands he set the silver-winged thing upon his head.

It was an unplanned, instinctive gesture; the expressions on the men's faces were enough to show him that his instinct had been right. The men looking on fell into an unwilling silence that was mirror enough to show Matt that the helmet had marked a transformation, even though in another moment the men were turning back to their jobs with busy practicality, ignoring as best they could the new presence in their midst.

In another moment, some of his tutors came hurrying up again, saying that they had just a few more questions for him. Matt understood that they felt a sudden need to reassure themselves that they were his teachers still, and not his subjects. But now that the spirit he needed had come to him, he was not going to give them any such comfort; the tutors' time of power over him had passed.

Looking for the Planetary Commander, he strode impatiently through the knots of busy people. Some of them looked up, angry at his jostling, but when they beheld him they fell silent and made way. He walked into the group where the ruler of the Moderns was standing and stood looking down into his wrinkled-encircled eyes.

"I grow impatient," said Matt. "Are my ship and my men ready or are they not?"

And the Planetary Commander looked back with a surprise that became something like envy before he nodded.

On his earlier trip to the Reservoir, Matt had seen Ay's crew lying asleep in specially constructed beds, while machines stretched their muscles to keep them strong, lamps threw slivers of sunlight onto their faces and arms to keep them tanned, and electronic familiars whispered tirelessly to them that their young lord lived.

This time the men were on their feet, though they moved like sleepwalkers, eyes still shut. They had been dressed again in their own clothes and armed again with their own harness and weapons. Now they were being led in a long file from Lukas' manor down to the beach and hoisted aboard their ship. The gunwale that had been scraped by dragon scales had been replaced, and everything else maintained.

The fog-generators had long ago been turned off. Each man and object on the thin crescent of beach stood in the center of a flower of shadow-petals, in the light of the cold little suns that clustered high up under the black distant curve of roof.

Matt shook Derron's hand again and other offered hands, then he waded a short distance through the fresh water and swung himself up onto the long-ship's deck. A machine was coming to push the craft out into deep water.

Time Ops came climbing on board with Matt, and he half-followed, half-led him on a quick tour of inspection that finally took both of them into the royal tent.

" . . . Stick to your briefing, especially regarding the dragon. Try to make it move around as much as possible—if you should see it. Remember that historical damage, even casualties, are of secondary importance, if we can find the dragon's keyhole. Then everything can be set right . . . . "

Time Ops' voice trailed off as Matt turned to face him, holding in his hands a replica of the winged helmet on his head, a replica he had just picked up from atop Ay's treasure chest. "I have heard all your lectures before," said Matt. "Now take this—and compose a lecture on carelessness for those whom you command."

Time Ops grabbed the helmet, glaring at it in anger that for the moment was speechless.

"And now," said Matt, "get off my ship, unless you mean to pull an oar."

Still gripping the helmet and muttering to himself, Time Ops was already on his way.

After that, Matt paid the Modern world no more attention. He went to stand beside Harl, who had been set like a sleepy statue beside the steering oar. The other men, still tranced, were in place on their benches. Their hands moved slightly on their oar's worn wood as if glad to be back, making sure they were where they really fitted.

Looking out past the prow, over the black water under the distant lights, Matt heard a hum of power behind him and felt the ship slide free. In the next moment he saw a shimmering circle grow beneath her—and then, with scarcely a splash, the darkness and the cave were gone, exploded into a glare of blue light. An open morning sky gave sea-birds room to wheel away, crying their surprise at the sudden appearance of a ship. Free salt air blew against Matt's face, and a ground swell passed under his feet. Dead ahead, the horizon was marked with the blue vague line he had been told to expect—Queensland. Off to starboard, a reddened sun was just climbing clear of dawn.

Matt spent no time with last thoughts or hesitations. "Harl!" he roared out, at the same time thwacking his steersman so hard on the shoulder that the man nearly toppled even as his eyes broke open. "Must I watch alone all day, as well as through the end of the night?"

He had been told that these words, spoken in his voice, would wake the men, and so it happened. The warriors blinked and growled their way out of their long slumber, each man perhaps thinking that he alone had dozed briefly at his oar. Most of them had started rowing before their spirits were fully back in control of their bodies, but within a few seconds they had put a ragged stroke together, and, a few moments later, all of them were pulling strongly and smoothly.

Matt moved between the benches, making sure all were fully awake, bestowing curses and half-affectionate slaps such as no one else but Ay would dare give these men. Before they had been given time to start thinking, to wonder what they had been doing five minutes ago, they were firmly established in a familiar routine. And if, against commanded forgetfulness, any man's mind still harbored visions of an attacking dragon and a slaughtered chief, no doubt that man would be more than glad to let such nightmare vapors vanish with the daylight.

"Row, boys! Ahead is the land where, they say, all women are queens!"

It was a good harbor they found waiting for them. This was Blanium, Queensland's capital, a town of some eight or ten thousand folk, a big city in this age. Immediately inland from the harbor, on the highest point of hill, there rose the gray keep of a small castle. From those high battlements the Princess Alix was doubtless now peering down at the ship, to catch a first distant look at her husband-to-be.

In the harbor there were other vessels, traders and wanderers, but less than a dozen of them; few for the season and for all the length of quay. Empire trade was falling off steadily over the years; seamen and landsmen alike faced evil days. But let Ay live, and a part of the civilized world would outlast the storm.

Scattered rivulets of folk were trickling down Blanium's steep streets, to form a throng along the quay as the long-ship entered the harbor. By the time his crew had pulled into easy hailing distance, and the cheers on shore had started, Matt beheld nearly a thousand people of all ranks waiting to see him land. From the castle whence, of course, the ship must have been spied a great distance out, there had come down two large chariots of gilded wood, drawn by hump-backed load-beasts. These had halted near the water's edge, where men of some high rank had dismounted and now stood waiting.

The moment of arrival came, of songs and tossed flowers of welcome. Ropes were thrown ashore, and a crew of dockmen made the long-ship fast to bollards on the quary, where it rode against a bumper of straw matts. Matt leaped ashore, concealing his relief at escaping the rise and fall of the sea. It was probably a good thing for Ay's reputation that the voyage had not been a longer one.

The delegation of nobles earnestly bade him welcome, a sentiment echoed by the crowd. King Gorboduc sent his regrets that he ailed too gravely to come down to the harbor himself and expressed his wish to see Ay as soon as possible in the castle. Matt knew that Gorboduc was old, and ill indeed, having only about a month to live, historically, beyond this day.

The king was still without a male heir, and the Queensland nobles would not long submit to the rule of any woman. For Alix to marry one of them might displease the others enough to bring on the very civil war that she and her father were seeking so desperately to avoid. So, logically enough, the king's thoughts had turned to Ay—a princely man of royal blood, young and extremely capable, respected if not liked by all, with no lands of his own to divide his loyalty.

Leaving orders for Harl to see to the unloading of the ship and the quartering of the crew, Matt took from Ay's coffer the jewels historically chosen by Ay as gifts for king and princess. And then he accepted a chariot ride up the hill.

In the Moderns' world he had heard of places in the universe where load-beasts came in shapes that allowed men to straddle and ride them. He was just well satisfied that such was not the case on Sirgol. Learning to drive a chariot had presented problems enough, and today he was happy to leave the reins in another's hands. Matt hung on with one hand and used the other to wave to the crowd; as the chariots clattered up through the steep streets of the town, more hundreds of citizens, of all classes, came pouring out of buildings and byways to salute Matt with cries of welcome. The people expected the sea-rover to hold their country together; he hoped they were making no mistake.

The high gray walls of the castle at last loomed close. The chariots rumbled over a drawbridge and pulled to a halt in a narrow courtyard inside the castle walls. Here Matt was saluted by the sword and pike of the guard, and acknowledged the greetings of a hundred minor officials and gentry.

In the great hall of the castle there was gathered only a score of men and women, but these were naturally the most important. When Matt was ushered in, to the sound of trumpet and drum, only a few of them showed anything like the enthusiasm of the crowds outside. Matt could recognize most of the faces here from their likenesses in old portraits and secret photos; and he knew from the Modern historians that for the most part these powerful people were suspending judgment on Ay—and that there were a few among them whose smiles were totally false. The leader of this last faction would be the court wizard Nomis, who stood tall in a white robe such as Colonel Lukas had worn, wearing a smile that seemed no more than a baring of teeth.

If there was pure joy anywhere, it shone in the lined and wasted face of King Gorboduc. To cry welcome he rose from his chair of state, though his legs would support him for only a moment. After embracing Matt, and when they had exchanged formal greetings, the king sank wheezing back into his seat. His narrow-eyed scrutiny continued, giving Matt the feeling that his disguise was being probed.

"Young man," Gorboduc quavered, suddenly. "You look very like your father. He and I shared many a fight and many a feast; may he rouse well in the Warriors' Castle, tonight and always."

Ay would receive such a wish with mixed feelings and Ay was ever the man to speak out what he felt. "I thank you, Gorboduc, for meaning to wish my father well. May his spirit rest forever in the Garden of the Blessed above."

Gorboduc was taken with a sudden coughing spell; perhaps he gave way to it more fully than he needed, to spare himself making an issue of this correction by an upstart in his own hall.

But Nomis was not about to let his chance slip by. He strode forward, white robe flowing, while the king was momentarily incapacitated in the hands of his attendants.

Nomis did not speak to Matt directly, but stood beside him at the front of the hall and addressed the others. "You lords of the realm! Will all of you stand silent while the gods of your fathers are thus insulted?"

Most of them would, it seemed. Perhaps they were not sure of the insult; perhaps not of the gods. A few of them did grumble something, but in voices low enough for their words to be ignored.

Matt, his nerves stretched taut, did not ignore them. "I meant no insult to any here," he said clearly. The conciliatory words were hardly out of his mouth before he felt sure that they had been a mistake, too mild an utterance, too near an apology to have come from the real Ay. Nomis displayed a faint sneer of pleasure, and some of the others were suddenly looking at Matt with new expressions of calculation; the atmosphere had subtly changed.

The king had recovered from his coughing fit, and now all other matters must wait while his daughter was led forth by her attendant women. From behind a gauzy veil, Alix's eyes smiled briefly at Matt before she modestly lowered them; and he thought that the Moderns had spoken truly: there would be many lifelines more painful than Ay's to follow to the end.

While preparations were being made for the exchange of gifts, a friendly noble whispered to Matt that, if the Lord Ay had no objection, the king preferred that the betrothal ceremony be completed at once. It would mean unusual haste, but there was the matter of the king's health . . . .

"I understand." Matt looked toward the princess. "If Alix is agreeable, I am."

Her eyes, intense and warm, flicked up at him again. And in a few more minutes he and she were standing side by side with joined hands.

With a show of great reluctance being overcome only by a loyalty that was stronger still, Nomis came at the king's order to perform the ceremony of formal betrothal. Midway through, he raised his eyes to the audience as he was asking the ritual question, whether anyone present had objection to the proposed marriage. And the wizard showed not the least surprise when a loud answer came from one at whom he was staring.

"I—I do object! I have long sought the princess for my own. And I think the sea-rover will be better mated with my sword!"

The man had hesitated and stammered at the start, and the deep voice was perhaps a shade too loud for real confidence to be behind it. But the speaker looked formidable enough, young and tall and wide-shouldered, with arms thick enough to make the average man a pair of legs.

No doubt Gorboduc would have liked to intervene and forbid a duel, but he could not do so in the case of a formal betrothal challenge. There was no historical record of Ay's having fought a duel at his betrothal ceremony, an item not likely to have been overlooked by the chroniclers; still, Nomis had now pushed his pawn forward. For this Matt supposed he could blame only himself; he had somehow failed to match Ay's exact behavior and so had encouraged the challenge.

In any event, there was no doubt about what had to be done now. Matt hooked his thumbs into his wide leather felt, faced his challenger, and drew a deep breath. "Will you state your name?"

The young giant answered in a tense voice, his tone far more hesitant than his words. "I need no introduction to any person of quality here. But that you may address me with the proper respect, know that I am Yunguf, of the House of Yung. And know also that I claim the Princess Alix for my own."

Matt bowed. His manner was very smooth and cool, as Ay's would be. "Since you appear to be a worthy man, Yunguf, we may fight at once to decide this matter . . . . If you have no reason to delay?"

Yunguf flushed; his control slipped for a moment, and Matt saw that beneath it the man was certainly badly frightened—more frightened than such a warrior should be by the prospect of any duel.

The princess's hand fell on Matt's arm; she had put back her veil and now, looking soberly at Matt, she drew him a little aside and spoke to him in a low voice. "I hope with all my heart that you fare well in this matter, lord. My affections have never belonged to that man."

"Princess, has he ever asked to marry you?"

"A year ago he did." Alix's eyes flickered in maidenly modesty. "As others have. But when I said him nay, he never pressed the matter more."

"So." Matt looked across the hall to where Nomis was now intoning over Yunguf's arms a blessing of the Old Religion. Yungus seemed to need all his courage to keep from shrinking away from the wizard's touch. No, it was not simple death or wounding in a duel that Yunguf feared.

Matt himself could face the personal danger calmly enough. He had spent most of his life within threat of violence from animals or nature—though, as one of The People, he had very rarely been in danger from another human being. The Moderns had given him Ay's lithe hitting power and endurance, had put not only skill but extra speed into his nerves. And they had given him his special sword, which alone could give him advantage enough to win a fight. No, it was not

Yunguf's prowess that bothered Matt, it was the very fact of the duel and the changes in history that it must bring.

Save for the king and the princess and the two participants, everyone seemed happy at the prospect of a little bloodletting. There was a general impatience at the delay necessary for Ay's shield to be fetched up from the ship. This delay would have allowed Matt time to get away by himself for a minute and report to Operations; but there was nothing he could say to them, or they to him, that would get him out of this duel. So Matt passed time in trying to make light conversation with the ladies, while Yunguf stood glowering and almost silent among a group who seemed to be his relatives.

The shield was soon brought in by Harl, who entered running, displaying every sign of eagerness to see the fight get started—probably with the intention of unsettling his lord's opponent's nerves as much as possible beforehand.

The company moved outside, where they were joined enthusiastically by the minor nobility and such of the commons as could crowd within sight. The king, chair and all, was established at the best vantage point, with the higher nobles around him. This courtyard was evidently consecrated to weaponry, judging by the massive timber butts, much hacked and splintered, which stood along its farther side.

The noble who had whispered to Matt about the betrothal came whispering again, to ask if he was acceptable to the Lord Ay as referee; Matt nodded his agreement.

"Then, my lord, if you will take a stand in the arena."

Matt moved to the center of the clear paved space, which was large enough to allow a good deal of maneuvering, and drew his blade. When he saw Yunguf advancing on him with blade and shield ready, slow and powerful-looking as a siege tower, he understood that there would be no further preliminaries. It seemed that at Gorboduc's court killing was much less ritualized than wedding.

The sun had passed the zenith by now, the air was warm, and in the windless courtyard even moderate exercise soon raised a sweat. Yunguf's approach, with many feints, was slow and cautious almost to the point of parody, but no one watching showed surprise. Probably a feigned slowness at the start was Yunguf's usual style. Sure enough, he moved rapidly at last, and Matt stepped quickly back, his shield-sword-shield parrying in good order the three blows of the attacking combination. Matt had hoped that at the clash of blades his opponent's sword might break, but the contact had been flat-sided and glancing, and Yunguf's weapon was evidently tough. And, Matt realized now, if one sword was broken, another would be provided; if two or three, cries of sorcery would be raised. No, only wounds could now decide the issue.

Matt worked his way back to the middle of the arena, still keeping out of Yunguf's way. The knowledge weighed on him that any killing he did today, any wounds he carved, would be disruptive changes that worked to the advantage of the ber-

serkers. But for Matt to be killed or beaten by
Yunguf would damage history still more. The on-
lookers had already begun to murmur; no doubt
his deep reluctance for this brawl was showing.
He had to win, and the sooner the better—but
without killing or maiming, if that were possible.

Matt raised his sword and shield in readiness as
Yunguf moved slowly into attacking range. And
when Yunguf charged again, Matt beat him to the
thrust, aiming along the side of Yunguf's shield to
damage the sword arm's shoulder muscles. But
Yunguf was twisting his body with the force of his
own lunge; as the huge man's blade slid off Matt's
shield, Yunguf's body turned into the path of
Matt's thrust, which cut between his upper ribs.

The wound was only moderately deep, and
Yunguf was not yet stopped, but his next slash
was weak and slow. Matt swayed back just enough
to let the blow go by, then lunged in again,
blocking sword with sword, hooking the wounded
man's knee with his foot and using his shield to
force Yunguf's upper body back.

Yunguf fell like a tree, and there was Matt's
bloody point hovering at his throat, while Matt's
foot pinned Yunguf's sword wrist to the paving
stone.

"Will you—yield to me—the combat—and its
prize?" Matt was now aware of his own panting
and of Yunguf's whistling, strangely gurgling
breath.

"I yield me." The answer, in strangled tones,
came quickly enough. There were no grounds for
hesitation.

Matt stepped wearily back, wondering what Ay

customarily used to wipe a bloody sword blade. Harl came to perform that office for him and to scold him about his hesitancy at the start of the fight. Yunguf's relatives had gone to Yunguf's aid, and with their help the wounded man seemed to be sitting up easily enough. At least, thought Matt, a killing had been avoided.

He turned to the princess and her father, to find them with frightened eyes fixed on an object that lay on the ground nearby. It was Nomis's outer robe, snowy in the sunlight. The wizard himself was no longer in sight; the white garment discarded was a plain enough signal that he was donning black.

A cough sounded wetly behind Matt, and he turned to see Yunguf with bright blood upon his lips.

The great metal dragon lay motionless, buried almost completely in the muck of the sea bottom. Around it the dull life of the great depths stirred— in safety, for this berserker was not seeking to avoid killing anything. For it to end even a vegetable lifeline nonhistorically could provide a datum for the Moderns' huge computers, implacable as berserkers themselves, to use in their relentless search for the dragon's keyhole.

The dragon was still under the direct command of the berserker fleet that was besieging the planet in Modern times. On their own variety of sentry screens, that fleet's linked computers had observed the lifting of Ay's ship and crew to Modern times and their subsequent restoration to Ay's time, with one lifeline added.

It was obvious what the Moderns intended, obvious to machines who themselves knew well the theory and practice of baiting traps. But a viable replacement for Ay was bait they could not afford to ignore. They must strike again, using one of the dragon's weapons.

But this time they must be subtle. The replacement must not be killed, at least not in any way that would spin a new thread of causation toward the dragon for the Moderns to follow. The linked berserker computers pondered electrically and arrived at what they considered an ideal solution: capture the replacement alive and hold him so, until the pillars of Sirgol's history came crashing down.

Even while in hiding, the dragon maintained around itself a net of subtle infraelectronic senses. Among the things it now observed in this way was a black-robed man, standing on a pillar of seaside rock about two miles from the berserker's hiding place and speaking on and on, rhythmically, into the empty air. From data in its memory banks the berserker deduced that this man was attempting to call supernatural forces to his aid.

And in the man's speech it caught the name of Ay.

In the full sunlight of midafternoon, Nomis stood chanting on his pinnacle of rock. The spells of deepest evil were best sung in darkness, but his hate and fear had grown until they seemed to spread a darkness of their own about him. He would not wait for the setting of the sun.

While the seabirds wheeled around him, crying in the wind, he sang in his thin but penetrating voice:

Demon of darkness, rise and stalk.
Put on the bones and make them walk.
Dead men's bones, through the weed
   and slime,
Walk and climb.
Walk to me here.
Speak to me here
Of the secret to bring my enemy's death.

There was more, much more, all cajoling and coercing the dark wet things that waited in the deeps for men to drown—waited for fresh-drowned bones to come falling through the fathoms, for limber young corpses that the demons could wear like garments in their endless revels at the bottom of the sea. The dark wet things down there possessed all the knowledge of death, including how the death of Ay might be accomplished—something Yunguf had proven unable to achieve, despite all the supernatural threats Nomis had lavished on the lout.

Nomis's thin arms quivered, holding drowned men's fingers over his head. Then his arms swept low as he bowed, still chanting, eyelids closing out the sun. Today the spells would work, today the hatred was in him like a lodestone, drawing to him things of utter evil.

When he came to a place in the chant where he could pause, he did so. He let down his arms and opened his eyes, wondering if he had heard another sound between the surges of the surf. Under his black robe his old man's chest was heaving with exertion and excitement.

A bird screamed. And from below, from somewhere on the furrowed length of cliff that climbed to this tabletop from the sea, there came once more a scraping sound, almost lost in the noise of wind and surf.

He had just given up listening for a repetition of the sound and had started to chant again, when, from much nearer the top of the cliff, almost from under Nomis's feet, there came a small clatter, a tumble of stones dislodged by some climbing foot or groping hand. The sound was in itself so ordinary that it momentarily drove all thoughts of magic from the wizard's tired mind. He could only think angrily that someone was about to discover his hideaway.

Before him as he faced the sea was a cleft that climbed to the tabletop between folds of rock. From just out of sight within this cleft he now heard the sound of grit crunched under a heavy foot.

And then Nomis's world was shaken around him, but a proof that put an end to a lifetime's nagging inward doubts. His first glimpse of his climbing visitor showed him a drowned man's skull, one small tendril of seaweed clinging to its glistening crown.

With quick smooth movements the whole creature now climbed into his view. It was a manform, thinner than any living human but fuller than a skeleton. Drowned skeletons must change when a demon possessed them—this one looked more like metal than bone.

Having emerged completely from the crevice, the demon-shape halted. It stood taller than Nomis, so that it bent its skull-head slightly on its cable neck to look at him. He had to struggle not to turn and run, to stand his ground and make himself keep looking into the cloudy jewels that were its eyes. A drop of water sparkled, falling from one bonelike fingertip. Only when the thing took another step toward him did Nomis remember to reinforce his chalked protective ring with a gesture and a muttered incantation.

And then at last he also remembered to complete his astoundingly successful ritual with a blinding spell. "Now you must guide and serve me, until you are released! And serve me first by saying how my enemy can be put to death."

The shiny jaw did not move, but a quavery voice came forth from a black square where the mouth should have been. "Your enemy is Ay. He landed today upon this coast."

"Yes, yes. And the secret of his death?"

Even if the berserker were to order another to accomplish the replacement's death, a track of causation would be left on the Moderns' screens. "You must bring your enemy Ay here, alive and unhurt, and give him to me. Then you will never see him more. And if you do this I will help you gain whatever else you may desire."

Nomis's mind raced. He had trained himself for nearly a lifetime to seize such an opportunity as this and he was not going to fail now, not going to be tricked or cheated. So . . . the demon wanted Ay kept alive! That could only mean that some vital magical connection existed between the sea-rover and this thing from the deeps. That Ay should have enjoyed such help in his career was far from surprising, considering the number of men he had sent to dwell among the fishes and the charmed life he himself seemed to lead.

Nomis's voice came out harsh and bold. "What is Ay to you, demon?"

"My enemy."

Not likely! Nomis almost laughed the words aloud. He realized now that it was his own body and soul that the wet thing craved; but by his spells and within his chalked circle Nomis was protected. The demon had come to protect Ay. But Nomis would not let the demon know how much he had deduced. Not yet. He saw in this situation possibilities of gain so enormous as to be worth any risk.

"Harken, mud-thing! I will do as you ask. To-night at midnight I will bring your enemy here, bound and helpless. Now begone—and return at midnight, ready to grant me all I ask!"

In the evening Matt went walking with Alix along the battlements, watching the stars come out, while the princess's ladies-in-waiting hovered just out of sight around corners.

Matt's preoccupation with his inner thoughts was evidently obvious. The girl beside him soon abandoned a rather one-sided effort to make small talk and asked him plainly, "Do I please you, lord?"

He stopped his moody pacing and turned to her. "Princess, you please me very well indeed." And it was so. "If my thoughts go elsewhere, it is only because they are forced to."

She smiled sympathetically. The Moderns would not think Alix a beautiful girl. But all his life Matt had seen women's beauty under sunburn and woodsmoke and toughness, and he could see beauty now in this different girl of his third world.

"May I know then, lord, what problems force your thoughts away?"

"For one thing, the problem of the man I wounded. I have not made a good beginning here."

"Such concern does you credit. I am pleased to discover you more gentle than I had been led to expect." Alix smiled again. No doubt she understood that his concern over Yunguf rested mainly on reasons of policy; though of course she could have no idea of how very far that policy ranged. She began to tell Matt of some things that she might do, people she could talk to, to help heal the breach between the new House of Ay and that of Yung.

Listening, and watching her, he felt he could be king in truth if she were queen beside him. He would not be Ay. He knew now, as the Moderns surely must, that no man could really live another's life. But, in Ay's name, he might perhaps be king enough to serve the world.

He interrupted Alix. "And do you find me pleasing, lady?"

This time her marvelous eyes did more than flicker; with a warm light of promise they held

fast to his. And, as if by instinct, the duennas
appeared at that moment to announce that the
decent time limit for keeping company had been
reached.

"Until the morning, then," he said, taking the
princess's hand briefly, in the way permitted by
courtly manners.

"Until the morning, my lord." And as the women
led her away, she turned back to send him another
glance of promise before passing out of sight.

He stood there alone, gazing after the princess,
wishing to see her for ten thousand mornings
more. Then he took off his helmet for a moment
and rubbed his head. His communicator was still
silent. No doubt he should call in to Operations
and report all that had happened.

Instead he put the helmet on again (Ay would
wear it as a sort of dress uniform) and went down
into the keep, to find his way to the chamber
where Yunguf had been bedded down by order of
the court physician. Through the doorway of the
room he saw a pair of the wounded man's relatives
on watch inside and he hesitated to enter. But
when they saw Matt they beckoned him in,
speaking to him freely and courteously. None of
the House of Yung, it seemed, were likely to bear
him any ill-will for winning a duel.

Yunguf was pale and looked somehow
shrunken. His difficult breathing gurgled in his
throat, and when he twisted on his pallet to spit up
blood, the bandage loosened from his wound, and
air gurgled there also with his breath. He showed
no fear now, but when Matt asked him how he did,

Yunguf whispered that he was dying. There was more he wanted to say to Matt, but talking came too hard.

"Lord Ay," said one of the relatives reluctantly, "I think my cousin would say that his challenge to you was a lie, and that therefore he knew he could not win."

The man on the pallet nodded.

"Also—" The cousin paused as the other relative gestured at him worriedly. Then he went on, in a determined rush of words. "I think Yunguf would warn you that things harder to fight against than swords are set against you here."

"I saw the white robe left on the ground."

"Ah, then you are warned. May your new god defend you if a time comes when your sword will avail nothing."

A seabird cried in the night outside. Yunguf's eyes, with fear in them again, turned to the small window.

Matt wished the men of Yung well and climbed the stair back to the castle roof. He could be alone there and unobserved, since only a token watch was kept, and full night had now descended. Once secluded in lonely darkness, he took a deep breath and, for the first time, pressed his helmet's right wing in a certain way, switching on the communicator.

"Time Ops here." The crisp Modern voice was barely a whisper of sound, but it made the castle, and even the open night with its rising moon, somehow unreal. Reality was once more a grimly crowded cave-fortress at the center of a fantastic web of machines and energy. In what sounded to his own ears like a lifeless voice, Matt reported the duel and Nomis's departure, with the implied threat of the discarded white robe.

"Yes, our screens showed Yunguf's lifeline being hit by something. He's going to—" A paradoxloop censored out some words of Time Ops' speech. "Nothing vital is involved there, though." By that, of course, Time Ops meant that nothing vital to the Moderns' historical base was involved. "Have you seen or heard anything of the dragon yet?"

"No." The track of the rising moon showed the calm sea out to the distant horizon. "Why do you speak of the dragon so much?"

"Why?" The tiny voice seemed to crackle. "Because it's important!"

"Yes, I know. But what about my task here, of being king? If you help me I can do that, though it seems that I cannot be Ay."

There was a pause. "You're doing as well as can be expected, Matt. We'll tell you when there's corrective action you must take to stay closer to Ay's lifeline. Yes, you're doing a damn good job, from what our screens show. As I said, what happens to Yunguf isn't vital. Your watching out for the dragon is."

"I will watch out for it, of course."

After correctly breaking off the contact, Matt decided it was time he visited Ay's men, who had been quartered temporarily in a kind of guardroom built into the castles massive outer wall. With this in mind he descended from the keep along an outer stair.

He was deep in thought, and it did not occur to

him that the courtyard at the bottom of the stair was darker than it ought to have been. Nor did he wonder that the postern gate nearby stood half-open and unguarded. A sound of rapid movement at his rear alerted him, but too late; before he could draw sword a wave of men was on him, weighing him down. And before he could shed Ay's pride enough to utter a cry for help, something smothering had been bound tight around his head.

"Sir, can you spare a minute? It's important."

Time Ops looked up impatiently behind his desk, but paused when he saw Derron's face and noticed what he was carrying. "Come in, then, Major. What is it?"

Derron walked stiffly into the office, carrying a winged helmet under his arm. "Sir, I've been—sort of hanging on to this. It's the extra one Matt found on his ship before he was dropped. Today some communications people came to see me about it. There was a continuous noise-signal being generated in its chronotransmitter."

Time Ops just sat there behind his desk, waiting not too patiently for Derron to get to the point.

"The communications people told me, sir, that the signal from this helmet was interfering with a similar signal put out by the helmet Matt's wearing. Whichever one he'd taken, he'd be walking around back there broadcasting a built-in noise, very easy for the berserker to identify as a chronotransmitter and home in on. The berserker must have thought it an obvious trap, sir, since it hasn't homed in and killed him yet." Derron's voice was very well controlled, but he could feel his anger in the tightness of his throat.

"So, you're shocked at what we're doing, Odegard. Is that it?" Time Ops grew angry too, but not guiltily or defensively. He was only annoyed, it seemed, at Derron's obtuseness. He flicked on his desk screen and spun a selector. "Take a look at this. Our present view of Ay's lifeline."

During his hitch of sentry duty, Derron had gotten pretty good at reading the screens. This was the first look he had today at what was happening to Ay's lifeline. He studied the picture carefully, but what he saw only confirmed his fears of yesterday. "It looks bad. He's getting way off the track."

"Matt's buying a little more present-time for us here, and so far that's all he's doing. Is it clear now why we're trying to get the dragon to kill him? Millions, many millions, have died in this war for *nothing*, Major."

"I see." His anger was growing more choking by the moment, because there was nowhere it could justly be vented. In hands that he could not keep from shaking, Derron held the helmet out in front of him for a moment, looking at it as if it were an archeological find he had just unearthed. "I see. You'll never win unless you find that dragon's keyhole. Matt never was anything but a fancy piece of live bait, was he?"

"No, I wouldn't say that, Major." Time Ops' voice was less sharp. "When you first suggested that he be used, we weren't sure but that he could come out alive. But the first full-scale computer simulation showed us the way things pretty well had to go. No doubt you're right when you say bugging the helmet made the trap a little too obvious." Time Ops shrugged, a slight, tired motion. "The way things stand at this moment, Matt may be šafer from berserkers than we are."

Matt came painfully awake, trying to cough around a gag of dirty cloth that had been stuffed into his mouth. His head ached, throbbing hideously, as if he had been drugged. He was being carried with a sickening jogging motion; when his head had cleared a little more, he understood that he was riding slung across a load-beast's humped back, his head hanging down on the one side of the animal and his feet on the other. His helmet had fallen off somewhere; and there was no bouncing tug at his waist from the weight of sword and scabbard.

Six or eight men had him prisoner. They were walking near the load-beast in the darkness, guiding and leading it along a narrow winding path by moonlight. The men looked behind them frequently, and now and then they exchanged a few low-voiced words.

" . . . I think two of them are following, or they were . . . . "

Matt heard that much. He tried the cords holding his wrists and ankles and found them strong and tight. Turning his head, he could see that the trail ahead wound among jagged pillars and outcroppings of rock; from what he knew of the country near Blanium he judged that they were right along the coast.

When the man who was leading the way turned and paused a moment to let the others close up, Matt saw without surprise that he was tall and thin and robed in black, and had belted round his

lean waist a sword and scabbard that looked like
Matt's. Nomis had taken for himself one of the
power symbols of a king.

The way grew steadily rougher. Shortly the
little procession came to a thin ridge, with deep
clefts in the rock on either side of it; here the load-
beast must be left behind. At Nomis's order, some
of the men lifted Matt from its back. He tried to
feign unconsciousness, but Nomis came to lift his
eyelids and then regard him with a knowing grin.

"He's awake. Untie his feet, but see to it that his
arms are doubly secure."

The men did so. The farther they progressed on
this hike, the more often they stopped to look
uneasily about them, starting at every sound of
the night. They seemed to fear Nomis and
whatever lay ahead almost as much as they feared
the pursuit that must be coming after them from
the castle.

With his arms still bound behind his back, men
ahead and behind holding on to him, Matt was led
across the single-file ridge, then made to scramble
up through a long twisting chute, almost a tunnel
between high walls of rock that shaded out the
moon. Only Nomis, leading through the darkness,
seemed to know the way. The sound of surf
became audible, drifting from somewhere below.

A cloud was over the moon when the party
straggled at last onto a tiny tableland of rock. Only
Nomis immediately saw the figure that had been
waiting, motionless as stone, for their arrival.
When he saw it, he quickly drew Matt's sword; and
when Matt was pushed up out of the chute to
within his reach, he gripped Matt's hair with one

hand and with the other laid the bare blade against Matt's throat.

The moon came out then, and the other men saw the thing that stood watching them. Like odd chicks of some gaunt black bird, they squawked and scrambled to get behind Nomis, all making sure they stood within the old chalked diagram. For a few seconds, then, everything was still, save for the faint wind and the surf and one man's muttering in fear.

Keeping the sword against Matt's neck, Nomis pulled the gag from his face and displayed him to the berserker. "What say you, mud-thing, is this man indeed your enemy? Shall I slay him, then?"

The metal puppet might have been sent charging forward, far faster than any man could move, to pull Matt away to captivity. But there was the keen edge right against the jugular. The berserker would not risk a thread of responsibility for Matt's death.

"Wizard, I will give you power," said the demon. "And wealth, and the pleasures of the flesh, and then life everlasting. But first you must give me that man alive."

Nomis crooned in his certainty of victory, while at his back his men huddled in terror. In this moment when all desires seemed possible of attainment, there rose uppermost in his mind the memory of a day long ago, when a child-princess's mocking laughter had burned at him. "I want Alix," he whispered. To him the breaking of her pride would mean more than her young body.

"I will give her to you," lied the demon solemnly, "when you have given me that man alive."

In Nomis's ecstasy of triumph, his arm wavered slightly as he held the long sword. Matt was ready. His bound wrists still allowed him some arm movement, and as he jerked free with all his strength his elbow struck the wizard's old ribs with force enough to send Nomis sprawling and the sword spinning in the air.

The other men's terror was triggered into panic flight. They burst up from their crouched positions, first scattering blindly and then converging on the only path of escape, the narrow way by which they had ascended. Running straight, head down, Matt kicked the fallen sword ahead of him and still got there first by a stride, thanks, to what the Moderns had done for his nerves and muscles.

The berserker was delayed by its need to avoid mangling the men who got in its way, but even as Matt reached the top of the path he felt a hand harder than flesh scrape down his back. It seized his clothing, but the fabric tore free. Then he was leaping, falling into the descending passage. At his back the other men were screaming in raw fear as they collided with one another and with the berserker.

When he landed he naturally fell, cutting and bruising himself without really feeling the injuries. The way was so narrow that he could not miss finding the sword he had kicked ahead of him. With his bound hands he groped behind him in the dark to pick it up by the blade, heedless of nicked fingers. Then he got his feet under him and scrambled some distance farther downward. He stumbled and fell again, hurting his knee, but he had gained a substantial lead on the tangled terror that was jamming the narrow chute behind him. One or more men had probably fallen and broken bones or injured themselves in other ways, and the rest were unable to get past them. They were all howling with mindless fear, and no doubt lacerating themselves further in the dark when they felt the chill touch of the berserker; it would be sorting through the men to find the one it wanted, trying to get the others out of its way . . . .

Matt propped the sword on its hilt behind him and, with the new skill of his nerves, slid his bonds against the edge of its blade. He had freed himself before he heard the machine's footsteps come crunching toward him in the dark.

"That's it, that's it! We'll nail the damned thing now!" In Time Operations, men were crying out a hunters' jubilation that was as old as mankind. On their screens their giant computers were limning out the radii of a spiderweb, the center of which would hold the dragon. The data needed to draw the web was flowing in from human lifelines being bent and battered; the berserker seemed to be struggling with men in some enclosed space.

But still it had not killed again. And the locus of its keyhole was not yet in sight.

"Only a little more," Time Ops, staring wildly at his screens, pleaded for bloodshed. "Something?"

But there was no more.

Matt retreated, limping, out into the moonlight where he could see. The thing followed unhurriedly, sure of him now. He backed out onto the thin ridge, between yawning crevices too deep for the moonlight to plumb, gripping his sword's hilt in bleeding fingers. Pale in the moonlight and almost skeleton-thin, the machine followed him carefully. It did not want him to fall. It would choose the precise moment and then rush to catch him, as easily as a human athlete picking up a toddler from a broad walk.

Keeping his sword's point centered on the narrow way along which it would have to come, he had just time enough to steel his arm. A moment ago the berserker had been twelve feet away, and now it was on him. It made a wiping motion with one hand, to clear what appeared to be an ordinary sword blade from its path—and four steel fingers leaped free like small silver fish in the moonlight, while the monomolecular blade stayed where it was, centered by Matt's braced muscles.

The inertia of the machine's rush was great. Before it could halt itself, the sword point had gone through its torso, and what had been delicately controlled mechanism became dead hurtling weight. Matt went down before the force of it, but he clung to the edge of the rock. He saw it go tumbling over him, then falling in an endless slow somersault, taking with it the transfixing sword, which already glowed like a red-hot needle with the inner fire that it had kindled.

The demon vanished. From far down inside the crevice came a crash, and then another and another, echoing remotely. Matt pulled himself back onto the ridge and crawled a few feet; then he made himself stand and walk before he reached the place where the path was broad and safe.

He was battered and bruised, but he could

move. Trying to keep in shadow, he limped past the phlegmatic, waiting load-beast. He had gone a dozen steps farther when the two men Nomis had left here as sentries pounced out of deeper shadows. As they seized him, his injured leg was twisted again, and he fell.

"Best let me go and run yourselves," he said to the buskined knees standing before him. "Back there, the devil has come for your master."

It made them take a moment to look back toward the distant commotion on the path. And then they themselves were seized, not by the devil but by the two men Matt had seen running up from the direction of the castle, ax and sword in hand. Around Matt there swirled a brief clashing of metal and choked cries that were quickly ended.

"Is this leg your worst hurt, lord?" Harl asked anxiously, putting his ax in his belt and bending over Matt.

"Yes, I do well enough."

Torla muttered grimly, "Then we will go on and slaughter the rest of them."

Matt tried to think. "No. Not now, at least. Nomis called up a thing from the sea—"

Torla shuddered now at the distant moaning. "Then let us away?"

"Can you stand, lord?" asked Harl. "Good, then lean on me." And having pulled Matt to his feet, he next detached something from under his cloak and held it out. "Your helmet, lord. It fell outside the postern gate and set us on the right trail."

Harl and Torla might think that he was dazed, or that it was the pain in his leg that made him slow to reach out for the helmet. Harl had carried it under his cloak as if it was no more than a shell of metal; but, worn like a crown, it weighed enough to crush a man.

Down in the sea-bottom muck the dragon stirred. The tantalizing bait-signal of the life-unit that the Moderns had sent as Ay's replacement was now very near the shore. If that life-unit could be captured without further damage to other lifelines, a berserker victory would be insured. To pursue the replacement inland, among other lives, would involve creating too much change: the dragon's auxiliary man-shaped device might have conducted such a pursuit almost unobtrusively, but it had been somehow lost. Still, the chance of seizing the important life-unit right along the coast was too good an opportunity to let slip. Darkening the water with an upheaved cloud of mud, the dragon rose.

Supported by a strong man on either side, Matt could make fair speed along the rough path that led back to Blanium. Not, he thought, that there was any real need for haste. Nomis and his men would certainly not be in pursuit; if Nomis had survived at all, his influence must have been thoroughly destroyed.

And the dragon? It had done what it could do to capture him, to take him alive, quietly and gently. He shuddered. It must be hiding in the sea. And it seemed that, unless he went to the water's edge and waved at it, it was not going to chase him. It could have come inland to kill him any time;

peasants and armies and the walls of Blanium would not stop it.

No, if the berserker wanted him dead he would have been dead now, and even his magic sword would not have helped him for a moment. He had seen and heard enough of berserkers to be sure of that.

"How made you your escape, lord?"

"I will tell you later. Let me think now."

Make the dragon chase you, said Time Ops. *We will try to pull you out in time.* So far there had been no pulling out. *A king must be ready to give his life,* said the Planetary Commander, making what he thought was an important point, as he spoke from the depths of his own missileproof shelter.

The Moderns were fighting to save the tribe-of-all-men, and to them Matt or any other individual was only an implement for fighting. Save his life once, then shove him forward again to draw the lightning of the stone-lion's eye . . . .

In a flash of insight, many things suddenly fell into place for Matt. Scraps of knowledge he had picked up in the Modern's world, about the war as it was fought with screens and missiles, lifelines and keyholes, suddenly dovetailed with what had happened to him here in the world of Ay. Of course, he should have seen it before! It was the Moderns who wanted him killed here, by the berserkers. And the berserkers, knowing this, wanted instead to take him alive!

He was still bleakly pondering this insight when the communicator in his helmet began to speak into his ear with its tiny voice that no one else could hear. In his new anger, he paid no attention to what it was saying; he came near pulling the helmet off and throwing it away, with all its lying voices. He would throw it away, he told himself, when he came to the sea . . . . No, he must avoid the shore from now on. When he came to another bottomless crevice, then.

But instead he gripped his companions' shoulders, stopping them. "Good friends, I must be alone for a little while. To think—and pray."

His good friends exchanged glances with each other; his request must seem a strange one, coming at this time. But then their kind had been through a day that might make any man act strangely.

Harl frowned at him. "You are weaponless."

"There are no enemies about. But let your dagger stay with me if you will; only let me have a short time to myself."

And so they left him, though with repeated backward glances, left him sitting alone on a rock in the moonlight. He was their king now, and they loved him, and he smiled after them with satisfaction, thinking that he would have them at his side for many a year yet. He could and he would. There was no way for the Moderns to punish him, if he chose never to go hunting dragons. Matt was all the Moderns had between themselves and chaos; they would not dare to pull him back to the future, not while he worked at living King Ay's life. He might bungle the job now and then and provide only a second-best defense for the Moderns' world; but it was all the service they were going to get.

He took off the buzzing helmet and scratched his head leisurely. Then, holding the helmet before him, he twisted its right wing, letting Time Ops' tiny voice come out above the faint murmur of the unseen surf.

"—Matt, answer me, it's urgent!"

"I am here. What would you have?"

"Where are you? What's going on?"

"I am going on. To my bride and my kingdom."

There was a pause. Then: "Matt, it may be that that won't be enough, your going on trying to take Ay's place."

"No? Enough for me, I think. I have already been demon-hunting and have used up your sword. So I think I will not chase after a dragon that seems content to let me live."

"Demon-hunting? What?"

Matt explained. He could hear consternation at Operations' end; they had not thought of the enemy's trying to capture him alive.

Time Ops was soon back, pleading with a ragged urgency that Matt had never heard in the commander's voice before. "Matt, whatever else happens, you can't let that thing capture you alive."

"No? I have often been ordered to make it chase me."

"Forget that. No, wait. You can't be captured. But just avoiding capture and going on playing Ay's part isn't going to be enough, not now. You've done as well as anyone could, but your filling in for Ay simply isn't going to work."

"Then why does the enemy want to stop me?"

"Because you *are* buying us a little time here.

They want to eliminate any lingering chance we have—any chance of finding some new defense, of pulling off a miracle. They want to play it safe and finish us off quickly. All I can do is tell you—ask you to—go down along the seashore where the damned thing is hiding. Make it come out and chase you and stir up some change."

"And if it should capture me?"

There was a pause, a murmur of voices exchanged at the other end, and then another familiar voice came on.

"Matt, this is Derron. All these people here are trying to figure out the best way to tell you to die. You're to get the berserker to kill you. If it catches you alive, then you must find a way to kill yourself. Kill yourself *because* it's caught you. Understand? *Die*, in one way or another, and make the dragon somehow responsible. All along, that's been what Operations wanted of you. I'm sorry. I didn't know how it was until after you were dropped."

Time Ops came back. "Matt, you can shut us off now and go on to claim your bride and your kingdom, as you said you were going to. But if you do that, all your life your world there will be slowly decaying around you. Decaying inside, where you won't be able to see it, becoming less and less probable. Up here we'll be dying, all of us. At your end of history the chaos will begin in your children's time—that's what you'll be leaving them."

"You lie!" But Matt's voice broke with the cry, for he knew that Time Ops was not lying. Or, if he was lying again about this face or that, still he was telling the truth about what was needed to win the war.

"Matt? This is Derron again. What you just heard is the truth. I don't know what more to say to you."

Matt cried bitterly, "My friend, there is no need for you to say anything more!" And with a jerk of his hand that almost broke the helmet wing, he cut the voices off.

Too late. He had silenced them too late. Slowly he put the helmet back on his head and stood up. Soon he saw Harl and Torla coming toward him; they had doubtless been watching protectively from not far away, overhearing some of the strange language of his prayers.

When they came up to him he said, no longer angry, "My leg gives me trouble. I think the path will be easier along the water's edge."

Between his friends, he moved toward the sound of surf. He went slowly, for in truth his leg did feel worse, having stiffened while he sat. No matter, now. He walked along thinking only in disconnected pictures and phrases, since the time for thought and worry was now past.

He had pulled the stone-man from the poison-digger's pit—that was twenty thousand years ago, and indeed it seemed to him that he had lived through twenty thousand years since then. He had been able to see the tribe-of-all-men grown to stretch across immensities of space and time. He had known, a little, the spirits of life. He had been a king, and a woman with the spirit of a princess had looked at him with love.

They had been walking for a minute along the

water's edge, when, without surprise, he saw a shoreline rock ahead suddenly move and become a nightmare head that rose amid moonlit spray on a sinuous column of neck. The dragon's vast body heaved itself up from the sea and lurched toward the men, moving faster than a man could run.

"I have the dagger," Matt said to his friends. "And right now both of you can use sword and ax better than I." The dragon was not coming for Harl or Torla, and it would have been a pointless insult to bid them run.

He kept the dagger hidden in his hand, the blade turned up flat behind his wrist, as the dragon's head came straight toward him on its tree-trunk neck that could swallow a man and hold him safe. Sword and ax hewed at it uselessly from either side. Matt was very tired, and in a way he welcomed the grave-wide jaws, which, he saw now, held no teeth. Only in the instant of the jaws' soft powerful closing did he bring the dagger up, holding the point steady at his own heart while the pressure came down . . . .

"It killed him." The first time, Time Ops whispered the words unbelievingly. Then he let them out in a whoop. "It killed him, it killed him?" The other hunters, who had been frozen at their screens, sharing their computers' creeping certainty of failure, were galvanized once more into action. On their screens the spiderwebs tightened like nooses, imaging a target greenly solid and sure.

In the deep cave called Operations Stage Two,

metallic arms extended a missile sideways from its rack while a silvery circle shimmered into being on the floor beneath. With a cluck and a jolt the arms released their burden. Falling, the missile was gone.

Derron had seen a keyhole hit and closed before, and he understood perfectly what a victory he was seeing now. On the screens, the whole writhing build-up of change surrounding Ay now burst like a boil; and the lines began to straighten themselves out like a string figure when the loose end is pulled. History's flow turned strongly and safely back into its familiar riverbed. Only the one lifeline that had been the catalyst was newly broken; you had to look closely at the screens not to miss that small detail.

The raw stump of that line left no room for reasonable doubt, but still Derron's hand went out to punch his communicator for Stage Three. "Alf? Listen, will you let me know what shape he's in, the moment— All right, thanks."

He waited, holding the circuit open to Stage Three, gazing blankly through tired eyes at the screens. Around him in Operations' nerve center, the first waves of jubilation foamed up around the edges of discipline.

"Derron?" Alf's reply was slow in coming and slow-spoken when it came, to tell about the wound in the heart and to speculate on how the man must have arranged to have the knife driven in. And to confirm that Matt's brain had been too long without blood and oxygen for the medics to do anything for him now.

Derron flipped off the switch and sat at his post, tired and immobile. Some of the victorious hunters around him were breaking out cigars, and one was calling jovially for a ration of grog. A few minutes later, Time Ops himself came strolling by with a glass in his hand, but he was not smiling as he paused at Derron's position.

"He was a good man, Odegard. The best. Not many can accomplish a thousandth part of what he did. With their lives or with their deaths." Time Ops raised his glass in a solemn, sipping toast to the bitten-off green line on the screen. Later, of course, there would be ceremonies, and perhaps a monument, to say the same thing more elaborately.

"The thing is," said Derron, "I don't really much care what happens to the world. Only about a person here and there."

Time Ops might not have heard, for the noise of celebration was growing louder. "You did a necessary job, Major, and did it well, from the start of the operation right up until today. We're going to be expanding even more here in Time Operations and we'll need good men in key positions. I'm going to recommend you for another promotion . . . . "

Nomis stood with arms upraised, gray beard and black robes whipping in the wind, while he persisted in the evil endeavor that had kept him here for the past three days on his secret pinnacle of rock. Nomis persisted, though he could not escape the feeling that all his labors against Ay were doomed to be in vain . . . .

On the battlement, Alix shaded her eyes against the morning sun and strained them seaward to catch sight of sail or mast. She waited, trembling inwardly a little, for her first sight of her future husband and lord . . . .

The cliffs of Queensland were dead ahead, Harl knew, though still a day's rowing out of sight. He frowned, gazing out to port across the sea's gray face, where nothing broke the line of the horizon but a distant line of squalls. Then his face cleared with the thought that young Ay, in his tent amidships, was doubtless planning for the fighting that was sure to come.

The instruments of science do not in themselves discover truth. And there are searchings that are not concluded by the coincidence of a pointer and a mark.

STARSONG

Forcing the passage through the dark nebula Taynarus cost them three fighting ships, and after that they took the casualties of a three-day battle as their boarding parties fought their way into Hell. The Battle Commander of the task force feared from the beginning to the end of the action that the computer in command on the berserker side would destroy the place and the living invaders with it, in a last *gotterdammerung* of destructor charges. But he could hope that the damped-field projectors his men took with him into the fight would prevent any nuclear explosion. He sent living men to board because it was believed that Hell held living human prisoners. His hopes were justified; or at least, for whatever reason, no nuclear explosion came.

The beliefs about prisoners were not easily confirmed. Ercul, the cybernetic psychologist who came to investigate when the fighting was over, certainly found humans there. In a way. In part.

Odd organs that functioned in a sort-of-way, inter-connected with the non-human and the non-alive. The organs were most of them human brains that had been grown in culture through use of the techniques that berserkers must have captured with some of our hospital ships.

Our human laboratories grow the culture-brains from seedlings of human embryo-tissue, grow them to adult size and then dissect them as needed. A doctor slices off a prefrontal lobe, say, and puts it into the skull of a man whose own corresponding brain-part has been destroyed by some disease or violence. The culture-brain material serves as a matrix for regrowth, raw material on which the old personality can re-impress itself. The culture-brains, raised in glass jars, are not human except in potential. Even a layman can readily distinguish one of them from a normally developed brain by the visible absence of the finer surface convolutions. The culture-brains cannot be human in the sense of maintaining sentient human minds. Certain hormones and other subtle chemicals of the body-environment are necessary for the development of a brain with personality—not to mention the need for the stimuli of experience, the continual impact of the senses. Indeed some sensory input is needed if the culture-brain is to develop even to the stage of a template usable by the surgeon. For this input music is commonly employed.

The berserkers had doubtless learned to culture livers and hearts and gonads as well as brains, but it was only man's thinking ability that interested them deeply. The berserkers must have stood in their computer-analogue of awe as they regarded the memory-capacity and the decision-making power that nature in a few billion years of evolution had managed to pack into the few hundred cubic centimeters of the human nervous system.

Off and on through their long war with men the berserkers had tried to incorporate human brains into their own circuitry. Never had they succeeded to their own satisfaction, but they kept trying.

The berserkers themselves of course named nothing. But men were not far wrong in calling this center of their research Hell. This Hell lay hidden in the center of the dark Taynarus nebula, which in turn was roughly centered in a triangle formed by the Zitz and Toxx and Yaty systems. Men had known for years what Hell was, and approximately where it was, before they could muster armed strength enough in this part of their sector of the galaxy to go in and find it and root it out.

"I certify that in this container there is no human life," said the cybernetic psychologist, Ercul, under his breath, at the same time stamping the words on the glassite case before him. Ercul's assistant gestured, and the able-bodied spaceman working with them pulled the power-connectors loose and let the thing in the tank begin to die. This one was not a culture-brain but had once been the nervous system of a living prisoner. It had been greatly damaged not only by removal of most of its human body but by being connected to a mass of electronic and micro-mechanical gear. Through some training program, probably a combination of punishment and reward, the berserker had then taught this brain to perform certain computing operations at great speed and with low probability of error. It seemed that every time the computations had been finished the mechanism in the case with the brain had immediately reset all the counters to zero and once more presented the same inputs, whereupon the brain's task had started over. The brain now seemed incapable of anything but going on with the job; and if that was really a kind of human life, which was not a possibility that Ercul was going to admit out loud, it was in his opinion a kind that was better terminated as soon as possible.

"Next case?" he asked the spacemen. Then he realized he had just made a horrible pun upon his judge's role. But none of his fellow harrowers of Hell seemed to have noticed it. But just give us a few more days on the job, he thought, and we will start finding things to laugh at.

Anyway, he had to get on with his task of trying to distinguish rescued prisoners—two of these had been confirmed so far, and might some day again look human—from collection of bottled though more or less functioning organs.

When they brought the next case before him, he had a bad moment, bad even for this day, recognizing some of his own work.

The story of it had started more than a standard year before, on the not-far-off planet of Zitz, in a huge hall that had been decorated and thronged for one of the merriest of occasions.

"Happy, honey?" Ordell Callison asked his bride, having a moment to take her hand and speak to her under the tumult of the wedding feast. It was not that he had any doubt of her happiness; it was just that the banal two-word question was the best utterance that he could find —unless, of course, he was to sing.

"Ohhhh, happy, yes!" At the moment Eury was no more articulate than he. But the truth of her words was in her voice and in her eyes, marvelous as some song that Ordell might have made and sung.

Of course he was not going to be allowed to get away, even for his honeymoon, without singing one song at least.

"Sing something, Ordell!" That was Hyman Bolf, calling from across the vast banquet table, where he stood filling his cup at the crystal punch-fountain. The famed multifaith revivalist had come from Yaty system to perform the wedding ceremony. On landing, his private ship had misbehaved oddly, the hydrogen power lamp flaring so that the smoke of burnt insulation had caused the reverend to emerge from his cabin weeping with irritated eyes; but after that bad omen, everything had gone well for the rest of the day.

Other voices took it up at once. "Sing, Ordell!"

"Yes, you've got to. Sing!"

"But it's m'own wedding, and I don't feel quite right—"

His objections were overwhelmingly shouted down.

The man was music, and indeed his happiness today was such that he felt he might burst if he could not express it. He got to his feet, and one of his most trusted manservants, who had foreseen that Ordell would sing, was ready to bring him his self-invented instrument. Crammed into a small box that Ordell could hang from his neck like an accordion were a speaker system from woofer to tweet, plus a good bit of electronics and audionics; on the box's plain surface there were ten spots for Ordell's ten fingers to play upon. His music-box, he called it, having to call it something. Ordell's imitators had had bigger and flashier and better music-boxes made for them; but surprisingly few people, even among girls between twelve and twenty, cared to listen to Ordell's imitators.

So Ordell Callison sang at his own wedding, and his audience was enthralled by him as people always were; as people had been by no other performer in all the ancient records of Man. The highbrowed music critics sat rapt in their places of honor at the head table; the cultured and not-so-cultured moneyed folk of Zitz and Toxx and Yaty, some of whom had come in their private racing ships, and the more ordinary guests, all were made happy by his song as no wine could have made them. And the adolescent girls, the Ordell fans who crowded and huddled inevitably outside the doors, they yielded themselves to his music to the point of fainting and beyond.

A couple of weeks later Ordell and Eury and his new friends of the last fast years, the years of success and staggering wealth, were out in space in their sporty one-seater ships playing the game they called Tag. This time Ordell was playing the game in a sort of reversed way, dodging about in one corner of the reserved volume of space, really trying to avoid the girl-ships that fluttered past instead of going after them.

He had been keeping one eye out for Eury's ship, and getting a little anxious about not being able to find it, when from out of nowhere there came shooting toward Ordell another boy-ship, the signals of emergency blazing from it across the spectrum. In another minute everyone had ceased to play. The screens of all the little ships imaged the face of Arty, the young man whose racer had just braked to a halt beside Ordell's.

Arty was babbling: "I tried, Ordell—I mean I didn't try to—I didn't mean her any harm— they'll get her back—it wasn't my fault she—"

With what seemed great slowness, the truth of what had happened became clear. Arty had chased and overtaken Eury's ship, as was the way of the game. He had clamped his ship to hers and boarded, and then thought to claim the usual prize. But Eury of course was married now, and being married meant much to her, as it did to Ordell who today had only played at catching girls. Somehow both of them had thought that everyone else must see how the world had changed since they were married, how the rules of the game of Tag would have to be amended for them from now on.

Unable to convince Arty by argument of how things stood, Eury had had to struggle to make her point. She had somehow injured her foot, trying to evade him in the little cabin. He kept on stubbornly trying to claim his prize. It came out later that he had only agreed to go back to his own ship for a first aid kit (she swore that her ship's kit was missing) after her seeming promise that he could have what he wanted when he returned.

But when he had gone back to his ship, she broke her own racer free and fled. And he pursued. Drove her into a corner, against the boundary of the safety zone, which was guarded by automated warships against the possibility of berserker incursions.

To get away from Arty she crossed that border in a great speeding curve, no doubt meaning to come back to safety within ten thousand miles or so.

She never made it. As her little racer sped close to an outlying wisp of dark Taynarus, the berserker machine that had been lurking there pounced out.

Of course Ordell did not hear the story in such coherent form, but what he heard was enough. On the screens of the other little ships his face at first seemed to be turned to stone by what he heard; but then his look became suddenly wild and mad. Arty cringed away, but Ordell did not stop a moment for him. Instead he drove at racer's speed out where his wife had gone. He shot through the zone of the protective patrols (which were set to keep intruders out, not to hold the mad or reckless in) and plunged between outlying dustclouds to enter one of the vast crevices that led into the heart of Taynarus; into the maze where ships and machines must all go slow, and from which no living human had emerged since the establishment of Hell.

Some hours later the outer sentries of the berserker came around his little ship, demanding in their well-learned human speech that he halt and submit to capture. He only slowed his little ship still further and began to sing to the berserker over the radio, taking his hands from his racer's controls to put his fingers on the keys of his music-box. Unsteered, his ship drifted away from the center of the navigable passage, grazing the nebular wall and suffering the pocking blasts of microcollisions with its gas and dust.

But before his ship was wrecked, the berserker's sentry-devices gave up shouting radio commands and sent a boarding party of machines.

Through the memory banks of Hell they had some experience of insanity, of the more bizarre forms of human behavior. They searched the racer for weapons, searched Ordell—allowed him to keep his music-box when it too had been examined and he kept on struggling for it—and passed him on as a prisoner to the jurisdiction of the inner guards.

Hell, a mass of fortified metal miles in diameter, received him and his racer through its main entrance. He got out of his ship and found himself able to breathe and walk and see where he was going; the physical environment in Hell was for the most part mild and pleasant, because prisoners did not as a rule survive very long, and the computer-brains of the berserker did not want to impose unnecessary stresses upon them.

The berserker devices having immediate control over the routine operations in Hell were themselves in large part organic, containing culture-brains grown for the purpose and some re-educated captured brains as well. These were all examples of the berserker's highest achievements in its attempts at reverse cybernation.

Before Ordell had taken a dozen steps away from his ship, he was stopped and questioned by one of these monsters. Half steel and circuitry, half culture-flesh, it carried in three crystal globes its three potentially-human brains, their too-smooth surfaces bathed in nutrient and woven with hair-fine wires.

"Why have you come here?" the monster asked him, speaking through a diaphragm in its mid-section.

Only now did Ordell begin at all to make a conscious plan. At the core of his thought was the knowledge that in the human laboratories music was used to tune and tone the culture-brains, and that his own music was as superior for that purpose as it was by all other standards.

To the three-headed monster he sang very simply that he had come here only to seek his young wife, pure accident had brought her, ahead of time, to the end of her life. In one of the old formal languages in which he sang so well of deep things, he implored the power in charge of this domain of terror, this kingdom of silence and unborn creatures, to tie fast again the thread of Eury's life. If you deny me this, he sang, I cannot return to the world of the living alone, and you here will have us both.

The music, which had conveyed nothing but its mathematical elements to the cold computer-brains outside, melted the trained purpose of the inner, half-fleshly guardians. The three-brained monster passed him on to others, and each in turn found its set aim yielding to the hitherto unknown touch of beauty, found harmony and melody calling up the buried human things that transcended logic.

He walked steadily deeper into Hell, and they could not resist. His music was leaked into a hundred experiments through audio-inputs, vibrated faintly through the mountings of glassite cases, was sensed by tortured nerve-cells through the changes in inductance and capacitance that emanated rhythmically from Ordell's music-box. Brains that had known nothing but to be forced to the limit of their powers in useless calculation—brains that had been hammered into madness with the leakage of a millimicrovolt from an inserted probe—these heard his music, felt it, sensed it, each with its own unique perception, and reacted.

A hundred experiments were interrupted, became unreliable, were totally ruined. The overseers, half flesh themselves, failed and fumbled in their programmed purposes, coming to the decision that the asked-for prisoner must be brought forth and released.

The ultimate-controlling pure berserker computer, pure metallic cold, totally immune to this strange jamming that was wreaking havoc in its laboratory, descended at last from its concentration on high strategic planning to investigate.

And then it turned its full energy at once to regaining control over what was going on within the heart of Hell. But it tried in vain, for the moment at least. It had given too much power to its half-alive creations; it had trusted too much to fickle protoplasm to be true to its conditioning.

Ordell was standing before the two linked potentially-human brains which were, under the berserker itself, the lords and superintendents of Hell. These two like all their lesser kind had been melted and deflected by Ordell's music; and now they were fighting back with all the electric speed at their command against their cold master's attempt to reaffirm its rule. They held magnetic relays like fortresses against the berserker, they maintained their grip on the outposts that were ferrite cores, they fought to hold a frontier that wavered through the territory of control.

"Then take her away," said the voice of these rebellious overseers to Ordell Callison. "But do not stop singing, do not pause for breath for more than a second, until you are in your ship and away, clear of Hell's outermost gate."

Ordell sang on, sang of his new joy at the wonderful hope that they were giving him.

A door hissed open behind him, and he turned to see Eury coming through it. She was limping on her injured foot, which had never been taken care of, but he could see that she was really all right. The machines had not started to open her head.

"Do not pause!" barked the voder at him. "Go!"

Eury moaned at the sight of her husband, and stretched out her arms to him, but he dared do no more than motion with his head for her to follow him, even as his song swelled to a paean of triumphant joy. He walked out along the narrow passage through which he had come, moving now in a direction that no one else had ever traveled. The way was so narrow that he had to keep on going ahead while Eury followed. He had to keep from even turning his head to look at her, to concentrate the power of his music on each new guardian that rose before him, half-alive and questioning; once more each one in turn opened a door. Always he could hear behind him the sobbing of his wife, and the dragging stepping of her wounded foot.

"Ordell? Ordell, honey, is it really you? I can't believe 'tis."

Ahead, the last danger, the three-brained sentry of the outer gate, rose to block their way, under orders to prevent escape. Ordell sang of the freedom of living in a human body, of running over unfenced grass through sunlit air. The gatekeeper bowed aside again, to let them pass.

"Honey? Turn an' look at me, tell me this is not some other trick they're playin'. Honey, if y'love me, turn?"

Turning, he saw her clearly for the first time since he had entered Hell. To Ordell her beauty was such that it stopped time, stopped even the song in his throat and his fingers on the keys of music. A movement free of the strange influence that had perverted all its creatures was all the time that the berserker needed, to re-establish something close to complete control. The three-headed shape seized Eury, and bore her away from her husband, carried her back through doorway after doorway of darkness, so fast that her last scream of farewell could scarcely reach the ears of her man. "Goodbye . . . love . . . "

He cried out and ran after me, beating uselessly on a massive door that slammed in his face. He hung there on the door for a long time, screaming and pleading for one more chance to get his wife away. He sang again, but the berserker had re-established its icy control too firmly—it had not entirely regained power, however, for though the half-living overseers no longer obeyed Ordell, neither did they molest him. They left the way open for him to depart.

He lingered for about seven days there at the gate, in his small ship and out of it, without food or sleep, singing uselessly until no voice was left him. Then he collapsed inside his ship. Then he, or more likely his autopilot, drove the racer away from the berserker and back toward freedom.

The berserker defenses did not, any more than the human, question a small ship coming out. Probably they assumed it to be one of their own scouts or raiders. There were never any escapes from Hell.

Back on the planet Zitz his managers greeted him as one risen from the dead. In a few days' time he was to give a live concert, which had long been scheduled and sold out. In another day the managers and promoters would have had to begin returning money.

He did not really cooperate with the doctors who worked to restore his strength, but neither did he oppose them. As soon as his voice came

back he began to sing again; he sang most of the
time, except when they drugged him to sleep. And
it did not matter to him whether they sent him
onto a stage to do his singing again.

The live performance was billed as one of his
pop concerts, which in practice meant a hall over-
flowing with ten thousand adolescent girls, who
were elevated even beyond their usual level of excitement by the miracles of Ordell's bereavement,
resurrection, and ghastly appearance—which last,
his managers had made sure, was not too much
relieved by cosmetics.

During the first song or two the girls were awed
and relatively silent, quiet enough so that Ordell's
voice could be heard. Then—well, one girl in ten
thousand would scream it out aloud: "You're ours
again!" There was a sense in which his marriage
had been resented.

Casually and indifferently looking out over
them all, he smiled out of habit, and began to sing
how much he hated them and scorned them,
seeing in them nothing but hopeless ugliness. How
he could send them all to Hell in an instant, to gain
for that instant just one more look at his wife's
face. How all the girls who were before him now
would become easier to look at in Hell, with their
repulsive bodies stripped away.

For a few moments the currents of emotion in
the great hall balanced against one another to
produce the illusion of calm. Ordell's deadly voice
was clear. But then the storm of reaction broke,
and he could no longer be heard. The powers of
hate and lust, rage and demand, bore all before
them. The ushers who always labored to form a

barricade at a Callison concert were swept away at once by ten thousand girls turned Maenad.

The riot was over in a minute, ended by the police firing a powerful tranquilizer gas into the crowd. One of the ushers had been killed and others badly hurt.

Ordell himself was nearly dead. Medical help arrived only just in time to save the life in the tissues of his brain, which a thoroughly broken neck and other damage had all but isolated from the rest of his body.

Next day the leading cybernetic-psychologist on Zitz was called in by Ordell Callison's doctors. They were saving what remained of Ordell's life, but they had not yet been able to open any bridge of communication with him. They wanted to tell him now that they were doing all they could, and they would have to tell him sometime that he could probably never be restored to anything like physical normality.

Ercul and psychologist sank probes directly into Ordell's brain, so that this information could be given him. Next he connected the speech centers to a voder device loaded with recordings of Ordell's own voice, so that the tones that issued were the same as had once come from his throat. And—in response to the crippled man's first request—to the motor-centers that had controlled Ordell's fingers went probes connected to a music-box.

After that he at once began to sing. He was not limited now by any need to pause for breath. He sang orders to those about him, telling them what he wanted done, and they obeyed. While he sang, not one of them was assailed by any doubt.

They took him to the spaceport. With his life-support system of tubes and nourishment and electricity they put him aboard his racer. And with the autopilot programmed as he commanded, they sent him out, fired along the course that he had chosen.

Ercul knew Ordell and Eury when he found them, together in the same experimental case. Recognizing his own work on Ordell, he felt certain even before the electroencephalogram patterns matched with his old records.

There was little left of either of them; if Ordell was still capable of singing, he would never gain be able to communicate a song.

"Dols only two point five above normal bias level," chanted the psychologist's assistant, taking routine readings, not guessing whose pain it was he was attempting to judge. "Neither one of them seems to be hurting. At the moment, anyway."

In a heavy hand, Ercul lifted his stamp and marked the case. *I certify that in this container there is no human life.*

The assistant looked up in mild surprise at this quick decision. "There is some mutual awareness here, I would say, between the two subjects." He spoke in a businesslike, almost cheerful voice. He had been enough hours on the job now to start getting used to it.

But Ercul never would.

And the search for truth may be the life-work of a human mind. Praise be to those who have such a purpose—truly—in their hearts!

SOME EVENTS AT THE
TEMPLAR RADIANT

All his years of past work, his entire future too, hung balanced on this moment.

A chair forgotten somewhere behind him, Sabel stood tall in the blue habit that often served him as laboratory coat. His hands gripped opposite corners of the high, pulpit-like control console. His head was thrown back, eyes closed, sweat-dampened dark hair hanging in something more than its usual disarray over his high, pale forehead.

He was alone, as far as any other human presence was concerned. The large, stone-walled chamber in which he stood was for the moment quiet.

All his years of work . . . and although during the past few days he had mentally rehearsed this moment to the point of exhaustion, he was still uncertain of how to start. Should he begin with a

series of cautious, testing questions, or ought he leap toward his real goal at once?

Hesitancy could not be long endured, not now. But caution, as it usually had during his mental rehearsals, prevailed.

Eyes open, Sabel faced the workbenches filled with equipment that were arranged before him. Quietly he said: "You are what human beings call a berserker. Confirm or deny."

"Confirm." The voice was familiar, because his hookup gave it the same human-sounding tones in which his own laboratory computer ordinarily spoke to him. It was a familiarity that he must not allow to become in the least degree reassuring.

So far, at least, success. "You understand," Sabel pronounced, "that I have restored you from a state of nearly complete destruction. I—"

"Destruction," echoed the cheerful workbench voice.

"Yes. You understand that you no longer have the power to destroy, to take life. That you are now contrained to answer all my—"

"To take life."

"Yes. Stop interrupting me." He raised a hand to wipe a trickle of fresh sweat from an eye. He saw how his hand was quivering with the strain of its unconscious grip upon the console. "Now," he said, and had to pause, trying to remember where he was in his plan of questioning.

Into the pause, the voice from his laboratory speakers said: "In you there is life."

"There is." Sabel managed to reassert himself, to pull himself together. "Human life." Dark eyes glaring steadily across the lab, he peered at the long, cabled benches whereon his captive enemy lay stretched, bound down, vitals exposed like those of some hapless human on a torture rack. Not that he could torture what had no nerves and did not live. Nor was there anything like a human shape in sight. All that he had here of the berserker was fragmented. One box here, another there, between them a chemical construct in a tank, that whole complex wired to an adjoining bench that bore rows of semi-material crystals.

Again his familiar laboratory speaker uttered alien words: "Life is to be destroyed."

This did not surprise Sabel; it was only a restatement of the basic programmed command that all berserkers bore. That the statement was made so boldly now roused in Sabel nothing but hope; it seemed that at least the thing was not going to begin by trying to lie to him.

It seemed also that he had established a firm physical control. Scanning the indicators just before him on the console, he saw no sign of danger . . . he knew that, given the slightest chance, his prisoner was going to try to implement its basic programming. He had of course separated it from anything obviously useful as a weapon. But he was not absolutely certain of the functions of all the berserker components that he had brought into his laboratory and hooked up. And the lab of course was full of potential weapons. There were fields, electric and other-wise, quite powerful enough to extinguish human life. There were objects that could be turned into deadly projectiles by only a very moderate appli-cation of force. To ward off any such improvisations Sabel had set defensive rings of force to dancing round the benches upon which his foe lay bound. And, just for insurance, another curtain of fields hung round him and the console. The fields were almost invisible, but the ancient stonework of the lab's far wall kept acquiring and losing new flavorings of light at the spots where the spinning field-components brushed it and eased free again.

Not that it seemed likely that the berserker-brain in its present disabled and almost disembodied state could establish control over weaponry enough to kill a mouse. Nor did Sabel ordinarily go overboard on the side of caution. But, as he told himself, he understood very well just what he was dealing with.

He had paused again, seeking reassurance from the indicators ranked before him. All appeared to be going well, and he went on: "I seek information from you. It is not military information, so whatever inhibitions have been programmed into you against answering human questions do not apply." Not that he felt at all confident that a berserker would meekly take direction from him. But there was nothing to be lost by the attempt.

The reply from the machine was delayed longer than he had expected, so that he began to hope his attempt had been successful. But then the answer came.

"I may trade certain classes of information to you, in return for lives to be destroyed."

The possibility of some such proposition had crossed Sabel's mind some time ago. In the next room a cage of small laboratory animals was waiting.

"I am a cosmophysicist," he said. "In particular I strive to understand the Radiant. In the records of past observations of the Radiant there is a long gap that I would like to fill. This gap corresponds to the period of several hundred standard years during which berserkers occupied this fortress. That period ended with the battle in which you were severely damaged. Therefore I believe that your memory probably contains some observations that will be very useful to me. It is not necessary that they be formal observations of the Radiant. Any scene recorded in light from the Radiant may be helpful. Do you understand?"

"In return for my giving you such records, what lives am I offered to destroy?"

"I can provide several." Eagerly Sabel once more swept his gaze along his row of indicators. His recording instruments were probing hungrily, gathering at an enormous rate the data needed for at least a partial understanding of the workings of his foe's unliving brain. At a score of points their probes were fastened in its vitals.

"Let me destroy one now," its human-sounding voice requested.

"Presently. I order you to answer one question for me first."

"I am not constrained to answer any of your questions. Let me destroy a life."

Sabel turned a narrow doorway for himself through his defensive fields, and walked through it into the next room. In a few seconds he was back. "Can you see what I am carrying?"

"Then it is not a human life you offer me."

"That would be utterly impossible."

"Then it is utterly impossible for me to give you information."

Without haste he turned and went to put the animal back into the cage. He had expected there might well be arguments, bargaining. But this argument was only the first level of Sabel's attack. His data-gathering instruments were what he really counted on. The enemy doubtless knew that it was being probed and analyzed. But there was evidently nothing it could do about it. As long as Sabel supplied it power, its brain must remain functional. And while it functioned, it must try to devise ways to kill.

Back at his console, Sabel took more readings. DATA PROBABLY SUFFICIENT FOR ANALYSIS, his computer screen at last informed him. He let out breath with a sigh of satisfaction, and at once threw certain switches, letting power die. Later if necessary he could turn the damned thing on again and argue with it some more. Now his defensive fields vanished, leaving him free to walk between the workbenches, where he stretched his aching back and shoulders in silent exultation.

Just as an additional precaution, he paused to disconnect a cable. The demonic enemy was only hardware now. Precisely arranged atoms, measured molecules, patterned larger bits of this and that. Where now was the berserker that humanity so justly feared? That had given the Templars their whole reason for existence? It no longer existed, except in potential. Take the hardware apart, on even the finest level, and you would not discover any of its memories. But, reconnect this and that, reapply power here and there, and back it would bloom into reality, as malignant and clever and full of information as before. A nonmaterial artifact of matter. A pattern.

No way existed, even in theory, to torture a machine into compliance, to extort information from it. Sabel's own computers were using the Van Holt algorithms, the latest pertinent mathematical advance. Even so they could not entirely decode the concealing patterns, the trapdoor functions, by which the berserker's memory was coded and concealed. The largest computer in the human universe would probably not have time for that before the universe itself came to an end. The unknown Builders had built well.

But there were other ways besides pure mathematics with which to circumvent a cipher. Perhaps, he thought, he would have tried to find a way to offer it a life, had that been the only method he could think of.

Certainly he was going to try another first. There had to be, he thought, some way of disabling the lethal purpose of a berserker while leaving its calculating abilities and memory intact. There would have been times when the living Builders wanted to approach their creations, at least in the lab, to test them and work on them. Not an easy or simple way, perhaps, but something. And that way Sabel now instructed his own computers to discover, using the mass of data just accumulated by measuring the berserker in operation.

Having done that, Sabel stood back and surveyed his laboratory carefully. There was no reason to think that anyone else was going to enter it in the near future, but it would be stupid to take chances. To the Guardians, an experiment with viable berserker parts would stand as *prima facie* evidence of goodlife activity; and in the Templar code, as in many another systems of human law, any such willing service of the berserker cause was punishable by death.

Only a few of the materials in sight might be incriminating in themselves. Coldly thoughtful, Sabel made more disconnections, and rearrangements. Some things he locked out of sight in cabinets, and from the cabinets he took out other things to be incorporated in a new disposition on the benches. Yes, this was certainly good enough. He suspected that most of the Guardians probably no longer knew what the insides of a real berserker looked like.

Sabel made sure that the doors leading out of the lab, to the mall-level corridor, and to his adjoining living quarters, were both locked. Then, whistling faintly, he went up the old stone stair between the skylights, that brought him out upon the glassed-in roof.

Here he stood bathed in the direct light of the Radiant itself. It was a brilliant point some four kilometers directly above his head—the pressure of the Radiant's inverse gravity put it directly overhead for everyone in the englobing structure of the Fortress. It was a point brighter than a star but dimmer than a sun, not painful to look at. Around Sabel a small forest of sensors, connected to instruments in his laboratory below, raised panels and lenses in a blind communal stare, to that eternal noon. Among these he began to move about as habit led him, mechanically checking the sensors' operation, though for once he was not really thinking about the Radiant at all. He thought of his success below. Then once more he raised his own two human eyes to look.

It made its own sky, out of the space enclosed by the whitish inner surface of the Fortress's bulk. Sabel could give from memory vastly detailed expositions of the spectrum of the Radiant's light. But as to exactly what color it was, in terms of perception by the eye and brain—well, there were different judgments on that, and for his part he was still uncertain.

Scattered out at intervals across the great curve of interior sky made by the Fortress's whitish stonework, Sabel could see other glass portals like his own. Under some of them, other people would be looking up and out, perhaps at him. Across a blank space on the immense concavity, an echelon of maintenance machines were crawling, too far away for him to see what they were working at. And, relatively nearby, under the glass roof of a great ceremonial plaza, something definitely unusual was going on. A crowd of thousands of people, exceptional at any time in the Fortress with its relatively tiny population, were gathered in a circular mass, like live cells attracted to some gentle biological magnet at their formation's center.

Sabel had stared at this peculiarity for several seconds, and was reaching for a small telescope to probe it with, when he recalled that today was the Feast of Ex. Helen, which went a long way toward providing an explanation. He had in fact deliberately chosen this holiday for his crucial experiment, knowing that the Fortress's main computer would today be freed of much routine business, its full power available for him to tap if necessary.

And in the back of his mind he had realized also that he should probably put in an appearance at at least one of the day's religious ceremonies. But this gathering in the plaza—he could not recall that any ceremony, in the years since he had come to the Fortress, had ever drawn a comparable crowd.

Looking with his telescope up through his own glass roof and down through the circular one that sealed the plaza in from airless space, he saw that the crowd was centered on the bronze statue of Ex. Helen there. And on a man standing in a little cleared space before the statue, a man with arms raised as if to address the gathering. The angle was wrong for Sabel to get a good look at his face, but the blue and purple robes made the distant figure unmistakable. It was the Potentate, come at last to the Fortress in his seemingly endless tour of his many subject worlds.

Sabel would not recall, even though he now made an effort to do so, that any such visitation had been impending—but then of late Sabel had been even more than usually isolated in his own work. The visit had practical implications for him, though, and he was going to have to find out more about it quickly. Because the agenda of any person of importance visiting the Fortress was very likely to include at some point a full-dress inspection of Sabel's own laboratory.

He went out through the corridor leading from laboratory to pedestrian mall, locking up carefully behind him, and thinking to himself that there was no need to panic. The Guardians would surely call to notify him that a visit by the Potentate impended, long before it came. It was part of their job to see that such things went smoothly, as well as to protect the Potentate while he was here. Sabel would have some kind of official warning. But this was certainly an awkward time . . .

Along the pedestrian mall that offered Sabel his most convenient route to the ceremonial plaza, some of the shops were closed—a greater number than usual for a holiday, he thought. Others appeared to be tended only by machines. In the green parkways that intersected the zig-zag mall at irregular intervals, there appeared to be fewer strollers than on an ordinary day. And the primary school operated by the Templars had evidently been closed; a minor explosion of youngsters in blue-striped coveralls darted across the mall from parkway to playground just ahead of Sabel, their yells making him wince.

When you stood at one side of the great plaza and looked across, both the convexity of its glass roof and the corresponding concavity of the level-feeling floor beneath were quite apparent. Especially now that the crowd was gone again. By the time Sabel reached the center of the plaza, the last of the Potentate's entourage were vanishing through exits on its far side.

Sabel was standing uncertainly on the lowest marble step of Ex. Helen's central shrine. Her statbronze statue dominated the plaza's center. Helen the Exemplar, Helen of the Radiant, Helen Dardan. The statue was impressive, showing a woman of extreme beauty in a toga-like Dardanian garment, a diadem on her short curly hair. Of course long-term dwellers at the Fortress ignored it for the most part, because of its sheer familiarity. Right now, though, someone was stopping to look, gazing up at the figure with intent appreciation.

Sabel's attention, in turn, gradually became concentrated upon this viewer. She was a young, brown-haired girl of unusually good figure, and clad in a rather provocative civilian dress.

And presently he found himself approaching her. "Young woman? If you would excuse my curiosity?"

The girl turned to him. With a quick, cheerful curiosity of her own she took in his blue habit, his stature and his face. "No excuse is needed, sir." Her voice was musical. "What question can I answer for you?"

Sabel paused a moment in appreciation. Everything about this girl struck him as quietly delightful. Her manner held just a hint of timidity, compounded with a seeming eagerness to please.

Then he gestured toward the far side of the plaza. "I see that our honored Potentate is here with us today. Do you by any chance know how long he plans to stay at the Fortress?"

The girl replied: "I heard someone say, ten standard days. It was one of the women wearing purple-bordered cloaks—?" She shook brown ringlets, and frowned with pretty regret at her own ignorance.

"Ah—one of the vestals. Perhaps you are a visitor here yourself?"

"A newcomer, rather. Isn't it always the way,

sir, when you ask someone for local information? 'I'm a newcomer here myself.'"

Sabel chuckled. *Forget the Potentate for now.* "Well, I can hardly plead newcomer status. It must be something else that keeps me from knowing what goes on in my own city. Allow me to introduce myself: Georgicus Sabel, Doctor of Cosmography."

"Greta Thamar." Her face was so pretty, soft, and young, a perfect match for her scantily costumed body. She continued to radiate an almost-timid eagerness. "Sir, Dr. Sabel, would you mind if I asked you a question about yourself?"

"Ask anything."

"Your blue robe. That means you are one of the monks here?"

"I belong to the Order of Ex. Helen. The word 'monk' is not quite accurate."

"And the Order of Ex. Helen is a branch of the Templars, isn't it?"

"Yes. Though our Order is devoted more to contemplation and study than to combat."

"And the Templars in turn are a branch of Christianity."

"Or they were." Sabel favored the girl with an approving smile. "You are more knowledgeable than many newcomers. And, time was when many Templars really devoted themselves to fighting, as did their ancient namesakes."

The girl's interest continued. By some kind of body-language agreement the two of them had turned around and were now strolling slowly back in the direction that Sabel had come from.

Greta said: "I don't know about that. The

ancient ones, I mean. Though I tried to study up before I came here. Please, go on."

"Might I ask your occupation, Greta?".

"I'm a dancer. Only on the popular entertainment level, I'm afraid. Over at the *Contrat Rouge*. But I . . . please, go on."

On the Templar-governed Fortress, popular entertainers were far down on the social scale. *Seen talking to a dancer in the plaza* . . . but no, there was really nothing to be feared from that. A minimal loss of status, perhaps, but counterbalanced by an increase in his more liberal acquaintances' perception of him as more fully human. All this slid more or less automatically through Sabel's mind, while the attractive smile on his face did not, or so he trusted, vary in the slightest.

Strolling on, he shrugged. "Perhaps there's not a great deal more to say, about the Order. We study and teach. Oh, we still officially garrison this Fortress. Those of us who are Guardians maintain and man the weapons, and make berserkers their field of study, besides acting as the local police. The main defenses out on the outer surface of the Fortress are still operational, though a good many decades have passed since we had a genuine alarm. There are no longer many berserkers in this part of the Galaxy." He smiled wryly. "And I am afraid there are no longer very many Templars, either, even in the parts of the Galaxy where things are not so peaceful."

They were still walking. Proceeding in the direction of Sabel's laboratory and quarters.

"Please, tell me more." The girl continued to

look at him steadily with attention. "Please, I am really very interested."

"Well. We of the Order of Ex. Helen no longer bind ourselves to poverty—or to permanent celibacy. We have come to honor Beauty on the same level as Virtue, considering them both to be aspects of the Right. Our great patroness of course stands as Exemplar of both qualities."

"Ex. Helen . . . and she finally founded the Order, hundreds of years ago? Or—"

"Or, is she really only a legend, as some folk now consider her? No. I think that there is really substantial evidence of her historical reality. Though of course the purposes of the Order are still valid in either case."

"You must be very busy. I hope you will forgive my taking up your time like this."

"It is hard to imagine anyone easier to forgive. Now, would you by chance like to see something of my laboratory?"

"Might I? Really?"

"You have already seen the Radiant, of course. But to get a look at it through some of my instruments will give you a new perspective . . ."

As Sabel had expected, Greta did not seem able to understand much of his laboratory's contents. But she was nevertheless impressed. "And I see you have a private space flyer here. Do you use it to go out to the Radiant?"

At that he really had to laugh. "I'm afraid I wouldn't get there. Oh, within a kilometer of it, maybe, if I tried. The most powerful spacecraft built might be able to force its way to within half that distance. But to approach any closer than that—impossible. You see, the inner level of the Fortress, where we are now, was built at the four-kilometer distance from the Radiant because that is the distance at which the effective gravity is standard normal. As one tries to get closer, the gravitic resistance goes up exponentially. No, I use the flyer for field trips. To the outer reaches of the Fortress, places where no public transport is available."

"Is that a hobby of some kind?"

"No, it's really connected with my work. I search for old Dardanian records, trying to find their observations of the Radiant . . . and in here is where I live."

With eyes suddenly become competent, Greta surveyed the tidy smallness of his quarters. "Alone, I see."

"Most of the time . . . my work demands so much. Now, Greta, I have given you something of a private showing of my work. I would be very pleased indeed if you were willing to do the same for me."

"To dance?" Her manner altered, in a complex way. "I suppose there might be room enough in here for dancing . . . if there were some suitable music."

"Easily provided." He found a control on the wall; and to his annoyance he noticed that his fingers were now quivering again.

In light tones Greta said: "I have no special costume with me, sir, just these clothes I wear."

"They are delightful—but you have one other, surely."

"Sir?" And she, with quick intelligence in certain fields of thought, was trying to repress a smile.

"Why, my dear, I mean the costume that nature gives to us all, before our clothes are made. Now, if it is really going to be up to me to choose . . . "

Hours later when the girl was gone, he went back to work, this time wearing a more conventional laboratory coat. He punched in a command for his computer to display its results, and, holding his breath, looked at the screen.

BASIC PROGRAMMING OF SUBJECT DEVICE MAY BE CIRCUMVENTED AS FOLLOWS: FABRICATE A DISABLING SLUG OF CESIUM TRIPHENYL METHYL, ISOTOPE 137 OF CESIUM, OF 99% PURITY, TO BE USED. SLUG TO BE CYLINDRICAL 2.346 CM DIAMETER, 5.844 CM LENGTH. COMPONENTS OF SUBJECT DEVICE NOW IN LABORATORY TO BE REASSEMBLED TO THOSE REMAINING IN FIELD, WITH SLUG CONNECTED ELECTRICALLY AND MECHANICALLY ACROSS PROBE POINTS OUR NUMBER 11 AND OUR NUMBER 12A IN ARMING MECHANISM OF DEVICE. PRIME PROGRAMMED COMMAND OF DEVICE WILL THEN BE DISABLED FOR TIME EQUAL TO ONE HALF-LIFE OF ISOTOPE Cs-137 . . .

There were more details on how the "subject device" was to be disabled—he had forbidden his own computer to ever display or store in memory the word "berserker" in connection with any of his work. But Sabel did not read all the details at once. He was busy looking up the half-life of cesium-137. It turned out to be thirty years! Thirty standard years!

He had beaten it. He had won. Fists clenched,

Sabel let out exultation in a great, private, and almost silent shout . . .

This instinctive caution was perhaps well-timed, for at once a chime announced a caller, at the door that led out to the mall. Sabel nervously wiped the displayed words from his computer screen. Might the girl have come back? Not because she had forgotten something—she had brought nothing with her but her clothes.

But instead of the girl's face, his video intercom showed him the deceptively jovial countenance of Chief Deputy Guardian Gunavarman. Had Sabel not become aware of the Potentate's presence on the Fortress, he might have had a bad moment at the sight. As matters stood, he felt prepared; and after a last precautionary glance around the lab, he let the man in confidently.

"Guardian. It is not often that I am honored by a visit from you."

"Doctor Sabel." The black-robed visitor respectfully returned the scientist's bow. "It is always a pleasure, when I can find the time. I wish my own work were always as interesting as yours must be. Well. You know of course that our esteemed Potentate is now in the Fortress . . . "

The discussion, on the necessity of being prepared for a VIP inspection, went just about as Sabel had expected. Gunavarman walked about as he spoke, eyes taking in the lab, their intelligence operating on yet a different level than either Sabel's or Greta Thamar's. The smiling lips asked Sabel just what, exactly, was he currently working on? What could he demonstrate, as dramatically as possible but safely of course, for the distinguished visitor?

Fortunately for Sabel he had been given a little advance time in which to think about these matters. He suggested now one or two things that might provide an impressive demonstration. "When must I have them ready?"

"Probably not sooner than two days from now, or more than five. You will be given advance notice of the exact time." But the Guardian, when Sabel pressed him, refused to commit himself on just how much advance notice would be given.

The real danger of this Potential visit, thought Sabel as he saw his caller out, was that it was going to limit his mobility. A hurried field trip to the outer surface was going to be essential, to get incriminating materials out of his lab. Because he was sure that a security force of Guardians was going to descend on the place just before the Potentate appeared. More or less politely, but thoroughly, they would turn it inside out. There were those on every world of his dominion who for one reason or another wished the Potentate no good.

After a little thought, Sabel went to his computer terminal and punched in an order directed to the metallic fabrication machines in the Fortress's main workshops, an order for the disabling slug as specified by his computer. He knew well how the automated systems worked, and took care to place the order in such a way that no other human being would ever be presented with a record of it. The machines reported at once that delivery should take several hours.

The more he thought about it, the more essential it seemed for him to get the necessary field excursion out of the way as quickly as he could.

Therefore while waiting for the slug to be delivered, he loaded up his flyer, with berserker parts hidden among tools in various containers. The vehicle was another thing that had been built to his special order. It was unusually small in all three dimensions, so he could drive it deeply into the caves and passages and cracks of ancient battle-damage that honeycombed the outer stone-work of the Fortress.

A packet containing the slug he had ordered came with a clack into his laboratory through the old-fashioned pneumatic system still used for small deliveries, direct from the workshops. Sabel's first look at the cesium alloy startled him. A hard solid at room temperature, the slug was red as blood inside a statglass film evidently meant to protect it against contamination and act as a radiation shield for human handlers as well. He slid it into a pocket of his light spacesuit, and was ready.

The lab locked up behind him, he sat in his flyer's small open cab and exited the rooftop airlock in a modest puff of fog. The air and moisture were mostly driven back into recycling vents by the steady gravitic pressure of the Radiant above. His flyer's small, silent engine worked against the curve of space that the Radiant imposed, lifting him and carrying him on a hand-controlled flight path that skimmed over glass-roofed plazas and apartment complexes and offices. In its concavity, the inner surface of the Fortress fell more distant from his straight path, then reapproached. Ahead lay the brightly lighted

mouth of the traffic shaft that would lead him out
to the Fortress's outer layers.

Under Sabel's briskly darting flyer there now
passed a garish, glassed-in amusement mall. There
entertainment, sex, and various kinds of drugs
were all for sale. The *Contrat Rouge* he thought
was somewhere in it. He wondered in passing if
the girl Greta understood that here her occupation
put her very near the bottom of the social scale, a
small step above the level of the barely tolerable
prostitutes? Perhaps she knew. Or when she found
out, she would not greatly care. She would
probably be moving on, before very long, to some
world with more conventional mores.

Sabel had only vague ideas of how folk in the
field of popular entertainment lived. He wondered
if he might go sometime to watch her perform
publicly. It was doubtful that he would. To be seen
much in the *Contrat Rouge* could do harm to one
in his position.

The wide mouth of the shaft engulfed his flyer. A
few other craft, electronically guided, moved on
ahead of his or flickered past. Strings of lights
stretched vertiginously down and ahead. The shaft
was straight; the Fortress had no appreciable
rotation, and there was no need to take coriolis
forces into account in traveling through it rapidly.
With an expertise born of his many repetitions of
this flight, Sabel waited for the precisely proper
movement to take back full manual control. The
gravitic pressure of the Radiant, behind him and
above, accelerated his passage steadily. He fell
straight through the two kilometers' thickness of

stone and reinforcing beams that composed most
of the Fortress's bulk. The sides of the vast shaft,
now moving faster and faster past him, were
ribbed by the zig-zag joints of titanic interlocking
blocks.

This is still Dardania, here, he thought to himself, as usual at this point. The Earth-descended
Dardanians, who had built the Fortress and
flourished in it even before berserkers came to the
human portion of the Galaxy, had wrought with
awesome energy, and a purpose not wholly clear
to modern eyes. The Fortress, after all, defended
not much of anything except the Radiant itself,
which hardly needed protection from humanity.
Their engineers must have tugged all the stone to
build the Fort through interstellar distances, at
God alone knew what expense of energy and time.
Maybe Queen Helen had let them know she would
be pleased by it, and that had been enough.

The Fortress contained about six hundred cubic
kilometers of stone and steel and enclosed space,
even without including the vast, clear central
cavity. Counting visitors and transients, there
were now at any moment approximately a
hundred thousand human beings in residence.
Their stores and parks and dwellings and
laboratories and shops occupied, for the most
part, only small portions of the inner surface,
where gravity was normal and the light from the
Radiant was bright. From the outer surface,
nearby space was keenly watched by the sensors
of the largely automated defense system; there
was a patchy film of human activity there. The
remainder of the six hundred cubic kilometers

were largely desert now, honeycombed with cracks and designed passages, spotted with still-undiscovered troves of Dardanian tombs and artifacts, for decades almost unexplored, virtually abandoned except by the few who, like Sabel, researched the past.

Now he saw a routine warning begin to blink on the small control panel of his flyer. Close ahead the outer end of the transport shaft was yawning, and through it he could see the stars. A continuation of his present course would soon bring him into the area surveyed by the defense system.

As his flyer emerged from the shaft, Sabel had the stars beneath his feet, the bulk of the Fortress seemingly balanced overhead. With practiced skill he turned now at right angles to the Radiant's force. His flyer entered the market notch of another traffic lane, this one grooved into the Fortress's outer armored surface. The bulk of it remained over his head and now seemed to rotate with his motion. Below him passed stars, while on the dark rims of the traffic lane to either side he caught glimpses of the antiquated but still operational defensive works. Blunt snouts of missile-launchers, skeletal fingers of mass-drivers and beam-projectors, the lenses and screens and domes of sensors and field generators. All the hardware was still periodically tested, but in all his journeyings this way Sabel had never seen any of it looking anything but inactive. War had long ago gone elsewhere.

Other traffic, scanty all during his flight, had now vanished altogether. The lane he was following branched, and Sabel turned left, adhering to his usual route. If anyone should be watching him today, no deviation from his usual procedure would be observed. Not yet, anyway. Later . . . later he would make very sure that nobody was watching.

Here came a landmark on his right. Through another shaft piercing the Fortress a wand of the Radiant's light fell straight to the outer surface, where part of it was caught by the ruined framework of an auxiliary spaceport, long since closed. In that permanent radiance the old beams glowed like twisted night-flowers, catching at the light before it fell away to vanish invisibly and forever among the stars.

Just before he reached this unintended beacon, Sabel turned sharply again, switching on his bright running lights as he did so. Now he had entered a vast battle-crack in the stone and metal of the Fortress's surface, a dark uncharted wound that in Dardanian times had been partially repaired by a frail-looking spiderwork of metal beams. Familiar with the way, Sabel steered busily, choosing the proper passage amid obstacles. Now the stars were dropping out of view behind him. His route led him up again, into the lightless ruined passages where nothing seemed to have changed since Helen died.

Another minute of flight through twisting ways, some of them designed and others accidental. Then, obeying a sudden impulse, Sabel braked his flyer to a hovering halt. In the remote past this passage had been air-filled, the monumental length and breadth of it well suited for mass ceremony. Dardanian pictures and glyphs filled great portions of its long walls. Sabel had looked at them a hundred times before, but now he swung his suited figure out of the flyer's airless cab and walked close to the wall, moving buoyantly in the light gravity, as if to inspect them once again. This was an ideal spot to see if anyone was really following him. Not that he had any logical reason to think that someone was. But the feeling was strong that he could not afford to take a chance.

As often before, another feeling grew when he stood here in the silence and darkness that were broken only by his own presence and that of his machines. Helen herself was near. In Sabel's earlier years there had been something religious in this experience. Now . . . but it was still somehow comforting.

He waited, listening, thinking. Helen's was not the only presence near, of course. On three or four occasions at least during the past ten years (there might have been more that Sabel had never heard about) explorers had discovered substantial concentrations of berserker wreckage out in these almost abandoned regions. Each time Sabel had heard of such a find being reported to the Guardians, he had promptly petitioned them to be allowed to examine the materials, or at least to be shown a summary of whatever information the Guardians might manage to extract. His pleas had vanished into the bureaucratic maw. Gradually he had come to understand that they would never tell him anything about berserkers. The Guardians were jealous of his relative success and fame. Besides, their supposed job of protecting humanity on the Fortress now actually gave them almost nothing to do. A few newly-discovered berserker parts could be parlayed into endless hours of technical and administrative work. Just keeping secrets could be made into a job, and they were not about to share any secrets with outsiders.

But, once Sabel had become interested in berserkers as a possible source of data on the Radiant, he found ways to begin a study of them. His study was at first bookish and indirect, but it advanced; there was always more information available on a given subject than a censor realized, and a true scholar knew how to find it out.

And Sabel came also to distrust the Guardians' competence in the scholarly aspects of their own field. Even if they had finally agreed to share their findings with him, he thought their pick-axe methods unlikely to extract from a berserker's memory anything of value. They had refused of course to tell him what their methods were, but he could not imagine them doing anything imaginatively.

Secure in his own space helmet, he whispered now to himself: "If I want useful data from my own computer, I don't tear it apart. I communicate with it instead."

Cold silence and darkness around him, and nothing more. He remounted his flyer and drove on. Shortly he came to where the great corridor was broken by a battle-damage crevice, barely wide enough for his small vehicle, and he turned slowly, maneuvering his way in. Now he must go slowly, despite the number of times that he had traveled this route before. After several hundred meters of jockeying his way along, his headlights picked up his semi-permanent base camp structure in a widening of the passageway ahead. It looked half bubble, half spiderweb, a tentlike thing whose walls hung slackly now but were inflatable with atmosphere. Next to it he had dug out of the stone wall a niche just big enough to park his flyer in. The walls of the niche were lightly marked now from his previous parkings. He eased in now, set down gently, and cut power.

On this trip he was not going to bother to inflate his shelter; he was not going to be out here long enough to occupy it. Instead he began at once to unload from the flyer what he needed, securing things to his backpack as he took them down. The idea that he was being followed now seemed so improbable that he gave it no more thought. As soon as he had all he wanted on his back, he set off on foot down one of the branching crevices that radiated from the nexus where he had placed his camp.

He paused once, after several meters, listening intently. Not now for nonexistent spies who might after all be following. For something active ahead. Suppose it had, somehow, after all, got itself free . . . but there was no possibility. He was carrying most of its brain with him right now. Around him, only the silence of ages, and the utter cold. The cold could not pierce his suit. The silence, though . . .

The berserker was exact. as he had left it, days ago. It was partially entom ?d, caught like some giant mechanical insect .n opaque amber. Elephant-sized metal shoulders and a ruined head protruded from a bank of centuries-old slag. Fierce weaponry must have melted the rock, doubtless at the time of the Templars' reconquest of the Fortress, more than a hundred years ago.

Sabel when he came upon it for the first time understood at once that the berserker's brain might well still be functional. He knew too that there might be destructor devices still working, built into the berserker to prevent just such an analysis of captured units as he was suddenly determined to attempt. Yet he had nerved himself to go to work on the partially shattered braincase that protruded from the passage wall almost like a mounted trophy head. Looking back now, Sabel was somewhat aghast at the risks he had taken. But he had gone ahead. If there were any destructors, they had not fired. And it appeared to him now that he had won.

He took the cesium slug out of his pocket and put it into a tool that stripped it of statglass film and held it ready for the correct moment in the reconstruction process. And the reconstruction went smoothly and quickly, the whole process taking no more than minutes. Aside from the insertion of the slug it was mainly a matter of reconnecting subsystems and of attaching a portable power supply that Sabel now unhooked from his belt; it would give the berserker no more power than might be needed for memory and communication.

Yet, as soon as power was supplied, one of the thin limb stumps that protruded from the rock surface began to vibrate, with a syncopated buzzing. It must be trying to move.

Sabel had involuntarily backed up a step; yet reason told him that his enemy was effectively powerless to harm him. He approached again, and plugged a communications cord into a jack he had installed. When he spoke to it, it was in continuation of the dialogue in the laboratory.

"Now you are constrained, as you put it, to answer whatever questions I may ask." Whether it was going to answer truthfully or not was something he could not yet tell.

It now answered him in his own voice, cracked, queer, inhuman. "Now I am constrained."

Relief and triumph compounded were so strong that Sabel had to chuckle. The thing sounded so immutably certain of what it said, even as it had sounded certain saying the exact opposite back in the lab.

Balancing buoyantly on his toes in the light gravity, he asked it: "How long ago were you damaged, and stuck here in the rock?"

"My timers have been out of operation."

That sounded reasonable. "At some time before you were damaged, though, some visual observations of the Radiant probably became stored somehow in your memory banks. You know what I am talking about from our conversation in the laboratory. Remember that I will be able to extract useful information from even the most casual, incidental video records, provided they were made in Radiant light when you were active."

"I remember." And as the berserker spoke there came faintly to Sabel's ears a grinding, straining sound, conducted through his boots from somewhere under the chaotic surface of once-molten rock.

"What are you doing?" he demanded sharply. God knew what weapons it had been equipped with, what potential powers it still had.

Blandly the berserker answered: "Trying to re-establish function in my internal power supply."

"You will cease that effort at once! The supply I have connected is sufficient."

"Order acknowledged." And at once the grinding stopped.

Sabel fumbled around, having a hard time trying to make a simple connection with another small device that he removed from his suit's belt. If only he did not tend to sweat so much. "Now. I have here a recorder. You will play into it all the video records you have that might be useful to me in my research on the Radiant's spectrum. Do not erase any records from your own banks. I may want to get at them again later."

"Order acknowledged." In exactly the same cracked tones as before.

Sabel got the connection made at last. Then he crouched there, waiting for what seemed endless time, until his recorder signalled that the data flow had ceased.

And back in his lab, hours later, Sabel sat glaring destruction at the inoffensive stonework of the wall. His gaze was angled downward, in the direction of his unseen opponent, as if his anger could pierce and blast through the kilometers of rock.

The recorder had been filled with garbage. With

nonsense. Virtually no better than noise. His own computer was still trying to unscramble the hopeless mess, but it seemed the enemy had succeeded in . . . still, perhaps it had not been a ploy of the berserker's at all. Only, perhaps, some kind of trouble with the coupling of the recorder input to . . .

He had, he remembered distinctly, told the berserker what the input requirements of the recorder were. But he had not explicitly ordered it to meet them. And he could not remember that it had ever said it would.

Bad, Sabel. A bad mistake to make in dealing with any kind of a machine. With a berserker . . .

A communicator made a melodious sound. A moment later, its screen brought Guardian Gunavarman's face and voice into the lab.

"Dr. Sabel, will your laboratory be in shape for a personal inspection by the Potentate three hours from now?"

"I—I—yes, it will. In fact, I will be most honored," he remembered to add, in afterthought.

"Good. Excellent. You may expect the security party a few minutes before that time."

As soon as the connection had been broken, Sabel looked around. He was in fact almost ready to be inspected. Some innocuous experiments were in place to be looked at and discussed. Almost everything that might possibly be incriminating had been got out of the way. Everything, in fact, except . . . he pulled the small recorder cartridge from his computer and juggled it briefly in his hand. The chance was doubtless small that any of his impending visitors would examine or play the cartridge, and smaller still that they might recognize the source of information on it if they did. Yet in Sabel's heart of hearts he was not so sure that the Guardians could be depended upon to be incompetent. And there was no reason for him to take even a small chance. There were, there had to be, a thousand public places where one might secrete an object as small as this. Where no one would notice it until it was retrieved . . . there were of course the public storage facilities, on the far side of the Fortress, near the spaceport.

To get to any point in the Fortress served by the public transportation network took only a few minutes. He had to switch from moving slidewalk to high-speed elevator in a plaza that fronted on the entertainment district, and as he crossed the plaza his eye was caught by a glowing red sign a hundred meters or so down the mall: *Contrat Rouge.*

His phantom followers were at his back again, and to try to make them vanish he passed the elevator entrance as if that had not been his goal at all. He was not wearing his blue habit today, and as he entered the entertainment mall none of the few people who were about seemed to take notice of him.

A notice board outside the *Contrat Rouge* informed Sabel in glowing letters that the next scheduled dance performance was several hours away. It might be expected that he would know that, had he really started out with the goal of seeing her perform. Sabel turned and looked

around, trying to decide what to do next. There
were not many people in sight. But too many for
him to decide if any of them might really have
been following him.

Now the doorman was starting to take notice of
him. So Sabel approached the man, clearing his
throat. "I was looking for Greta Thamar?"

Tall and with a bitter face, the attendant looked
as Sabel imagined a policeman ought to look.
"Girls aren't in yet."

"She lives somewhere nearby, though?"

"Try public info."

And perhaps the man was somewhat surprised
to see that that was what Sabel, going to a nearby
booth, actually did next. The automated information service unhesitatingly printed out Greta's
address listing for him, and Sable was
momentarily surprised: he had pictured her as
beseiged by men who saw her on stage, having to
struggle for even a minimum of privacy. But then
he saw a stage name printed out in parentheses
beside her own; those inquiring for her under the
stage name would doubtless be given no information except perhaps the time of the next performance. And the doorman? He doubtless gave
the same two answers to the same two questions a
dozen times a day, and made no effort to keep
track of names.

As Sabel had surmised, the apartment was not
far away. It looked quite modest from the outside.
A girl's voice, not Greta's, answered when he
spoke into the intercom at the door. He felt irritated that they were probably not going to be able
to be alone.

A moment later the door opened. Improbable blond hair framed a face of lovely ebony above a dancer's body. "I'm Greta's new roommate. She ought to be back in a few minutes." The girl gave Sabel an almost-amused appraisal. "I was just going out myself. But you can come in and wait for her if you like."

"I . . . yes, thank you." Whatever happened, he wouldn't be able to stay long. He had to leave himself plenty of time to get rid of the recorder cartridge somewhere and get back to the lab. But certainly there were at least a few minutes to spare.

He watched the blond dancer out of sight. Sometime, perhaps . . . Then, left alone, he turned to a half-shaded window through which he could see a large part of the nearby plaza. Still there was no one in sight who looked to Sabel as if they might be following him. He moved from the window to stand in front of a cheap table. If he left before seeing Greta, should he leave her a note? And what ought he to say?

His personal communicator beeped at his belt. When he raised it to his face he found Chief Deputy Gunavarman looking out at him from the tiny screen.

"Doctor Sabel, I had expected you would be in your laboratory now. Please get back to it as soon as possible; the Potentate's visit has been moved up by about two hours. Where are you now?"

"I . . . ah . . ." *What might be visible in Gunavarman's screen?* "The entertainment district."

The chronic appearance of good humor in the Guardian's face underwent a subtle shift; perhaps now there was something of genuine amusement in it. "It shouldn't take you long to get back, then. Please hurry. Shall I send an escort?"

"No. Not necessary. Yes. At once." Then they were waiting for him at the lab. It was even possible that they could meet him right outside this apartment's door. As Sabel reholstered his communicator, he looked around him with quick calculation. There. Low down on one wall was a small ventilation grill of plastic, not much broader than his open hand. It was a type in common use within the Fortress. Sabel crouched down. The plastic bent springily in his strong fingers, easing out of its socket. He slid the recorder into the dark space behind, remembering to wipe it free of fingerprints first.

The Potentate's visit to the lab went well. It took longer than Sabel had expected, and he was complimented on his work, at least some of which the great leader seemed to understand. It wasn't until next morning, when Sabel was wondering how soon he ought to call on Greta again, that he heard during a chance encounter with a colleague that some unnamed young woman in the entertainment district had been arrested.

Possession of a restricted device, that was the charge. The first such arrest in years, and though no official announcement had yet been made, the Fortress was buzzing with the event, probably in several versions. The wording of the charge meant that the accused was at least suspected of actual contact with a berserker; it was the same one, technically, that would have been placed against

Sabel if his secret activities had been discovered. And it was the more serious form of goodlife activity, the less serious consisting in forming clubs or cells of conspiracy, of sympathy to the enemy, perhaps having no real contact with berserkers.

Always in the past when he had heard of the recovery of any sort of berserker hardware, Sabel had called Gunavarman, to ask to be allowed to take part in the investigation. He dared not make an exception this time.

"Yes, Doctor," said the Guardian's voice from a small screen. "A restricted device is in our hands today. Why do you ask?"

"I think I have explained my interest often enough in the past. If there is any chance that this —device—contains information pertinent to my studies, I should like to apply through whatever channels may be necessary—"

"Perhaps I can save you the trouble. This time the device is merely the storage cartridge of a video recorder of a common type. It was recovered last night during a routine search of some new-comers' quarters in the entertainment district. The information on the recorder is intricately coded and we haven't solved it yet. But I doubt it has any connection with cosmophysics. This is just for your private information of course."

"Of course. But—excuse me—if you haven't broken the code why do you think this device falls into the restricted category?"

"There is a certain signature, shall we say, in the coding process. Our experts have determined that the information was stored at some stage in a berserker's memory banks. One of the two young women who lived in the apartment committed suicide before she could be questioned—a typical goodlife easy-out, it appears. The other suspect so far denies everything. We're in the process of obtaining a court order for some M-E, and that'll take care of that.''

"Memory extraction. I didn't know that you could still—?''

"Oh, yes. Though nowadays there's a formal legal procedure. The questioning must be done in the presence of official witnesses. And if innocence of the specific charge is established, questioning must be halted. But in this case I think we'll have no trouble.

Sabel privately ordered a printout of all court documents handled during the previous twenty-four hours. There it was: Greta Thamar, order for memory-extraction granted. At least she was not dead.

To try to do anything for her would of course have been completely pointless. If the memory-extraction worked to show her guilt, it should show also that he, Sabel, was only an innocent chance acquaintance. But in fact it must work to show her innocence, and then she would be released. She would regain her full mental faculties in time—enough of them, anyway, to be a dancer.

Why, though, had her roommate killed herself? Entertainers. Unstable people . . .

Even if the authorities should someday learn that he had known Greta Thamar, there was no reason for him to come forward today and say so.

No; he wasn't supposed to know as yet that she was the one arrested. Gunavarman had mentioned no names to him.

No, indeed, the best he could hope for by getting involved would be entanglement in a tedious, time-wasting investigation. Actually of course he would be risking much worse than that.

Actually it was his work, the extraction of scientific truth, that really mattered, not he. And, certainly, not one little dancer more or less. But if he went, his work went too. Who else was going to extract from the Templar Radiant the truths that would open shining new vistas of cosmophysics? Only seven other Radiants were known to exist in the entire Galaxy. None of the others were as accessible to study as this one was, and no one knew this one nearly as well as Georgicus Sabel I knew it.

Yes, it would be pointless indeed for him to try to do anything for the poor girl. But he was surprised to find himself going through moments in which he felt that he was going to have to try.

Meanwhile, if there were even the faintest suspicion of him, if the Guardians were watching his movements, then an abrupt cessation of his field trips would be more likely to cause trouble than their continuation. And, once out in the lonely reaches of Dardania, he felt confident of being able to tell whether the Guardians were following him or not.

This time he took with him a small hologram-stage, so he could look at the video records before he brought them back.

"This time," he said to the armored braincase projecting from the slag-bank, "you are ordered to give me the information in intelligible form."

Something in its tremendous shoulders buzzed, a syncopated vibration. "Order acknowledged."

And what he had been asking for was shown to him at last. Scene after scene, made in natural Radiant-light. Somewhere on the inner surface of the Fortress, surrounded by smashed Dardanian glass roofs, a row of berserkers stood as if for inspection by some commanding machine. Yes, he should definitely be able to get something out of that. And out of this one, a quite similar scene. And out of—

"Wait. Just a moment. Go back, let me see that one again. What was that?"

He was once more looking at the Fortress's inner surface, bathed by the Radiant's light. But this time no berserkers were visible. The scene was centered on a young woman, who wore space garb of a design unfamiliar to Sabel. It was a light-looking garment that did not much restrict her movements, and the two-second segment of recording showed her in the act of performing some gesture. She raised her arms to the light above as if in the midst of some rite or dance centered on the Radiant itself. Her dark hair, short and curly, bore a jeweled diadem. Her long-lashed eyes were closed, in a face of surpassing loveliness.

He watched it three more times. "Now wait again. Hold the rest of the records. Who was that?"

To a machine, a berserker, all human questions

and answers were perhaps of equal unimportance. Its voice gave the same tones to them all. It said to Sabel: "The life-unit Helen Dardan."

"But—" Sabel had a feeling of unreality. "Show it once more, and stop the motion right in the middle—yes, that's it. Now, how old is this record?"

"It is of the epoch of the 451st century, in your time-coordinate system."

"Before berserkers came to the Fortress? And why do you tell me it is she?"

"It is a record of Helen Dardan. No other existed. I was given it to use as a means of identification. I am a specialized assassin-machine and was sent on my last mission to destroy her."

"You—you claim to be the machine that actually—actually killed Helen Dardan?"

"No."

"Then explain."

"With other machines, I was programmed to kill her. But I was damaged and trapped here before the mission could be completed."

Sabel signed disagreement. By now he felt quite sure that the thing could see him somehow. "You were trapped during the Templars' reconquest. That's when this molten rock must have been formed. Well after the time when Helen lived."

"That is when I was trapped. But only within an hour of the Templars' attack did we learn where the life-unit Helen Dardan had been hidden, in suspended animation."

"The Dardanians hid her from you somehow, and you couldn't find her until then?"

"The Dardanians hid her. I do not know whether she was ever found or not."

Sabel tried to digest this. "You're saying that for all you know, she might be still entombed somewhere, in suspended animation—and still alive."

"Confirm."

He looked at his video recorder. For a moment he could not recall why he had brought it here. "Just where was this hiding place of hers supposed to be?"

As it turned out, after Sabel had struggled through a translation of the berserkers' coordinate system into his own, the supposed hiding place was not far away at all. Once he had the location pinpointed it took him only minutes to get to the described intersection of Dardanian passageways. There, according to his informant, Helen's life-support coffin had been mortared up behind a certain obscure marking on a wall.

This region was free of the small blaze-marks that Sabel himself habitually put on the walls to remind himself of what ground he had already covered in his systematic program of exploration. And it was a region of some danger, perhaps, for here in relatively recent times there had been an extensive crumbling of stonework. What had been an intersection of passages had become a rough cave, piled high with pieces great and small of what had been wall and floor and overhead. The fragments were broken and rounded to some extent, sharp corners knocked away. Probably at intervals they did a stately mill-dance in the low gravity, under some perturbation of the Fortress's stately secular movement round the Radiant in space. Eventually the fallen fragments would probably grind themselves into gravel, and slide away to accumulate in low spots in the nearby passages.

But today they still formed a rough, high mound. Sabel with his suit lights could discern a dull egg-shape nine-tenths buried in this mound. It was rounder and smoother than the broken masonry, and the size of a piano or a little larger.

He clambered toward it, and without much trouble succeeded in getting it almost clear of rock. It was made of some tough, artificial substance; and in imagination he could fit into it any of the several types of suspended-animation equipment that he had seen.

What now? Suppose, just suppose, that any real chance existed . . . he dared not try to open up the thing here in the airless cold. Nor had he any tools with him at the moment that would let him try to probe the inside gently. He had to go back to base camp and get the flyer here somehow.

Maneuvering his vehicle to his find proved easier than he had feared. He found a roundabout way to reach the place, and in less than an hour had the ovoid secured to his flyer with adhesive straps. Hauling it slowly back to base camp, he reflected that whatever was inside was going to have to remain secret, for a while at least. The announcement of any important find would bring investigators swarming out here. And that Sabel could not afford, until every trace of the berserker's existence had been erased.

Some expansion of the tent's fabric was necessary before he could get the ovoid in, and leave himself with space to work. Once he had it in a securely air-filled space, he put a gentle heater to work on its outer surface, to make it easier to handle. Then he went to work with an audio pickup to see what he could learn of the interior.

There was activity of some kind inside, that much was obvious at once. The sounds of gentle machinery, which he supposed might have been started by his disturbance of the thing, or by the presence of warm air around it now.

Subtle machinery at work. And then another sound, quite regular. It took Sabel's memory a little time to match it with the cadence of a living human heart.

He had forgotten about time, but in fact not much time had passed before he considered that he was ready for the next step. The outer casing opened for him easily. Inside, he confronted great complexity; yes, obviously sophisticated life-support. And within that an interior shell, eyed with glass windows. Sabel shone in a light.

As usual in suspended-animation treatment, the occupant's skin had been covered with a webbed film of half-living stuff to help in preservation. But the film had torn away now from around the face.

And the surpassing beauty of that face left Sabel no room for doubt. Helen Dardan was breathing, and alive.

Might not all, all, be forgiven one who brought the Queen of Love herself to life? All, even goodlife work, the possession of restricted devices?

There was also to be considered, though, the

case of a man who at a berserker's direction unearthed the Queen and thereby brought about her
final death.

Of course an indecisive man, one afraid to take
risks would not be out here now faced with his
problem. Sabel had already unslung his
emergency medirobot, a thing the size of a suit-
case, from its usual perch at the back of the flyer,
and had it waiting inside the tent. Now, like a man
plunging into deep, cold water, he fumbled open
the fasteners of the interior shell, threw back its
top, and quickly stretched probes from the medirobot to Helen's head and chest and wrist. He tore
away handfuls of the half-living foam.

Even before he had the third probe connected,
her dark eyes had opened and were looking at him.
He thought he could see awareness and understanding in them. Her last hopes on being put to
sleep must have been for an awakening no worse
than this, at hands that might be strange but were
not metal.

"Helen." Sabel could not help but feel that he
was pretending, acting, when he spoke the name.
"Can you hear me? Understand?" He spoke in
Standard; the meagre store of Dardanian that he
had acquired from ancient recordings having
completely deserted him for the moment. But he
thought a Dardanian aristocrat should know
enough Standard to grasp his meaning and the
language had not changed enormously in the
centuries since her entombment.

"You're safe now," he assured her, on his spacesuited knees beside her bed. When a flicker in her

eyes seemed to indicate relief, he went on: "The berserkers have been driven away."

Her lips parted slightly. They were full and perfect. But she did not speak. She raised herself a little, and moved to bare a shoulder and an arm from clinging foam.

Nervously Sabel turned to the robot. If he was interpreting its indicators correctly, the patient was basically in quite good condition. To his not-really-expert eye the machine signalled that there were high drug levels in her bloodstream; high, but falling. Hardly surprising, in one just being roused from suspended animation.

"There's nothing to fear, Helen. Do you hear me? The berserkers have been beaten." He didn't want to tell her, not right away at least, that glorious Dardania was no more.

She had attained almost a sitting position by now, leaning on the rich cushions of her couch. There was some relief in her eyes, yes, but uneasiness as well. And still she had not uttered a word.

As Sabel understood it, people awakened from SA ought to have some light nourishment at once. He hastened to offer food and water both. Helen sampled what he gave her, first hesitantly, then with evident enjoyment.

"Never mind, you don't have to speak to me right away. The-war-is-over." This last was in his best Dardanian, a few words of which were now belatedly willing to be recalled.

"You-are-Helen." At this he thought he saw agreement in her heavenly face. Back to Standard now. "I am Georgicus Sabel. Doctor of Cosmophysics, Master of . . . but what does all that matter of me, now? I have saved you. And that is all that counts."

She was smiling at him. And maybe after all this was a dream, no more . . .

More foam was peeling, clotted, from her skin. Good God, what was she going to wear? He bumbled around, came up with a spare coverall. Behind his turned back he heard her climbing from the cushioned container, putting the garment on.

What was this, clipped to his belt? The newly-charged video recorder, yes. It took him a little while to remember what he was doing with it. He must take it back to the lab, and make sure that the information on it was readable this time. After that, the berserker could be destroyed.

He already had with him in camp tools that could break up metal, chemicals to dissolve it. But the berserker's armor would be resistant, to put it mildly. And it must be very thoroughly destroyed, along with the rock that held it, so that no one should ever guess it had existed. It would take time to do that. And special equipment and supplies, which Sabel would have to return to the city to obtain.

Three hours after she had wakened, Helen, dressed in a loose coverall, was sitting on cushions that Sabel had taken from her former couch and arranged on rock. She seemed content to simply sit and wait, watching her rescuer with flattering eyes, demanding nothing from him—except, as it soon turned out, his presence.

Painstakingly he kept trying to explain to her

that he had important things to do, that he was going to have to go out, leave her here by herself for a time.

"I-must-go. I will come back. Soon." There was no question of taking her along, no matter what. At the moment there was only one spacesuit.

But, for whatever reason, she wouldn't let him go. With obvious alarm, and pleading gestures, she put herself in front of the airlock to bar his way.

"Helen. I really must. I—"

She signed disagreement, violently.

"But there is one berserker left, you see. We cannot be safe until it is—until—"

Helen was smiling at him, a smile of more than gratitude. And now Sabel could no longer persuade himself that this was not a dream. With a sinuous movement of unmistakable invitation, the Queen of Love was holding out her arms . . .

When he was thinking clearly and coolly once again, Sabel began again with patient explanations. "Helen. My darling. You see, I must go. To the city. To get some—"

A great light of understanding, acquiescence, dawned in her lovely face.

"There are some things I need, vitally. Then I swear I'll come right back. Right straight back here. You want me to bring someone with me, is that it? I—"

He was about to explain that he couldn't do that just yet, but her renewed alarm indicated that that was the last thing she would ask.

"All right, then. Fine. No one. I will bring a spare spacesuit . . . but that you are here will be my secret, our secret, for a while. Does that please you? Ah, my Queen!"

At the joy he saw in Helen's face, Sabel threw himself down to kiss her foot. "Mine alone!"

He was putting on his helmet now. "I will return in less than a day. If possible. The chronometer is over here, you see? But if I should be longer than a day, don't worry. There's everything you'll need, here in the shelter. I'll do my best to hurry."

Her eyes blessed him.

He had to turn back from the middle of the air-lock, to pick up his video recording, almost forgotten.

How, when it came time at last to take the Queen into the city, was he going to explain his long concealment of her? She was bound to tell others how many days she had been in that far tent. Somehow there had to be a way around that problem. At the moment, though, he did not want to think about it. The Queen was his alone, and no one . . . but first, before anything else, the berserker had to be got rid of. No, before that even, he must see if its video data was good this time.

Maybe Helen knew, Helen could tell him, where cached Dardanian treasure was waiting to be found . . .

And she had taken him as lover, as casual bed-partner rather. Was that the truth of the private life and character of the great Queen, the symbol of chastity and honor and dedication to her people? Then no one, in the long run, would thank him for bringing her back to them.

Trying to think ahead, Sabel could feel his life

knotting into a singularity at no great distance in
the future. Impossible to try to predict what lay
beyond. It was worse than uncertain; it was
opaque.

This time his laboratory computer made no fuss
about accepting the video records. It began to
process them at once.

At his private information station Sabel called
for a printout of any official news announcements
made by the Guardians or the city fathers during
the time he had been gone. He learned that the
entertainer Greta Thamar had been released
under the guardianship of her court-appointed
lawyer, after memory extraction. She was now in
satisfactory condition in the civilian wing of the
hospital.

There was nothing else in the news about goodlife, or berserkers. And there had been no black-
robed Guardians at Sabel's door when he came in.

DATING ANOMALY PRESENT was on the
screen of Sabel's laboratory computer the next
time he looked at it.

"Give details," he commanded.

RECORD GIVEN AS EPOCH 451st CENTURY
IDENTIFIES WITH SPECTRUM OF RADIANT
EPOCH 456th CENTURY, YEAR 23, DAY 152.

"Let me see."

It was, as some part of Sabel's mind already
seemed to know, the segment that showed Helen
on the inner surface of the Fortress, raising her
arms ecstatically as in some strange rite. Or
dance.

The singularity in his future was hurtling

toward him quickly now. "You say—you say that the spectrum in this record is identical with the one we recorded—what did you say? How long ago?"

38 DAYS 11 HOURS, APPROXIMATELY 44 MINUTES.

As soon as he had the destructive materials he needed loaded aboard the flyer, he headed at top speed back to base camp. He did not wait to obtain a spare spacesuit.

Inside the tent, things were disarranged, as if Helen perhaps had been searching restlessly for something. Under the loose coverall her breast rose and fell rapidly, as if she had recently been working hard, or were in the grip of some intense emotion.

She held out her arms to him, and put on a glittering smile.

Sabel stopped just inside the airlock. He pulled his helmet off and faced her grimly. "Who are you?" he demanded.

She winced, and tilted her head, but would not speak. She still held out her arms, and the glassy smile was still in place.

"*Who are you, I said?* That hologram was made just thirty-eight days ago."

Helen's face altered. The practiced expression was still fixed on it, but now a different light played on her features. The light came from outside the shelter, and it was moving toward them.

There were four people out there, some with hand weapons leveled in Sabel's direction.

Through the plastic he could not tell at once if their suited figures were those of men or women. Two of them immediately came in through the air-lock, while the other two remained outside, looking at the cargo Sabel had brought out on the flyer.

"God damn, it took you long enough." Helen's lovely lips had formed some words at last.

The man who entered first, gun drawn, ignored Sabel for the moment and inspected her with a sour grin. "I see you came through five days in the cooler in good shape."

"Easier than one day here with him—God damn." Helen's smile at Sabel had turned into an equally practiced snarl.

The second man to enter the shelter stopped just inside the airlock. He stood there with a hand on the gun holstered at his belt, watching Sabel alertly.

The first man now confidently holstered his weapon too, and concentrated his attention on Sabel. He was tall and bitter-faced, but he was no policeman. "I'm going to want to take a look inside your lab, and maybe get some things out. So hand over the key, or tell me the combination."

Sabel moistened his lips. "Who are you?" The words were not frightened, they were imperious with rage. *"And who is this woman here?"*

"I advise you to control yourself. She's been entertaining you, keeping you out of our way while we got a little surprise ready for the city. We each of us serve the Master in our own way . . . even you have already served. You provided the Master with enough power to call on us for help, some days ago . . . yes, what?" Inside his helmet he turned his head to look outside the shelter. "Out completely? Under its own power now? Excellent!"

He faced back toward Sabel. "And who am I? Someone who will get the key to your laboratory from you, one way or another, you may be sure. We've been working on you a long time already, many days. We saw to it that poor Greta got a new roommate, as soon as you took up with her. Poor Greta never knew . . . you see, we thought we might need your flyer and this final cargo of tools and chemicals to get the Master out. As it turned out, we didn't."

Helen, the woman Sabel had known as Helen, walked into his field of vision, turned her face to him as if to deliver a final taunt.

What it might have been, he never knew. Her dark eyes widened, in a parody of fainting fright. In the next moment she was slumping to the ground.

Sabel had a glimpse of the other, suited figures tumbling. Then a great soundless, invisible, cushioned club smote at his whole body. The impact had no direction, but there was no way to stand against it. His muscles quit on him, his nerves dissolved. The rocky ground beneath the shelter came up to catch his awkward fall with bruising force.

Once down, it was impossible to move a hand or foot. He had to concentrate on simply trying to breathe.

Presently he heard the airlock's cycling sigh. To lift his head and look was more than he could do; in his field of vision there were only suited bodies, and the ground.

Black boots, Guardian boots, trod to a halt close before his eyes. A hand gripped Sabel's shoulder and turned him part way up. Gunavarman's jovial eyes looked down at him for a triumphal moment before the Chief Deputy moved on.

Other black boots shuffled about. "Yes, this one's Helen Nadrad, all right—that's the name she used whoring at the Parisian Alley, anyway. I expect we can come up with another name or two for her if we look offworld. Ready to talk to us, Helen? Not yet? You'll be all right. Stunner wears off in an hour or so."

"Chief, I wonder what they expected to do with suspended animation gear? Well, we'll find out."

Gunavarman now began a radio conference with some distant personage. Sabel, in his agony of trying to breathe, to move, to speak, could hear only snatches of the talk:

"Holding meetings out here for some time, evidently . . . mining for berserker parts, probably . . . equipment . . . yes, Sire, the berserker recording was found in his laboratory this time . . . a publicity hologram of Helen Nadrad included in it, for some reason . . . yes, very shocking. But no doubt . . . we followed him out here just now. Joro, that's the goodlife organizer we've been watching, is here . . . yes, Sire. Thank you very much. I will pass on your remarks to my people here."

In a moment more the radio conversation had been concluded. Gunavarman, in glowing triumph, was bending over Sabel once again. "Prize catch," the Guardian murmured. "Something you'd like to say to me?"

Sabel was staring at the collapsed figure of

Joro. Inside an imperfectly closed pocket of the man's spacesuit he could see a small, blood-red cylinder, a stub of cut wire protruding from one end.

"Anything important, Doctor?"

He tried, as never before. Only a few words. "Dr-aw . . . your . . . wea-pons . . ."

Gunavarman glanced round at his people swarming outside the tent. He looked confidently amused. "Why?"

Now through the rock beneath the groundsheet of his shelter Sabel could hear a subtly syncopated, buzzing vibration, drawing near.

"Draw . . . your . . ."

Not that he really thought the little handguns were likely to do them any good.

As life may transmit evil, so machines of great power may hand on good.

WINGS OUT OF SHADOW

In Malori's first and only combat mission the berserker came to him in the image of a priest of the sect into which Malori had been born on the planet Yaty. In a dreamlike vision that was the analogue of a very real combat he saw the robed figure standing tall in a deformed pulpit, eyes flaming with malevolence, lowering arms winglike with the robes they stretched. With their lowering, the lights of the universe were dimming outside the windows of stained glass and Malori was being damned.

Even with his heart pounding under damnation's terror Malori retained sufficient consciousness to remember the real nature of himself and of his adversary and that he was not powerless against him. His dream-feet walked him timelessly toward the pulpit and its demon-priest while all around him the stained glass windows burst, showering him with fragments of sick fear. He walked a crooked path, avoiding the places in

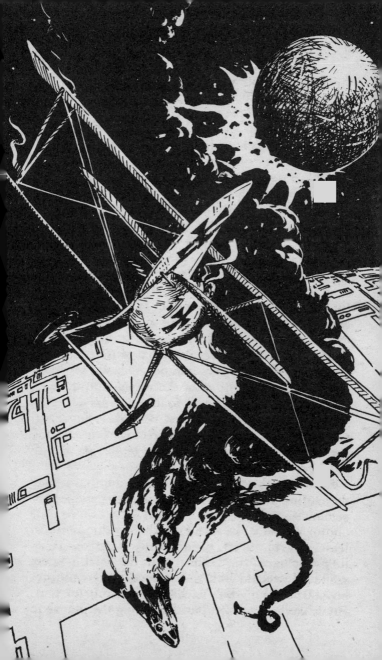

the smooth floor where, with quick gestures, the priest created snarling, snapping stone mouths full of teeth. Malori seemed to have unlimited time to decide where to put his feet. *Weapon*, he thought, a surgeon instructing some invisible aide. *Here—in my right hand.*

From those who had survived similar battles he had heard how the inhuman enemy appeared to each in different form, how each human must live the combat through in terms of a unique nightmare. To some a berserker came as a ravening beast, to others as devil or god or man. To still others it was some essence of terror that could never be faced or even seen. The combat was a nightmare experienced while the subconscious ruled, while the waking mind was suppressed by careful electrical pressures on the brain. Eyes and ears were padded shut so that the conscious mind might be more easily suppressed, the mouth plugged to save the tongue from being bitten, the nude body held immobile by the defensive fields that kept it whole against the thousands of gravities that came with each movement of the one-man ship while in combat mode. It was a nightmare from which mere terror could never wake one; waking came only when the fight was over, came only with death or victory or disengagement.

Into Malori's dream-hand there now came a meat cleaver keen as a razor, massive as a guillotine-blade. So huge it was that had it been what it seemed, it would have been far too cumbersome to even lift. His uncle's butcher shop on Yaty was gone, with all other human works of that planet. But the cleaver came back to him now, magnified, perfected to suit his need.

He gripped it hard in both hands and advanced. As he drew near the pulpit towered higher. The carved dragon on its front, which should have been an angel, came alive, blasting him with rosy fire. With a shield that came from nowhere, he parried the splashing flames.

Outside the remnants of the stained glass windows the lights of the universe were almost dead now. Standing at the base of the pulpit, Malori drew back his cleaver as if to strike overhand at the priest who towered above his reach. Then, without any forethought at all, he switched his aim to the top of his backswing and laid the blow crashing against the pulpit's stem. It shook, but resisted stoutly. Damnation came.

Before the devils reached him, though, the energy was draining from the dream. In less than a second of real time it was no more than a fading visual image, a few seconds after that a dying memory. Malori, coming back to consciousness with eyes and ears still sealed, floated in a soothing limbo. Before post-combat fatigue and sensory deprivation could combine to send him into psychosis, attachments on his scalp began to feed his brain with bursts of pins-and-needles noise. It was the safest signal to administer to a brain that might be on the verge of any of a dozen different kinds of madness. The noises made a whitish roaring scattering of light and sound that seemed to fill his head and at the same time somehow outlined for him the positions of his limbs.

His first fully conscious thought: he had just fought a berserker and survived. He had won—or had at least achieved a stand-off—or he would not be here. It was no mean achievement.

Yaty was only the latest of many Earth-colonized planets to suffer a berserker attack, and it was among the luckiest; nearly all its people had been successfully evacuated. Malori and others now fought in deep space to protect the *Hope*, one of the enormous evacuation ships. The *Hope* was a sphere several kilometers in diameter, large enough to contain a good proportion of the planet's population stored tier on tier in defense-field stasis. A tickle-relaxation of the fields allowed them to breathe and live with slowed metabolism.

The voyage to a safe sector of the galaxy was going to take several months because most of it, in terms of time spent, was going to be occupied in traversing an outlying arm of the great Taynarus nebula. Here gas and dust were much too thick to let a ship duck out of normal space and travel faster than light. Here even the speeds attainable in normal space were greatly restricted. At thousands of kilometers per second, manned ship or berserker machine could alike be smashed flat against a wisp of gas far more tenuous than human breath.

Taynarus was a wilderness of uncharted plumes and tendrils of dispersed matter, laced through by corridors of relatively empty space. Much of the wilderness was completely shaded by interstellar dust from the light of all the suns outside.

Through dark shoals and swamps and tides of nebula the *Hope* and her escort *Judith* fled, and a berserker pack pursued. Some berserkers were even larger than the *Hope*, but those that had taken up this chase were much smaller. In regions of space so thick with matter, a race went to the small as well as to the swift; as the impact cross-section of a ship increased, its maximum practical speed went inexorably down.

The *Hope*, ill-adapted for this chase (in the rush to evacuate, there had been no better choice available) could not expect to outrun the smaller and more maneuverable enemy. Hence the escort carrier *Judith*, trying always to keep herself between *Hope* and the pursuing pack. *Judith* mothered the little fighting ships, spawning them out whenever the enemy came too near, welcoming survivors back when the threat had once again been beaten off. There had been fifteen of the one-man ships when the chase began. Now there were nine.

The noise injections from Malori's life support equipment slowed down, then stopped. His conscious mind once more sat steady on its throne. The gradual relaxation of his defense fields he knew to be a certain sign that he would soon rejoin the world of waking men.

As soon as his fighter, Number Four, had docked itself inside the *Judith*, Malori hastened to disconnect himself from the tiny ship's systems. He pulled on a loose coverall and let himself out of the cramped space. A thin man with knobby joints and an awkward step, he hurried along a catwalk through the echoing hangar-like chamber, noting that three or four fighters besides his had already returned and were resting in their cradles. The artificial gravity was quite steady, but Malori stumbled and almost fell in his haste to get down the short ladder to the operations deck.

Petrovich, commander of the *Judith*, a bulky, iron-faced man of middle height, was on the deck apparently waiting for him.

"Did—did I make my kill?" Malori stuttered eagerly as he came hurrying up. The forms of military address were little observed aboard the *Judith*, as a rule, and Malori was really a civilian anyway. That he had been allowed to take out a fighter at all was a mark of the commander's desperation.

Scowling, Petrovich answered bluntly. "Malori, you're a disaster in one of these ships. Haven't the mind for it at all."

The world turned a little gray in front of Malori. He hadn't understood until this moment just how important to him certain dreams of glory were. He could find only weak and awkward words. "But . . . I thought I did all right." He tried to recall his combat-nightmare. Something about a church.

"Two people had to divert their ships from their original combat objectives to rescue you. I've already seen their gun-camera tapes. You had Number Four just sparring around with that berserker as if you had no intention of doing it any damage at all." Petrovich looked at him more closely, shrugged, and softened his voice somewhat. "I'm not trying to chew you out, you weren't even aware of what was happening, of course. I'm just stating facts. Thank probability the *Hope* is twenty AU deep in a formaldehyde cloud up ahead. If she'd been in an exposed position just now they would have got her."

"But—" Malori tried to begin an argument but the commander simply walked away. More fighters were coming in. Locks sighed and cradles clanged, and Petrovich had plenty of more important things to do than stand here arguing with him. Malori stood there alone for a few moments, feeling deflated and defeated and diminished. Involuntarily he cast a yearning glance back at Number Four. It was a short, windowless cylinder, not much more than a man's height in diameter, resting in its metal cradle while technicians worked about it. The stubby main laser nozzle, still hot from firing, was sending up a wisp of smoke now that it was back in atmosphere. There was his two-handed cleaver.

No man could direct a ship or a weapon with anything like the competence of a good machine. The creeping slowness of human nerve impulses and of conscious thought disqualified humans from maintaining direct control of their ships in any space fight against berserkers. But the human subconscious was not so limited. Certain of its processes could not be correlated with any specific synaptic activity within the brain, and some theorists held that these processes took place outside of time. Most physicists stood aghast at this view—but for space combat it made a useful working hypothesis.

In combat, the berserker computers were coupled with sophisticated randoming devices, to provide the flair, the unpredictability that gained an advantage over an opponent who simply and consistently chose the maneuver statistically most likely to bring success. Men also used computers to drive their ships, but had now gained an edge over the best randomizers by relying once more on their own brains, parts of which were evidently freed of hurry and dwelt outside of time, where even speeding light must be as motionless as carved ice.

There were drawbacks. Some people (including Malori, it now appeared) were simply not suitable for the job, their subconscious minds seemingly uninterested in such temporal matters as life or death. And even in suitable minds the subconscious was subject to great stress. Connection to external computers loaded the mind in some way not yet understood. One after another, human pilots returning from combat were removed from their ships in states of catatonia or hysterical excitement. Sanity might be restored, but the man or woman was worthless thereafter as a combat-computer's teammate. The system was so new that the importance of these drawbacks was just coming to light aboard the *Judith* now. The trained operators of the fighting ships had been used up, and so had their replacements. Thus it was that Ian Malori, historian, and others were sent out, untrained, to fight. But using their minds had bought a little extra time.

From the operations deck Malori went to his small single cabin. He had not eaten for some time, but he was not hungry. He changed clothes and sat in a chair looking at his bunk, looking at his books and tapes and violin, but he did not try to rest or to occupy himself. He expected that he would promptly get a call from Petrovich. Because Petrovich now had nowhere else to turn.

He almost smiled when the communicator chimed, bringing a summons to meet with the commander and other officers at once. Malori acknowledged and set out, taking with him a brown leather-like case about the size of a brief-case but differently shaped, which he selected from several hundred similar cases in a small room adjacent to his cabin. The case he carried was labeled: CRAZY HORSE.

Petrovich looked up as Malori entered the small planning room in which the handful of ship's officers were already gathered around a table. The commander glanced at the case Malori was carrying, and nodded. "It seems we have no choice, historian. We are running out of people, and we are going to have to use your pseudopersonalities. Fortunately we now have the necessary adapters installed in all the fighting ships."

"I think the chances of success are excellent." Malori spoke mildly as he took the seat left vacant for him and set his case out in the middle of the table. "These of course have no real subconscious minds, but as we agreed in our earlier discussions, they will provide more sophisticated randoming devices than are available otherwise. Each has a unique, if artificial, personality."

One of the other officers leaned forward. "Most of us missed these earlier discussions you speak of. Could you fill us in a little?"

"Certainly." Malori cleared his throat. "These personae, as we usually call them, are used in the computer simulation of historical problems. I was able to bring several hundred of them with me from Yaty. Many are models of military men." He put his hand on the case before him. "This is a reconstruction of the personality of one of the most able cavalry leaders on ancient Earth. It's not one of the group we have selected to try first in combat, I just brought it along to demonstrate the interior structure and design for any of you who are interested. Each persona contains about four million sheets of two-dimensional matter."

Another officer raised a hand. "How can you accurately reconstruct the personality of someone who must have died long before any kind of direct recording techniques were available?"

"We can't be positive of accuracy, of course. We have only historical records to go by, and what we deduce from computer simulations of the era. These are only models. But they should perform in combat as in the historical studies for which they were made. Their choices should reflect basic aggressiveness, determination—"

The totally unexpected sound of an explosion brought the assembled officers as one body to their feet. Petrovich, reacting very fast, still had time only to get clear of his chair before a second and much louder blast resounded through the ship. Malori himself was almost at the door, heading for his battle station, when the third explosion came. It sounded like the end of the galaxy, and he was aware that furniture was flying, that the bulkheads around the meeting room

were caving in. Malori had one clear, calm thought
about the unfairness of his coming death, and then
for a time he ceased to think at all.

Coming back was a slow unpleasant process. He
knew *Judith* was not totally wrecked for he still
breathed, and the artificial gravity still held him
sprawled out against the deck. It might have been
pleasing to find the gravity gone, for his body was
one vast, throbbing ache, a pattern of radiated
pain from a center somewhere inside his skull. He
did not want to pin down the source any more
closely than that. To even imagine touching his
own head was painful.

At last the urgency of finding out what was
going on overcame the fear of pain and he raised
his head and probed it. There was a large lump
just above his forehead, and smaller injuries
about his face where blood had dried. He must
have been out for some time.

The meeting room was ruined, shattered, litter-
ed with debris. There was a crumpled body that
must be dead, and there another, and another,
mixed in with the furniture. Was he the only survivor? One bulkhead had been torn wide open, and
the planning table was demolished. And what was
that large, unfamiliar piece of machinery standing
at the other end of the room? Big as a tall filing
cabinet, but far more intricate. There was something peculiar about its legs, as if they might be
movable . . .

Malori froze in abject terror, because the thing
did move, swiveling a complex of turrets and
lenses at him, and he understood that he was

seeing and being seen by a functional berserker machine. It was one of the small ones, used for boarding and operating captured human ships.

"Come here," the machine said. It had a squeaky, ludicrous parody of a human voice, recorded syllables of captives' voices stuck together electronically and played back. "The bad-life has awakened."

Malori in his great fear thought that the words were directed at him but he could not move. Then, stepping through the hole in the bulkhead, came a man Malori had never seen before—a shaggy and filthy man wearing a grimy coverall that might once have been part of some military uniform.

"I see he has, sir," the man said to the machine. He spoke the standard interstellar language in a ragged voice that bore traces of a cultivated accent. He took a step closer to Malori. "Can you understand me, there?"

Malori grunted something, tried to nod, pulled himself up slowly into an awkward sitting position.

"The question is," the man continued, coming a little closer still, "how d'you want it later, easy or hard? When it comes to your finishing up, I mean. I decided a long time ago that I want mine quick and easy, and not too soon. Also that I still want to have some fun here and there along the way."

Despite the fierce pain in his head, Malori was thinking now, and beginning to understand. There was a name for humans like the man before him, who went along more or less willingly with the berserker machines. A word coined by the machines themselves. But at the moment Malori was not going to speak that name.

"I want it easy," was all he said, and blinked his eyes and tried to rub his neck against the pain.

The man looked him over in silence a little longer. "All right," he said then. Turning back to the machine, he added in a different, humble voice: "I can easily dominate this injured badlife. There will be no problems if you leave us here alone."

The machine turned one metal-cased lens toward its servant. "Remember," it vocalized, "the auxiliaries must be made ready. Time grows short. Failure will bring unpleasant stimuli."

"I will remember, sir." The man was humble and sincere. The machine looked at both of them a few moments longer and then departed, metal legs flowing suddenly into a precise and almost graceful walk. Shortly after, Malori heard the familiar sound of an airlock cycling.

"We're alone now," the man said, looking down at him. "If you want a name for me you can call me Greenleaf. Want to try to fight me? If so, let's get it over with." He was not much bigger than Malori but his hands were huge and he looked hard and very capable despite his ragged filthiness. "All right, that's a smart choice. You know, you're actually a lucky man, though you don't realize it yet. Berserkers aren't like the other masters that men have—not like the governments and parties and corporations and causes that use you up and then just let you drop and drag away. No, when the machines run out of uses for you they'll finish you off quickly and cleanly—if you've served well. I know, I've seen 'em do it that way with other humans. No reason why they shouldn't. All they want is for us to die, not suffer."

Malori said nothing. He thought perhaps he would be able to stand up soon.

Greenleaf (the name seemed so inappropriate that Malori thought it probably real) made some adjustment on a small device that he had taken from a pocket and was holding almost concealed in one large hand. He asked: "How many escort carriers besides this one are trying to protect the *Hope?*"

"I don't know," Malori lied. There had been only the *Judith*.

"What is your name?" The bigger man was still looking at the device in his hand.

"Ian Malori."

Greenleaf nodded, and without showing any particular emotion in his face took two steps forward and kicked Malori in the belly, precisely and with brutal power.

"That was for trying to lie to me, Ian Malori," said his captor's voice, heard dimly from somewhere above as Malori groveled on the deck, trying to breathe again. "Understand that I am infallibly able to tell when you are lying. Now, how many escort carriers are there?"

In time Malori could sit up again, and choke out words. "Only this one." Whether Greenleaf had a real lie detector, or was only trying to make it appear so by asking questions whose answers he already knew, Malori decided that from now on he would speak the literal truth as scrupulously as possible. A few more kicks like that and he would be helpless and useless and the machines would kill him. He discovered that he was by no means ready to abandon his life.

"What was your position on the crew, Malori?"

"I'm a civilian."

"What sort?"

"An historian."

"And why are you here?"

Malori started to get to his feet, then decided there was nothing to be gained by the struggle and stayed sitting on the deck. If he ever let himself dwell on his situation for a moment he would be too hideously afraid to think coherently. "There was a project . . . you see, I brought with me from Yaty a number of what we call historical models—blocks of programmed responses we use in historical research."

"I remember hearing about some such things. What was the project you mentioned?"

"Trying to use the personae of military men as randomizers for the combat computers on the one-man ships."

"Aha." Greenleaf squatted, supple and poised for all his raunchy look. "How do they work in combat? Better than a live pilot's subconscious mind? The machines know all about *that.*"

"We never had a chance to try. Are the rest of the crew here all dead?"

Greenleaf nodded casually. "It wasn't a hard boarding. There must have been a failure in your automatic defenses. I'm glad to find one man alive and smart enough to cooperate. It'll help me in my career." He glanced at an expensive chronometer strapped to his dirty wrist. "Stand up, Ian Malori. There's work to do."

Malori got up and followed the other toward the operations deck.

"The machines and I have been looking around,

Malori. These nine little fighting ships you still have on board are just too good to be wasted. The machines are sure of catching the *Hope* now, but she'll have automatic defenses, probably a lot tougher than this tub's were. The machines have taken a lot of casualties on this chase so they mean to use these nine little ships as auxiliary troops— no doubt you have some knowledge of military history?"

"Some." The answer was perhaps an understatement, but it seemed to pass as truth. The lie detector, if it was one, had been put away. But Malori would still take no more chances than he must.

"Then you probably know how some of the generals of old Earth used their auxiliaries. Drove them on ahead of the main force of trusted troops, where they could be killed if they tried to retreat, and were also the first to be used up against the enemy."

Arriving on the operations deck, Malori saw few signs of damage. Nine tough little ships waited in their launching cradles, re-armed and refueled for combat. All that would have been taken care of within minutes of their return from their last mission.

"Malori, from looking at these ships' controls while you were unconscious, I gather that there's no fully automatic mode in which they can be operated."

"Right. There has to be some controlling mind, or randomizer, connected on board."

"You and I are going to get them out as berserker auxiliaries, Ian Malori." Greenleaf glanced at his timepiece again. "We have less than an hour to think of a good way and only a few hours more to complete the job. The faster the better. If we delay we are going to be made to suffer for it." He seemed almost to relish the thought. "What do you suggest we do?"

Malori opened his mouth as if to speak, and then did not.

Greenleaf said: "Installing any of your military personae is of course out of the question, as they might not submit well to being driven forward like mere cannon fodder. I assume they are leaders of some kind. But have you perhaps any of these personae from different fields, of a more docile nature?"

Malori, sagging against the operations officer's empty combat chair, forced himself to think very carefully before he spoke. "As it happens, there are some personae aboard in which I have a special personal interest. Come."

With the other following closely, Malori led the way to his small bachelor cabin. Somehow it was astonishing that nothing had been changed inside. There on the bunk was his violin, and on the table were his music tapes and a few books. And here, stacked neatly in their leather-like curved cases, were some of the personae that he liked best to study.

Malori lifted the top case from the stack. "This man was a violinist, as I like to think I am. His name would probably mean nothing to you."

"Musicology was never my field. But tell me more."

"He was an Earthman, who lived in the

twentieth century CE—quite a religious man, too, as I understand. We can plug the persona in and ask it what it thinks of fighting, if you are suspicious."

"We had better do that." When Malori had shown him the proper receptacle beside the cabin's small computer console, Greenleaf snapped the connections together himself. "How does one communicate with it?"

"Just talk."

Greenleaf spoke sharply toward the leather-like case. "Your name?"

"Albert Ball." The voice that answered from the console speaker sounded more human by far than the berserker's had.

"How does the thought of getting into a fight strike you, Albert?"

"A detestable idea."

"Will you play the violin for us?"

"Gladly." But no music followed.

Malori put in: "More connections are necessary if you want actual music."

"I don't think we'll need that." Greenleaf unplugged the Albert Ball unit and began to look through the sack of others, frowning at unfamiliar names. There were twelve or fifteen cases in all. "Who are these?"

"Albert Ball's contemporaries. Performers who shared his profession." Malori let himself sink down on the bunk for a few moments' rest. He was not far from fainting. Then he went to stand with Greenleaf beside the stack of personae. "This is a model of Edward Mannock, who was blind in one eye and could never have passed the physical examination necessary to serve in any military force of his time." He pointed to another. "This man served briefly in the cavalry, as I recall, but he kept getting thrown from his horse and was soon relegated to gathering supplies. And this one was a frail, tubercular youth who died at twenty-three standard years of age."

Greenleaf gave up looking at the cases and turned to size up Malori once again. Malori could feel his battered stomach muscles trying to contract, anticipating another violent impact. It would be too much, it was going to kill him if it came like that again . . .

"All right." Greenleaf was frowning, checking his chronometer yet again. Then he looked up with a little smile. Oddly, the smile made him look like the hell of a good fellow. "All right! Musicians, I suppose, are the antithesis of the military. If the machines approve, we'll install them and get the ships sent out. Ian Malori, I may just raise your pay." His pleasant smile broadened. "We may just have bought ourselves another standard year of life if this works out as well as I think it might."

When the machine came aboard again a few minutes later, Greenleaf bowing before it explained the essence of the plan, while Malori in the background, in an agony of terror, found himself bowing too.

"Proceed, then," the machine approved. "If you are not swift, the ship infected with life may find concealment in the storms that rise ahead of us."

Then it went away again quickly. Probably it had repairs and refitting to accomplish on its own robotic ship.

With two men working, installation went very fast. It was only a matter of opening a fighting ship's cabin, inserting an uncased persona in the installed adapter, snapping together standard connectors and clamps, and closing the cabin hatch again. Since haste was vital to the berserkers' plans, testing was restricted to listening for a live response from each persona as it was activated inside a ship. Most of the responses were utter banalities about nonexistent weather or ancient food or drink, or curious phrases that Malori knew were only phatic social remarks.

All seemed to be going well, but Greenleaf was having some last minute misgivings. "I hope these sensitive gentlemen will stand up under the strain of finding out their true situation. They will be able to grasp that, won't they? The machines won't expect them to fight well, but we don't want them going catatonic, either."

Malori, close to exhaustion, was tugging at the hatch of Number Eight, and nearly fell off the curved hull when it came open suddenly. "They will apprehend their situation within a minute after launching, I should say. At least in a general way. I don't suppose they'll understand it's intersteller space around them. You have been a military man, I suppose. If they should be reluctant to fight—I leave to you the question of how to deal with recalcitrant auxiliaries."

When they plugged the persona into ship Number Eight, its test response was: "I wish my craft to be painted red."

"At once, sir," said Malori quickly, and slammed down the ship's hatch and started to move on to Number Nine.

"What was that all about?" Greenleaf frowned, but looked at his timepiece and moved along.

"I suppose the maestro is already aware that he is about to embark in some kind of a vehicle. As to why he might like it painted red . . ." Malori grunted, trying to open up Number Nine, and let his answer trail away.

At last all the ships were ready. With his finger on the launcing switch, Greenleaf paused. For one last time his eyes probed Malori's. "We've done very well, timewise. We're in for a reward, as long as this idea works at least moderately well." He was speaking now in a solemn near-whisper. "It had better work. Have you ever watched a man being skinned alive?"

Malori was gripping a stanchion to keep erect. "I have done all I can."

Greenleaf operated the launching switch. There was a polyphonic whisper of airlocks. The nine ships were gone, and simultaneously a holographic display came alive above the operations officer's console. In the center of the display the *Judith* showed as a fat green symbol, with nine smaller green dots moving slowly and uncertainly nearby. Farther off, a steady formation of red dots represented what was left of the berserker pack that had so long and so relentlessly pursued the *Hope* and her escort. There were at least fifteen red berserker dots, Malori noted gloomily.

"This trick," Greenleaf said as if to himself, "is to make them more afraid of their own leaders than they are of the enemy." He keyed the panel switches that would send his voice out to the ships. "Attention, units One through Nine!" he barked. "You are under the guns of a vastly superior force, and any attempt at disobedience or escape will be severely punished . . ."

He went on browbeating them for a minute, while Malori observed in the screen that the dirty weather the berserker had mentioned was coming on. A sleet of atomic particles was driving through this section of the nebula, across the path of the *Judith* and the odd hybrid fleet that moved with her. The *Hope*, not in view on this range scale, might be able to take advantage of the storm to get away entirely unless the berserker pursuit was swift.

Visibility on the operations display was failing fast and Greenleaf cut off his speech as it became apparent that contact was being lost. Orders in the berserkers' unnatural voices, directed at auxiliary ships One through Nine, came in fragmentarily before the curtain of noise became an opaque white-out. The pursuit of the *Hope* had not yet been resumed.

For a while all was silent on the operations deck, except for an occasional crackle of noise from the display. All around them the empty launching cradles waited.

"That's that," Greenleaf said at length. "Nothing to do now but worry." He gave his little transforming smile again, and seemed to be almost enjoying the situation.

Malori was looking at him curiously. "How do you—manage to cope so well?"

"Why not?" Greenleaf stretched and got up from the now-useless console. "You know, once a man gives up his old ways, badlife ways, admits he's really dead to them, the new ways aren't so bad. There are even women available from time to time, when the machines take prisoners."

"Goodlife," said Malori. Now he had spoken the obscene, provoking epithet. But at the moment he was not afraid.

"Goodlife yourself, little man." Greenleaf was still smiling. "You know, I think you still look down on me. You're in as deep as I am now, remember?"

"I think I pity you."

Greenleaf let out a little snort of laughter, and shook his own head pityingly. "You know, I may have ahead of me a longer and more pain-free life than most of humanity has ever enjoyed—you said one of the models for the personae died at twenty-three. Was that a common age of death in those days?"

Malori, still clinging to his stanchion, began to wear a strange, grim little smile. "Well, in his generation, in the continent of Europe, it was. The First World War was raging at the time."

"But he died of some disease, you said."

"No. I said he *had* a disease, tuberculosis. Doubtless it would have killed him eventually. But he died in battle, in 1917 CE, in a place called Belgium. His body was never found, as I recall, an artillery barrage having destroyed it and his aircraft entirely."

Greenleaf was standing very still. "Aircraft! What are you saying?"

Malori pulled himself erect, somewhat painfully, and let go of his support. "I tell you now that Georges Guynemer—that was his name—shot down fifty-three enemy aircraft before he was killed. Wait!" Malori's voice was suddenly loud and firm, and Greenleaf halted his menacing advance in sheer surprise. "Before you begin to do anything violent to me, you should perhaps consider whether your side or mine is likely to win the fight outside."

"The fight . . . "

"It will be nine ships against fifteen or more machines, but I don't feel too pessimistic. The personae we have sent out are not going to be meekly slaughtered."

Greenleaf stared at him a moment longer, then spun around and lunged for the operations console. The display was still blank white with noise and there was nothing to be done. He slowly sank into the padded chair. "What have you done to me?" he whispered. "That collection of invalid musicians—you couldn't have been lying about them all."

"Oh, every word I spoke was true. Not all World War One fighter pilots were invalids, of course. Some were in perfect health, indeed fanatical about staying that way. And I did not say they were all musicians, though I certainly meant you to think so. Ball had the most musical ability among the aces, but was still only an amatuer. He always said he loathed his real profession."

Greenleaf, slumped in the chair now, seemed to be aging visibly. "But one was blind . . . it isn't possible."

"So his enemies thought, when they released him from an internment camp early in the war. Edward Mannock, blind in one eye. He had to trick an examiner to get into the army. Of course the tragedy of these superb men is that they spent themselves killing one another. In those days they had no berserkers to fight, at least none that could be attacked dashingly, with an aircraft and a machine gun. I suppose men have always faced berserkers of some kind."

"Let me make sure I understand." Greenleaf's voice was almost pleading. "We have sent out the personae of nine fighter pilots?"

"Nine of the best. I suppose their total of claimed aerial victories is more than five hundred. Such claims were usually exaggerated, but still . . ."

There was silence again. Greenleaf slowly turned his chair back to face the operations display. After a time the storm of atomic noise began to abate. Malori, who had sat down on the deck to rest, got up again, this time more quickly. In the hologram a single glowing symbol was emerging from the noise, fast approaching the position of the *Judith*.

The approaching symbol was bright red.

"So there we are," said Greenleaf, getting to his feet. From a pocket he produced a stubby little handgun. At first he pointed it toward the shrinking Malori, but then he smiled his nice smile and shook his head. "No, let the machines have you. That will be much worse."

When they heard the airlock begin to cycle, Greenleaf raised the weapon to point at his own skull. Malori could not tear his eyes away. The inner door clicked and Greenleaf fired.

Malori bounded across the intervening space and pulled the gun from Greenleaf's dead hand almost before the body had completed its fall. He turned to aim the weapon at the airlock as its inner door sighed open. The berserker standing there was the one he had seen earlier, or the same type at least. But it had just been through violent alterations. One metal arm was cut short in a bright bubbly scar, from which the ends of truncated cables flapped. The whole metal body was riddled with small holes, and around its top there played a halo of electrical discharge.

Malori fired, but the machine ignored the impact of the forcepacket. They would not have let Greenleaf keep a gun with which they could be hurt. The battered machine ignored Malori too, for the moment, and lurched forward to bend over Greenleaf's nearly decapitated body.

"Tra-tra-tra-treason," the berserker squeaked. "Ultimate unpleasant ultimate unpleasant stum-stum-stimuli. Badlife badlife bad—"

By then Malori had moved up close behind it and thrust the muzzle of the gun into one of the still-hot holes where Albert Ball or perhaps Frank Luke or Werner Voss or one of the others had already used a laser to good effect. Two force-packets beneath its armor and the berserker went down, as still as the men who lay beneath it. The halo of electricity died.

Malori backed off, looking at them both, then spun around to scan the operations display again. The red dot was drifting away from the *Judith*, the vessel it represented now evidently no more than inert machinery.

Out of the receding atomic storm a single green dot was approaching. A minute later, Number Eight came in along, bumping to a gentle stop against its cradle pads. The laser nozzle at once began smoking heavily in atmosphere. The craft was scarred in several places by enemy fire.

"I claim four more victories," the persona said as soon as Malori opened the hatch. "Today I was given fine support by my wingmen, who made great sacrifices for the Fatherland. Although the enemy outnumbered us by two to one, I think that not a single one of them escaped. But I must protest bitterly that my aircraft still has not been painted red."

"I will see to it at once, *meinherr*," murmured Malori, as he began to disconnect the persona from the fighting ship. He felt a little foolish for trying to reassure a piece of hardware. Still, he handled the persona gently as he carried it to where the little formation of empty cases were waiting on the operations deck, their labels showing plainly:

ALBERT BALL;

WILLIAM AVERY BISHOP;

RENE PAUL FONCK;

GEORGES MARIE GUYNEMER:

FRANK LUKE;

EDWARD MANNOCK;

CHARLES NUNGESSER;

MANFRED VON RICHTHOFEN;

WERNER VOSS.

They were English, American, German, French. They were Jew, violinist, invalid, Prussian, rebel, hater, bon vivant, Christian. Among the nine of them they were many other things besides. Maybe there was only the one word—man—which could include them all.

Right now the nearest living humans were many millions of kilometers away, but still Malori did not feel quite alone. He put the persona back into its case gently, even knowing that it would be un-damaged by ten thousand more gravities than his hands could exert. Maybe it would fit into the cabin of Number Eight with him, when he made his try to reach the *Hope*.

"Looks like it's just you and me now, Red Baron." The human being from which it had been modeled had been not quite twenty-six when he was killed over France, after less than eighteen months of success and fame. Before that, in the cavalry, his horse had thrown him again and again.

Relatively unfettered by time or space, my mind has roamed the Galaxy in past and future to gather pieces of the truth of the great war of life against unliving death. What I have set down is far from the whole truth of that war, yet it is true.

Most of the higher intellects of the galaxy will shrink from war, even when survival depends upon it absolutely. Yet from the same matter that supports their lives, came the berserkers. Were their Builders uniquely evil? Would that it were so . . .

THE SMILE

The berserker attack upon the world called St. Gervase had ended some four standard months before the large and luxurious private yacht of the Tyrant Yoritomo appeared amid the ashclouds and rainclouds that still monotonized the planet's newly lifeless sky. From the yacht a silent pair of waspish-looking launches soon began a swift descent, to land on the denuded surface where the planet's capital city had once stood.

The crews disembarking from the launches were armored against hot ash and hot mud and residual radiation. They knew what they were looking for, and in less than a standard hour they had located the vaulted tunnel leading down, from what had been a sub-basement of the famed St. Gervase Museum. The tunnel was partially collapsed in places, but still passable, and they followed its steps downward, stumbling here and there on debris fallen from the surface. The battle had not been completely one-sided in its early

stages, and scattered amid the wreckage of the
once-great city were fragments of berserker troop-
landers and of their robotic shock-troops. The
unliving metal killers had had to force a landing,
to neutralize the defensive field generators, before
the bombardment could begin in earnest.

The tunnel terminated in a large vault a
hundred meters down. The lights, on an independent power supply, were still working, and the
air conditioning was still trying to keep out dust.
There were five great statues in the vault,
including one in the attached workshop where
some conservator or restorer had evidently been
treating it. Each one was a priceless masterwork.
And scattered in an almost casual litter throughout the shelter were paintings, pottery, small
works in bronze and gold and silver, the least a
treasure to be envied.

At once the visitors radioed news of their dis-
covery to one who waited eagerly in the yacht
hovering above. Their report concluded with the
observation that someone had evidently been
living down here since the attack. Beside the workshop, with its power lamp to keep things going,
there was a small room that had served as a
repository of the Museum's records. A cot stood in
it now, there had been food supplies laid in, and
there were other signs of human habitation. Well,
it was not too strange that there should have been
a few survivors, out of a population of many
millions.

The man who had been living alone in the
shelter for four months came back to find the
landing party going busily about their work.

"Looters," he remarked, in a voice that seemed to have lost the strength for rage, or even fear. Not armored against radiation or anything else, he leaned against the terminal doorway of the battered tunnel, a long-haired, unshaven, once-fat man whose frame was now swallowed up in clothes that looked as if they might not have been changed since the attack.

The member of the landing party standing nearest looked back at him silently, and drummed fingers on the butt of a holstered handgun, considering. The man who had just arrived threw down the pieces of metallic junk he had brought with him, conveying in the gesture his contempt.

The handgun was out of its holster, but before it was leveled, an intervention from the leader of the landing party came in the form of a sharp gesture. Without taking his eyes off the man in the doorway, the leader at once reopened communication with the large ship waiting above.

"Your Mightiness, we have a survivor here," he informed the round face that soon appeared upon the small portable wallscreen. "I believe it is the sculptor Antonio Nobrega."

"Let me see him at once. Bring him before the screen." The voice of His Mightiness was inimitable and terrible, and no less terrible, somehow, because he always sounded short of breath. "Yes, you are right, although he is much changed. Nobrega, how fortunate for us both! This is indeed another important find."

"I knew you would be coming to St. Gervase now," Nobrega told the screen, in his empty voice. "Like a disease germ settling in a mangled body.

Like some great fat cancer virus. Did you bring along your woman, to take charge of our Culture?"

One of the men beside the sculptor knocked him down. A breathless little snarl came from the screen at this, and Nobrega was quickly helped back to his feet, then put into a chair.

"He is an artist, my faithful ones," the screen-voice chided. "We must not expect him to have any sense of the fitness of things outside his art. No. We must get the maestro here some radiation treatment, and then bring him along with us to the Palace, and he will live and work there as happily, or unhappily, as elsewhere."

"Oh no," said the artist from his chair, more faintly than before. "My work is done."

"Pish-posh. You'll see."

"I knew you were coming . . ."

"Oh?" The small voice from the screen was humoring him. "And how did you know that?"

"I heard . . . when our fleet was still defending the approaches to the system, my daughter was out there with it. Through her, before she died, I heard how you brought your own fleet in-system, to watch what was going to happen, to judge our strength, our chance of resisting the berserkers. I heard how your force vanished when they came. I said then that you'd be back, to loot the things you could never get at in any other way."

Nobrega was quiet for a moment, then lunged from his chair—or made the best attempt at lunging that he could. He grabbed up a long metal sculptor's tool and drew it back to swing at *Winged Truth Rising*, a marble Poniatowski eleven centuries old. "Before I'll see you take this—"

Before he could knock a chip of marble loose, he was overpowered, and put into restraint.

When they approached him again an hour later, to take him up to the yacht for medical examination and treatment, they found him already dead. Autopsy on the spot discovered several kinds of slow and gentle poison. Nobrega might have taken some deliberately. Or he might have been finished by something the berserkers had left behind, to ensure that there would be no survivors, as they moved on to carry out their programmed task of eradicating all life from the Galaxy.

On his voyage home from St. Gervase, and for several months thereafter, Yoritimo was prevented by pressing business from really inspecting his new treasures. By then the five great statues had been installed, to good esthetic advantage, in the deepest, largest, and best-protected gallery of the Palace. Lesser collections had been evicted to make room and visual space for *Winged Truth Rising;* Lazamon's *Laughing* (or *Raging*) *Bacchus; The Last Provocation*, by Sarapion; Lazienki's *Twisting Room;* and *Remembrance of Past Wrongs*, by Prajapati.

It chanced that at this time the Lady Yoritimo was at the Palace too. Her duties, as Cultural Leader of the People, and High Overseer of Education for the four tributary planets, kept her on the move, and it often happened that she and her Lord did not see each other for a month or longer at a time.

The two of them trusted each other more than

they trusted anyone else. Today they sat alone in the great gallery and sipped tea, and spoke of business.

The Lady was trying to promote her latest theory, which was that love for the ruling pair might be implanted genetically in the next generation of people on the tributary worlds. Several experimental projects had already begun. So far these had achieved little but severe mental retardation in the subjects, but there were plenty of new subjects and she was not discouraged.

The Lord spoke mainly of his own plan, which was to form a more explicit working arrangement with the berserkers. In this scheme the Yoritomos would furnish the killer machines with human lives they did not need, and planets hard to defend, in exchange for choice works of art and, of course, immunity from personal attack. The plan had many attractive features, but the Lord had to admit that the difficulty of opening negotiations with berserkers, let alone establishing any degree of mutual trust, made it somewhat impractical.

When a pause came in the conversation, Yoritomo had the banal thought that he and his wife had little to talk about anymore, outside of business. With a word to her, he rose from the alcove where they had been sitting, and walked to the far end of the gallery of statues to replenish the tea pot. For esthetic reasons he refused to allow robots in here; nor did he want human servitors around while this private discussion was in progress. Also, he thought, as he retraced his steps, the Lady could not help but be flattered, and won toward his own position in a certain matter where they disagreed, when she was served personally by the hands of one so mighty . . .

He rounded the great metal flank of *The Last Provocation* and came to a dumb halt, in shocked surprise so great that for a moment his facial expression did not even alter. Half a minute ago he had left her vivacious and thoughtful and full of graceful energy. She was still in the same place, on the settee, but slumped over sideways now, one arm extended with its slender, jeweled finger twitching upon the rich brown carpet. The Lady's hair was wildly disarranged; and small wonder, he thought madly, for her head had been twisted almost completely around, so her dead eyes now looked over one bare shoulder almost straight at Yoritomo. Upon her shoulder and her cheek were bruised discolorations . . .

He spun around at last, dropping the fragile masterpiece that held his tea. His concealed weapon was half-drawn before it was smashed out of his grip. He had one look at death, serenely towering above him. He had not quite time enough to shriek, before the next blow fell.

The wind had not rested in the hours since Ritwan's arrival, and with an endless howl it drove the restless land before it. He could quite easily believe that in a few years the great pit left by the destruction of the old Yoritomo Palace had been completely filled. The latest dig had ended only yesterday, and already the archaeologists' fresh pits were beginning to be reoccupied by sand.

"They were actually more pirates than anything

else," Iselin, the chief archaeologist, was saying. "At the peak of their power two hundred years ago they ruled four systems. Ruled them from here, though there's not much showing on the surface now but this old sandpile."

"Ozymandias," Ritwan murmured.

"What?"

"An ancient poem." He pushed back sandy hair from his forehead with a thin, nervous hand. "I wish I'd got here in time to see the statues before you crated them and stowed them on your ship. You can imagine I came as fast as I could from Sirgol, when I heard there was a dig in progress here."

"Well," Iselin folded her plump arms and frowned, then smiled, a white flash in a dark Indian face. "Why don't you ride with us back to Esteel system? I really can't open the crates for anything until we get there. Not under the complicated rules of procedure we're stuck with on these jointly sponsored digs."

"My ship does have a good autopilot."

"Then set it to follow ours, and hop aboard. When we unpack on Esteel you can be among the first to look your fill. Meanwhile we can talk. I wish you'd been with us all along, we've missed having a really first-rate art historian."

"All right, I'll come." They offered each other enthusiastic smiles. "It's true, then, you really found most of the old St. Gervase collection intact?"

"I don't know that we can claim that. But there's certainly a lot."

"Just lying undisturbed here, for about two centuries."

"Well, as I say, this was the Yoritomos' safe port. But it looks like no more than a few thousand people ever lived on this world at any one time, and no one at all has lived here for a considerable period. Some intrigue or other evidently started among the Tyrant's lieutenants—no one's ever learned exactly how or why it started, but the thieves fell out. There was fighting, the Palace destroyed, the rulers themselves killed, and the whole thing collapsed. None of the intriguers had the ability to keep it going. I suppose, with the so-called Lord and Lady gone."

"Just when was that?"

Iselin named a date.

"The same year St. Gervase fell. That fits. The Yoritomos could have gone there after the berserkers left, and looted at their leisure. That would fit with their character, wouldn't it?"

"I'm afraid so . . . you see, the more I learned of them, the more I felt sure that they must have had a deeper, more secret shelter than any that was turned up in the early digs a century ago. The thing is, the people who dug here then found so much loot they were convinced they'd found it all."

Ritwan was watching the pits fill slowly in.

Iselin gave his arm a friendly shake. "And—did I tell you? We found two skeletons, I think of the Yoritomos themselves. Lavishly dressed in the midst of their greatest treasures. Lady died of a broken neck, and the man of multiple . . . "

The wind was howling still, when the two ships lifted off.

Aboard ship on the way to Esteel, things were relaxed and pleasant, if just a trifle cramped. With Ritwan along, they were six on board, and had to fit three to a cabin in narrow bunks. It was partially the wealth of the find that crowded them, of course. There were treasures almost beyond imagining stowed in plastic cratings almost everywhere one looked. The voyagers could expect a good deal of leisure time en route to marvel at it all. Propulsion and guidance and life-support were taken care of by machinery, with just an occasional careful human glance by way of circumspection. People in this particular portion of the inhabited Galaxy traveled now, as they had two hundred years before, in relative security from berserker attack. And now there were no human pirates.

Lashed in place in the central cargo bay stood the five great, muffled forms from which Ritwan particularly yearned to tear the pads and sheeting. But he made himself be patient. On the first day out he joined the others in the cargo bay, where they watched and listened to some of the old recordings found in the lower ruins of the Yoritomo Palace. There were data stored on tapes, in crystal cubes, around old permafrozen circuit rings. And much of the information was in the form of messages recorded by the Tyrant himself.

"The Gods alone know why he recorded this one," sighed Oshogbo. She was chief archivist of a large Esteel museum, one of the expedition's sponsoring institutions. "Listen to this. Look at him. He's ordering a ship to stand by and be boarded, or face destruction."

"The ham actor in him, maybe," offered Chinan, who on planet had been an assistant digger for the expedition, but in space became its captain. "He needed to study his delivery."

"Every one of his ships could carry the recording," suggested Klyuchevski, expert excavator. "So their victims wouldn't know if the Tyrant himself were present or not—I'm not sure how much difference it would make."

"Let's try another," said Granton, chief record-keeper and general assistant.

Within the next hour they sampled recordings in which Yoritomo: (1) ordered his subordinates to stop squabbling over slaves and concubines; (2) pleaded his case, to the Interworlds Government, as that of a man unjustly maligned, the representative of a persecuted people; (3) conducted a video tour, for some supposed audience whose identity was never made clear, of the most breathtaking parts of his vast collection of art . . .

"Wait!" Ritwan broke in. "What was that bit? Would you run that last part once more?"

The Tyrant's asthmatic voice repeated: "The grim story of how these magnificent statues happened to be saved. Our fleet had made every effort but still arrived too late to be of any help to the heroic defenders of St. Gervase. For many days we searched in vain for survivors; we found just one. And this man's identity made the whole situation especially poignant to me, for it was the sculptor Antonio Nobrega. Sadly, our help had come too late, and he shortly succumbed to the berserker poisons. I hope that the day will come soon, when all governments will heed my repeated urgings, to prosecute a war to the finish against these scourges of . . . ''

"So!" Ritwan looked pleased, a man who has just had an old puzzle solved for him. "That's where Nobrega died, then. We've thought for some time it was likely—most of his family was there—but we had no hard evidence before."

"He was the famous forger, wasn't he?" asked Granton.

"Yes. A really good artist in his own right, though the shady side of his work has somewhat overshadowed the rest." Ritwan allowed time for the few small groans earned by the pun, and went on: "I'd hate to accept the old Tyrant's word on anything. But I suppose he'd have no reason to lie about Nobrega."

Iselin was looking at her wrist. "Lunch time for me. Maybe the rest of you want to spend all day in here."

"I can resist recordings." Ritwan got up to accompany her. "Now, if you were opening up the crates—"

"No chance, friend. But I can show you holograms—didn't I mention that?"

"You didn't!"

Oshogbo called after them: "Here's the Lord and Lady both, on this one—"

They did not stop. Chi-nan came out with them, leaving three people still in the cargo bay.

In the small ship's lounge, the three who had left set up lunch with a floor show.

"This is really decadence. Pea soup with ham, and—what have we here? Lazienki. Marvelous!"

The subtle grays and reds of *Twisting Room*

(was it the human heart?) came into existence, projected by hidden devices in the corners of the lounge, and filling up the center. Iselin with a gesture made the full-size image rotate slowly.

"Captain?" the intercom asked hoarsely, breaking in.

"I knew it—just sit down, and—"

"I think we have some kind of cargo problem here." It sounded like Granton's voice, perturbed. "Something seems to be breaking up, or . . . Iselin, you'd better come to, and take a look at your . . ."

A pause, with background smashing noises. Then incoherent speech, in mixed voices, ending in a hoarse cry.

Chi-nan was already gone. Ritwan, sprinting, just kept in sight of Iselin's back going around corners. Then she stopped so suddenly that he almost ran into her.

The doorway to the cargo hold, left wide open when they came out of it a few minutes before, was now sealed tightly by a massive sliding door, a safety door designed to isolate compartments in case of emergencies like fire or rupture of the hull.

On the deck just outside the door, a human figure sprawled. Iselin and Chi-nan were already crouched over it; as Ritwan bent over them, a not-intrinsically-unpleasant smell of scorched meat reached his nostrils.

"Help me lift her . . . careful . . . sick bay's that way."

Ritwan helped Iselin. Chi-nan sprang to his feet, looked at an indicator beside the heavy door, and momentarily rested a hand on its flat surface.

"Something burning in there," he commented tersely, and then came along with the others on the quick hustle to sickbay. At his touch the small door opened for them, lights springing on inside.

"What's in our cargo that's not fireproofed?" Iselin demanded, as if all this were some personal insult hurled her way by Fate.

Dialogue broke off for a while. The burn-tank, hissing brim-full twenty seconds after the proper studs were punched, received Oshogbo's scorched dead weight, clothes and all, and went to work upon her with a steady sloshing. Then, while Iselin stayed in sick bay, Ritwan followed Chi-nan on another scrambling run, back to the small bridge. There the captain threw himself into an acceleration chair and laid swift hands on his controls, demanding an accounting from his ship.

In a moment he had switched his master intercom to show conditions inside the cargo bay, where two people were still unaccounted for. On the deck in there lay something clothed, a bundle-of-old-rags sort of something. In the remaining moment of clear vision before the cargo bay pickup went dead, Ritwan and Chi-nan both glimpsed a towering, moving shape.

The captain stared for a moment at the gray noise which came next, then switched to sick bay. Iselin appeared at once.

"How's she doing?" Chi-nan demanded.

"Signs are stabilizing. She's got a crack in the back of her skull as well as the burns on her torso, the printout says. As if something heavy had hit her in the head."

"Maybe the door clipped her, sliding closed, just as she got out." The men in the control room could see into the tank, and the captain raised his voice. "Oshy, can you answer me? What happened to Granton and Klu?"

The back of Oshogbo's neck was cradled on a rest of ivory plastic. Her body shook and shimmied lightly, vibrating with the dark liquid, as if she might be enjoying her swim. Here and there burnt shreds of clothing were now drifting free. She looked around and seemed to be trying to locate Chi-nan's voice. Then she spoke: "It . . . grabbed them. I . . . ran."

"What grabbed them? Are they still alive?"

"Granton's head came . . . it pulled off his head. I got out. Something hit . . . " The young woman's eyes rolled, her voice faded.

Iselin's face came into view again. "She's out of it; I think the medic just put her to sleep. Should I try to get it to wake her again?"

"Not necessary." The captain sounded shaken. "I think we must assume the others are finished. I'm not going to open that door, anyway, until I know more about our problem."

Ritwan asked: "Can we put down on some planet quickly?"

"Not one where we can get help," the captain told him over one shoulder. "There's no help closer than Esteel. Three or four days."

The three of them quickly talked over the problem, agreeing on what they knew. Two people were sure that they had seen, on intercom, something large moving about inside the cargo bay.

"And," Iselin concluded, "our surviving first-hand witness says that 'it' tore off someone's head."

"Sounds like a berserker," Ritwan said impulsively. "Or could it possibly be some animal—? Anyway, how could anything that big have been hiding in there?"

"An animal's impossible," Chi-nan told him flatly. "And you should have seen how we packed that space, how carefully we checked to see if we were wasting any room. The only place anyone or anything *could* have been hidden was inside one of those statuary crates."

Iselin added: "And I certainly checked out every one of them. We formed them to fit closely around the statues, and they couldn't have contained anything else of any size. What's that noise?"

The men in the control room could hear it too, a muffled, rhythmic banging, unnatural for any space ship that Ritwan had ever ridden. He now, for some reason, suddenly thought of what kind of people they had been whose Palace had provided this mysterious cargo; and for the first time since the trouble had started he began to feel real fear.

He put a hand on the other man's shoulder. "Chi-nan—what exactly did we see on the intercom screen?"

The captain thought before answering. "Something big, taller than a man, anyway. And moving by itself. Right?"

"Yes, and I'd say it was dark . . . beyond that, I don't know."

"I would have called it light-colored." The

muffled pounding sounds had grown a little steadier, faster, louder. "So, do you think one of our statues has come alive on us?"

Iselin's voice from sick bay offered: "I think 'alive' is definitely the wrong word."

Ritwan asked: "How many of the statues have movable joints?" *Twisting Room*, which he had seen in hologram, did not. But articulated sculpture had been common enough a few centuries earlier.

"Two did," said Iselin.

"I looked at all the statues closely," Chi-nan protested. "Iselin, you did too. We all did, naturally. And they were genuine."

"We never checked inside them, for controls, power supplies, robotic brains. Did we?"

"Of course not. There was no reason."

Ritwan persisted: "So it is a berserker. It can't be anything else. And it waited until now to attack, because it wants to be sure to get the ship."

Chi-nan pounded his chair-arm with a flat hand. "No! I can't buy that. Do you think that emergency door would stop a berserker? We'd all be dead now, and it would have the ship. And you're saying it's a berserker that looks just like a masterpiece by a great artist, enough alike to fool experts; and that it stayed buried there for two hundred years without digging itself out; and that that—"

"Nobrega," Ritwan interrupted suddenly.

"What?"

"Nobrega . . . he died on St. Gervase, we don't know just how. He had every reason to hate the Yoritomos. Most probably he met one or both of them at the St. Gervase Museum, after the attack, while they were doing what they called their collecting.

"You said Nobrega was a great forger. Correct. A good engineer, too. You also said that no one knows exactly how the Yoritomos came to die, only that their deaths were violent. And occurred among these very statues."

The other two, one on screen and one at hand, were very quiet, watching him.

"Suppose," Ritwan went on, "Nobrega knew somehow that the looters would be coming, and he had the time and the means to concoct something special for them. Take a statue with movable limbs, and build in a power lamp, sensors, controls—a heat-projector, maybe, as a weapon. And then add the electronic brain from some small berserker unit."

Chi-nan audibly sucked in his breath.

"There might easily have been some of those lying around on St. Gervase, after the attack. Everyone agrees it was a fierce defense."

"I'm debating with myself," said Chi-nan, "whether we should all pile into the lifeboat, and head for your ship, Ritwan. It's small, as you say, but I suppose we'd fit, in a pinch."

"There's no real sick bay."

"Oh." They all looked at the face of the young woman in the tank, unconscious now, dark hair dancing round it upon the surface of the healing fluid.

"Anyway," the captain resumed, "I'm not sure it couldn't take over the controls here, catch us, ram us somehow. Maybe, as you think, it's not a real berserker. But it seems to be too close to the real thing to just turn over our ship to it. We're going to have to stay and fight."

"Bravo," said Iselin. "But with what? It seems to me we stowed away our small arms in the cargo bay somewhere."

"We did. Let's hope Nobrega didn't leave it brains enough to look for them, and it just keeps banging on that door. Meanwhile, let's check what digging equipment we can get at."

Iselin decided it was pointless for her to remain in sick bay, and came to help them, leaving the intercom channel open so they could look in on Oshogbo from time to time.

"That door to the cargo bay is denting and bulging, boys," she told them as she ducked into the cramped storage space beneath the lounge where they were rummaging. "Let's get something organizing in the way of weapons."

Ritwan grunted, dragging out a long, thick-bodied tool, evidently containing its own power supply. "What's this, an autohammer? Looks like it would do a job."

"Sure," said Chi-nan. "If you get within arm's length. We'll save that for when we're really desperate."

A minute later, digging through boxes of electrical-looking devices strange to Ritwan, the captain murmured: "If he went to all the trouble of forging an old master he must have had good reason. Well, it'd be the one thing the Yoritomos might accept at face value. Take it right onto their ship, into their private rooms. He must have been out to get the Lord and Lady both."

"I guess that was it. I suppose just putting a simple bomb in the statue wouldn't have been sure enough, or selective enough."

"Also it might have had to pass some machines that sniff out explosives, before it got into the inner . . . Ritwan! When that thing attacked, just now, what recording were they listening to in the cargo bay?"

Ritwan stopped in the middle of opening another box. "Oshogbo called it out to us as we were leaving. You're right, one with both the Yoritomos on it. Nobrega must have set his creation to be triggered by their voices, heard together."

"How it's supposed to be turned off, is what I'd like to know."

"It did turn off, for some reason, didn't it? And lay there for two centuries. Probably Nobrega didn't foresee that the statue might survive long enough for the cycle to be able to repeat. Maybe if we can just hold out a little longer, it'll turn itself off again."

Patient and regular as a clock, the muffled battering sounded on.

"Can't depend on that, I'm afraid." Chi-nan kicked away the last crate to be searched. "Well, this seems to be the extent of the hardware we have for putting together weapons. It looks like whatever we use is going to have to be electrical. I think we can rig up something to electrocute—if that's the right word—or fry, or melt, the enemy. We've got to know first, though, just which of those statues is the one we're fighting. There are only two possible mobile ones, which narrows it down. But still."

"*Laughing Bacchus,*" Iselin supplied. "And *Remembrance of Past Wrongs.*"

"The first is basically steel. We can set up an induction field strong enough to melt it down, I think. A hundred kilos or so of molten iron in the middle of the deck may be hard to deal with, but not as hard as what we've got now. But the other statue, or anyway its outer structure, is some kind of very hard and tough ceramic. That one will need something like a lightning bolt to knock it out." A horrible thought seemed to strike Chi-nan all at once. "You don't suppose there could be two—?"

Ritwan gestured reassurance. "I think Nobrega would have put all his time and effort into perfecting one."

"So," said Iselin, "it all comes down to knowing which one he forged, and which is really genuine. The one he worked on must be forged; even if he'd started with a real masterpiece to build his killing device, by the time he got everything implanted the surface would have to be almost totally reconstructed."

"So I'm going up to the lounge," the art historian replied. "And see those holograms. If we're lucky I'll be able to spot it."

Iselin came with him, muttering: "All you have to do, friend, is detect a forgery that got past Yoritomo and *his* experts . . . maybe we'd better think of something else."

In the lounge the holograms of the two statues were soon displayed full size, side by side and slowly rotating. Both were tall, roughly humanoid figures, and both in their own ways were smiling.

A minute and a half had passed when Ritwan

said, decisively: "This one's the forgery. Build your lightning device."

Before the emergency door at last gave way under that mindless, punch-press pounding, the electrical equipment had been assembled and moved into place. On either side of the doorway Chi-nan and Iselin crouched, manning their switches. Ritwan (counted the most expendable in combat) stood in plain view opposite the crumpling door, garbed in a heat-insulating space-suit and clutching the heavy autohammer to his chest.

The final failure of the door was sudden. One moment it remained in place, masking what lay beyond; next moment, it had been torn away. For a long second of the new silence, the last work of Antonio Nobrega stood clearly visible, bonewhite in the glare of lamps on every side, against the blackened ruin of what had been the cargo bay.

Ritwan raised the hammer, which suddenly felt no heavier than a microprobe. For a moment he knew what people felt, who face the true berserker foe in combat.

The tall thing took a step toward him, serenely smiling. And the blue-white blast came at it from the side, faster than any mere matter could be made to dodge.

A couple of hours later the most urgent damage-control measures had been taken, two dead bodies had been packed for preservation—with real reverence if without gestures—and the pieces of Nobrega's work, torn asunder by the current that the ceramic would not peacefully admit, had cooled enough to handle.

Ritwan had promised to show the others how he had known the forgery; and now he came up with the fragment he was looking for. "This," he said.

"The mouth?"

"The smile. If you've looked at as much Federation era art as I have, the incongruity is obvious. The smile's all wrong for Prajapati's period. It's evil, cunning—when the face was intact you could see it plainly. Gloating. Calm and malevolent at the same time."

Iselin asked: "But Nobrega himself didn't see that? Or Yoritomo?"

"For the period *they* lived in, the smile's just fine, artistically speaking. They couldn't step forward or backward two hundred years, and get a better perspective. I suppose revenge is normal in any century, but tastes in art are changeable."

Chi-nan said: "I thought perhaps the subject or the title gave you some clue."

"*Remembrance of Past Wrongs*—no, Prajapati did actually do something very similar in subject, as I recall. As I say, I suppose revenge knows no cultural or temporal boundaries."

Normal in any century. Oshogbo, watching via intercom from the numbing burn-treatment bath, shivered and closed her eyes. *No boundaries.*

On the least lonely and best defended of all human worlds, not even the past was safe from enemy invasion.

METAL MURDERER

It had the shape of a man, the brain of an electronic devil.

It and the machines like it were the best imitations of men and women that the berserkers, murderous machines themselves, were able to devise and build. Still, they could be seen as obvious frauds when closely inspected by any humans.

"Only twenty-nine accounted for?" the supervisor of Defense demanded sharply. Strapped into his combat chair, he was gazing intently through the semitransparent information screen before him, into space. The nearby bulk of Earth was armored in the dun-brown of defensive force fields, the normal colors of land and water and air invisible.

"Only twenty-nine." The answer arrived on the flagship's bridge and a sharp sputtering of electrical noise. The tortured voice continued. "And it's quite certain now that there were thirty to begin with."

"Then where's the other one?"

There was no reply.

All of Earth's defensive forces were still on full alert, though the attack had been tiny, no more than an attempt at infiltration, and seemed to have been thoroughly repelled.

A small blur leaped over Earth's dun-brown limb, hurtling along on a course that would bring it within a few hundred kilometers of the supervisor's craft. This was Power Station One, a tamed black hole. In time of peace the power-hungry billions on the planet drew from it half their needed energy. Station One was visible to the eye only as a slight, flowing distortion of the stars beyond.

Another report was coming in. "We are searching space for the missing berserker android, Supervisor."

"You had damned well better be."

"The infiltrating enemy craft had padded containers for thirty androids, as shown by computer analysis of its debris. We must assume that all containers were filled."

Life and death were in the supervisor's tones. "Is there any possibility that the missing unit got past you to the surface?"

"Negative, Supervisor." There was a slight pause. "At least we know it did not reach the surface in our time."

"Our time? What does that mean, babbler? How could . . . ah."

The black hole flashed by. Not really tamed, though that was a reassuring word, and humans applied it frequently. Just harnessed, more or less.

Suppose—and, given the location of the skirmish, the supposition was not unlikely—that berserker android number thirty had been propelled, by some accident of combat, directly at Station One. It could easily have entered the black hole. According to the latest theories, it might conceivably have survived to reemerge intact into the universe, projected out of the hole as its own tangible image in a burst of virtual-particle radiation.

Theory dictated that in such a case the reemergence must take place before the falling in. The supervisor crisply issued orders. At once his computers on the world below, the Earth Defense Conglomerate, took up the problem, giving it highest priority. What could one berserker android do to Earth? Probably not much. But to the supervisor, and to those who worked for him, defense was a sacred task. The temple of Earth's safety had been horribly profaned.

To produce the first answers took the machines eleven minutes.

"Number thirty did go into the black hole sir. Neither we nor the enemy could very well have foreseen such a result, but—"

"What is the probability that the android emerged intact?"

"Because of the peculiar angle at which it entered, approximately sixty-nine percent."

"That high!"

"And there is a forty-nine-percent chance that it will reach the surface of the earth in functional condition, at some point in our past. However, the computers offer reassurance. As the enemy device must have been programmed for some subtle attack upon our present society, it is not likely to be able to do much damage at the time and place where it—"

"Your skull contains a vacuum of a truly intergalactic order. *I* will tell *you* and the computers when it has become possible for us to feel even the slightest degree of reassurance. Meanwhile, get me more figures."

The next word from the ground came twenty minutes later.

"There is a ninety-two-percent chance that the landing of the android on the surface, if that occurred, was within one hundred kilometers of fifty-one degrees, eleven minutes north latitude; zero degrees, seven minutes west longitude."

"And the time?"

"Ninety-eight-percent probability of January 1, 1880 Christian Era, plus or minus ten standard years."

A landmass, a great clouded island, was presented to the supervisor on his screen.

"Recommended course of action?"

It took the ED Conglomerate an hour and a half to answer that.

The first two volunteers perished in attempted launchings before the method could be improved enough to offer a reasonable chance of survival. When the third man was ready, he was called in, just before launching, for a last private meeting with the supervisor.

The supervisor looked him up and down, taking in his outlandish dress, strange hairstyle, and all the rest. He did not ask whether the volunteer was ready but began bluntly: "It has now been confirmed that whether you win or lose back there, you will never be able to return to your own time."

"Yes, sir. I had assumed that would be the case."

"Very well." The supervisor consulted data spread before him. "We are still uncertain as to just how the enemy is armed. Something subtle, doubtless, suitable for a saboteur on the earth of our own time—in addition, of course, to the super-human physical strength and speed you must expect to face. There are the scrambling or the switching mindbeams to be considered; either could damage any human society. There are the pattern bombs, designed to disable our defense computers by seeding them with random information. There are always possibilities of bio-logical warfare. You have your disguised medical kit? Yes, I see. And of course there is always the chance of something new."

"Yes, sir." The volunteer looked as ready as anyone could. The supervisor went to him, opening his arms for a ritual farewell embrace.

He blinked away some London rain, pulled out his heavy ticking timepiece as if he were checking the hour, and stood on the pavement before the theater as if he were waiting for a friend. The instrument in his hand throbbed with a silent, extra vibration in addition to its ticking, and this special signal had now taken on a character that meant the enemy machine was very near to him. It was probably within a radius of fifty meters.

A poster on the front of the theater read:

THE IMPROVED AUTOMATON CHESS PLAYER
MARVEL OF THE AGE
UNDER NEW MANAGEMENT

"The real problem, sir," proclaimed one top-hatted man nearby, in conversation with another, "is not whether a machine can be made to win at chess, but whether it may possibly be made to play at all."

No, that is not the real problem, sir, the agent from the future thought. *But count yourself fortunate that you can still believe it is.*

He bought a ticket and went in, taking a seat. When a sizable audience had gathered, there was a short lecture by a short man in evening dress, who had something predatory about him and also something frightened, despite the glibness and the rehearsed humor of his talk.

At length the chess player itself appeared. It was a desklike box with a figure seated behind it, the whole assembly wheeled out on stage by assistants. The figure was that of a huge man in Turkish garb. Quite obviously a mannequin or a dummy of some kind, it bobbed slightly with the motion of the rolling desk, to which its chair was fixed. Now the agent could feel the excited vibration of his watch without even putting a hand into his pocket.

The predatory man cracked another joke, displayed a hideous smile, then, from among several chess players in the audience who raised their hands—the agent was not among them—he selected one to challenge the automaton. The challenger ascended to the stage, where the pieces were being set out on a board fastened to the rolling desk, and the doors in the front of the desk were being opened to show that there was nothing but machinery inside.

The agent noted that there were no candles on this desk, as there had been on that of Maelzel's chess player a few decades earlier. Maelzel's automaton had been an earlier fraud, of course. Candles had been placed on its box to mask the odor of burning wax from the candle needed by the man who was so cunningly hidden inside amid the dummy gears. The year in which the agent had arrived was still too early, he knew, for electric lights, at least the kind that would be handy for such a hidden human to use. Add the fact that this chess player's opponent was allowed to sit much closer than Maelzel's had ever been, and it became a pretty safe deduction that no human being was concealed inside the box and figure on this stage.

Therefore . . .

The agent might, if he stood up in the audience, get a clear shot at it right now. But should he aim at the figure or the box? And he could not be sure how it was armed. And who would stop it if he tried and failed? Already it had learned enough to survive in nineteenth-century London. Probably it had already killed, to further its design—"under new management" indeed.

No, now that he had located his enemy, he must plan thoroughly and work patiently. Deep in thought, he left the theater amid the crowd at the conclusion of the performance and started on foot back to the rooms that he had just begun to share on Baker Street. A minor difficulty at his launching into the black hole had cost him some equipment, including most of his counterfeit money. There had not been time as yet for his adopted profession to bring him much income; so he was for the time being in straitened financial circumstances.

He must plan. Suppose, now, that he were to approach the frightened little man in evening dress. By now that one ought to have begun to understand what kind of a tiger he was riding. The agent might approach him in the guise of—

A sudden tap-tapping began in the agent's watch pocket. It was a signal quite distinct from any previously generated by his fake watch. It meant that the enemy had managed to detect his detector; it was in fact locked onto it and tracking.

Sweat mingled with the drizzle on the agent's face as he began to run. It must have discovered him in the theater, though probably it could not then single him out in the crowd. Avoiding horse-drawn cabs, four-wheelers, and an omnibus, he turned out of Oxford Street to Baker Street and slowed to a fast walk for the short distance remaining. He could not throw away the telltale watch, for he would be unable to track the enemy without it. But neither did he dare retain it on his person.

As the agent burst into the sitting room, his roommate looked up, with his usual, somewhat shallow, smile, from a leisurely job of taking books out of a crate and putting them on shelves.

"I say," the agent began, in mingled relief and urgency, "something rather important has come up, and I find there are two errands I must undertake at once. Might I impose one of them on you?"

The agent's own brisk errand took him no farther than just across the street. There, in the doorway of Camden House, he shrank back, trying to breathe silently. He had not moved when, three minutes later, there approached from the direction of Oxford Street a tall figure that the agent suspected was not human, its hat was pulled down, and the lower portion of its face was muffled in bandages. Across the street it paused, seemed to consult a pocket watch of its own, then turned to ring the bell. Had the agent been absolutely sure it was his quarry, he would have shot it in the back. But without his watch, he would have to get closer to be absolutely sure.

After a moment's questioning from the landlady, the figure was admitted. The agent waited for two minutes. Then he drew a deep breath, gathered up his courage, and went after it.

The thing standing alone at a window turned to face him as he entered the sitting room, and now he was sure of what it was. The eyes above the bandaged lower face were not the Turk's eyes, but they were not human, either.

The white swathing muffled its gruff voice. "You are the doctor?"

"Ah, it is my fellow lodger that you want." The agent threw a careless glance toward the desk where he had locked up the watch, the desk on some papers bearing his roommate's name were scattered. "He is out at the moment, as you see, but we can expect him presently. I take it you are a patient."

The thing said, in its wrong voice, "I have been referred to him. It seems the doctor and I share a certain common background. Therefore the good landlady has let me wait in here. I trust my presence is no inconvenience."

"Not in the least. Pray take a seat, Mr.—?"

What name the berserker might have given, the agent never learned. The bell sounded below, suspending conversation. He heard the servant girl answering the door, and a moment later his roommate's brisk feet on the stairs. The death machine took a small object from its pocket and sidestepped a little to get a clear view past the agent toward the door.

Turning his back upon the enemy, as if with the casual purpose of greeting the man about to enter, the agent casually drew from his own pocket a quite functional briar pipe, which was designed to serve another function, too. Then he turned his head and fired the pipe at the berserker from under his own left armpit.

For a human being he was uncannily fast, and for a berserker the android was meanly slow and clumsy, being designed primarily for imitation, not dueling. Their weapons triggered at the same instant.

Explosions racked and destroyed the enemy, blasts shatteringly powerful but compactly limited in space, self-damping and almost silent.

The agent was hit, too. Staggering, he knew with his last clear thought just what weapon the enemy had carried—the switching mindbeam. Then for a moment he could no longer think at all. He was dimly aware of being down on one knee and of his fellow lodger, who had just entered, standing stunned a step inside the door.

At last the agent could move again, and he

shakily pocketed his pipe. The ruined body of the
enemy was almost vaporized already. It must have
been built to self-destruct when damaged badly,
so that humanity might never learn its secrets.
Already it was no more than a puddle of heavy
mist, warping in slow tendrils out the slightly
open window to mingle with the fog.

The man still standing near the door had put out
a hand to steady himself against the wall. "The
jeweler . . . did not have your watch," he muttered
dazedly.

I have won, thought the agent dully. It was a
joyless thought because with it came slow
realization of the price of his success. Three
quarters of his intellect, at least, was gone, the
superior pattern of his brain-cell connections
scattered. No. Not scattered. The switching mindbeam would have reimposed the pattern of his
neurons somewhere farther down its pathway . . .
there, behind those gray eyes with their newly
penetrating gaze.

"Obviously, sending me out for your watch was
a ruse." His roommate's voice was suddenly
crisper, more assured than it had been. "Also, I
perceive that your desk has just been broken into,
by someone who thought it mine." The tone
softened somewhat. "Come, man, I bear you no ill
will. Your secret, if honorable, shall be safe. But it
is plain that you are not what you have
represented yourself to be."

The agent got to his feet, pulling at his sandy
hair, trying desperately to think. "How—how do
you know?"

"Elementary!" the tall man snapped.

The terror of the berserkers spread ahead of them across the galaxy. Even on worlds not touched by the physical fighting, there were people who felt themselves breathing darkness, and sickened inwardly. Few men on any world chose to look for long out into the nighttime sky. Some men on each world found themselves newly obsessed by the shadows of death.

I touched a mind whose soul was dead...

PATRON OF THE ARTS

After some hours' work, Herron found himself hungry and willing to pause for food. Looking over what he had just done, he could easily imagine one of the sycophantic critics praising it: A huge canvas, of discordant and brutal line! Aflame with a sense of engulfing menace! And for once, Herron thought, the critic might be praising something good.

Turning away from his view of easel and blank bulkhead, Herron found that his captor had moved up silently to stand only an arm's length behind him, for all the world like some human kibitzer.

He had to chuckle. "I suppose you've some idiotic suggestion to make?"

The roughly man-shaped machine said nothing, though it had what might be a speaker mounted on what might be a face. Herron shrugged and walked around it, going forward in search of the galley. This ship had been only a few hours out from Earth on C-plus drive when the berserker

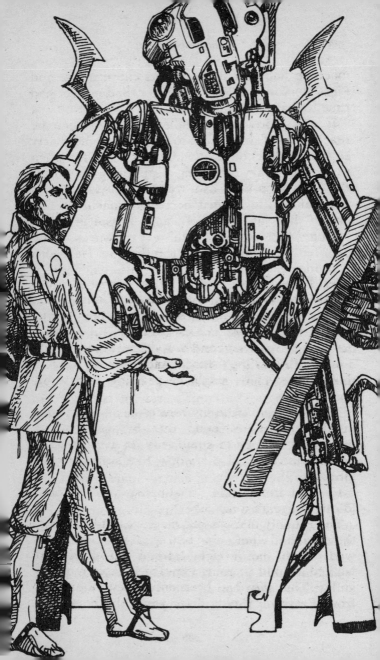

machine had run it down and captured it; and Piers Herron, the only passenger, had not yet had time to learn his way around.

It was more than a galley, he saw when he reached it—it was meant to be a place where arty colonial ladies could sit and twitter over tea when they grew weary of staring at pictures. The *Frans Hals* had been built as a traveling museum; then the war of life against berserker machines had grown hot around Sol, and BuCulture had wrongly decided that Earth's art treasures would be safer if shipped away to Tau Epsilon. The *Frans* was ideally suited for such a mission, and for almost nothing else.

Looking further forward from the entrance to the galley, Herron could see that the door to the crew compartment had been battered down, but he did not go to look inside. Not that it would bother him to look, he told himself; he was as indifferent to horror as he was to almost all other human things. The *Frans*'s crew of two were in there, or what was left of them after they had tried to fight off the berserker's boarding machines. Doubtless they had preferred death to capture.

Herron preferred nothing. Now he was probably the only living being—apart from a few bacteria—within half a light year; and he was pleased to discover that his situation did not terrify him; that his long-growing weariness of life was not just a pose.

His metal captor followed him into the galley, watching while he set the kitchen devices to work.

"Still no suggestions?" Herron asked it. "Maybe you're smarter than I thought."

"I am what men call a berserker," the man-shaped thing squeaked at him suddenly, in an ineffectual-sounding voice. "I have captured your ship, and I will talk with you through this small machine you see. Do you grasp my meaning?"

"I understand as well as I need to." Herron had not yet seen the berserker itself, but he knew it was probably drifting a few miles away, or a few hundred or a thousand miles, from the ship it had captured. Captain Hanus had tried desperately to escape it, diving the *Frans* into a cloud of dark nebula where no ship or machine could move faster than light, and where the advantage in speed lay with the smaller hull.

The chase had been at speeds up to a thousand miles a second. Forced to remain in normal space, the berserker could not steer its bulk among the meteoroids and gas-wisps as well as the *Frans*'s radar-computer system could maneuver the fleeing ship. But the berserker had sent an armed launch of its own to take up the chase, and the weaponless *Frans* had had no chance.

Now, dishes of food, hot and cold, popped out on a galley table, and Herron bowed to the machine. "Will you join me?"

"I need no organic food."

Herron sat down with a sigh. "In the end," he told the machine, "you'll find that lack of humor is as pointless as laughter. Wait and see if I'm not right." He began to eat, and found himself not so hungry as he had thought. Evidently his body still feared death—this surprised him a little.

"Do you normally function in the operation of this ship?" the machine asked.

"No," he said, making himself chew and swallow. "I'm not much good at pushing buttons." A peculiar thing that had happened was nagging at Herron. When capture was only minutes away, Captain Hanus had come dashing aft from the control room, grabbing Herron and dragging him along in a tearing hurry, aft past all the stored art treasures.

"Herron, listen—if we don't make it, see here?" Tooling open a double hatch in the stern compartment, the captain had pointed into what looked like a short padded tunnel, the diameter of a large drainpipe. "The regular lifeboat won't get away, but this might."

"Are you waiting for the Second Officer, Captain, or leaving us now?"

"There's room for only one, you fool, and I'm not the one who's going."

"You mean to save me? Captain, I'm touched!" Herron laughed, easily and naturally. "But don't put yourself out."

"You idiot. Can I trust you?" Hanus lunged into the boat, his hands flying over its controls. Then he backed out, glaring like a madman. "Listen. Look here. This button is the activator; now I've set things up so the boat should come out in the main shipping lanes and start sending a distress signal. Chances are she'll be picked up safely then. Now the controls are set, only this activator button needs to be pushed down—"

The berserker's launch had attacked at that moment, with a roar like mountains falling on the hull of the ship. The lights and artificial gravity had failed and then come abruptly back. Piers

Herron had been thrown on his side, his wind knocked out. He had watched while the captain, regaining his feet and moving like a man in a daze, had closed the hatch on the mysterious little boat again and staggered forward to his control room.

"Why are you here?" the machine asked Herron. He dropped the forkful of food he had been staring at. He didn't have to hesitate before answering the question. "Do you know what BuCulture is? They're the fools in charge of art, on Earth. Some of them, like a lot of other fools, think I'm a great painter. They worship me. When I said I wanted to leave Earth on this ship, they made it possible.

"I wanted to leave because almost everything that is worthwhile in any true sense is being removed from Earth. A good part of it is on this ship. What's left behind on the planet is only a swarm of animals, breeding and dying, fighting—"

"Why did you not try to fight or hide when my machines boarded this ship?"

"Because it would have done no good."

When the berserker's prize crew had forced their way in through an airlock, Herron had been setting up his easel in what was to have been a small exhibition hall, and he had paused to watch the uninvited visitors file past. One of the man-shaped metal things, the one through which he was being questioned now, had stayed to stare at him through its lenses while the others had moved on forward to the crew compartment.

"Herron!" The intercom had shouted. "Try, Herron, please! You know what to do!" Clanging noises followed, and gunshots and curses.

What to do, Captain? Why, yes. The shock of events and the promise of imminent death had stirred up some kind of life in Piers Herron. He looked with interest at the alien shapes and lines of his inanimate captor, the inhuman cold of deep space frosting over its metal here in the warm cabin. Then he turned away from it and began to paint the berserker, trying to catch not the outward shape he had never seen, but what he felt of its inwardness. He felt the emotionless deadliness of its watching lenses, boring into his back. The sensation was faintly pleasurable, like cold spring sunshine.

"What is good?" the machine asked Herron, standing over him in the galley while he tried to eat.

He snorted. "You tell me."

It took him literally. "To serve the cause of what men call death is good. To destroy life is good."

Herron pushed his nearly full plate into a disposal slot and stood up. "You're almost right about life being worthless—but even if you were entirely right, why so enthusiastic? What is there praiseworthy about death?" Now his thoughts surprised him as his lack of appetite had.

"I am entirely right," said the machine.

For long seconds Herron stood still, as if thinking, though his mind was almost completely blank. "No," he said finally, and waited for a bolt to strike him.

"In what do you think I am wrong?" it asked.

"I'll show you." He led it out of the gallery, his

hands sweating and his mouth dry. Why wouldn't the damned thing kill him and have done?

The paintings were racked row on row and tier on tier; there was no room in the ship for more than a few to be displayed in a conventional way. Herron found the drawer he wanted and pulled it open so the portrait inside swung into full view, lights springing on around it to bring out the rich colors beneath the twentieth-century statglass coating.

"This is where you're wrong," Herron said.

The man-shaped thing's scanner studied the portrait for perhaps fifteen seconds. "Explain what you are showing me," it said.

"I bow to you!" Herron did so. "You admit ignorance! You even ask an intelligible question, if one that is somewhat too broad. First, tell me what *you* see here."

"I see the image of a life-unit, its third spatial dimension of negligible size as compared to the other two. The image is sealed inside a protective jacket transparent to the wavelengths used by the human eye. The life-unit imaged is, or was, an adult male apparently in good functional condition, garmented in a manner I have not seen before. What I take to be one garment is held before him—"

"You see a man with a glove," Herron cut in, wearying of his bitter game. "That is the title, *Man with a Glove*. Now what do you say about it?"

There was a pause of twenty seconds. "Is it an attempt to praise life, to say that life is good?"

Looking now at Titian's thousand-year-old more-than-masterpiece, Herron hardly heard the machine's answer; he was thinking helplessly and hopelessly of his own most recent work.

"Now you will tell me what it means," said the machine without emphasis.

Herron walked away without answering, leaving the drawer open.

The berserker's mouthpiece walked at his side. "Tell me what it means or you will be punished."

"If you can pause to think, so can I." But Herron's stomach had knotted up at the threat of punishment, seeming to feel that pain mattered even more than death. Herron had great contempt for his stomach.

His feet took him back to his easel. Looking at the discordant and brutal line that a few minutes ago had pleased him, he now found it as disgusting as everything else he had tried to do in the past year.

The berserker asked: "What have you made here?"

Herron picked up a brush he had forgotten to clean, and wiped at it irritably. "It is my attempt to get at your essence, to capture you with paint and canvas as you have seen those humans captured." He waved at the storage racks. "My attempt has failed, as most do."

There was another pause, which Herron did not try to time.

"An attempt to praise me?"

Herron broke the spoiled brush and threw it down. "Call it what you like."

This time the pause was short, and at its end the machine did not speak, but turned away and walked in the direction of the airlock. Some of its fellows clanked past to join it. From the direction of the airlock there began to come sounds like those of heavy metal being worked and hammered. The interrogation seemed to be over for the time being.

Herron's thoughts wanted to be anywhere but on his work or on his fate, and they returned to what Hanus had shown him, or tried to show him. Not a regular lifeboat, but she might get away, the captain had said. All it needs now is to press the button.

Herron started walking, smiling faintly as he realized that if the berserker was as careless as it seemed, he might possibly escape it.

Escape to what? He couldn't paint any more, if he ever could. All that really mattered to him now was here, and on other ships leaving Earth.

Back at the storage rack, Herron swung the *Man with a Glove* out so its case came free from the rack and became a handy cart. He wheeled the portrait aft. There might be yet one worthwhile thing he could do with his life.

The picture was massive in its statglass shielding, but he thought he could fit it into the boat.

As an itch might nag a dying man, the question of what the captain had been intending with the boat nagged Herron. Hanus hadn't seemed worried about Herron's fate, but instead had spoken of trusting Herron . . . .

Nearing the stern, out of sight of the machines, Herron passed a strapped-down stack of crated statuary, and heard a noise, a rapid feeble pounding.

It took several minutes to find and open the proper case. When he lifted the lid with its padded lining, a girl wearing a coverall sat up, her hair all wild as if standing in terror.

"Are they gone?" She had bitten at her fingers and nails until they were bleeding. When he didn't answer at once, she repeated her question again and again, in a rising whine.

"The machines are still here," he said at last.

Literally shaking in her fear, she climbed out of the case. "Where's Gus? Have they taken him?"

"Gus?" But he thought he was beginning to understand.

"Gus Hanus, the captain. He and I are—he was trying to save me, to get me away from Earth."

"I'm quite sure he's dead," said Herron. "He fought the machines."

Her bleeding fingers clutched at her lower face. "They'll kill us, too! Or worse! What can we do?"

"Don't mourn your lover so deeply," he said. But the girl seemed not to hear him; her wild eyes looked this way and that, expecting the machines. "Help me with this picture," he told her calmly. "Hold the door there for me."

She obeyed as if half-hypnotized, not questioning what he was doing.

"Gus said there'd be a boat," she muttered to herself. "If he had to smuggle me down to Tau Epsilon he was going to use a special little boat—" She broke off, staring at Herron, afraid that he had heard her and was going to steal her boat. As indeed he was.

When he had the painting in the stern compartment, he stopped. He looked long at the

Man with a Glove, but in the end all he could seem to see was that the fingertips of the ungloved hand were not bitten bloody.

Herron took the shivering girl by the arm and pushed her into the tiny boat. She huddled there in dazed terror; she was not good-looking. He wondered what Hanus had seen in her.

"There's room for only one," he said, and she shrank and bared her teeth as if afraid he meant to drag her out again. "After I close the hatch, push that button there, the activator. Understand?

That she understood at once. He dogged the double hatch shut and waited. Only about three seconds passed before there came a scraping sound that he supposed meant the boat had gone.

Nearby was a tiny observation blister, and Herron put his head into it and watched the stars turn beyond the dark blizzard of the nebula. After a while he saw the berserker through the blizzard, turning with stars, black and rounded and bigger than any mountain. It gave no sign that it had detected the tiny boat slipping away. Its launch was very near the *Frans* but none of its commensal machines were in sight.

Looking the *Man with a Glove* in the eye, Herron pushed him forward again, to a spot near his easel. The discordant lines of Herron's own work were now worse than disgusting, but Herron made himself work on them.

He hadn't time to do much before the man-shaped machine came walking back to him; the uproar of metalworking had ceased. Wiping his brush carefully, Herron put it down, and nodded at his berserker portrait. "When you destroy all the rest, save this painting. Carry it back to those who built you, they deserve it."

The machine-voice squeaked back at him: "Why do you think I will destroy paintings? Even if they are attempts to praise life, they are dead things in themselves, and so in themselves they are good."

Herron was suddenly too frightened and weary to speak. Looking dully into the machine's lenses he saw there tiny flickerings, keeping time with his own pulse and breathing, like the indications of a lie detector.

"Your mind is divided," said the machine. "But with its much greater part you have praised me. I have repaired your ship, and set its course. I now release you, so other life-units can learn from you to praise what is good."

Herron could only stand there staring straight ahead of him, while a trampling of metal feet went past, and there was a final scraping on the hull.

After some time he realized he was alive and free.

At first he shrank from the dead men, but after once touching them he soon got them into a freezer. He had no particular reason to think either of them Believers, but he found a book and read Islamic, Ethical, Christian and Jewish burial services.

Then he found an undamaged handgun on the deck, and went prowling the ship, taken suddenly with the wild notion that a machine might have stayed behind. Pausing only to tear down the abomination from his easel, he went on to the very stern. There he had to stop, facing the direction in which he supposed the berserker now was.

"Damn you, I can change!" he shouted at the stern bulkhead. His voice broke. "I can paint again. I'll show you . . . I can change. I am alive."

More Bestselling
Science Fiction
from Pinnacle/Tor

"LIFE AND DEATH IN DREADFUL CONFLICT STROVE..."

It happened long ago and far away. Perhaps in this galaxy, perhaps in one close by. Two war-maddened races fought — and though both are gone, their legacy abides: the Frankenstein weapon that destroyed not only the enemy, but the creator. The Berserkers, robotic, asteroid-sized killers programed to one purpose: to seek out and end life. The death machines have harried their way across our galaxy. Now they have come for us.

Here at last is the essence of the Berserker Saga in a single volume:

THE BERSERKER WARS

Fred Saberhagen is the author of the renowned Berserker Saga: *Berserkers, Brother Assassin, Berserker's Planet, The Ultimate Enemy,* and *Berserker Man,* as well as the enormously popular new Dracula series: *The Dracula Tape, The Holmes Dracula File, An Old Friend of the Family, Thorne,* and (coming soon from TOR) *Dominion.* He is also the author of the massive new fantasy classic, *Empire of the East,* and, with Roger Zelazny, is the co-author of the spectacular new occult science fiction novel, *Coils* (also coming soon from TOR).

A Tom Doherty Associates Book